PRAISE FOR
CHILDREN OF PARANOIA

"A generations-long war that's claimed thousands of lives, waged in perfect secrecy beneath the clueless noses of people like me? Oh, hell yeah. *Children of Paranoia* is a claustrophobic, relentless, fascinating ride that will have you eyeballing everyone you pass in the street. I can't wait for the sequel."

—Marcus Sakey, author of *The Two Deaths of Daniel Hayes*

"Trevor Shane's *Children of Paranoia* is a gripping journey into a secret war where literally anyone could kill you. Like *The Bourne Identity* turned inside out, his protagonist navigates a world where banal choices like going to the ATM have life-and-death consequences. Filled with sharp plotting and vivid action, this book will stay with you long after you've raced to the end."   —Chris Farnsworth, author of *Blood Oath*

"What keeps the reader relentlessly glued to *Children of Paranoia* are the unrelenting suspense and complex characters. It is definitely a roller-coaster ride that one won't soon forget." —New York Journal of Books

"Shane's work here is impressive. He certainly knows how to stage an action scene and how to ratchet up tension. If you're in the market for an exciting, propulsive read . . . *Children of Paranoia* would make an excellent choice."   —*The Saturday Evening Post*

"*Children of Paranoia* functions neatly as a surreal variant on the noir thriller where evil lurks in every shadow and happiness either remains tantalizingly just out of reach or could be snatched away in an instant."
—Shelf Awareness

continued . . .

"An action-packed story of war, intrigue, and twists and turns."
—*The Parkersburg News and Sentinel* (Parkersburg, WV)

"[*Children of Paranoia*] is an interesting but poignant metaphor for the senselessness of killing, be it by rival street gangs, feuding families, or entire countries . . . a powerful story."   —*Suspense Magazine*

"Well-written and exciting. . . . The plot takes some interesting and un-expected turns."   —Geek Speak Magazine

"Fast-paced . . . a thought-provoking, enjoyable read that will stay with readers when the last page is done."   —Monsters and Critics

"An exceptional story."   —Fresh Fiction

"[*Children of Paranoia*] will please lovers of adventure and action."
—Examiner.com

"*Children of Paranoia*, the first installment of a planned trilogy, never flags, and kept this reader's attention rapt until its end, by which time Irene's winds had died down and the rain had long since stopped."
—*Psychology Today*

CHILDREN OF THE UNDERGROUND

THE CHILDREN OF PARANOIA SERIES

TREVOR SHANE

 NAL NEW AMERICAN LIBRARY

New American Library
Published by the Penguin Group
Penguin Group (USA) Inc., 375 Hudson Street,
New York, New York 10014, USA

USA | Canada | UK | Ireland | Australia | New Zealand | India | South Africa | China

Penguin Books Ltd., Registered Offices: 80 Strand, London WC2R 0RL, England
For more information about the Penguin Group visit penguin.com.

First published by New American Library,
a division of Penguin Group (USA) Inc.

First Printing, April 2013

 REGISTERED TRADEMARK—MARCA REGISTRADA

THE LIBRARY OF CONGRESS HAS CATALOGED THE HARDCOVER EDITION OF THIS TITLE AS FOLLOWS:
Shane, Trevor.
Children of the underground / Trevor Shane.
p. cm.—(The children of paranoia series)
ISBN 978-0-451-23929-7 (pbk.)
1. Mothers of kidnapped children—Fiction. I. Title.
PS3619.H35465C48 2013
813'.6—dc23   2012032443

Printed in the United States of America

Set in Janson Text

"And then what happened?" the young girl asked
the old woman sitting across the table from her.

CHILDREN OF PARANOIA
BOOK II

Dear Christopher,
I finally found him. It took me almost nine
months, but I finally found him. Now he's
gone again. All I have left of him is the
blood-soaked washcloth in the bathroom sink.
Let's pray that he comes back. Let's pray that
he agrees to help me find you.

Love,
Mom

CHILDREN OF THE UNDERGROUND

One

I remembered the smell of blood. When there's enough of it, it's a pungent smell that you can never forget. When the scent hit me, so many memories came flooding back.

I drove into Grand Case before noon. I brought a magazine with me, imagining that I could hide behind it as I searched strangers' faces for the man that I saw on the pier. I was excited, not only at the prospect of finally finding him, but at the prospect of playing the game. For the first time in months, I felt like I had a chance to win.

Grand Case is small enough that I knew I would find Michael if he showed up. What I didn't know was how he'd react to meeting me. I knew that there was a chance that he would blame me for your father's death. There was a chance that he wouldn't want anything to do with me. I didn't know how I was going to react to meeting him either. I'd spent nine months without the War, without violence or blood or terror. I'd need courage to go back. Sometimes life doesn't give you choices, Christopher. I made fun of your father for telling me that once, but he was right. Even if you have choices, sometimes you have only one worth making. I had to go back to the War. It's the only way that I can save you from it.

When I got to Grand Case, I parked my car and walked toward

the water. It was a quick walk from the street to the beach. The beach at Grand Case coils its way around the bay in an almost perfect semicircle. From where I stepped onto the sand, I could see every bar, every restaurant, every sunbather, every ounce of sand as they all wrapped themselves around the blue water of the bay. I took off my shoes and began to walk, digging my toes into the soft white sand. I walked the length of the beach twice, checking the inside of each restaurant and bar to see if Michael was already inside. When I didn't see him, I found a spot in the sand that afforded me a clear view of everything. I sat down and began scanning the faces of the people around me.

I sat in that spot for four hours before I saw Michael. When I did, it was as thrilling and as frightening as it had been the day before. I had so much riding on this man that I'd never met. I spotted him coming out of the water. I recognized his face. I noticed the deep scar on his side from where someone had driven a knife into his ab-domen while he was saving your father's life. It was shaped like a pair of eternally silent lips. I recognized his taut, muscular frame from the docks. Michael wasn't big, but he looked strong and agile. Watching him gave me faith that he could help me. I thought for a moment that everything was going to work out. I didn't know that the next twenty-four hours were going to dissolve into a nightmare.

The beach was quiet and uncrowded. Michael was fifty yards from me, but only a few people stood between us. I could hear the cries of the seagulls and the wind blowing through the flags on the boats an-chored in the bay, but I didn't hear any other sound. The water was calm. Michael stretched out in the sand and slept. Other than the rise and fall of his chest, his body didn't move. While he was sleeping, I took a cigarette out of my bag and lit it to calm my nerves. I was in the middle of my third cigarette when Michael sat up, put on his shirt, and walked toward one of the restaurants overlooking the beach. I tossed my half-smoked cigarette in the sand, dusted myself off, and followed him. My plan was to let Michael get three drinks into him before I confronted him. I planned on telling him who I was and then telling him how often and how fondly your father spoke about him. I was ready to tell Michael that your father's last wish was that Michael could have a chance to meet you. I was ready to lie. I was ready to do whatever it took.

By the time I walked up the steps leading from the beach into the shade of the restaurant, Michael was already sitting at the bar with a drink in front of him. I did my best to avoid staring at him. I sat down at a table overlooking the water. The waiter asked what I'd like to drink. I'd learned from your father's journal that he was never supposed to drink on a job. I remembered the stories where your father and his friends ordered club soda so that they could look like they were drinking. I needed a drink, though. I ordered a margarita, thinking it would at least make me look like I was on vacation.

The restaurant was about half-full when I walked in, but it was quickly crowding up. The day was slipping slowly into night. Men came in wearing loud Hawaiian-print shirts, and the women came in wearing airy, spaghetti-strap dresses. Michael ordered a second beer. I ordered a salad so that the waiter wouldn't kick me off my table. I tried to eat some of the salad, realizing that I hadn't eaten anything since breakfast, but my throat closed up. I couldn't swallow. One drink down, two to go, I told myself. Then I saw one of the others for the first time.

He was sitting at a table in the corner of the restaurant. He appeared to be alone. He had a glass of wine on his table but it looked full, not even sipped. A plate of untouched seafood-strewn pasta sat in front of the man. He was doing what I was doing. He was watching Michael. At first I thought that I was imagining things. I've had fits of paranoia before. When I was on the run with your father, they were frequent. I would suddenly feel every eye on me and think that that everyone was out to get me. Maybe my brain could sense that I was near the War again. Your father taught me to trust my instincts, so I kept one eye on Michael and one eye on the man in the corner. I wasn't imagining things. He followed every move that Michael made with a measured ease, turning away only when Michael turned toward him. Unlike me, he was no amateur. Michael didn't seem to notice him.

My mind raced. I tried to think of what I should do. I felt like I was trapped in one of your father's stories, only I was unprepared. The man in the corner glanced at his watch. He reached out in front of him and appeared to take a sip of wine. He was older than me but younger than Michael. He had a thin face. His hair and eyes were dark. He looked at his watch again as if he were waiting for someone.

I put my half-empty margarita back down on the table, vowing not to drink another drop. I'd thought that the only thing I had to fear was Michael's reaction to meeting me. I'd been naive. I never thought I had to be afraid that someone else would get to Michael before I did. If anything happened to Michael, I was lost. He was all I had.

That's when the second man walked through the door.

The second man and his partner were about the same age. I noticed the second man walk into the restaurant and glance at his partner in the corner. They made eye contact, and the man in the corner tapped on his watch and shook his head as if to admonish his partner for being late. The second man was bigger than the first. He had broad shoulders and deep-set eyes. He glanced at Michael and began walking toward him. He was only a few steps away. I wanted to shout. I wanted to warn Michael, but I couldn't find the courage to speak. The new guy reached Michael and kept walking. He eventually found a place at the end of the bar. I began breathing again.

The second man ordered a beer, though I would have bet my life that he wasn't going to drink it. I looked at Michael again. He seemed oblivious to it all. He drank his beer alone. The only person Michael spoke to was the bartender. He wasn't nearly as alone as he thought he was. I felt frozen, trapped, watching everything that was happening like it was a movie. Your father taught me how to run. He never taught me how to fight. I had to do something. I had to warn Michael. The restaurant was getting louder, and the bar was getting more crowded. It was growing harder to keep an eye on Michael, let alone the others. I tried to think about what Michael would have done if our roles were reversed.

I stood up from my table and began walking toward the bar. At first, my legs nearly gave out beneath me. I ignored the others as I walked. I pushed my way through the bodies of some revelers on the way to the bar. They smelled like a mix of red wine and coconut oil. At last, I got past the final person and saw that the barstool next to Michael was still free. I hadn't had time to plan what I was going to say to him. *Run* or *They're after you* was all I could think of. Before I sat down on the stool next to Michael, I glanced at the thin-faced man in the corner. He was staring at me. He looked nervous. He wasn't expecting me. I turned away from him, trying to ignore the unease in my stomach.

I sat down on the barstool and turned to face Michael. As I did, the waiter who had served me my drink and my salad called out, "Miss," and held the check in his hand. "You forgot to pay." As he spoke the words, Michael turned and stared at me. Our faces were only inches apart. He was looking into me, through me. I wanted to say something, but I froze beneath his stare.

Without looking away from me, Michael yelled to the bartender, "Jerry, I gotta run. I'll get you next time. Okay?" Then Michael stood up and began walking away.

The bartender laughed. "Sure thing, Michael. I'll put it on your tab." Michael walked toward the door leading to the street. I never opened my mouth. I never warned him. I never had a chance. I froze for a second and then looked over at the man in the corner. He had taken out his wallet and was dropping money on the table to cover his bill. I looked back toward the man at the end of the bar, but he wasn't there. He was already gone. He must have gone out through the entrance to the beach as soon as he saw Michael leave. The man in the corner rushed toward the door to the street, leaving a wad of bills on the table. I sat there frozen with panic.

"Miss, your bill?" my waiter called out to me again, waving the paper above his head. I didn't have time for him. I turned and ran to the door. I wasn't going to lose Michael. I was too close. I didn't care that the thin-faced man stood between me and Michael or that the man with the sunken eyes was lurking somewhere in the darkness.

I made it out of the front door just in time to see the thin-faced man disappear into a crowd to my right. I followed him, moving as quickly as I could through the throngs of bodies now littering the street. I could hear the dissonant mix of reggae and jazz music echoing out of the restaurants as I passed them. I wove through the crowd. I heard tourists laughing and bellowing out to each other. It was safe amid the people. All Michael had to do was stay in the crowd and he'd be safe. He didn't have to run. I couldn't see the thin-faced man anymore. I kept moving, searching the faces of the people as I passed them. I came to a vacant little street that led away from the water. Dark, quiet buildings lined the street. The gaps between the buildings were empty except for shadows. I looked down the street. The only thing I saw was the silhouette of a man walking slowly away from the crowds. He was alone. It was Michael. I could tell by the way that he moved. He was walking away from safety and into the darkness. I didn't know where the others were. I'd lost them. All

I knew was that they were out there. Michael was walking right into danger and he didn't even know it. I watched him until he turned down a smaller, darker alleyway branching off the side street. I broke into a run. I ran toward Michael. My feet stamped hard on the ground as I tried to follow the direction that his shadow had moved. I followed him into the darkness. I turned down the second, darker alley. Then I froze. Everything around me became quiet. The alley was empty, lit only by the half-moon reflecting off the broken windows around me.

I remembered to be afraid. I ducked into the shadow of one of the buildings. I didn't dare move. I listened. I heard the murmuring sound of people whispering to each other over the faint sound of music from the restaurants only a few blocks away. Then I heard footsteps, light footsteps, running away from the whispers. I couldn't figure out what was happening. I needed to save Michael. Without him, I had no way to find you. I moved. I jumped from one shadow to the next, from one gap between buildings to another. Each time I stopped, I listened. I heard nothing but silence.

I breathed slowly, deliberately, trying to control my anxiety, trying to remain hidden. Sheltered in the deep darkness between two buildings, I leaned forward and peered around the corner. All I saw was moonlight shining down on the street. Then I heard a noise. It took me a moment—one horrible, frozen moment—to realize where the noise was coming from. Something was behind me, hidden in the shadows. I didn't hear any footsteps, only a whooshing sound, like the wind. I saw a quick flash of light in front of me, the moonlight reflecting off a metal object as it moved by my face. Before I had a chance to react, I felt the hot blade of a knife pressing deep into my neck. I inhaled, trying not to breathe, knowing that any movement and the knife might break my skin. Then I felt an arm move across my body, clenching my arms at my sides in one strong, viselike grip. The arm pulled me backward until I was pressed up against a body. I couldn't move. I closed my eyes, trying to remember you one more time, thinking that it would all be over soon.

I couldn't see anything in the darkness. "You've got ten seconds to tell me why I shouldn't kill you," a voice whispered into my ear. I recognized the voice. I would have fallen if Michael hadn't literally been holding me up with the arm he had wrapped around my torso.

"People are following you," I whispered back to him.

"I know," he replied. "You're one of them."

I became confused. In my rush to warn Michael, I'd forgotten that he didn't know who I was. "No," I stammered, "I'm not one of *Them*." I said the word *Them* like your father used to say it, like it was the world's greatest insult.

"Then who are you?" Michael asked. I could feel the pressure on my neck from the blade of the knife ease up slightly. My eyes were getting used to the darkness. I could almost see the knife blade now.

"I'm Joe's girlfriend," I answered.

Michael took the knife from my throat and spun me around until I was facing him. He kept a powerful grip on both my arms. For a moment, he just looked at me, staring at me through the darkness. We were close enough that I could see the expression on his face. He looked confused, surprised, and angry all at once. Your father had never been easy to read, but he wore only one emotion at a time. In one look, Michael wore hundreds.

"Stay here," Michael whispered to me. "Don't move. No matter what happens, don't move. If you move for any reason, I'll know that I can't trust you." I didn't know how to respond, so I simply nodded. I felt his hands release my arms. Then he disappeared into the shadows. I stood there for a moment, relieved to no longer have a knife blade jutting into my skin but afraid because I was alone again.

He had known that people were following him. I didn't know how it was possible, but he had known.

I stood alone in the darkness and listened to the night. I stayed as still as I could, trying not to move a muscle, hoping that my stillness would hide me.

Everything was quiet. I don't know how long the quiet lasted. It was impossible to measure the passage of time. Then I heard something moving toward me—the sound of barely audible footsteps. Whoever was coming was placing each footfall carefully on the gravel, trying to move silently. I heard the footsteps only because my senses were heightened by the darkness. Then I saw a shadow move through the street in front of me. I held my breath. It was the man with the deep-set eyes. He was holding a gun out in front of him. His hands were trembling. All he had to do was look in my direction and I would have been at his mercy. I had never felt so vulnerable before. I stood there in the shadows, not daring to move. Losing Michael's trust now would be worse than death. Then, without warning, the man standing in front of me broke into a run, his feet pounding on the gravel. The footsteps sounded as loud to me as a drum. BOOM BOOM BOOM BOOM they went and then, only seconds later, they stopped as abruptly as they started. I stayed as quiet as possible, trying to listen to see if I could hear what was happening. The sounds drifted toward me through the night air. I heard something that sounded far too short to be a fight. I heard the sound of feet sliding across gravel followed by a deep, guttural grunt. Then, even though I'd never heard it before, I heard the unmistakable sound of a knife piercing someone's skin. I heard a quick sound, almost like a popping noise, as the knife punctured the skin, and then I heard the knife slide deeper into flesh. I stood there frozen. Then I heard a huffing sound, followed by the piercing sound of the knife a second time. Everything was quiet for a moment. Finally, I heard the last breath, gasping and horrid. Nothing else in the world sounds like the last breath of a dying man. I had almost forgotten what it sounded like. I wish I had. As someone else's breathing stopped, I breathed again. Someone was dead. I had stood there in the darkness and listened to them die. I only prayed that it wasn't Michael.

Then everything was silent again. I still didn't move, standing as Michael had ordered me to, hidden from the world only by the shadows, and waited for Michael's return. Michael didn't get to me first, though. The man with the dark eyes found me first. I saw him before he saw me. He was moving down the street, trying to jump from shadow to shadow. The fact that he was still out there searching for something meant either that Michael was still alive or that they were done with him and were looking for me. I watched the man. His movements were clumsy. He looked younger than he had at the restaurant. For some reason, as he tried to make his way through the darkness, he didn't look much older than a boy, a scared and frightened boy. Like his partner, he held a gun. Without even realizing it at first, he turned toward me. He stared directly into the alleyway. He stopped moving, trying to let his eyes focus. Every single piece of my body told me to run but I didn't. If Michael was going to test me, I was going to pass. The man took another step toward me, still unsure of what he was seeing. He lifted his gun and pointed it at me. I thought he might pull the trigger, firing blindly into the alleyway just to be safe, but he didn't. He simply walked toward me, no longer bothering to hide himself in the shadows. "Don't move," he shouted as he walked closer, though I could still hear confusion in his voice. He made it across the street and stopped just shy of the entrance to the alley where I was standing.

He could see me now. He aimed the gun at my chest. We were standing less than five feet apart. "It's you," he said, his voice full of shock and anger. "The bitch from the restaurant." He lifted the gun so that it was pointed at my head. "Where's your friend?" he asked. I didn't answer. I didn't move. I stared into the barrel of the gun and was not afraid. No one could hurt me more than I'd already been hurt. "Okay, I'm giving you until three to answer me, and then I pull the trigger.

"One," he counted. I stared at him. I felt stronger than I'd ever felt before. "Two."

Michael moved so fast that I didn't see him. He must have made a sound, but I didn't hear him either. All I knew was that the instant before the dark-eyed man said, "Three," the gun wasn't pointing at me anymore. Instead, it was pointing up toward the sky. The dark-eyed man's whole body was turned so that I could see his silhouette framed by the light from the street. Michael appeared, standing in front of the dark-eyed man. A knife blade was protruding through the fingers of Michael's right hand. Michael's left hand was clamped onto the dark-eyed man's wrist, pulling the gun up toward the sky. Michael took his knife blade and jammed it into the dark-eyed man's throat. That's when I smelled the blood. That's when I remembered what it smelled like. It smelled like a mixture of life and death. Then Michael twisted the knife like a corkscrew and the dark-eyed man fell to his knees. I could see the blood now too, dripping from the man's neck onto the ground. In the moonlight, it looked dark and inhuman. Michael pulled the knife out of the man's throat. He wiped the blood off the knife on the dead man's shirt. Michael let go and the dead man fell to the ground with a thud.

Michael turned to me. "What the fuck are you doing?" he shouted. "Are you fucking nuts?"

"You told me not to move," I answered.

"I meant not to move from here," Michael said, pointing around the dark alley I'd been standing in. "I didn't mean not to move at all. Jesus Christ." I didn't know what to say. I'd done what he told me to do.

"I wanted you to trust me," I said.

Michael stared at me like I was crazy. He shook his head. "Help me get rid of these bodies," he ordered me. "The other one is in a garbage can at the end of the street." He bent down and threw the dark-eyed man's body over his shoulder without another word. "Don't worry," he said, "I've done this before." His assurance didn't make me feel any better.

It took longer to get rid of the bodies than it had taken Michael to kill them. We dumped the bodies in the trough of water surrounding the landing strip of the Grand Case Airport. I tried looking down into the water as we dropped the bodies in, wondering how many more bodies were down there, but all I could see was my own reflection on top of the shiny black water. By the time we were finished, it was the darkest part of the night. It wouldn't be long before morning.

We barely spoke to each other as we worked. When we were done, Michael asked where I was staying. I told him. "Good," he said. "I'm staying with you."

TWO

I waited until the sun came up before daring to get out of bed. Even with the shades drawn, the sun burst through cracks in the windows and the walls. I heard birds. I heard the squawking of the seagulls first and then the singing of the songbirds in the trees outside our room. Michael was still lying frozen on the floor. Michael had slept on the floor in front of the motel room door without a blanket or pillow. He simply folded his hands behind his head and closed his eyes. I didn't sleep. I had too much adrenaline pumping through my system. It had been a long time since I'd been that close to death. I had a feeling that I should start getting used it again.

I climbed out of bed as quietly as I could and walked into the bathroom. I wanted to wash my face and brush my teeth. I wanted to look at myself in the mirror. The mirror hadn't been my friend for some time. I almost didn't recognize the woman in the glass. She looked tired, sad, and lost. I ran water, as cold as I could get it, and splashed some on my face. I took out the soap and scrubbed my hands clean. I used the same soap to wash my face. I brushed my teeth. I felt better. I felt slightly cleansed. A thousand more days and maybe I could feel clean.

I opened the bathroom door and walked back toward the bed.

My eyes darted to the spot on the floor in front of the door. It was empty. Michael was gone. My heart dropped in my chest. I lifted my eyes. The chain lock still hung between the door and the wall. The windows. I turned and looked toward the windows to see if any were open.

"I'm still here," a voice echoed from the corner of the room. I turned and looked. Michael was sitting in a chair along the back wall. "I haven't gone anywhere yet." He was sunk low in the chair, with one foot resting on the chair's armrest. The light shining in through the blinds drew shadows on his face. I wanted to finally say something to him, but the words failed me again. Michael took his foot off the armrest and leaned forward in his chair, placing his elbows on his knees. "What are you doing here?" he asked.

"I'm Joe's girlfriend," I repeated, as if that answered his question.

"I know. I recognized you from your picture."

"What picture?" I asked, confused.

"In Joe's file," Michael answered. "When you and Joe went on the run, they sent his file out to everyone—his friends, his enemies, everyone." I knew about the file. I'd seen it on the kid that your father shot in Ohio. I remember how surreal it was when I saw my own picture in it. "I remember looking through the file, trying to figure out why Joe ran. I read your bio. I saw your picture." Michael looked up at me. "You look different." He paused. "You look older." His voice was somber, not like I expected.

"I am older," I told him. "Is that when you left the War, when you got Joe's file?" I asked.

"I haven't left the War," Michael answered with a liar's smile. He looked at his hands. They were still stained with blood. "I just stopped taking orders." I wondered if he'd gotten blood in his hair while he slept with his head in his hands. I went into the bathroom and got a wet washcloth. I handed it to Michael. He started rubbing the blood off his hands. The washcloth turned a dark pink. "But yeah"—Michael nodded now—"that's when I stopped taking orders."

"Did they send a file out on you too?" I asked. "Is that how those people last night found you?"

"No," Michael replied. "I haven't been cut loose. They just aren't protecting me anymore."

"So who were those guys?" I asked.

"Word's gotten out that I'm holed up on this island." Michael finished scrubbing his hands and placed the blood-soaked washcloth on the table next to the chair. "So they've been coming, trying to make a name for themselves by taking me out. It was only a trickle at first, one every few weeks. There are more of them now, and they come in bunches—two at a time, sometimes three. It's like a rat problem."

"And you kill them all?" I asked.

"Well, first I ask them to leave," Michael said. I deserved the sarcasm.

"How can you keep it up?"

"I can't," Michael said. "Eventually someone's going to get the drop on me." His dark blue eyes flared up for a moment as a streak of sunlight snuck in through the blinds. "It won't be easy for them, though." We were quiet for a moment. "You still haven't answered my question," Michael said, breaking the silence. "Why are you here?"

I couldn't think of a diplomatic way to do this. "I need your help," I answered.

"My help with what?"

"I need you to help me get my son back." I swallowed hard, trying to fight the tears I felt in my eyes. "I need you to help me get Joe's son back."

"What good's that going to do?" Michael stood up and walked

over to the window. He pulled back the shades with one hand and peeked outside.

"I want to save him. I want to take him away from the War."

Michael smiled again. It was a sad smile. He shook his head. "You can't save him from the War. The War's in his blood. He was born into it. He's a child of paranoia, just like I am, just like Joe was. No matter how hard you try, the War will find him."

"I don't believe that," I responded.

"Believe what you want, little girl," Michael said. "What you believe doesn't change the truth." The words stung.

"You realize that if we don't get him, Joe's son is going to grow up on the other side."

"I don't see how that's any of my business," Michael said, but I could see something in his eyes. He cared. I saw it, if only for a second.

"How is that not your business? If we don't find him, Joe's son is going to grow up to be your enemy. He's going to grow up to be one of those kids that you sink in that lake."

"Oh, I don't think so, Maria," Michael laughed. "I'll be long dead by the time your son starts fighting. I'm sure of that."

"His name is Christopher," I said, searching for words that Michael wouldn't have an answer for. "Joe died trying to keep him out of the War."

"Joe was a dreamer," Michael answered.

"Funny, that's what he said about you."

"Yeah, I was a dreamer too," Michael replied. "Now Joe's dead and I'm not a dreamer anymore."

"Wait. I have something for you." I walked over to the closet and reached up to the top shelf. I pulled down your father's journal. I hadn't planned on giving the journal to Michael. The idea just came to me. If I couldn't convince Michael to help you, maybe your father could. I handed Michael the journal. The pages were worn where I had read them over and over again. "It's Joe's journal. I asked Joe to write it." I crammed the crumpled pages that I'd written about the day they stole you into the back of the journal. Michael deserved to know how his friend had died.

Michael held the journal in his hands. He looked down at it, unsure if he actually wanted it. He reached up and rubbed the stubble on his cheeks. "Am I in it?" he asked, his voice weak.

"It's how I found you," I told him.

"Can I take this?" Michael asked, lifting the journal in one hand. He was leaving. I couldn't make him stay. I could only try to make him come back.

"Only if you promise to return it."

"I promise," Michael said. "You can count on me."

"I know," I said. "That's why I'm here." I reached out and grabbed Michael's hand and squeezed it tightly against the book. His hand felt thick and weathered.

He looked down at my hand on top of his and then turned to go. He walked toward the door and unchained the lock. "Am I safe here?" I asked before he left.

"You thought I stayed here last night to protect you?" Michael said as he opened the door. I was nearly blinded by the sun. The room flooded with light. "You've got a lot to learn, Maria. I stayed here last night for my protection, not yours." Michael stepped into the daylight. "You'll be safe. They're after me. Now that Joe's gone, nobody cares about you anymore." Then Michael walked out the door, closing it behind him.

He hasn't come back yet. I have to believe he will. I have no choice.

Three

Twelve of them were sleeping in the house that night. As far as Evan and Addy knew, they were the only two that made it out alive. Dutty was gone. So were Soledad and Kevin. So were the others.

Evan woke up in a strange bed, the smoke choking his lungs. He could already feel the heat from the fire. It took him a moment before he remembered where he was. Then he heard the gunshots. Everything was chaos. He heard running and screaming. The smoke filling the room made it hard for him to see. He looked across the room to the other bed. It was empty. His friend's absence only added to the madness. Evan sat up in his bed and shouted his friend's name. There was no answer. Evan's shout was followed immediately by a coughing fit as the smoke crept into his lungs and his body tried to expel it. More gunfire. Evan rolled off the bed and onto the floor. He yelled his friend's name again, sure that this time he'd get an answer.

Addy heard Evan calling out through the smoke. She was already making her way toward him. It was a relief to hear his voice. Addy crawled along the floor beneath the smoke and bullets. She knew what room Evan was in, but until she heard his voice, she had no idea if he was still there and still alive. Hell, she had no idea if the room would still be there. For all she knew, the room could have already been eaten by the fire. She tried to crawl quickly, but her inability to pull in a full breath slowed her down.

She felt the heat and smoke in her lungs, leaving little room for air. Her eyes stung. Tears ran down the sides of her face. She heard more gunshots. She didn't know if the bullets were finding targets or were simply cutting like missiles through the smoke. She heard Evan call out again. She knew that he wasn't calling out for her but she was going to him anyway. She'd made a promise.

Addy crawled toward the sound of Evan's voice. As she neared him, she saw his body slumped on the ground next to the bed. He was only ten feet in front of her. She could see his chest heaving, trying, like hers, to find usable air. "Evan, are you okay?" Addy shouted through the dark gray haze, though her shout came out not much louder than a raspy whisper.

"Addy," Evan called out, his eyes searching for her through the chaos. "I'm okay. What about—?" Evan began.

Addy cut Evan off before he could finish. She knew what he was going to ask. He was going to ask about him. "He's gone," she shouted at him, shaking her head. She knew what the words implied. She knew what Evan would think when he heard them. She wanted him to think it. At that moment, death was better than the truth—it was more expedient anyway.

Evan could barely believe what he'd heard. How could his best friend be gone? Evan froze. It didn't make sense. Things like this didn't happen—not where Evan came from. Addy saw Evan freeze. She'd expected it. She knew Evan wasn't used to any of this, not like her. He hadn't grown up with the violence and the death and the paranoia. If they were going to escape the fire and the bullets, she knew that she was going to have to lead him out.

Addy crawled closer to Evan, pulling her body next to his. He was lying on the floor, his face as close to the carpet as he could get it. He was trying to catch his breath, like a drowning man gasping for air. "We've got to find a way out of here!" Addy shouted at Evan, trying to break through his paralysis. "We've got to make a run for it!" Addy reached out and grabbed Evan's hand. Evan felt her hand land on top of his. In the growing heat of the room, Addy's hand felt almost cool. "Are you ready?" she asked him. He was young and strong and wasn't about to let himself die lying on the floor. He didn't ask Addy where they were running. He simply nodded.

They stood up together and ran.

Addy's plan was for them to run for the door. She couldn't think of any other way out. She probably should have known that their attackers would have the door covered. Once standing, Evan and Addy could barely see anything but smoke and, dancing amid the smoke, the red lasers from the sights of their attackers' guns. Even holding hands, Evan and Addy had trouble seeing each other. They could hear the crackling of the burning fire, though, and they could hear the gunshots. They kept running. As they neared the door, the sound of the gunshots became more frequent and they could hear the sounds of people moaning. Then Evan lost his footing and toppled to the floor, pulling Addy down to the ground with him. Evan looked back. He'd tripped over a body. Now that he was on the ground, below the line of smoke, he could see the bodies lining the hallway. He counted four of them. Then he heard a scream, and both he and Addy knew that it was the scream of someone being eaten by the fire. More bullets flew in through the open door. Whoever was attacking them was literally trying to smoke them out of the house. The attackers stood outside with their guns and their uniforms, waiting for anyone who managed to escape the fire through the door. They must have started the fire by shooting some sort of firebomb through a window while everyone was sleeping. Then they watched the door, picking people off as they ran out, like plastic targets in a carnival game. The gunshots weren't single shots. They were rips of automatic fire, sounding like a snare drum from hell, gunning down everyone who emerged from the smoke. Evan looked at the bodies, trying to see if he could identify the body of his friend, but even below the smoke it was far too hazy to tell.

Evan and Addy were still clutching each other's hands. "The window," Evan shouted. *It was on the other side of the room, away from the door.*

"They must have that covered too," Addy yelled before coughing a violent, spastic cough.

Evan looked around them. He couldn't see any flames, only smoke, but he learned quickly that he didn't need to see the flames in order to feel their heat. His skin was roasting. "We burn in here or we take our chances with the window," he said to Addy. More gunshots echoed through the air like an exclamation point on Evan's words. The screams seemed to have stopped for the time being.

"We'll have to break the window," Addy said. "We'll never get it open." Each word was an effort. "We can throw something out to distract them and then jump."

"There's a chair in the corner," Evan said. He crawled over and grabbed the chair before dragging it back to Addy.

"We'll do it together," Addy said to Evan. "On one, we break the window." She took a breath. "On two, we throw the chair out. On three, we jump." They both knew that they couldn't fit through the window at the same time. "I'll go first," Addy said, aware that if their attackers had the window covered, going first was a death sentence.

"Okay," Evan said. They didn't talk about their ability to run with lungs full of hot ash. They would either run or they would die. It wasn't something they needed to discuss.

Evan and Addy stood up, their heads lifting into the blinding smoke again. They each held on to one side of the chair. "One," Addy called out, and they swung the chair in the direction of the window. Even through the smoke, their aim was true. The window shattered. They held on to the chair, knowing they would need it to create their diversion. As soon as the glass broke, smoke was sucked out of the cracks in the glass. For a split second, Addy and Evan felt like they could breathe again. A split second after that, they heard gunshots pummeling the wall next to the window. It didn't matter. They had no time for backup plans. "Two," Addy called out, and they threw the chair out the broken window. As the chair fell toward the ground, it was chased by another rip of gunfire. "Three," Addy yelled, and jumped out the window. Without a moment's hesitation, Evan jumped after her.

Addy's leg caught on some glass as she leapt through the window, cutting a small gash into her skin, but she barely noticed. The fresh, smoke-free air acted like an elixir, a cure-all to any pain. When Addy landed, she heard the sound of the bullets hitting the wall next to her. She rolled away from the sound. From where they were positioned, their attackers didn't have a direct line of sight at Addy and Evan. Instead, the attackers were shooting at them at an angle, plugging holes into the already ravished building but missing their true targets. Evan landed only a short moment after Addy. In that moment, Addy's eyes began to clear. She closed her eyes tightly and let the tears wash away the ash. When she opened her eyes again, she could see the two men with guns running toward them. They were wearing LAPD SWAT uniforms. Addy reached down and grabbed Evan. "Run," she shouted with as much force as she could muster. Then she dragged Evan to his feet and they ran.

Four

I have a book that I bring with me wherever I go. I read it every day. It describes the stages of a baby's development. Every morning I wake up and count the days since you were born, so that I can read about each new thing that you might be doing that month or that week. I read it so that I know everything I'm missing. Since they stole you from me, I missed your first smile. I missed hearing you laugh for the first time. I missed watching you learn how to crawl. I've missed so much already. I don't want to miss any more.

I remember kneeling on the dirt in our front yard in New Mexico, my head resting in your father's lap after the life slipped out of him. I could still taste his last breath on my lips. I couldn't move. I wished that they'd killed me too. I knelt there, looking at the horizon in the direction they had taken you. It didn't seem real. They came out of nowhere and stole you from me. For nine months you grew inside me and then, after only a few weeks, they came and took you away. The last image I have of you, crying as that brute held you upside down by your leg, your body covered in your father's blood, will be burned in my memory forever. I can still hear you cry in my sleep. As much as that sound hurts me, I never want to forget it. It's all I have of you.

I don't know how long I knelt there before finally getting up and stumbling back to the empty house. I remember the sky was dark. My knees ached. They were covered in hard red dirt. My whole body throbbed. When I got to the house, I did the only thing that I could think of to do. I called for help. I picked up the phone and dialed 911. I told them that my one-month-old son had been kidnapped and that his father had been murdered. I didn't tell them who your father was. I didn't tell them about the War or the Rules. I didn't tell them that they took you from me because I was under eighteen and that, according to the Rules of the War, any baby born to a mother under eighteen had to be given to the other side. I didn't tell them that your father's best friend took you so that he could give you to your father's enemies. It would make me sound crazy. I told them only what would make sense in a sane world. Then I sat down and waited for the sirens. I was convinced that the world would help me, but the world isn't on our side, Christopher. At best, it's neutral. At worst, it's against us.

I knew something was wrong when the sirens never came. Eventually, a single police car pulled up in front of our house, carrying only two police officers. No posse was coming. They weren't going to round up the townsfolk to chase after the men who had taken you. The police car pulled up the driveway slowly and stopped without a sound.

I stood on the front porch and watched as two officers stepped out of the car. They didn't look at me. They stood next to each other for a moment, staring at the car. I could see the shattered windshield and your father's body by the moonlight from the porch. The police officers were closer to the carnage, only a few feet from the car. One of the officers, a lanky blond man wearing aviator sunglasses despite the darkness, walked over to the car and began circling it. He started on the passenger's side, walking slowly as he went, looking inside each of the unbroken windows on the passenger's side. He ran a finger along the car as he walked, as if inspecting for dust. He passed the trunk, turned, and began walking toward the open driver's-side door.

When the blond officer finally made it to the open driver's-side door, he knelt down and peered inside. He knelt there for a moment, staring at your father's lifeless body. Then he angled his head so that he could look through the bullet hole in the front windshield. He knelt down like that without moving for some time before standing up and slamming the driver's-side door shut. That instant before he slammed that door was the last time I saw your father, except for in my dreams.

The inspection complete, the blond officer walked back to his partner. His partner was shorter than him and had darker skin. He wore dark sunglasses that matched his partner's. The blond officer leaned into his partner. They spoke in whispers. Then they finally turned toward me and started walking up to the porch. As they walked toward me, I remembered the other two dead bodies on the porch that I hadn't mentioned when I called 911, the bodies of the men that your father killed while trying to save you. They were mere inches from my feet. How was I going to explain them? I could feel my heart pounding in my chest as the officers walked toward me, getting closer with each step. Everything was wrong. The police were wrong. The silence was wrong. I'd made a mistake. The cops hadn't come to help me. I was alone.

The cops stopped at the bottom of the steps leading up to the house. I could barely make out the name printed on the badge of the darker-skinned officer. It said GONZALEZ. The blond officer's badge didn't have a name on it. When they stopped walking, Officer Gonzalez took a quick glance down at the bodies. The blond officer didn't even bother. Somehow they'd known what to expect. "You called the police, ma'am?" Officer Gonzalez said. His voice was calm and oddly formal. I didn't know how to respond to his question. Of course I called the police. My yard was littered with dead bodies. I suddenly felt like the script for this moment was written somewhere, but no one had bothered to tell me my lines.

"They killed my husband," I was able to mumble eventually, no longer caring what I was supposed to say. Fuck their script.

"Officer Heywood here," Officer Gonzalez said, motioning to the blond officer. The blond officer didn't move, standing there like some sort of grotesque statue. "Officer Heywood inspected the car and determined that your husband died in an accident." Officer Gonzalez looked up at me when he said the words *your husband* to let me know that he knew that your father and I weren't married. They knew everything. They were in on it.

"An accident?" My voice was trembling now. "There's a bullet hole in the windshield!" They can't cover it all up, I kept telling myself. They can't.

"We see all sorts of crazy crash patterns in windshields, ma'am. Sometimes it makes it look like things that didn't happen, happened."

I tried to stare into the officer's eyes to shame him, but all I could see in his sunglasses was my own pathetic reflection. "And what about my son?" I asked, fearing that I already knew the answer to the question. "What are you going to do about my son?"

Officer Gonzalez took a pen and a pad of paper out of his pocket. He flipped through a couple of pages. "As far as our records show," he said, holding the tip of the pen to the paper, "you don't have a son." The words hurt worse than if he'd punched me in the stomach.

"I have a son," I said, knowing that it wouldn't help, saying it just to hear the words. "I have a son and they took him!"

Officer Gonzalez took off his sunglasses. He had soft brown eyes that turned down at the sides. His voice remained painfully calm. "Did your son have a social security number?" he asked. I shook my head. "Do you have any of his medical records? Do you have the hospital records of his birth?" I shook my head again. You weren't born in a hospital. You were born at home. They knew that. Your father demanded that you be born off the grid. He thought that it would protect you. He thought that if no one could find a record of your birth, they might leave us alone. He was wrong. He should have known that they would use it against us. They use everything against us.

"No," I answered, my voice broken. I wanted to collapse on the floor and roll into a ball. If it weren't for the dead bodies already lying around me, I might have. "I don't have anything. I don't have any records," I said, looking Officer Gonzalez in the eyes, gathering what little strength I had, "but Christopher exists and he's my son, and don't you dare tell me different."

Officer Gonzalez returned my stare. I saw pity in his eyes. "Go home," he said, shaking his head. "Forget all of this ever happened. This isn't your fight. Go home."

I could feel my lips trembling. "What about them?" I asked, gently kicking one of the bodies at my feet.

"We'll take care of them," the blond officer answered.

"Go inside," Officer Gonzalez ordered me. "We're going to call someone to tow your car away and to clean up the mess here." He looked down at the bodies again as he spoke. "I'll knock when we're done. Then we'll be out of your hair."

I didn't know what else to do, so I obeyed. I went inside. I sat on the couch and cried. An hour later, I heard a knock at the door. I didn't bother to answer it. I waited for the silence. I needed the silence. Then I stood up and walked to the front door again. I opened it and looked out. The bodies on the porch were gone. The car with your father's body in it was gone. They'd cleansed the death from the yard. It was dark outside and cold. I could feel a breeze blow across the porch. I hugged my arms around my shoulders but I knew I wouldn't feel warm again, not for a long time. I noticed a short note, written on Officer Gonzalez's notebook paper, stuffed into the knocker on the front door. I took it down, unfolded it. *Don't be a hero*, it read. *It won't end well. Go back to where you belong.*

I took the note and crumpled it in my hand. I tossed it down onto the ground in front of the porch. The wind picked it up and I watched as it sailed away into the night.

I don't remember how long I stayed at the house in New Mexico. It might have been a week. It might have been longer. I had never felt so hopeless in my life. Eventually, I picked up your father's journal and began rereading it. I read it over and over again. I searched inside it for clues, for anything that I could grab hold of that might lead me to you. I still had all of the money that your father and I had been saving. It was meant for you, for your future. If I didn't use it, you'd have no future. I needed to move. I needed inertia. I wasn't getting any closer to you wallowing in my own misery in New Mexico. I read your father's journal one more time. Two days later, I walked into town and got on a bus heading for New Jersey.

The bus ride to New Jersey took three days. I had to switch buses three times. It was the cheapest route I could find. For three days, I practiced what I was going to say to the woman who was, by blood, your grandmother. I was ready to tell her about every characteristic that you shared with your father—the way your ears stuck out a little, the slant of your eyes, the thickness of your lips. I was ready to beg for her help. I was ready to get down on my knees and plead with the woman who'd taken everything I'd ever loved from me.

The bus let me off five miles from your father's old house. I had been there only once before, but I remembered how to get there. The walk took me a couple hours, but it felt good to move again after three days cooped up on the bus. It had been a long journey and I felt ready for almost anything, except for what I found.

The house was empty, stripped completely bare. It wasn't merely that no one was home. Everything was gone. The house looked like it had never been lived in. I noticed the curtains first. I walked up the driveway toward the house and I could see that the curtains were missing. When I stepped closer and peered through the windows, I saw that all the furniture was gone. I went to the side door and placed my hand on the doorknob. I twisted it and it gave way easily. The door swung open, creaking on its hinges. I stepped inside. The house already had a musty odor. A thin layer of dust had collected on the countertops in the kitchen. I walked over to one of the cabinets and opened it. Everything that should have been inside was gone— the plates, the glasses. Only ring stains on the wood where the cups used to be remained. I began moving more quickly. I ran upstairs to your father's room. It was empty too. All of the things that his mother had saved for him since his childhood were gone—his trophies, his pictures. I went into his sister's room, the one that I'd slept in, the one his mother had kept as a shrine to his murdered sister. Nothing. I felt my heart drop. It felt like they had killed your father all over again. I walked back into your father's bedroom and crouched down in a corner and cried. It's amazing how much you can cry before running out of tears.

I stayed there, in the house where your father grew up, for three days. I slept on the floor in the sleeping bag that I carried with me. I didn't eat. I didn't want to leave. Leaving meant leaving your father forever.

Eventually, I had to leave. I wasn't going to let myself die in that house. I wouldn't give them that satisfaction. I went to Manhattan to be surrounded by people. Nobody ever told me how lonely it is to be surrounded by strangers. Days turned into weeks. Weeks turned into months. I had always been the smart kid, the overachiever—prizes, awards, university at sixteen. Everything in my life had been so easy, but none of that mattered. I couldn't solve this problem with a pencil and eraser. I got lonely enough once that I called my parents. I couldn't tell them about Joseph. I couldn't tell them about the War. I couldn't even tell them about you. I didn't dare risk pulling them into this mess. All I could tell them was that I was okay. All I could do was lie to them. My mother cried when I spoke with her. I wanted to tell her not to cry. I wanted to tell her that the only thing that I knew in the world was that crying doesn't help.

According to my book, sometime while I was in New York, you smiled for the first time.

After New York I headed back to Montreal, to the apartment where your father and I shared our first weekend together. It was the only lead I could think of. Whoever owned that apartment was part of the War. It wasn't much to go on, but it was something.

Montreal was cold when I arrived. I'd come a long way from New Mexico. It was dark outside when I stepped off the bus. I headed straight for the apartment. The lights inside the apartment were still on. I could see the light from the sidewalk across the street. I remembered standing in almost that exact same spot and looking up at that window before the first night that I ever spent with your father. I never told him this, but I had stood there for a moment, looking up at the window, and I almost ran away. If I'd run your father would probably still be alive but you wouldn't exist. I'm glad I didn't run. I know that your father would feel the same way.

I decided that I should wait until morning to confront whoever lived in the apartment, but I didn't have the strength to leave. Instead I pulled my jacket tight around my neck and sat down on a bench. Shadows were moving inside the apartment. I watched them dance along the walls. The lights went out around midnight. Once the apartment was dark, I leaned back on the bench and shoved my hands into the pockets of my coat. I think I slept a bit, but I can't be sure. In the morning, some warmth returned. I sat in silence and watched the front door to the apartment building. The building had eight apartments, but only one mattered.

I stopped the first man who came out of the apartment building and asked him if he could tell me who owned apartment 3A. He told me that the woman was about my height and had straight blond hair. I saw the woman come out of the building about an hour and a half later. I followed her, not wanting to confront her yet, not wanting to scare her away. She walked downtown from her apartment and disappeared into a tall office building downtown. I waited outside. I decided that I'd talk to her when she came out for lunch. I tried to calm my nerves.

Around lunchtime, the woman came out of the building, along with throngs of others. I followed her again. She walked about four blocks and then got in line at a place that sold chopped salads for the amount of money that I survived on for days. I got in line behind her. I felt how much I stood out. I'd been wearing the same clothes for three days. I hadn't looked at my hair since I left New York. I waited a few minutes, slowly shuffling forward as the line moved. The woman didn't speak to anyone. When we were nearing the front of the line, I reached out and touched her shoulder. "Excuse me," I said, trying to act as casual as possible. "Don't you live at ———?" I named the address of her apartment.

"Yes, I do," she said with a slight francophone accent. "Why do you ask?"

"I stayed in one of the apartments there once. I thought that maybe I'd seen you." I instantly saw the paranoia in her face. I'd said something wrong. The War breeds paranoia. I knew that. "Don't worry," I said to her in a whisper. "I'm a friend."

"I don't know what you mean," she answered, a nervous tremble seeping into her voice. "When was it that you stayed in my apartment building?"

"About a year ago," I answered.

"Then you couldn't have seen me there. My husband and I bought our apartment only two months ago." She looked me up and down now. "Who are you?" She stepped out of the queue and started hurrying away from me. I followed her. I couldn't let her go. She began walking faster to try to get away from me, but she was wearing heels. I caught up to her when we got back to the plaza in front of her office building. When she turned toward the entrance, I reached out, grabbed her arm, and twisted it so that she was forced to turn and face me.

"I need your help," I said, sounding as desperate as I was. "Please."

"What do you want from me?" the woman shrieked, trying to pull her arm from my grip. I was holding on too tight.

"I need to know about the War," I blurted out. "I need to know where they took my son." I was raving like a madman, near tears. I could see fear in the woman's eyes but it wasn't the right kind of fear. She wasn't afraid of me because she knew something. She was afraid of me because she didn't. To her, I was just a crazy woman grabbing her on the street, rambling about wars and missing children.

"Let me go!" the woman screamed. A crowd formed around us.

"You bought your apartment two months ago?" I asked.

"Yes," she replied.

"Who did you buy it from?"

"It was a bank sale, a foreclosure. We never knew anything about the owners." I let go of the woman's arm. She didn't run. Something in my voice had caught her off guard.

"They just abandoned the place?" I asked. I didn't expect anyone to answer me. I already knew the answer. They'd left it because of me. This woman was as innocent and naïve as I had been a year ago. I could see it in her eyes.

"Do you need help?" the woman asked me, her fear turning into pity. Pity isn't something that I can stomach.

"Yes," I answered her, "but not from you." I turned away from her and away from the crowd that had gathered around us. I walked away as quickly as I could. They had wiped the world clean. If I hadn't seen everything with my own eyes, even I would have begun to doubt that the War existed. That's what they wanted. Everything that could connect me to the War was gone. They made it disappear. The only thing that they couldn't take away from me was my memory of you.

I stayed in Montreal even longer than I had stayed in New York. I got a job. I rented an apartment. I saved some money. At night, I read your father's journal over and over again. I pretended that your father was trying to help me find you. While I was in my apartment in Montreal, you probably rolled over for the first time. You probably started saying the word *Mama* to a woman that wasn't me. Unless I find you in another month or two, I'll likely miss your first steps. One night while reading your father's journal, it hit me. Michael could help me. I just had to find him. That's how I ended up in St. Martin.

Five

The morning that I first saw Michael, my plan was to search Orient Beach again. Based on its reputation alone, it was the obvious choice. If Michael was on the island at all, it only made sense that he'd be on its most famous nude beach. I'd already searched Orient Beach once, the first day I got to the island. I roamed through the masses of naked bodies, looking for someone who I had never seen before. All I had to go on was a name that I wasn't sure Michael was using anymore and that scar on his abdomen. I could have easily missed him the first time. I decided to give it another chance.

I lasted only a couple of hours. All those people walking around naked, without cares or anything to hide. I felt like an alien, like a germ. I had enough to hide for everybody. So did Michael. Maybe that's why he wasn't there. I had to leave. I headed to the city of Marigot to get more sunscreen and supplies. I've been staying in this same cheap motel for five days now, living on peanut butter sandwiches. After restocking, I planned on heading out to another beach, one that I hadn't been to before. I never made it to the second beach. Instead I spent the afternoon reading through your father's journal again, trying to confirm that the man I saw actually was THE Michael.

Michael wasn't where I expected to find him. He was working on the docks in Marigot, loading supplies onto a cruise ship. I was walking by, heading for the convenience store, when I heard someone call out his name. I didn't hear anything else, only his name. It echoed over the din from the crowds in the market, and I heard it as clearly as if somebody had whispered it in my ear. "Michael." The word sounded teasingly sweet. I almost dropped my bags when I heard it. I tried staying realistic. How many Michaels were there in the world? A million? What were the odds that this was the one I was looking for? I walked closer and looked at the four men working on the pier. They were all lean and muscular. They had the builds of people who pushed and lifted things for a living, their bodies drenched in a thick, workingman's sweat. One of the men had a tank top on. The other three were shirtless. "Get a move on, Michael," I heard one of them yell with a slight Creole accent. "I've got a date I don't want to be late for."

"Relax," Michael answered, almost out of breath from his work, "I hear your mom doesn't even own a watch." The other two men laughed. Michael was pushing a large crate on a dolly across the pier toward the boat. The crate rattled as it moved over the slats of wood. I could see only his back as his muscles tensed and he leaned lower to push the crate faster. "You could always help me push. You know?" This time, all three of the other men laughed. I couldn't take my eyes off this Michael. I tried willing him to turn around. What are the odds? I asked myself. What are the odds that this is the man that I'm looking for? But somehow I knew.

"Who put a stick up your ass?" the Creole man called back to Michael.

"I'm just tired," Michael replied. He had pushed the crate all the way to the plank leading up the ship. The other two men took it from there.

"You off tomorrow?" the Creole man asked.

"Yeah," Michael replied. He didn't sound like I expected. I expected him to sound more boisterous, more alive. I stepped over to one side of the pier so that I could hide behind one of the pylons and watch this Michael. I knew where the scar needed to be. Your father told me the story so many times. I didn't understand why the details were so important then. Now I do.

"So, Michael, whatchya goin' to do on your day off?"

"I'm going to Grand Case to lie on the beach and get drunk," Michael answered. Then he turned toward me. I looked for the scar on his right side, slightly above his waistline. As Michael turned I could see the folds on his abdomen where his skin bubbled up surrounding a deep slit. It looked like he had a pair of lips on the side of his stomach.

I stayed on the pier for another hour at least, watching Michael. They had tried to wipe the world clean, to cleanse any connection I had to the War. They failed. I finally found something that they failed to erase. I needed to make a plan. I needed to figure out the best way to approach him. I figured I had one shot. He was going to Grand Case the next day. So was I.

Six

Addy and Evan made it as far as they could on foot. Even out in the fresh night air, they were both still struggling to breathe. They had made it out of the fire, but the fire was still inside of them. Addy kept scanning the streets for a place for them to hide. Hiding was the one thing in the world that she knew how to do really well. She was learning how to fight. She was trying to learn how to rebel. But, to her growing shame, what she knew how to do best was run and hide. It was what she'd been trained to do.

As they ran down the empty city street, Addy spotted a deserted building with a door that appeared loose on its hinges. She knew that the odds were good that it wasn't locked and, even if it was, Addy was certain that she could kick through the lock. Addy was pulling Evan behind her by his hand. She'd grabbed his hand after he killed the cop and she still hadn't let it go. "Come on," she urged him. "We need to rest. We need to get inside." She guided the two of them toward the dilapidated doorway. Before reaching for the door, Addy looked back. She could see the smoke billowing up in the moonlight from the house where they'd been asleep not long ago. She wished she knew what the fuck was going on.

When they reached the door, Addy pulled on it, but it wouldn't give. She couldn't tell if it was locked or merely rusted shut. She didn't care. She *lifted up her leg and kicked the door near the doorknob. The door swung open. She pulled Evan inside. Once inside, Addy sat Evan down on the floor. She let go of his wrist. She began moving around the building as quickly as her choked lungs would allow her. She was checking the windows to see if anyone could see them hiding from outside the building. The windows were all boarded up. Satisfied that they were hidden from view, Addy began looking for an escape route. She found another door down the stairs in the back. It led to a concrete yard surrounded by a tall chain-link fence. With a little strength, she thought that she and Evan could climb over the fence if they had to. It wasn't much of an escape route, but it would have to do. Convinced that this was the best that they could hope for at the moment, Addy returned to Evan. Evan hadn't moved. He looked up at her when she came back into the room. It was dark. Only a little gray light from outside slipped through the cracks in the boarded-up windows. Evan could see a bit of light pass through Addy's hair in the darkness. Her hair was as red as the flames that had engulfed the house. He tried to imagine what she looked like before she dyed her hair. Addy and Evan were still close enough to the madness that they could hear the sirens. Fire trucks. Police cars. Ambulances. Addy wondered how long they'd been blaring like that. Until that moment, she hadn't noticed them.*

"What are we going to do?" Evan asked Addy. His fear was evident in his voice. After what he'd just done, he had reason to be afraid.

Addy walked over to one of the windows and peered out through the cracks in the boards. She was trying to see the smoke from inside their hiding place. She couldn't. The angle was all wrong. Addy tried to think of what they should do next. She and Evan might have been the only two to make it out of their house, but she knew that there were other houses with other people across the city. Addy feared that those houses had been raided too. She knew that this wasn't an ordinary raid. For all Addy knew, every house in Los Angeles had been raided. For all Addy knew, she and Evan were the only rebels left in the whole state. She could check her phone—she'd managed to save it from the fire—but she knew that there wouldn't be any news yet. "We get our strength," Addy said to Evan, trying to sound strong, "and then we get the fuck out of here."

"Where are we going to go?" Evan shook his head. "I don't understand what's going on. What were cops doing there? Why were they trying to kill us?"

"I don't know," Addy answered him. She was trying to figure it out too. Could all of those policemen have been part of the War? She turned back to Evan. "How did you know how to do that?" she asked him. She was taking inventory, trying to figure out everything that they had going for them.

Evan knew what Addy was asking him about. Evan tried to replay what happened in his head. He remembered it like he was remembering a scene from a movie. The man in the uniform was catching up to them. Even with his helmet and vest on, even carrying one of the biggest guns Evan had ever seen, he was catching up to them. He and Addy were running up a hill, leading away from the highway. The ground was rough and dry and covered in the hard, dead roots of whatever used to live on that embankment. Even though the man in the uniform was catching up to them, they probably would have made it to the top of the hill if Addy hadn't tripped on one of withered, dead roots. If they could have gotten to the top of the hill, Evan thought that they could have gotten away cleanly. The cop seemed reluctant to shoot them from a distance.

Evan heard Addy fall. He heard the thump as her body hit the ground. He heard her cry out. The cry was a high, quick whimper that was almost over before it started, as if Addy nearly caught the sound before letting it escape her body. It was close to nothing, but Evan heard it. For the first time since Evan had met Addy, she sounded scared. It was the sound of her fear that made Evan look back.

When he looked back, he saw Addy lying on the ground. She was beginning to lift herself up. She was already on one knee, but the cop was so close to her now. Evan had stopped running. Maybe he was even moving back toward Addy already. He couldn't remember. The cop lifted the gun and aimed it at Addy's head. The cop wasn't going to stop her or arrest her or take her in or do whatever else cops did in the movies. The cop was going to shoot Addy in the head in cold blood. Evan knew that. Evan had heard the cops shoot the others. He heard the bullets tear into their bodies. He didn't want to hear that sound again.

The cop didn't see Evan coming. He didn't sense that he was in danger. He lifted up his gun to shoot Addy and, moments later, he was lying on the ground, dead. Evan acted to save Addy. He acted on instinct. He didn't do what he did intentionally. Addy knew that. Addy also knew that it didn't matter.

Evan had taken the gun first, grabbing it by the nozzle and pulling it away from the cop's hands. Evan was surprised how easily the cop let the gun go, but his surprise was nothing compared to the cop's. Two swings. The cop got in two swings with his empty fists, but the cop was no match for Evan. Evan was quicker and stronger. The cop died on the ground, a sharp rock buried into his skull. It took only seconds. Evan had never killed a man before, but when he did it, he did it with glorious efficiency. How did he know how to do that? "I've been training for years," he said to Addy in response to her question, "with him."

Addy looked at the cracks in the boards covering the windows again. "What do you know about the War?" she asked Evan.

Evan shook his head. "Just what I've been told. That there are supposed to be rules. That innocent bystanders are supposed to be left out of it."

Addy looked at Evan, beginning to understand. "You thought it was a game, didn't you?" she asked. She didn't need him to answer. What has this poor, innocent kid been dragged into? she thought. These battles didn't need to be his battles, but they were his battles now, whether he liked it or not.

Addy could see in Evan's face that he didn't think that the War was a game anymore.

Evan sat in humbled silence.

"We have to leave here before daybreak," Addy said to Evan as she continued to stare out the boarded-up window, listening for encroaching danger.

Seven

I haven't stepped outside my motel room since Michael left. I can't risk missing him. I haven't seen or heard any sign from Michael. I'm trying to stay calm. I'm trying to breathe. He has to come back. He has your father's journal. I've been watching TV, hoping that it would help to kill the time, but I can't concentrate on it. I've been watching the BBC mostly. The newscasters keep talking about flooding in Asia and riots in Africa. No one mentions the War. A world exists out there for you, Christopher. It is full of hardship and trouble, but it isn't this. It's getting dark outside. I'm getting into bed. I could use the sleep.

I was pulled out of sleep by the sound of the phone ringing next to the bed. I'd been dreaming. I don't know what I was dreaming about, but my head was a jumble. The phone rang again and I lunged toward it, unsure of how many rings I'd already slept through.

"Hello," I said when I got the phone near my mouth.

"Did you get some sleep?" Michael asked. I could hear the sounds of the docks behind him.

"More than last night," I answered. I wasn't in the mood for small talk. I wanted him to end my agony and come out and tell me that he was going to help me. I had to play the game, though.

"Good," he said with an urgency that I hadn't heard in his voice the previous morning. "You're going to need it."

"Why? What's going on?" I asked.

"Do you know Sunset Beach Bar?" he asked.

"The one by the airport?" I responded. Sunset Beach Bar was on my list of places to go to look for Michael. I hadn't made it that far down the list yet. It was famous because it was close enough to the airport that when the massive planes came in, people claimed that you could sit at the bar and almost reach up and touch them.

"Yeah," Michael answered. "Meet me there at noon today. Bring everything you have with you."

"Everything?" I asked, not that it mattered. Everything I had wasn't much. I was simply trying to gauge Michael's intentions.

"Everything," he answered.

"What's going on?" I asked. "Are you going to help me or not?" I was losing my stamina for intrigue.

"We'll talk at the bar," Michael said. I could hear the horn of a cruise liner behind him. "Noon." Then I heard a click and the line went dead. I got up and took everything I owned and threw it in my duffel bag. Your father had taught me to travel light. Packing took me less than five minutes. I looked at the clock. It was only half past eight.

I didn't care how much time I had. I needed to go. I grabbed my bag, flung it over my shoulder, and walked outside. The sun was shocking. I felt like I was walking free after days in solitary confinement. I had to remind myself that I'd been in that room for only a little more than twenty-four hours. The world around me was shining, reflecting the bright sunlight. I went to the motel office and checked out. My finances were running dangerously low.

Maho Beach, where Sunset Beach Bar was, was only about a half an hour drive from the motel, so instead of heading straight there, I stopped for breakfast. Breakfast killed about forty-five minutes. After I finished, I decided to go to the bar. Killing time anywhere else seemed pointless.

Michael showed up fifteen minutes late. At noon, I started to worry. I worried that he'd changed his mind and was standing me up. I worried that he'd been ambushed on the way to the bar and I'd never see him again. I worried that the whole thing was a setup, that he had no intention of meeting me, that he hated me for what I did to Joe. At five after twelve, I took out a cigarette and lit it. I inhaled. The chemicals did nothing to ease my anxiety. A few minutes later, I heard his voice.

"How long have you been here?" Michael asked, sneaking up on me from behind for the second time in two days.

I turned and looked at him. He had a duffel bag with him. I'd left mine in the car. "About two hours," I told him. "So what's going on?"

"We're leaving," Michael replied.

"The bar?" I asked, wondering why we met there only to leave.

"No," Michael answered. He sat on a bar stool next to mine. "The island."

"So, you're going to help me," I said, letting some hope slip into my voice. I assumed that's why we were leaving the island together.

"No." Michael shook his head. I felt my heart crashing into my stomach. "I can't help you," he continued. "I don't know how. I don't know where your son is, and I don't have the slightest idea how to find out. It's not my fight anyway." Michael reached down into the outside pocket of his duffel bag. "But I might be able to take you to some people that can help you." He handed me a bunch of postcards that he'd pulled from his bag. I looked at the picture on the back of one. It was a picture of the Lincoln Memorial at dusk. Streaks of golden light glowed in the tide pool in front of the Memorial. I flipped it over.

Michael, we can help you escape the War, it read. *Follow the directions below and we'll find you.* Below the words was a short poem that didn't appear to have any connection to the rest of the message. I flipped it to the back of the pile and read the next postcard. This one had a picture of the Washington Monument lit up at night like a giant sword pushing up through the earth. The message was similar. *We can help you escape. We know who you are. Follow the directions below if you're interested.* I flipped to another and another. They were all the same.

"How many of these do you have?" I asked Michael.

"Since I've been here, I've gotten about a dozen. I got the first one about three months in. I got it right after the first person came down here to try to kill me."

"What are they?" I asked, looking over the postcards again.

"My only guess is that they're from the Underground."

"What's the Underground?"

"They're former soldiers who've teamed up to try to wash people."

"Wash people?" I asked.

"Clean them. Help them disappear. They take people who want out of the War and they make them vanish. They turn them into innocents."

"And you think that they can help me?"

"I don't know." Michael shrugged. "But I don't have any better ideas." A plane flew overhead. The sound was intense, like standing inside the jet's engine. I looked up at the plane as it flew over us. Michael ignored it. He took that second when everyone else was looking up to glance around the bar.

"And you're going to take me to them?" I asked, wondering why he'd bother.

"Sure," he said.

"Why?"

"Because I need to get off the island too."

"Why do you need to get off the island?" I asked. Michael was making me nervous.

"Because there are more of Them here," he said. "I don't know how many, but more." Michael's voice dropped to a whisper. "I saw them following me. There are at least four of them. I can't beat all four of them—not at once."

"And that's why you're going to help me?" I asked.

Michael shrugged. His eyes met mine for a moment. "You have better options?"

"Okay," I said. "Okay." It wasn't what I'd been hoping for, but it was something. Maybe the Underground would be able to help me. "So what's the plan?" I asked. Michael glanced at the people around us. He put up one finger, telling me to wait for a moment. Then another plane roared overhead. As the sound grew louder, Michael spoke.

"Do you have your car here?" he asked over the sound of the jet engine. I nodded. He stood up from the bar and grabbed his duffel bag. The airplane was directly over our heads. "Meet me there in ten minutes." I nodded again. Michael walked off. He didn't look back.

I sat alone at the bar for another five minutes. I looked around at the vacationers in their bathing suits. They looked happy. I looked at each of their faces, wondering which ones I could trust and which ones I couldn't. Then I paid for my drinks, got up, and walked to the car.

I didn't see Michael when I got to the car. I'd already learned that didn't mean he wasn't there. I tried my best to act casual, walking up to the driver's-side door. I unlocked the door and sat down in the driver's seat. As soon as I did, one of the rear doors opened. I looked back in time to see Michael jump into the backseat. "Holy shit," I gasped. "You scared the crap out of me. Where did you come from?" Michael threw his duffel bag on the floor of the car and then ducked down in the backseat, closing the door quietly behind him. "What are you doing?" I asked, turning toward him.

"Look forward," he said, "and drive." I didn't ask any more questions. I put the key in the ignition and drove.

"Where am I going?"

"North. Toward Grand Case," Michael said. I put the car into gear and turned out of the parking lot. I had no desire to go back to Grand Case after what happened the other night, but I headed in that direction. Before long we were on the main road, driving past Mullet Bay and Cupecoy Beach.

"I feel stupid, Michael. Are you going to tell me what's going on?" I stared at the road, glancing periodically at my rearview mirror. A yellow, open-top jeep was following close behind us.

"I told you. They're here. They're looking for me. You're just a woman on vacation." I started to feel like I was being used. I checked my rearview mirror again. The jeep was closer, close enough that I could see the driver.

"Michael," I said, looking in my rearview mirror again to make sure I wasn't hallucinating. "I think we're being followed."

I heard Michael mutter something under his breath. "What makes you think that we're being followed?"

"I recognize the driver from the bar. He was there. He was looking at us."

"What does he look like?" Michael asked.

"I don't know," I said. "He looks like a regular guy."

Then Michael described him. "Brown hair," he said. "Short and curly. Black-rimmed sunglasses." It wasn't much of a description, but it was accurate.

"Yeah," I said.

"Fuck," Michael muttered. "How do you feel?" he asked me.

How was I supposed to answer that? My hands were trembling. "Fine," I said. I could hear Michael moving behind me. I heard a click. "What are you doing?" I asked.

"I want you to slow down," Michael answered, "and see if they drive past us." I peeked down at him through the rearview mirror. He had pulled the back of one of the seats forward, opening up a passageway to the trunk.

"What if they don't drive past us?"

"Then pull over. See if they drive past us then."

"What are you doing?" I asked again.

"I'm hiding in the trunk," Michael answered.

"What if they don't drive past us when I pull over?"

"Talk your way out of it. Forget that I'm here."

"What if they go for the trunk?"

"Then hit the gas and don't stop." Peeking in the rearview mirror, I could see that Michael had already pushed his legs into the trunk. I started to slow the car down. The yellow jeep slowed down too.

"They're not passing us," I said to Michael. Then I heard the click again. I looked behind me. The backseat was empty. Michael was in the trunk. He'd pulled the seat back into place. His duffel bag was gone too. It was like he'd never been there. I drove slower and slower. The jeep kept slowing down with me. A second man was in the passenger's seat. I didn't recognize him. He had straight brown hair. He wasn't wearing sunglasses, so I could see his eyes. He was watching me. Pulling over was a bad idea. I could feel it. Still, I did what Michael told me to do.

We had just passed Baie Rouge. I pulled over by a bluff overlooking the ocean. I could see the whitecaps on the waves in the water. When I turned off the car, I could hear the ocean churn. The jeep pulled over behind me. I wanted to ask Michael if he was sure this was a good idea, but it was too late.

The two men got out of the jeep behind me and started walking toward my car. The passenger walked about twenty paces past the car and then turned around to face me. The driver walked up to my window. He leaned in toward me, eyeing the inside of the car. "You okay, lady?" he asked after seeing that the car was otherwise empty. His shirt was untucked and hung over the waist of his pants. It did little to hide the gun tucked into his waistband.

"I'm fine," I said, trying to keep my voice from trembling. "I was letting you pass. You seemed to be in a rush."

"You're the lady from the bar," the man said, feigning surprise. I didn't respond. "Where's your friend?" he asked.

"That guy? Not my type. I don't go for scruffy guys." I looked at the other man standing twenty feet in front of the car, with his hands at his sides.

"Really? Because you guys looked pretty cozy." The man reached down and placed a hand on the car door. "Maybe you should get out of the car."

"No," I answered. "I'm not getting out of the car with two strange men." I shook my head. "I really need to get going." I turned the key in the ignition, restarting the car.

"Open your trunk," the man shouted at me when I started the car. He moved the front of his shirt, displaying to me the butt of his gun.

"No," I said, knowing that my lack of a poker face might get Michael killed.

"We're not going to hurt you," the man said. "Just open your trunk."

"No," I said again, and put the car in drive.

"Fine," the man said. He pulled the gun out from his waistband. He walked behind the car. I could see him in the rearview mirror.

He lifted his gun and aimed it at the trunk. He was standing only about ten feet behind the car. I looked in front of me. The other man had pulled out a gun too. I had only a second before the trunk was going to be littered with bullets. It was either them or Michael. Working on instinct, I put the car in reverse and slammed on the gas. It took a second for the wheels to catch. I could hear them screeching even before the car started moving. When the wheels caught, we moved fast, lunging backward. I looked into the rearview mirror. The man was holding his gun in front of him, getting larger and larger as the car sped toward him. He had underestimated me. He didn't think I'd fight. That's because he didn't know what I had to fight for. I squeezed the steering wheel so tightly that my forearms began to ache.

The man behind me got one wild shot off before I heard the thump as his body hit the back window. The window didn't break but the whole car shook when his body hit. I tried not to think about how badly he might be hurt. I looked in front of me. The other man was running toward the car now. He had the gun in his right hand. I looked down at the transmission again and put it into drive. I slammed on the gas for a second time. I aimed the car right for him. He lifted his gun and aimed it at me. I could almost feel the spot where the bullet would have hit if he'd fired. It burned my skin. He didn't shoot. At the last second, right before I hit him, the man tried to dive out of the way. By jumping, he kept me from hitting him dead-on. I only clipped him. Some part of his body ricocheted off the front corner of the windshield and his body careened off to the side. I pulled the car back onto the road. I checked the rearview mirror one more time. The driver of the jeep, the one I'd backed into, was on the ground—moving but not getting up. The other man was lying there, as still as a corpse.

I hit the gas. My foot was still pushed all the way to the floor when I heard a clicking from the backseat again. I'd almost forgotten that Michael was hiding there. "Slow down," he said, popping his head out. "You don't want to draw attention to yourself." With that, I felt all the muscles in my body relax. I eased my foot off the gas until we were moving at a normal speed.

"Where exactly are we going?" I asked.

"The Grand Case Airport," Michael said. "I have friends who can get us on a plane to Miami." I didn't want to go back to the Grand Case Airport. I didn't want to see the water where we'd dumped those bodies. But if it meant getting off the island, I was willing.

"Okay," I said, steering the car around another winding turn in the road. My hands were still trembling.

"You all right?" Michael asked, still dangling there, half in the trunk, half in the backseat. I had seen a lot of things since your father and I started running, but up until that point, I had never hurt anyone. I didn't answer Michael's question. He knew better than to ask it again.

Eight

The hum of the airplane's engine outside my window was strangely soothing, almost loud enough to drown out the voices in my head. "Are you okay?" I heard Michael ask over the din of the engine. I opened my eyes. We were flying above some low-lying clouds. They were soft and white and looked surreal and perfect. Through the breaks in the clouds I could look down at the water. For miles in every direction, all I could see was blue water.

I looked over at Michael. He was sitting in a seat on the other side of the thin aisle from me. If I reached out my hand, I could touch him. "I'm fine," I said, with no force behind the words.

"You're mad at me," Michael said.

I could feel tears rushing into my eyes, but I was determined to hold them back. "You used me," I said, sure now that Michael's plan all along was to use me as cover for his escape.

"Sure," Michael replied. "I used you to get off the island, and you're using me to take you to people who might be able to help you."

I could barely believe he was comparing the two. "I was honest with you. I asked for your help. And I didn't make you hurt anyone." I looked away, staring at the wall in front of me, caught between looking at Michael and staring out the window at the reminder of my own insignificance.

Michael laughed. "Is that what this is about? It's about those thugs you hit with the car. You didn't seem to mind too much when I took care of the guy pointing the gun at you the other night." I didn't want to respond. The more we spoke, the angrier I got.

"Let's drop it," I said.

"Listen, Maria," Michael said. His voice had the same inflections as your father's. I could hear their shared youths in Michael's voice. "If you really want to get your son back, you have to be ready to fight. Nobody's going to hand your kid back to you. You can't rely on anybody else to do your dirty work." He was right. I have to become colder.

"I'm just not used to it," I said. "I've never hurt anyone before."

"Well, you'll get used to it. You'll be surprised how easy it is to get used to."

"Do you think they died?" I asked.

"I don't think about it at all," Michael answered. Then there was silence. The only sound was the sound of the airplane's engine. I wanted Michael to reach out and grab my hand and tell me that everything was going to be okay. I stared out the window again. The plane was too small for Michael and me to escape each other, even if we wanted to. I heard movement and looked over to see Michael leaning down, unzipping his duffel bag. "I think I have something of yours," he said, reaching into his duffel bag and pulling out your father's journal. He'd promised to return the journal. He kept his promise.

"Did you read it?" I asked. If he read it, I thought he'd have to help me. If he knew how much your father loved you, he'd have to love you too.

"Yeah."

"What did you think?" I asked, expecting no more than a full conversion.

"I think you're a little minx," he said through a slightly crooked smile.

"What are you talking about?" I asked. When I realized, I could feel the warmth run to my cheeks. "You mean the sex?" I asked.

Michael merely smirked at me.

"It wasn't like that," I told him. "It wasn't like Joe wrote it. It wasn't like a cheesy romance novel." I looked over at Michael. For the first time since I'd met him, Michael was acting like the Michael from your father's stories. "Joe must have been trying to impress me with what he wrote. Or maybe he was afraid that I'd be insulted if he wrote the truth."

"What was the truth?"

I thought back to that first weekend I spent with your father, the weekend that we made you. I decided I would tell Michael this one thing. "It was beautiful. It just wasn't like Joe wrote it. It was clumsier and more tender. And scarier. It was so much scarier. And more special," I finished, nodding. "So much more special."

"Well, thanks for ruining that for me," Michael replied with a smile. I could feel some of the tension break.

"What about the rest of what Joe wrote?"

"You want to know what I thought?"

"Yes," I said.

"I was glad that Joe never gave up fighting, that he just found something different to fight for. It hurt when he ran off. I didn't understand it."

"Do you understand it now?" I asked. I wanted him to say yes. I wanted him to sing it.

"No," Michael answered, shaking his head. "I still don't understand why he ran. I'm just glad that he kept on fighting." Michael is so different from your father.

I looked down at my hands. "It takes a baby's eyes a few months to develop," I blurted out. "Until they're into their third month, they can't really recognize people—not by sight anyway." I looked up at Michael with pleading eyes. "So Christopher has no idea what I look like. If I'm lucky, he may remember my voice, but he won't know why he remembers it." I started to cry. "He'll be a year old in a few months. When babies are a year old, they start to fear strangers. That means that when I meet my son again, he's going to be afraid of me." Then he did it. Michael reached out and put his hand on top of mine, but he didn't tell me that everything was going to be okay. He didn't say a word.

Nine

I studied the postcards, trying to figure out what they might mean, as Michael drove. I read the one with the picture of the White House on it:

> *Michael, don't be afraid. We can protect you.*
> *Don't doubt the rust,*
> *Don't doubt the fall,*
> *Don't doubt the clock*
> *That is ticking on the wall.*
> *On the fifth day, freedom can be found in Malcolm's park.*

None of the postcards are signed. Each one seems more cryptic than the next. I flipped over the one with the picture of the Lincoln Memorial:

> *Michael, you don't have to be alone.*
> *Five is a lot,*
> *Three is not many,*
> *One is too little,*
> *Four is just plenty.*
> *On the third day, freedom can be found on Einstein's lap.*

We rented a car when we landed in Miami. All of the postcards are from Washington, D.C., so that's where we're headed. We plan on stopping for the night in Fayetteville, North Carolina, to give us more time to try to decipher the postcards' riddles and to get some rest.

I asked Michael what he thought the postcards meant. He said that he had no idea. I asked him how he knew it wasn't a trap. "I don't," he answered. "You can never *know* that it's not a trap. Sometimes you roll the dice and you take your chances." He kept his eyes on the road in front of him.

Then I asked him what he knew about the Underground.

"*Know* is a tricky word. I've heard rumors. I don't know what's true. Like I said, until I started getting these postcards, I thought it was a myth. What I've heard is that they're just the disaffected, the nonbelievers. Since they don't believe, they try to help other people who don't believe either."

"Don't believe in the War, you mean?"

"Yeah." Michael nodded. "Well, they believe it exists." Michael smiled. "They just don't believe it's worth fighting."

"Have you ever heard of them reaching out to someone before?"

"No," Michael said. "But I know a lot of people who died in the War and I've seen only so many bodies, if you know what I mean."

"So you think that some of the people you were told were killed might have run to the Underground?" Is that what he had hoped had happened to your father? Had I killed his hope by telling him what actually happened?

"No," Michael answered. "All I'm saying is that if I don't see a body, I suppose anything is possible."

The drive from Miami to Fayetteville is supposed to take us about twelve hours. Hopefully by then, I'll have figured out what some of the writing on these postcards means.

Ten

Addy took out her phone again. Evan was lying in the sand next to her, sound asleep. She looked down at his face and at the stubble on his chin. She liked how the stubble looked, even with the eighteen-year-old's empty patches along his jawline. In front of her, the sunlight glistened over the calm, seemingly endless ocean. Addy could hardly believe how serene the ocean looked. After everything that happened over the past two days, she half expected the sea to be boiling over. Addy and Evan had made it all the way up to Santa Barbara. They snuck out of their hiding place before dawn and hitched a ride up Route 1 out of Los Angeles. Addy made Evan hide in the shadows along the side of the highway while she flagged down a ride. He jumped out only after a car had pulled over. Their plan—Addy's plan—was to take the ride as far as the driver would let them go. That got them as far north as Santa Barbara. It was far enough for now. For the moment, Addy felt safe from the fire and the smoke and the men with guns.

Addy had known enough to keep her phone, her money, and her identification on her before the fire. She'd had enough experience being forced to stand up and run without having time to gather her things that she learned to always keep everything within reach at all times. Sleeping with empty pockets or without her hand curled around the strap of a duffel bag were luxuries Addy had nearly forgotten. Evan had never learned those lessons.

He grew up innocent, free from the running and the paranoia. Unlike Addy, when Addy and Evan ran from the burning house, Evan left everything behind. Addy prayed that Evan's cell phone and ID melted into the ground as the house burned down. Addy hoped that Evan could still have what she knew she would never have: the chance to disappear into the world without having to be afraid of every stranger he walked near for the rest of his life. His only chance was to remain anonymous. If they found his wallet, that chance was lost. He would be a marked man, just like the rest of them.

Sitting on the beach, Addy checked her e-mail on her phone. She'd checked it a few times already during the car ride up to Santa Barbara. When Evan found out that Addy still had her phone, he could barely contain his excitement. He saw the phone and assumed that Addy could simply call for help. The phone, Evan thought, would be their savoir. What Addy knew that Evan didn't understand was that it doesn't help to be connected to a world you don't belong to. People in Addy's world didn't give each other their phone numbers. They didn't text each other about how their days were going. It was too dangerous. Everything was monitored. Everything was tapped. Addy knew that her phone would not be their savoir. It was only a tool. They would have to save themselves.

Addy looked down at her phone. She still didn't have any messages. She didn't expect to. Addy was almost certain that everyone in the world who knew how to contact her had died in the raid. She didn't know how to contact anyone that she knew was still alive either. She kept checking her e-mail anyway, hoping for a miracle. Since her e-mail was still empty and Evan still asleep, Addy took the opportunity to see if she could find any clues about what had happened the night before in Los Angeles. She didn't want to look while Evan was awake. She wanted to see if she could find anything first. She was used to scanning the news for coded language about the War. She was good at deciphering the misinformation and the cover-ups. It was like a cipher. What Addy expected to find was a story buried deep beneath the headlines about an electrical fire in a small house in central L.A. or a freak accident at a meth lab. The information she'd found before had always been buried. She always had to dig. She didn't think this story would be different. She never expected to see Evan's picture on the top of every Web site she went to looking for news.

She read. The headlines were all a derivation of the same thing: TERRORIST GROUPS RAIDED *or* DEADLY TERRORIST GROUP STING. *Addy's worst fears were confirmed. Their house wasn't the only one that had been raided. Three separate SWAT team raids had taken place across Los Angeles. The raids were coordinated. At least twenty-eight people were killed. It didn't mention how many were taken into custody. Addy felt sick. The queasiness in her stomach grew with each word. It wasn't the facts—the three raids, that it was an actual SWAT team, even the twenty-eight dead—that frightened Addy the most. What scared her the most was the simple fact that the story was everywhere in big, bold letters. It wasn't supposed to be like this. The War wasn't supposed to be out in the open like this. Nothing was hidden. Nothing had been covered up. Either the raids had nothing to do with the War—and Addy knew that wasn't possible—or someone wasn't playing fair anymore. Addy kept clicking from one site to the next, scrolling through stories more quickly than she could actually read the words. It wasn't possible that all of the law enforcement officers involved in the raid were part of the War—too many had taken part. They were genuine LAPD working in conjunction with the FBI. The fucking FBI. Addy read the description of the raid. The words were almost identical on each site. The quotes had come down from somewhere. The raids were described as "coordinated attacks on the compounds of a growing, dangerous domestic terrorist organization." The stories differed on motive. Some said it was unclear. Some hypothesized that the terrorists were anarchists. They all echoed the fact that authorities had reason to believe that the terrorists were planning additional attacks on American soil. Some of the stories included pictures of the dead. Addy knew many of them. She saw Dutty's picture and Soledad's. Addy might have taken a moment to mourn if she believed that she had any time to be sad.*

Addy recognized other pictures too. She recognized the picture of the single fallen hero of the stories, the cop that Evan killed. She recognized him because she'd stared into his face over the barrel of a gun right before his life was taken from him. He was the authorities' only casualty. Twenty-eight deaths to one. Addy wondered if anyone else would question those numbers. Every time a site had a picture of the fallen officer, it had a picture of Evan too. The picture was a couple of years old, probably from Evan's driver's license. They must have found it on the floor of the burning house. The articles included Evan's real, full name. The articles branded him. He didn't need to have been born into the War. Now he was a terrorist and a cop killer. Sending Evan home to his parents and the peace and quiet of the small town he grew up in was no longer an option. In only a few short days, Evan had gone from an innocent eighteen-year-old boy to the most wanted man in the country.

Addy tried to think of what to do. She would have been able to clean Evan all by herself if Evan was still anonymous, but he was more than not anonymous now. He was infamous. She looked around them at the surrounding beach. The sun was rising higher in the sky. The air was warming up. People were beginning to make their way to the beach. Addy felt the eyes on her. She knew that someone might recognize Evan. His picture was everywhere. Addy needed help. She needed serious help. The Underground. Addy would have to go back to the Underground, if anybody was left. She worried that the Underground might have been raided into oblivion too. She wondered if the raids were bigger than just Los Angeles, but circumstance simply made Los Angeles dominate the news. She had no way of knowing. It was a new game now, and Addy no longer knew the rules.

Before turning off her phone, Addy checked her e-mail one last time. This time, she had a message. It was from an e-mail address that she didn't recognize. The e-mail itself didn't contain any words. It simply had a link to a Web site with a thirty-character URL made up entirely of gibberish. Addy hesitated for a moment, wondering if it was some sort of trap—if they'd be able to trace her if she clicked the link. In the end, she was too curious, too thirsty for information not to take the risk. A new page opened. The new page had a bright yellow background and dark green font. Addy recognized the colors. They were the colors of the revolution. Only eight words appeared on the entire page. Someone must have sent this message out to everyone who may or may not have escaped the raids. Someone had Addy's e-mail address. The message read simply,

THE REVOLUTION IS DEAD. LONG LIVE THE REVOLUTION . . .

Addy didn't know what the message meant. Maybe it was simply meant to let everyone know that people were still out there. If it had a greater meaning, it was lost on Addy. She didn't need a greater meaning. It was enough for Addy to know that she and Evan weren't alone.

The crowds began to pour onto the beach. It was only a matter of time before someone recognized Evan. Addy reached down and shook Evan awake. His eyes opened.

"You ready?" Addy asked. She didn't wait for an answer. She didn't even know why she bothered asking the question. Whether Evan was ready or not was no longer relevant. "Let's go," she said.

Addy didn't tell Evan what she'd learned. Not yet. She made him keep his face hidden as they walked, but she didn't tell him why. She was afraid of how he'd react. She was already dealing with enough unknowns. For now, Addy simply wanted to get the two of them moving again. The revolution is dead. Long live the revolution. Someone was out there still sending messages. Addy just had to figure out how to stay alive and keep Evan alive long enough to find them.

"Where are we going?" Evan asked.

"Have you ever heard of the Underground?" Addy answered.

Eleven

We're going to Meridian Hill Park. I made Michael stop on the way to Fayetteville to get a Washington, D.C., guidebook. I've found landmarks that match five of the six clues in the postcards. I think the references to the days match up with days of the week. I don't think the pictures on the postcards mean anything, and I still can't figure out what the poems mean. Today is Friday. The fifth day.

> *Don't doubt the rust,*
> *Don't doubt the fall,*
> *Don't doubt the clock*
> *That is ticking on the wall.*
> *On the fifth day, freedom can be found in Malcolm's park.*

Meridian Hill Park is also known as Malcolm X Park. I thought the poem might be a reference to a clock or a sundial or something. When I told Michael what I'd figured out, he told me that it all seemed kind of obvious. Even without figuring out what the poems meant, the other clues weren't hard to decipher. It made me more nervous that we were walking into a trap. I wasn't worried about myself. They weren't allowed to hurt me. I was worried about Michael. I told him that he didn't have to come, that he shouldn't come, that it was too risky. He told me that he owed it to me to stay with me until I found the Underground, since I helped him get out of St. Martin. Once we found the Underground he'd go back to his own life, whatever that meant.

Michael turned off the highway. I could see the monuments on the other side of the river. I knew each one by name from studying their pictures on the postcards and my tourism book. I could see the Jefferson Memorial and the Lincoln Memorial. I could see the Washington Monument jutting into the cloudless blue sky. We crossed the bridge into the city and drove past the monuments. We drove right between the Capitol Building, sitting like a giant ivory castle at the end of a long stretch of grass, and the Washington Monument. We headed north. I looked over at Michael. He was drumming his hands on the steering wheel. Every so often he'd lift his back off the seat and lean forward toward the steering wheel with his whole body. "What are you doing?" I asked.

"Stretching," he said.

"Stretching for what?" I asked.

"Just in case," he replied without looking at me. I didn't ask him to elaborate.

We drove around a circle with a fountain in the middle. It was a beautiful spring day. Throngs of people were sitting around the fountain, probably drinking iced coffees while absorbing the sun. "We need a plan," Michael said to me as we turned off the circle and started driving up a hill, still going north.

"I thought we were going to Meridian Park," I said to him.

"Going to Meridian Park isn't a plan. The plan is what we're going to do once we get to the park." I stared at him blankly. I had no idea what he was talking about. "If this is a trap, and I'm not saying it is, it was a trap set for me, not you. The only way you get pulled in is if you're too close to me." He paused to think. I could see the wheels turning in his head. "Here's what we do. I'll go into the park first and find someplace where I can see the whole park without being afraid that someone might sneak up behind me. You wait five minutes and then come in. This way you can look for whatever it is you think you're looking for, and I can keep an eye on you. Once you're in the park, you have to pretend that you don't know me. Anything else is too dangerous." Pretend I didn't know him? I didn't know him. Still, I wasn't ready to split up. My heart rate sped up when the car stopped. "Got it?" Michael asked, putting the car in park.

It all seemed so crazy. It was a beautiful day. Quiet. Serene. I tried to think of everything bad that had ever happened to me. I'd been through enough to know that how beautiful a day it was didn't matter. "I got it," I said.

Michael got out of the car. Before closing the door, he leaned down and looked over at me. "Five minutes," he said. I nodded. He closed the door. I looked at my watch. It was a little after two o'clock. I marked the exact minute so I'd know when I could leave. Then I watched Michael walk away. I tried to concentrate on the plan and the clues. *Don't doubt the rust. Don't doubt the fall. Don't doubt the clock that is ticking on the wall.* I tried to clear my mind of everything else, but it was impossible. You were in my head. Joseph was there too and now, surprisingly, so was Michael. For a moment, I didn't care why he was helping me. I was just glad not to be alone anymore. I closed my eyes. When I opened them, five minutes had passed.

I got out of the car. To be safe, I reached in and grabbed my backpack. It had my journal, your father's journal, and the baby-development book in it. I took the postcards from the Underground as well, slipping them inside the pages of your father's journal. Then I started walking toward the park. I could see the steps in the front of the park, two long flights leading up to a large field of grass at the top. I started walking up the steps, looking for anything that might be a clue. I didn't see anything, but I didn't linger. I wanted to get to where I could see Michael. Then I could take my time.

I got to the top of the steps. I could see the whole field, surrounded by benches. Behind the benches were trees that separated the park from the road. I looked down one side of the field. It was full of people—old people and young people, parents playing with their children. I didn't see Michael. I looked down the other side. Michael was in the middle of the park, standing up, leaning against a broad tree. From where he was standing, Michael could see almost the whole park, and the tree would hide him from anyone standing behind him. I took a deep, relieved breath.

I kept looking for clues, stopping in every nook to see if I could find anything that might mean *something*. I studied each bench for engravings or markings. Every few steps, I would look up again to make sure Michael was still watching me. He never looked back at me, though he appeared to be annoyed that I was risking our cover by paying so much attention to him. I didn't care. Knowing he was there made me feel safe. With him there, the park seemed pleasant, full of sunshine and laughter. I didn't believe that any of the people around us could be the enemy, not at that moment.

I circled the park once and didn't find anything. I started to think that maybe the clues weren't as simple as they appeared. Maybe we'd come to the wrong place. I wasn't ready to give up yet. I started to circle the park again. A cool breeze blew by, shaking the leaves on the trees. I decided to sit down at the next bench to think. I looked up at Michael. He still hadn't moved.

I looked around again from my new perspective. At one end of the park a young mother was playing with her baby. The baby couldn't have been much more than a year old. The mother was sitting down in the grass. The baby was sitting a few feet away from her. I couldn't hear her over the rustle of the wind through the leaves, but I could see that she was singing to her baby. Every so often the baby pushed himself up onto his feet, lifting himself into a standing position. Once on his feet, the baby bounced up and down to the sound of his mother's voice. Then he'd fall. Each time he fell, his mother would clap and he would look up at her and start clapping too. Then he would stand up again. The wind stopped and I could hear what the mother was singing. "If you're happy and you know it, clap your hands." Then the boy fell again, but this time, instead of falling backward, he fell to his side, putting his hands down right before his head hit the ground. Even though he caught himself, he started crying. He cried because he was afraid. I could hear him crying. The mother leapt toward him and lifted him off the ground. I wanted to leap toward him too. Instead, a sudden, muffled sound broke my concentration. I looked up. It sounded like someone was calling my name. I had no idea how long I'd been watching the child. Five minutes? Ten?

Michael wasn't standing by the tree anymore. I looked up just in time to see two men pulling him to the ground. One was standing behind him with his hand clamped over Michael's mouth. The other was aiming something at Michael's chest. He pulled the trigger and a split second latter, Michael's body convulsed. Why wasn't anyone helping him? The two men started dragging Michael's limp body away. I looked around. It was getting late. Most of the people were already gone. Only a few stragglers were left, and no one saw what was happening to Michael—no one except for me.

I stood up and started running toward Michael. "Stop," I screamed as loud as I could. One of the men, the one with the weapon in his hand, looked up at me. I saw panic in his eyes. I ran faster. I didn't know what I was going to do when I caught them, but

I ran. The two men worked faster. One lifted Michael's legs while the other grabbed him beneath his armpits. "Michael," I yelled. The man carrying Michael's legs looked toward me again but he wasn't looking at me. He was looking behind me.

Without slowing down, I turned my head and looked behind me. Someone was chasing me. He was wearing a suit and sunglasses and had an earpiece in his ear. He was running fast. I didn't understand why I was being chased. I stared at the man for a second, and then I felt someone else's hand reach out and grab my arm. The grip was like a vise. My body stopped with a jerk. The man who grabbed me was dressed exactly like the other one. I looked up at the spot where Michael's body had been, but he was gone. They'd gotten him. First they'd taken you and now they'd taken him. I started to scream. People around us were staring now. They didn't see what happened to Michael but they could see me, standing in the middle of the park, being kidnapped by two men. Still, no one did anything to help me. I screamed again. A few people stared at me. Others looked away when my pleading eyes met theirs.

"Please come with us, ma'am," one of the men said. I struggled, trying to break free of his grip. The man holding me reached out and lifted me off the ground. He began carrying me outside the park. I kicked my legs, but it was no use. He was so strong. They carried me toward a car parked on the street right outside the park. It was a big, dark sedan. The man with the free hands took a quick look around to see if anyone was still watching him. Then he opened the trunk. The trunk was large and empty. It was covered with a black liner. They threw me inside the trunk and slammed it closed.

It was dark. I screamed and kicked, but it was hopeless. They knew what they were doing. They'd made sure that it was impossible to open the trunk from inside. I heard the engine start. I could feel when we started moving and when the car turned. Whenever the driver hit the brakes, the entire trunk glowed an eerie red from the car's brake lights. I listened to see if I could hear the men in the car, but either I couldn't hear them or they didn't speak. My knees were jammed up into my chest. The next time they hit the brakes, I looked at my watch.

We drove for more than two hours. My legs began cramping. I had curled into the most comfortable position I could, a fetal position facing toward the back of the car. Even though it was nearly six o'clock when they finally opened the trunk, the light was momentarily blinding. Once my eyes adjusted to the light, I saw the two men in suits standing over me. "You can get out now," the one who had grabbed me said in a deep, authoritative voice. I could still feel his grip on my arm.

My muscles and joints were stiff, but I climbed out of the trunk. One of the men offered me his hand, and I took it. My feet hit the ground and I stretched the cramps out of my arms and legs. I looked around me. We were near a ranch-style house surrounded by woods. "Where am I?" I asked.

"Come with us," one of them said instead of answering my question. They started walking toward the house.

I followed them. Then I remembered. "No," I replied, stopping in my tracks. "What have you done with Michael?"

The two men looked at me. Then they looked at each other. The one who had ordered me to follow them said, "If he wants to see you, we'll let him."

"So he's okay?" I asked, not willing to let myself feel any relief yet.

"He'll be okay," one of the men said. "Now please come with us." I followed them, knowing that I didn't have any options. They were faster than me and stronger than me, and I had no idea where I was. The inside of the house looked more like an office building than a home. People were milling around. They were dressed more casually than the men who had grabbed me—wearing jeans and T-shirts—but they all appeared to be working, standing over desks, staring down at papers. Some of them looked at me as I walked. Most didn't. The two men led me down a long hallway and then down a thin flight of stairs. At the bottom of the stairs was a windowless room with a couch, a table, a television, and a watercooler. Attached to the room was a tiny windowless bathroom. The only way to see in or out of the room was through a small, reinforced window in the door. It was a cell. "Step inside," one of the men said.

"What's going on?" I asked, doubting that I was going to get a straight answer. "What are you going to do with me?"

One of the men grabbed my elbow. He was gentler now than he had been in the park, but I could still feel his authority. "No one is going to hurt you," he said. "We just need you to wait in here."

I began to mutter another protest, but before I could get the words out, they had closed the door. I reached for the doorknob and tried to turn it, but the door was locked. I shouted and banged on the door, but I could feel from the door's weight that no one was going to hear me. I looked out through the tiny window in the door. All I could see was the empty staircase. Four hours later, the light at the top of the staircase went dark.

In the morning, a new person came to the door. She came alone, carrying a tray with cereal and juice. When she first opened the door, I looked her up and down, wondering if I could take her. Even if I could, where would I run to? Besides, I knew better than to underestimate these people.

She didn't bother to close the door behind her. She placed the tray on the table and sat down next to me. "We thought you might be hungry, Maria," she said, sliding the tray toward me. I ate.

Whatever was going to happen to me, I thought I'd need my strength. The woman sat and watched me eat.

"What have you done with Michael?" I asked when I was finished, deciding that I would simply repeat the question until I got an answer.

"He's fine," she said. "He's here with us."

"But they shot him. I saw it."

"It was a Taser," the woman answered, "painful but not harmful to someone in Michael's condition. We don't normally use them, but things didn't go as we expected yesterday."

"Nobody helped us," I said out loud, remembering what happened.

"It's amazing what you can get away with in D.C. with a dark suit and an earpiece, Maria."

"How do you know my name?"

"Michael told us who you are," she answered, "but we already knew a lot about you."

"Who are you?"

"We're trying to help," she answered. She smiled when she spoke.

"What now?" I asked.

"When Michael wakes up, Clara wants to talk to you both."

"Who's Clara? Why is Michael still asleep? Are you sure he's okay?"

"Michael's fine. He was up late last night. We were trying to get him to talk to us. He refused to tell us anything without you there. Eventually, we gave up." The woman stood up and walked toward the door. "I'm going to leave the door open," she said. "But we'd appreciate it if you stayed here until we come back to get you." I nodded. Michael was here. I had no reason to leave. The woman walked away, leaving the door open as promised.

When the woman and another man came for me, they led me

back up the flight of stairs to the main floor and through the maze of desks and computers. I tried to listen to the conversation of one man who was talking on the phone, but he was speaking Spanish. We turned down another hallway. I could see a room at the end. Inside, a confident-looking gray-haired woman sat behind a large desk.

"That's Clara?" I whispered to the woman in front of me, not knowing why I whispered.

"Yes," she answered.

When we stepped into the room, I saw Michael sitting in a chair. He stood up when he saw me and put his arms around me. I grabbed him and held him tightly. We had touched only two times before, and one of those times Michael was holding a knife to my throat, but I held him now like I would fall if I let him go. "Are you okay, Maria?" he asked.

"I'm fine," I said. "How are you?"

"Alive," Michael answered.

I eased my grip on him and stepped back. "Who are these people?" I asked, knowing that he would tell me the truth.

"They're the Underground," Michael answered. "They're the people we're looking for." I looked around the room at the faces of the man and the woman who escorted me here. I looked at the woman behind the desk. I expected them to look different.

"Please sit down," the woman behind the desk said, motioning to the two chairs facing her. It was impossible to tell how old the woman was. Her gray hair was pulled back into a ponytail, but the skin on her face was taut. She looked strong. Michael sat back down. I sat in the other chair. The woman closed the door behind us, but both she and her colleague stayed inside, standing by the door. "My name is Clara," the woman behind the desk said to me.

"Is that your real name?" Michael asked before I had time to respond.

Clara looked at Michael. "It's nice to see that you're talking now, Michael. It's not my given name, if that's what you mean. We all take pseudonyms when we start working here, hoping that if word got out, it might help to protect our families." She looked at Michael again. "My given name doesn't mean anything anymore." I glanced out the windows behind the woman at the thick, green forest.

"Do you have any other questions you'd like to get out of the way, Michael?" Clara asked. From her tone of voice, I got the impression that she'd had this conversation before.

"Whose side were you on?" Michael asked without looking away from her.

"It doesn't matter," Clara answered. She picked up a pen and rolled it between her fingers.

"It matters to me," Michael answered.

"It shouldn't. People here come from both sides of the War. Any other questions?" Clara asked, looking at Michael. When Michael didn't say anything, she looked at me.

"What do the poems mean?" I asked.

"What poems?" Clara asked.

"The ones on the postcards."

"Nothing," Clara said. "They don't mean anything. We have a system. We target certain people that we think could use our help. When we identify one of these people, on either side"—she looked at Michael—"we send them the postcards. The only important information in the letters is the place and the day. We keep a list of who might show up and send teams out to pick them up if they do. The poems simply distract people. They're easier to contact if they have something else on their mind."

"So, what happened yesterday?" I asked, confused.

"Simple. When we reached out to Michael, he ran. Our teams know that when that happens, the safest thing to do is to subdue the target and bring him in. If he gets away, we have to worry about our own safety. Secrecy is what keeps us alive. We thought Michael might be running from us so that he could turn us in. We didn't know that he was running to you."

"How do you know who to target?" I asked.

"We have spies," Clara answered. "We have spies in the intelligence groups on both sides. They tell us about the people who get into trouble and the people who run."

"You have spies?" Michael asked, as if the idea had never occurred to him.

"Yes," Clara answered. "There are spies all over this War. Both sides have spies working inside the other's organizations. There are double agents. It's like any other war." Clara laughed. "And we have spies too. That's how we heard about you, Michael."

They had spies. They could have helped us. They could have hidden us. They could have hidden me and you and your father and we could still be together. We could be a normal family. "If you have spies," I said, staring at Clara, "why didn't you help me and Joseph?"

Clara stared back at me. Her eyes were full of regret. "We tried, Maria. We tried to help you, but it was too dangerous. All we could do was try to warn you when they got close. We did that once. When you were in Charleston, one of our spies reached out and warned Joseph that they were coming for you. We were still monitoring you, waiting for it to be safe to contact you, but you were constantly being watched. Then it was too late."

I felt my heart breaking all over again. People had been trying to help us. It made the pain worse. "I'm sorry, Maria," Clara said. I nodded to her, but I wasn't able to accept her apology.

"If you believe so much in your cause, why don't you fight for it?" Michael asked.

"You can't fight war with war. I believe that. And what do you think, Michael?" Clara asked. "You came to us, remember. We just told you how to get here."

"I think you're a cult," Michael answered.

"If that's what you think," Clara began, "why did you stop fighting?"

Michael shook his head. "I didn't stop fighting. I just stopped taking orders." It was the same line that he'd fed me.

Clara sat there for a few moments, tapping the pen in her hand on her desk. She was staring at Michael, seemingly trying to determine if he was worth her effort. "Do you even know what you're fighting for, Michael?"

"I know why I fight," Michael answered with pride.

"Sure you do," Clara responded. "But the War. Do you have any idea what the War is about?"

"I've heard stories," Michael said, wary of falling into Clara's trap.

"Slaves?" Clara asked. Michael nodded his head in affirmation. "And you're the good guys, trying to keep the other side from enslaving the world?" Michael didn't respond. "You don't really believe the slave story. Do you, Michael? You're better than that."

"How can you be so sure that it's not true?" Michael asked.

"I know that story's a bunch of horseshit because I've heard people on both sides tell it. And no matter who tells it, they're always the hero and the people on the other side are always the ones trying to enslave the world."

"Okay," Michael said to Clara, "then what is the War about?"

Clara shook her head. "I have no idea. That's why I do this. All I know is that a lot of people get a lot of power from this War, people who would be nothing without this War but who are, instead, virtually kings. Those people, the really powerful people, they don't have much incentive to end the War, and every reason to keep it going."

"So you're saying that they don't want to win?" Michael asked.

Clara nodded.

"I can't believe that," Michael said. He was staring down at the floor. "I know too many people who've already died to believe that."

"We can help you, Michael. We can get you out. We couldn't do it for Joseph, but we can help you."

Michael sat there in silence. No one in the room said anything. Then Michael spoke. "I don't want your help."

"Then why are you here?" Clara asked.

"For her," Michael said, motioning toward me.

Clara glanced at me for less than a second. "She's not part of this, Michael. We can't do anything to help her."

"My son," I said, not knowing how to finish the sentence. Clara looked at me again and then looked right back at Michael. I was holding my breath.

"Michael?" I pleaded.

Michael was sitting low in his chair, sliding farther down as Clara tried to dismantle his entire world. He sat back up. "I want you to help Maria find her son," Michael said to Clara. I began to breathe again.

"That's not what we do," Clara said. She leaned back in her chair, shaking her head.

"You have spies," I said, talking quickly. "You can find out where he is. You can find out where they've taken him."

"I can't risk my spies on that," Clara answered. "We're in the business of helping people escape the War. We're not in the kidnapping business."

"But my son will be part of this War," I said. I leaned in toward Clara's desk. I was in a panic. If she wouldn't help me, who would? "If I don't save him, he'll be a part of the War. You can save him from the War now. You don't have to wait."

Clara shook her head. "Your son already is part of the War, Maria—whether you like it or not. When he's old enough to make his own decisions, hopefully we'll still be here to help him. But he's got to decide for himself."

"Why?" I asked. It didn't make any sense. These people seemed as brainwashed as everyone else. They're not innocent. You still are. You can still be saved. If they couldn't see that, then they're still blind.

"That's how it works," Clara answered. I couldn't even think of a way to respond.

"What can you tell us?" Michael asked, breaking the silence. "Do you have any idea where Maria's son is?"

"No," Clara answered. She looked at Michael. "Are you sure this is what you want, Michael?"

"Tell us what you know," Michael answered.

Clara glanced at me again. I braced myself for what she was going to say next. "We don't know where your son is, Maria," she said. "We don't even know where they're keeping that information. We don't track children. We concentrate on saving people who want to be saved." She took out a blank piece of paper. "All I can do is explain the system for you." She started drawing on the paper. She drew one large box in the middle of the page surrounded by a circle of smaller boxes. "It's a shockingly low-tech, paper-only system," she said. "There are different locations, each with different information." She pointed to the boxes on the outer rim of the page. "There's redundancy built in. No one piece of information is kept in only one spot." She drew letters in each of the boxes. A few of the boxes contained some of the same letters. "Both sides are afraid of having one of their intelligence cells raided, so they won't centralize the actual information. Then there are central hubs that contain the keys that map out the information." Clara pointed to the box in the middle of the page. "If you want to find out where your son is, you need to find out where they keep that information." She pointed to all the boxes on the edge of the page, the ones with the letters in them. "To do that, you either need to go to the central location to find that information or you need to find someone who already knows it. The central location is nearly impenetrable. So I'd suggest trying to find someone who might know where the information is first."

"Then what?" I asked. "What do we do when we find out where they keep the information?"

"You either break in and get the information or you bribe someone to get it for you. This War is not as pure as Michael thinks."

"I can't do that on my own," I muttered at Clara. "I need your help."

"I'm sorry, Maria," she said. "I can't risk one of my men on a child who's in no immediate danger."

They didn't realize how important this was, because it seemed small to them. They didn't realize that it was my whole world. I felt cold, like I'd been stripped naked and pushed into icy water.

Clara turned back to Michael. "If you want to escape, we can help you." Then she looked at me. "If you want to go the other way, if you want to go deeper inside the War, you have to do that by yourself."

Michael stood up. "Take us back to D.C.," he said.

"Are you sure that's what you want?" Clara said. "We're not going to contact you again. If you leave now, you're on your own forever."

Michael didn't need to think about it. "Take us back to D.C.," he repeated. "You've got nothing for me here."

"I'm sorry to hear that," Clara said, standing up. I stood up too. "Good luck to the two of you," Clara said. She reached her hand out to me. I shook it. Her grip was fierce. She shook Michael's hand too. "Marcus and Dorothy will show you out," Clara said, her voice sounding slightly defeated. She motioned toward the man and woman standing by the door.

Marcus opened the door. "Take them back in the van," Clara said as Michael and I walked out. "You'll have to hood them." Marcus nodded. Clara sat back down at her desk, took out another piece of paper, and began working again before we were even out the door. We were already forgotten. She had already moved on.

Marcus and Dorothy escorted us outside the ranch. Two other people were assigned to drive us back. Dorothy gave me a hug before we left. "Good luck," she whispered in my ear.

They put canvas hoods over each of our heads before letting us into the van. We understood the risk that we posed to them now, so we bowed our heads as they hooded us. I had a million questions for Michael, but they would have to wait until we were alone again. Having already fulfilled his promise to me, I just had to hope that Michael would let that happen.

Twelve

Addy and Evan were lying next to each other in the darkness. Addy believed in the power of the darkness. It covered them. It kept them safe. Addy knew all too well that if you stood in the light while everything around you was dark, then you were blind while everyone else could see. If you turned off the light, at least everyone else was blind too.

Evan lay on his back and lifted his hand into the dark air in front of him. He splayed his fingers wide apart and slowly moved his hand closer and closer to his face. He was trying to see how close to his face he'd have to bring his own hand before he could see it. He saw a shadow when his hand was about six inches away. The shadow didn't get any clearer until Evan's hand was nearly touching the tip of his nose. The darkness was thicker than any Evan could remember.

They were making their way east. That was the plan. That's all that Evan knew. They'd been traveling for most of the day, hitching rides, never taking any one ride for much more than a hundred miles. To Evan, the whole concept seemed antiquated and silly. He felt like he was in an old black-and-white movie with actors wearing white T-shirts tucked into their jeans and cigarette packs rolled up in the sleeves. Addy told Evan that she thought it was the safest way for them to travel, that trains, planes, even buses were little more than glorified mousetraps. Once on one, Addy said, there was no way for them to escape. "How is a stranger's car any different?" Evan had asked.

"We'll take rides only from people driving alone," Addy answered.

"And how does that help us escape?" Evan asked.

"There's two of us and one of them," Addy answered. "And I've seen what you can do when you're cornered." Simultaneous rushes of pride and disgust ran through Evan's body when Addy said the words. It was like a chill running down his spine.

Evan wasn't sure how far they'd made it that first day. They'd caught four separate rides. He knew that they were somewhere in Arizona. He'd seen the signs when they crossed the border from California, but never any signs informing them that they were leaving. "What if someone recognizes me?" Evan had asked Addy between the first and second ride. They didn't have much time for idle conversation. Addy hadn't had any time to tell Evan more about the Underground. She didn't have time to tell Evan about her plan. All she had time to tell him was that they had to run because he'd been marked. Addy made sure that she found the time to tell Evan that his picture and real name were the lead stories on all the news feeds. She wanted to light another fire under him so that he'd be ready for anything. She wanted to find out what else he was capable of.

"If someone recognizes you," Addy answered Evan's question, "then we'll know that they've been paying too close attention."

It wasn't until they were lying together in the darkness in the shell of an old, abandoned trailer that they had a slow moment to talk. Evan had been thinking all day about the question Addy had asked him that morning. "Have you ever heard of the Underground?" She hadn't elaborated at the time after Evan said no. Instead, she changed the subject. Later in the day, when he'd pressed her for details about what the Underground was and what it had to do with him, she simply said, "I'll tell you later." It was later.

"Are you going to tell me about the Underground?" Evan asked Addy as they stared straight ahead of each other into the nothingness.

"I think they can help us," Addy responded. Evan heard her voice as if it was unmoored, as if it was floating through to him from far away.

"Who are they?" Evan asked.

"The Underground are former fighters in the War that have banded together to try to help others escape. No one knows how long the Underground has been around. Some people say that it's almost as old as the War itself."

Evan was confused. "Escape what?"

"Escape the War," Addy answered. "As long as the War has existed, there have been people who wanted nothing to do with it, who didn't want to fight. Sometimes people call them the nonbelievers. Some of the nonbelievers tried to run away, some got killed, and some banded together to try to help others like them."

"How do they help them escape?"

"They take them away. They teach them how to hide. They teach them how to run. The Underground has connections and networks all over the world. I think they can help us, Evan. I think that they can keep us safe."

"How do you know about them? How are we supposed to find them?"

"I used to work for them," Addy said. Her voice made it sound almost like she was confessing a sin.

"You used to work for them, but you left. What happened?" Evan asked, even though he probably could have guessed. Addy didn't seem like the type to find value in running. Evan understood. Running didn't make much sense to him either.

"I didn't want to do it anymore," Addy told him. "I didn't want to just teach people how to hide. I wanted to make it so people didn't even have to hide anymore. You can't believe in things halfway, Evan. If we were right to try to help people escape from the War, then we're even more right to fight to end it."

A quiet moment passed between them while Evan thought. "So, you left the Underground because you didn't think that they were doing enough.

You left it to become a rebel," Evan said into empty space. Evan didn't come up with the word rebel on his own. He'd heard Addy and the others use it.

"I guess you could put it that way. I wasn't alone, though," Addy said. "A lot of people like me left the Underground to try to fight against the War. You met some of them. We thought we were finally ready to fight back."

Evan took another moment. He inhaled the darkness. "But you said the Underground's been around for almost as long as the War. Why now? After all this time, why are people trying to fight back now?"

"It didn't start all of a sudden. The rumblings began about seventeen years ago. Something inspired more and more people to start leaving the War. Something caught hold." Addy paused, choosing her words carefully, trying to decide what to reveal to Evan and what to hold back. "When people left the War, they ran to the Underground, but the flood of people was too much for the Underground to handle. They couldn't hide them all. People started getting caught, and not just one person here and one there. A lot of people were caught and killed. The leaders of the War thought that would be the end of it, but every time they caught and killed someone whose only crime was trying to run away, everyone else who'd ever thought about running got angrier and more righteous. It took years before there seemed to be enough people to try to fight, enough of us to make a difference. We'd grown sick of listening to faceless voices ordering us around, telling us to kill. And the alternative, spending our lives hiding, cowering in fear, didn't seem much better. We thought we could end the War." She shook her head. She'd been so naive. "The unrest has been building for almost seventeen years. It's a wasteland out there, Evan. You probably don't even see it. You guys outside of the War don't seem to see anything even though you're surrounded by it, but it's a wasteland. We were just waiting for a spark to light the fire."

Evan wanted to put all the pieces that Addy was giving him together, but could do little more than try to figure out how he fit into the puzzle. He'd absorbed so much new information over the past few weeks that he could cling only to what seemed the most urgent and necessary for his own survival. He didn't have the endurance to try to guess what had happened seventeen years ago to start the unrest, let alone what had happened more recently to spark the fire. He focused on what was practical. "So why should we go to the Underground now?" Evan asked.

"You saw what happens when we fight them," Addy answered. "The two sides of the War work together and they fight back twice as hard. They have more people, more power, more weapons. That SWAT team wasn't part of the War, Evan. They broke all the rules. They went outside the War to try to stop us. Your picture should never have been in the news. I know how to hide people from the War. I don't know how to hide people from the rest of the world. We need help from the Underground. We need time to regroup."

Evan stared straight ahead of him and tried to think about everything. He thought about what his life would be like if he had to spend the rest of it in hiding. He thought about the person he wanted to be and whether that person was the type of person who runs or the type of person who fights. He thought about why he'd come to California in the first place. He tried not to think of the sound of the screams of the people he heard die in the fire, or the sounds of the bullets hitting the bodies. He tried not to think about his lost friend. "Once we regroup," Evan said after thinking and not thinking about everything, "are we going to fight again?"

Addy didn't know how to answer that question. Instead, she shifted her body in the darkness. Even before she moved, Addy's body was close to Evan's. Evan heard Addy move and then felt one of her hands press against his chest. Slowly, Addy slid her hand up toward Evan's neck. She used Evan's body to guide her, even though she couldn't see. When Addy's hand made it to Evan's neck, she knew even without being able to see where she needed to aim. Addy leaned into Evan, pressing her chest against his, and kissed him hard on the lips. It wasn't the first time they'd kissed. While their lips were still pressed together, Evan's hands fumbled over Addy's body. It wouldn't be the first time they had sex either. The first time was before the fire. It was before Evan and Addy and the others had attacked the intelligence cell. It was before Addy knew how brave and strong Evan could be. At the time, Addy thought Evan was a goofy, guileless boy. She seduced him the first time on a lark. She did it because she thought he was cute in an innocent sort of way. She did it because it made her feel powerful. She did it because what the fuck?

Evan was different this time. She could feel it in her body. Evan slid one hand under the waistband of her pants. He was more confident this time. Their lips separated for a moment as Addy gasped and bit down on her lower lip. Addy reached down too, searching through the darkness for the button to Evan's pants. Addy was still in control but not like she had been the first time. Nothing was the same as the first time. This time, Addy seduced Evan because he had saved her life. This time, Addy seduced him because of how quickly he had accepted his fate as a wanted man. This time, she seduced him because Evan's strength and instincts excited her. This time, she seduced him because, after everything that had happened, he was still willing to fight. Both times she wanted him. Addy'd spent most of her life trying to be brave enough to go after what she wanted.

Evan knew that Addy had taken advantage of him the first time. He had been afraid but he had his reasons for not objecting, reasons that went beyond the obvious facts that he was an eighteen-year-old boy and she was a beautiful twenty-two-year-old woman. Evan let Addy take advantage of him the first time because Evan had never in his life met someone as alive as Addy. God, was she alive.

The darkness surrounded Addy and Evan. Inside the darkness, they could feel each other's skin and hear each other's breath. They were on the run from the world, hiding in an abandoned trailer in the middle of nowhere. In all their lives, neither of them had ever felt more isolated, and neither of them had ever felt less alone.

Thirteen

The light stung my eyes. They pulled off our hoods while the van was still moving. If I craned my neck, I could make out the tip of the Washington Monument over the driver's head. We were back in D.C. I recognized the man who took off our hoods. He was the man who threw me in the trunk a day earlier.

"Where are you taking us?" I asked the man.

"Back to the park," the man said without looking at me, "where we found you. Unless there's somewhere else we should drop you off."

"You can take us back to our car," Michael said to the man. "We're parked just off Sixteenth Street."

"Are the two of you still traveling together," the man asked, staring at me with steely gray eyes, "or do you want to be dropped off somewhere else, ma'am?" I looked over at Michael, unsure how to answer him.

"Just take us to the car," Michael answered. "We'll figure out where we're going from there."

The man with the gray eyes looked at me again. I nodded to show consent. "Whatever you say," the man said. Then he told the driver where to go. I looked at the driver's eyes in the rearview mirror. I didn't recognize him. I wonder how many of them there are in the Underground. I've always wondered how many people are fighting the War. Now I also have to wonder how many people are against it. The deeper I go, the more questions I have and the fewer answers I get.

I looked over at Michael, trying to will him to look at me, hoping that he would give me some sort of sign that we were still in this together. He didn't. He alternated staring at the floor and out the front windshield. I hated him for not looking at me. I had an urge to kick him in his shin. I remembered a warning he had given me during the drive up from Florida. "After this, after we find these people, I'm gone. You need to start having your own plans for everything. Even when you have a plan, things don't go right half the time; without a plan you're completely fucked." The problem was that he was my plan. I needed him.

We pulled up behind the rental car. They knew where it was. At first nobody moved. Then the gray-eyed man turned back to us one more time. "Are you sure this is what you want?" he asked.

"I don't think I was given a choice," I responded.

"I wasn't talking to you," the gray-eyed man said. He looked at Michael, giving him one more chance to run away—one more chance to leave the hate and the violence and the death forever.

Michael stared back into those gray eyes. "I'm sure that I want you to let me out of this van."

"You're the boss," the gray-eyed man replied. He motioned to the driver, who got out of the van and opened the back doors. Light and air rushed in. "You're free to go," the gray-eyed man said to us, motioning toward the open doors. "The only rule now is," he said as Michael and I stood up, "don't mention us to anyone." He was focusing on Michael. They knew as well as I did that I had no one to tell.

"I'm a pariah," Michael answered with a shrug. "Who's going to listen to me anyway?" I followed Michael onto the street. The driver held out a hand to help me down. When I was back on solid ground, he let go of my hand and got back into the van without saying a word.

"We'll be watching you," the gray-eyed man said to us before reaching out to close the back doors. I couldn't tell if he meant that as a favor or a threat. My head was swirling. The gray-eyed man got back in the van and they drove away, leaving Michael and me alone on the side of the road. It suddenly dawned on me how clever their system with the postcards was. The only way anyone could find them was if they came looking first.

Michael started walking toward the passenger's side of the car. Until then, he'd always driven. He threw me the car keys. "What's going on?" I asked, confused and scared.

"You're going to drive me to the train station," he said. I clutched the keys into my palm so hard that they dug into my skin.

"What?" I said, still not willing to believe that Michael was leaving me.

"Get in the car," Michael ordered. I unlocked the car and got in. Michael climbed in next to me. We closed our doors, shutting off the sounds from the world. It was quiet. No one could hear us now.

"Where are you going?" I figured he owed me that much.

He didn't. "You don't need to know that. Just drop me off at the train station. You can keep the car. It's not in my real name anyway. Tell me where you're going and I'll try to stay in touch with you."

"That's not fair," I said, almost stumbling on my words. "How come I have to tell you where I'm going but you don't have to tell me where you're going?" Michael grabbed the keys from my hand. He pushed the keys into the ignition and turned them. The engine revved on.

"Because you don't want to know where I'm going," Michael answered. "Drive." My hands began to shake. I knew how to get to the train station. I'd basically memorized the city when trying to decipher the postcards.

We drove for a few minutes in silence before I found the courage to speak again. "I have nowhere to go, Michael," I said as I turned the car around and headed back downtown.

"Don't tell *me* that you have nowhere to go. You've got plenty of places to go," Michael answered. "You've got a family in Canada. You can lead a normal life. Go there." I kept driving, afraid to do anything else. I decided that I wasn't going to the train station, though. The traffic thinned out and we drove for a few minutes along the reservoir before Michael got suspicious. "Where are we?" Michael asked when he realized that we weren't headed to the train station.

"I'm not letting you run from me that easily," I said. I pulled the car into the parking lot for the FDR Memorial. "Do you have any idea how long I've been looking for you?"

"Yeah," Michael answered. "A couple of months."

I stopped the car. I stared at Michael so that he could feel the rage in my eyes. "No, not just a couple of months. I've been looking for you for almost my son's entire life, you bastard. You're not leaving me like this."

"I have to," Michael said. He grabbed his duffel bag from the backseat and stepped out of the car. I jumped out after him before he could run away.

"Why?" I shouted.

He walked back to me until his face was only a few inches from mine. "Because I'm going back. I'm reenlisting."

I couldn't believe what I was hearing. "After all of that?" I yelled. "After Clara told you that everything you've been force-fed about this War is bullshit, you're going back? Why would you want to go back to the War now?"

When Michael spoke, his voice was a few decibels quieter than mine. "First of all, just because Clara said something is bullshit doesn't mean it's bullshit. Second, weren't you listening when they told you that they weren't going to help you find your son?" What did he mean, *weren't you listening*? I wanted to slap him. I nodded instead. "Then why the fuck would you give two shits about what Clara said?" I had no answer. Michael was looking at me now, acknowledging me the way I wanted him to do so badly when we were back in the van. I wasn't sure I wanted it anymore. His eyes were on fire. "One thing, Maria," Michael said, lifting a finger for emphasis. "They said one thing back there that matters. They said that to find your son, you're going to have to find someone who might know where they keep that information."

"So?" I said, utterly confused. What did that have to do with Michael reenlisting in the War?

"You read Joe's journal, Maria," Michael said, looking around us to make sure that no one else could hear him. "You know that I wasn't a high flyer in the War. I've only ever had two things going for me. One, I'm good at killing people. And two, I have friends who know how to play the game and who might know something."

It finally dawned on me what Michael was saying. "Jared? Are you saying that you're going to try to help me by finding Jared?" Michael nodded. "That's insane. I don't care if he was your friend. He said he was Joe's friend too and then he killed him. He's the one who took Christopher in the first place!"

Michael grabbed my shoulders. "Keep your voice down," he ordered. "I warned you that you wouldn't want to know where I'm going, but you don't have a lot of options. Let me take care of this. Go home. I'll find you when I know something." For a moment, I was tempted by the idea of running away and leaving my fate in someone else's hands. If it was only my future that was at risk, I might have done it.

I looked at Michael. He was going to help me. Even if his plan was crazy, at least he was going to help me. I wasn't alone. "Why do you think he'll help us?"

"If I reenlist, he'll find me. I don't know if he'll tell me anything, but I know he'll come find me."

"How can you know that?"

"Because he's my friend." Michael's voice was soft. I could see in his eyes that he knew what I thought about referring to Jared as a friend. "I wouldn't expect you to understand."

"But why Jared?" I asked.

"Because after those people refused to help us, he's the only friend I've got."

"Are you sure Jared will know something?"

"I've never known him not to."

Fourteen

Michael and I sat across from each other, only the small hotel desk between us. We stared at the phone for at least fifteen minutes before Michael picked it up to make his call. Even I knew that once Michael dialed the phone, everything would change. There would be no going back. Michael remembered the last code they'd given him. He said that it was something soldiers never forgot.

Michael wasn't happy when I demanded that he let me help him. I refused to back down. I wasn't going to simply put your fate in his hands and walk away. Still, Michael had a number of specific conditions before he consented. First, he told me that I had to stay hidden at all times. This made sense. If they knew he was working with me, they'd know to question his motives. I'd seen what they did to people whose motives they no longer trusted.

Second, Michael demanded that I get into better physical condition. He said that he didn't want me holding him back. He wanted me to be able to fend for myself. "What do I need to do? Get stronger?" I asked.

"Strength helps," Michael said, "but it almost never comes down to physical strength. People live or die because they have endurance and are mentally strong enough to keep a level head when everything around them is going to hell. You can't keep a level head if you don't know what you're capable of. That, and you have to be able to run. If you can run from a fight, you're almost always better off running than fighting. You can't control everything, but I don't want you dying on me because you got tired."

Third on his list, "No more smoking."

"I don't really smoke," I told him. "I only do it to calm my nerves."

"Well, no more. It's too expensive. It's going to slow you down." I nodded in response. "And it makes you smell bad." I could feel the blood rush to my cheeks, making me blush. I wondered why he cared how I smelled. Then he told me.

"Half of running is hiding, and you can't hide when they can smell you." At first I thought he was kidding. "How do you think I found you that night in St. Martin?" I didn't answer him, too embarrassed to admit that I knew what he was going to say. "I could smell you," he said. My cheeks were on fire.

"Okay," I said. "We can stop talking about it."

"Okay," he answered.

"Any other conditions?" I asked.

"Yeah, you have to remember that I'm not Joe. I'm never going to be Joe." I wanted to tell him that he didn't have to remind me that he wasn't your father. I kept my mouth shut. He isn't your father, but I do see something in him that I saw in your father. Michael pretends to be a machine, but I can tell that he's decent.

"Is that all?" I asked.

"For now," he answered.

He picked up the phone sitting on the desk between us and dialed. As he went through the code to be patched through, I could hear the fear in his voice. In everything we'd already been through together, I had never heard that before. I knew he wasn't afraid of killing or dying. He was simply afraid that they'd forgotten him or that they were going to tell him that they didn't need him anymore. When Michael finished going through the code, three seemingly random names, the line went quiet for a long time. I imagined people scrambling on the other end of the line, trying to find anyone who could take this call, anyone who remembered Michael. It took ten minutes before someone picked up. I watched Michael as he waited. He was taking deep breaths, trying to control his anxiety. Then I heard a man's voice come through the receiver. "Hello, Michael. We've been waiting for you." Michael nodded and his breathing relaxed.

We were on a train to New York only hours later. They wanted him to come in. They have offices in New York. Michael is supposed to go to the office tomorrow. They'd never asked Michael to come in before. Michael had never heard of them asking anyone to come in before. For almost seven years, Michael did everything they asked. He killed over and over again in their name, and they just kept sending him out on jobs. Then he became a deserter, and now they want him to come in. I asked him if he was sure it was safe.

"When are you going to stop asking me questions that I don't have the answers to?" Michael answered, but the fear in his voice was gone. They'd remembered him.

Michael's appointment was at eleven o'clock in the building above Grand Central Station. Michael wanted me to stay at the hotel we'd rented, but I refused. I felt a need to be closer to him than that, like if I were closer to him, I could somehow protect him. There were benches littered throughout Grand Central Station. With everyone around me either coming or going, I figured I could simply sit on one and wait without having anyone notice me. I picked a bench near a coffee shop. I have no idea how long he'll be inside. Michael still wasn't nervous this morning. I was. Michael dressed for the meeting, wearing a crisp, pressed shirt with black pants and black shoes.

"I feel like I'm going on a job interview," Michael joked as he stared at himself in the mirror and straightened the cuffs of his shirt.

"Have you ever gone on a job interview?" I asked him.

"No," he said. "Have you?" I shook my head. We were quite a pair.

"Remember everything," I told him. "Remember everything they say. Remember how everything looks, how everyone acts. We don't know what's going to be useful for us. I want you to tell me everything when you get back." Somewhere inside that building might be information that leads us to you. Michael nodded.

We went out drinking together last night. Michael made me. How could I refuse him after everything he's risking for me, everything he's risking for you? We went to a bar in the East Village where Michael knew I wouldn't get carded. He drinks like a frat boy. He was downing something he called an Irish Car Bomb—a shot of Irish whiskey mixed with Baileys, dripped into a half a pint of Guinness—all night. He made me drink two with him. It tastes kind of like a milk shake. When I asked him if he thought he was too old for a drink like that, he told me that, "You're only as old as you feel." When I told him that I must be a hundred years old then, he simply said, "We have time to make you young again." He should know that you are the only thing that will do that, though. I have to hope that's what he meant.

This morning, we took the subway together to Grand Central Station. When we got here, we went our separate ways. We didn't talk. We didn't even look at each other after we got off the subway, in case someone was watching us. I came here. Michael headed for the elevators. I felt a twinge in my stomach when I could no longer see him. I hope this isn't one giant mistake. I hope Michael knows what he's doing. I hope I didn't just watch our last hope walk into a nightmare he can't escape from.

Fifteen

I waited there, across from the coffee shop, for six hours. I was okay for the first three. For the first two hours, I kept myself busy updating this journal. I killed another hour rereading select parts of your father's journal. There wasn't much left in it for me. I'd practically memorized it already. After three hours, I started to get nervous. I never thought whatever it was that Michael was doing or whatever they were doing to Michael would take that long. I didn't know what to do. I knew what floor Michael had gone to. I imagined myself going up and bursting through the doors, demanding to know what they'd done with Michael, but I was either too scared or too smart to do that. So I waited, burning through coffee after coffee. I looked at the face of every person who walked past me, wondering who were the ones going up to those floors where they planned the War and who were the innocent ones with normal jobs and normal families. Sitting there, sipping my coffee and counting down the minutes, I had no way of telling the difference. I was dying for a cigarette. I hadn't had one since Michael demanded that I quit.

Then at ten after five, I saw Michael walking away from the elevators. I had an urge to jump up and run to him. I controlled it. I watched Michael as he walked toward the subway. He had a thick manila envelope in his hand. He looked exhausted. His gait was slow and unsteady. What had they done to him? I wanted to know everything, but I knew I had to wait. I'd already been waiting ten months for information. I could handle another hour.

I followed Michael, staying close enough not to lose him but far enough to avoid arousing suspicion. I watched him as he got on the subway. Michael stood on the subway, hanging on to a pole and riding most of the way with his eyes closed. They had him for six hours. They must have done something to him. He looked like a shadow of the man who had walked into the building.

Even when we got back to the hotel, I still waited, letting Michael go up to the room first. I tried to give him time to compose himself. Then I walked up, unlocked the door with my key, and stepped inside.

Michael was sitting on one of the beds. The room was in complete disarray. The drawers had been pulled out of each of the cabinets. Our clothes and the rest of the contents of our bags were strewn across the floor. Michael lifted his head and looked at me when I walked through the door. "They were here," he said as I looked around the room. For a second, I felt like I was going to throw up.

"I can see that." I bent down and started picking up my clothes and throwing them back in my bag. "So what are we going to do?" I asked, wondering why Michael's voice had no sense of urgency.

"What do you mean?" he asked, looking up from the bed.

"They know about me!" I shouted. "They were in our room. They know I was here. We've got to leave." I picked up Michael's duffel bag and threw it toward him.

"They don't know that it's you," Michael said, tossing his duffel bag back onto the floor. "I told them that I met a girl in St. Martin, some gold digger that I was trying impress with an expensive hotel room."

"And they believed you?"

"Yeah. It's not really out of character for me."

"How can you be sure?"

"Because they had me locked in an interrogation room while they searched the place. When they came back, they said that everything I'd told them checked out." We'd gotten lucky. I had the journals and the postcards from Underground with me. If I'd left them in the room, Michael would probably be dead already.

"What happened?" All I wanted to know was if he learned anything useful, but I didn't want to be so crass as to come out and ask. Not yet. He looked too weak.

"As soon as I went inside, I was escorted to a large room. I barely saw anything. It was like going into any other office building. There was a reception desk with two receptionists. There were offices and secretaries. They have at least three whole floors of the building, probably more. The room they took me to was like a conference room with a long wooden table, but the chair at the head of the table was welded to the floor and had leather straps on its arms. I spent hours in that room, strapped into that chair."

"What did they ask you?"

"They asked why I ran away. They asked about my loyalties. They asked if I was still willing to fight. They asked what I thought about Joe's betrayal." Michael looked at me when he said those words. I didn't flinch. I was learning to control my reactions. "They asked me why I came back."

"What did you tell them?"

"I told them what they wanted to hear," Michael said.

"Did you convince them?"

"For now," Michael said, his eyes too weak to be as certain as I wanted them to be. "I need to rest, Maria. I'm going to get into a bath. We can talk more when I'm done."

"Okay," I answered.

Michael began unbuttoning his shirt. He was moving slowly, like his whole body was sore. When his shirt was unbuttoned, he bent one shoulder back and slowly lifted the shirt from it. That's when I saw the discolored bandages on his back. I couldn't tell if the discoloration was blood or something else. Michael dropped his other shoulder and pulled his shirt down off his back. The bandages with their dark stains ran across the entire upper part of this back.

"What did they do to you?"

"Take a look for yourself," he said, turning his back to me.

I walked over to him. I ran my hand over the sinews on his shoulders. Then I grabbed some of the tape holding the bandages on and I pulled it back. His skin was raised from one shoulder blade to the other, and scabs were already beginning to form. It looked like they had tortured him. "What is this?" I asked.

"Branding," he answered. I pulled away and looked. From a few feet away I could see that the blisters on his back were in the shapes of letters. They had written a message in his skin.

"You mean they burned you?"

"Yeah." It looked painful.

I blew on the blisters, hoping to cool them down. I could hear Michael sigh as he felt my breath hit the bare skin on his back. Then I leaned back again and read the words that they had burnt into his skin. "*Eu Loito Porque Eu Me Lembro*," I read out loud. The words were broken down into three lines. *Eu Loito* was on the top, *Porque* in the middle, and *Eu Me Lembro* on the bottom.

"I fight because I remember," Michael translated for me.

"What language is that?" I asked.

"Galician," he answered. "But don't ask me why, because I don't know."

"So, this was your punishment."

"It wasn't a punishment," Michael said. He stood up and walked over to the bathroom. "It was a test."

"What were they testing?" I asked, struggling to believe that someone could come up with a test so cruel.

"My loyalty," Michael answered.

"Did you pass?" I asked

"I didn't flinch when I smelled my skin burning or when I heard it sizzle beneath the hot metal." Michael pointed to the manila envelope I had seen him carrying earlier. It was sitting on top of the dresser. "My first new job is in that packet. I don't think they would have given me that if I failed." I looked at the envelope. Michael was going to kill whoever's name was in that envelope. "It's going to take a few jobs before they really trust me again." Michael looked at me as he spoke, making sure that I knew that this was only the beginning of the plan. We still had a long way to go.

"The words on your back," I asked. "What are you supposed to be remembering?" I thought maybe they finally told him the reasons for the War.

"Whatever it was that made me want to fight in the first place," Michael answered. Then he walked into the bathroom and closed the door behind him. I looked at the envelope lying on the top of the dresser. Michael must have known that I was going to look inside it. Why else would he have mentioned it and left it there? I heard the water running in the bathroom as Michael filled up the bathtub. As the water ran, I picked up the envelope and tore it open. I poured the contents of the envelope out onto my bed.

Eu loito porque eu me lembro. I don't need scars on my back to remind me why I'm fighting.

Sixteen

Michael's first target was a fat man. It was strange looking at the details of a life, laid out so meticulously, knowing that it was these details that would ensure that the life would soon be over. I thought of something my father used to tell me: the devil is in the details. If he only knew. It felt like we were being shown everything about this man's life so that we'd know exactly what we were taking away. The envelope contained dozens of pictures taken from different angles, showing the fat man doing various things. I couldn't even begin to imagine how they'd gotten some of the photos. They seemed so close, almost intimate. I found photos of his house somewhere in the country. One of the last pictures showed the fat man's three Doberman pinschers.

The fat man was five feet, eleven inches tall and weighed a touch over four hundred pounds. He was forty-seven years old. He was single. He lived alone, not counting his dogs. On the physical condition line, he was listed simply as *unfit*. In the section where the target's skills are noted, it said *Intelligence/strategy management*. I scanned down the page to the subsection titled *Combat Skills*. I looked across the page at the words *None known*. Then I flipped to the next page.

The reports contained page after page of the target's professional and personal history. I skimmed them, knowing that Michael would be out of his bath soon. The target was the younger of two sons. His father had been the head of intelligence for the Eastern seaboard for more than twenty years. He was killed in a raid when a boat that he was on blew up, killing him and three of his enemies. The story in the press was that the boat blew up due to a gas leak and some faulty wiring. According to the report given to Michael, the fat man's father sacrificed his own life to save critical intelligence for his side. Their father a hero, his sons quickly moved up the ranks in the War. His older son became a soldier and was killed in action at the age of twenty-nine. He had more than twenty confirmed kills when he died. His younger son, Michael's target, went into intelligence. He had no combat experience. He'd never fought a single fight in his life. Instead he rose through the ranks based on his father's and his brother's reputations. Despite having no fighting experience of his own, it was the fat man's job to identify individuals or families for "customized, small-scale extermination." He was one of the ones who picked their targets—he drafted the list of the dead.

I heard Michael unplug the bath and heard the water swirling down the drain. I had gotten through most of the contents of the envelope. I glanced at the remaining pages, trying to absorb what information I could. The fat man was a bit of a recluse. He saw other people only for work. His identity had been discovered just a few months ago. It had been a tip. He'd been betrayed by someone on his own side, someone with a grudge. They had gathered all this information in a few months. I flipped to the last page of the envelope. It was titled *Personal Connection*. Only one entry was on the page, about halfway to the bottom. A year was listed. It was nineteen years ago. I read the sentence opposite the year and felt my heart stop for a moment. The bathroom door opened. I flinched when it did, looking up at Michael. He stepped out of the bathroom with a towel wrapped around his waist. "I feel better," he said, looking at the contents of the envelope in front of me. Then he walked over to his duffel bag and took out a hairbrush and some deodorant. When he did, I got a clear view of his back. He had kept the bandages off, airing out the blisters and scabs. "So what did you learn?" He rubbed deodorant under his arms and walked back to the bathroom with his hairbrush. He left the bathroom door open. "Who do they want me to kill?" he asked.

I started to say the fat man's name, but Michael cut me off before I could even finish the first syllable. "No," he said. The word was sharp and cutting. I looked at Michael reflection in the mirror. He was shaking his head. "We never use their names. The targets don't get names."

I hesitated, thinking about asking him why, but I knew. It wasn't because the targets didn't deserve names; it was because naming them might make it harder. "Then what should I call him?"

"Pick a defining characteristic."

I could see Michael's reflection in the bathroom mirror as he brushed his hair. "He's fat," I said. I could hear the nervousness in my own voice.

Michael laughed. "Then we'll call him the fat man. Tell me more."

"He lives in some town north of here called New Paltz."

"I know the town. I used to hike there," Michael said. He finished combing his hair and took out a razor and some shaving cream. "Keep going."

"He lives alone," I said, "but he's got guard dogs." My voice trailed off, not knowing what else to say. Michael was shaving in long slow strokes from the bottom of his neck up. He looked at my reflection in the mirror, waiting for me to continue. "He's never fought. He works in intelligence."

"What does he do?" Michael asked. His voice was calm. Half his face was now cleanly shaven.

"He decides who they're going to kill. He analyzes their intelligence and picks the people they should target." I could see Michael nodding to himself in the mirror, either because he now understood why they wanted this man dead or because he now knew that he wouldn't have any qualms killing him. Maybe it was both.

"Anything else?" he asked as he whisked the last bit of shaving cream off of his face with his razor.

"Yes," I answered, my voice weak.

"What is it?"

The last page. "He's the one who decided to have your mother and father killed." I watched Michael's face in the mirror. I didn't want to see him any more hurt than he already was, but his expression didn't change.

"They gave me some crap to rub on the blisters on my back," he said, ending a painful silence. "I can't reach back there."

"I'll do it," I told him.

"After that, we're going to have to find you another place to stay." He said the words so casually that it took a second for them to sink in. Even when I finally understood the words, they did nothing but confuse me. I thought he was kicking me out because of something I said.

"What?" I mumbled. "Why?"

"You can't stay here," Michael answered. "They were here. They went through our things. They came once already. They'll come again. We were lucky that you weren't here this time. If they find you, it's all over." Michael came over and sat on the bed with his back to me. He handed me a tube of some sort of antibacterial gel. I squeezed some out onto my fingers and rubbed it gently on the raised skin on Michael's back. I could feel the muscles in his back tense up and then relax as I touched them. "I'll stay here," Michael said. "Leaving would look suspicious. We'll have to find you someplace where you can stay cheap, where we can pay in cash. We can't leave any paper trail." I didn't care where I stayed. I'd been staying in flea-bitten, pay-by-the-hour motels for most of the past seven months. I could deal with the lack of amenities. All the same, I didn't have any desire to be alone again. I didn't tell Michael that, though.

"Why don't you stay with me?" I asked. "You can keep this hotel room, but you can stay with me. If they come looking for you, you can say that you were out."

"We'll see," Michael answered. My fingernail caught on the edge of one of his blisters. His back tensed but he didn't flinch. "Let's find you your place. Then let me do this first job. Then we'll see."

"Okay." I had to settle for what I could get. "Can I ask you a question?" Michael nodded. "Do you know why they gave you this person to kill? Why now?"

"They're trying to retrain me," Michael said. "It's like I'm eighteen again. The first job they give you is someone utterly unsympathetic, someone who clearly deserves to die. If they can make it personal"—Michael paused—"all the better. The first person that I ever killed was a sixty-five-year-old man. Before the job, they showed me a video of the guy killing an unarmed nineteen-year-old girl with a crowbar. That's all I knew." I finished rubbing the gel onto his back. He stood up and walked over to his bag to get some clothes. "So I killed the old bastard. Hopefully, there's no video of what I did to that old man to inspire any of their soldiers."

Michael got dressed. We found a place for me to stay, a small apartment in Alphabet City that the owners are basically running as an unlicensed hotel. They didn't ask questions. We paid for four nights up front and told them that I'd probably be staying longer.

Michael went back to his hotel room. He promised that he'd stop by in the morning to check on me.

I can't sleep. My mind keeps racing back to the pictures of the fat man. He looks harmless. If he wasn't so fat, he'd look like a million other people you might see on the street. One of the pictures was taken through a store window. The fat man was inside, talking to the woman behind the counter. He was smiling, reaching into his pocket for money. Sensing that sleep wasn't coming, I took out the baby-development book. Since I met Michael, you've crossed over into another month. You're more than nine months old now. You're probably standing up. I should sleep. Hopefully, it will be your image that haunts my sleep and not the fat man's.

Seventeen

I made Michael go over his entire plan with me. "It's sweet. You're worried about me," he said when I pressed him.

"I'm worried that you're not taking this seriously enough."

"You don't have to worry about that."

"Just go over the plan one more time."

"I'm going to go at night," he said. "According to our information, he leaves two of his guard dogs outside at night and keeps one in the house. I'm going to bring some hamburger meat for the dogs outside and use it to drug them. I'll bring some rope with me so that I can tie them up once they're drugged."

"Why do you need to tie up the dogs if you already drugged them?" I asked.

"I'm going to give them tranquilizers. I'll tie them up while they're unconscious so that I can get out without having to deal with them if the drugs wear off. The dog on the inside will be a bit harder, but I think that I can collar him and lock him in another room."

"It seems like a lot of work for a couple of dogs."

"I'm not killing any fucking dogs," Michael said. It was clear from the look on his face that it wasn't up for discussion.

"Won't the fat man hear you by the time you get rid of the third dog?"

"Sure, but that dog stays on the ground floor and the mark will be on the second floor, so there's no way for him to escape without going through me. He's a fat man with no fighting experience. Maybe he'll take out a gun that he doesn't know how to aim. If he does, he'll end up shooting at shadows. Once the dogs are out of the way, the fat man doesn't scare me."

"How are you going to kill him?" I asked. The question made me queasy until I reminded myself what the fat man did for a living.

"Knife," Michael answered.

"Isn't that messy?"

Michael laughed. "You sound like Joe." The words weren't an insult. They were full of nostalgia. "Look, everyone has their preferred methods for this stuff. Joe was a strangler. He strangled people because it was neat. He strangled people because he didn't like messes. Knives are bloody, but if you know how to use them, they're quick. You can reduce your victim's pain and terror. It's a trade-off. I've always been okay dealing with the mess."

"Why not a gun?"

"We don't use guns—not if we think there's any other way. Guns are hard to cover up and easy to trace. If you want me to get back in their good graces, then guns aren't an option."

"Okay," I conceded. "Will you call me when the job is over?" Michael shook his head. "Then how am I going to know that you're okay?"

"See? I knew you were worried about me," Michael answered,

smiling. "You have to have a little faith, Maria. They'll be moni-toring this job to see how I do. I can't take chances contacting you. You stay here. I'll come back as soon as it's safe."

"If you wait until it's safe, you'll never come back," I said, only half joking. Michael half chuckled in response.

"I have something for you," he said to me, changing the subject. He reached into his pocket.

"Don't give me anything. I'm already asking too much of you. I don't want to owe you any more than I already do." Michael pulled a wallet-sized picture out of his pocket and handed it to me. It was one of Joseph's old class pictures. It was a bit scuffed at the edges, but even though I'd never seen this picture before, I recognized Joe's eyes immediately. "Wow. How old is he in this picture?"

"Thirteen," Michael said, "three years before I met him. I nicked it from his mother's dresser the first time I was ever invited to his house." I smiled at that, knowing that Michael deserved the photo so much more than Joe's mom ever did. "It sounds weird, but when I was a kid, I used to like to pretend that me and Joe had been friends ever since we were little kids. I used to like to pretend that it was more than the War that brought us together."

I held the photo in my hand. "Why are you giving this to me?"

"Because I know that you don't have any pictures."

"Of Joseph?" I asked.

"Of Christopher," Michael answered. "I thought you might be able to see some of Christopher in Joe's picture."

I felt a knot twist in my throat. I could see you. Looking at that picture was like looking into a time machine and seeing you in twelve years. "Do you have any other pictures of Joseph?" I asked. Michael shook his head. "Then I can't keep this," I said, even though I wanted to keep it. "It means too much to you."

"You can give it back to me when you find your kid and you don't need the picture anymore."

"I will," I promised. "Thank you," I added, hoping that Michael realized how much I was trying to thank him for. I keep the picture in this journal. I look at it frequently. I can't wait to give it back.

Eighteen

I avoided looking at the clock on the stove until a couple minutes past eight, when Michael was probably crawling through the woods toward the back of the fat man's house. It's hot, hotter than it should be in April in New York. This apartment doesn't have air-conditioning. I brought a fan to try to get the air moving around the place. It helps a little. It doesn't cool the air down, but it feels good blowing over my skin. It's too hot to close the windows. I can hear the incessant sounds of traffic outside. Horns honk. People shout out of car windows. In between the blaring of horns and the sounds of car engines, I can hear people talking out on the sidewalk. I'm alone, sitting here, trying to keep cool.

I memorized Michael's plan so that I can watch the clock and know what he's doing at any given moment. The crawling through the woods behind the fat man's house is more dangerous than it sounds. The fat man lives on the edge of acres and acres of rocky cliffs and trees. Some of the rock ledges rise over three feet above the ground with nothing on the other side but air. Michael has a small flashlight to help him navigate through the darkness, but he also memorized his approach and his escape route to try to avoid the cliffs, in case he has to run.

I watched another hour slip by on the clock. Michael should be coming up to the fence behind the fat man's house. He's supposed to flick his flashlight off before getting too close to the fence so the dogs won't notice him. He's supposed to stop in the woods and pack the tranquilizers in the hamburger meat and then make his way toward the house, following the light from the fat man's windows. Without his flashlight, Michael will have to feel his way through the darkness, reaching from tree to tree, listening for the dogs so that he knows he's headed in the right direction. The dogs will smell him before he can see them. They'll start to bark into the darkness. The barking should help. Michael can follow the sound of the barking. He just has to be sure to move fast enough to throw the meat over and head back into the woods before the barking gets too suspicious.

My mind keeps racing with every possible thing that could go wrong. I feel like I don't have control over my own thoughts. I'm worried about Michael, for you, for us, for him too. I keep imagining him tripping in the darkness, falling over a cliff, or even more ludicrous scenarios like him being eaten by a bear or a mountain lion. I'm also worried about the practical problems like making sure that each dog eats the right amount of the tranquilizers. If one dog eats too much, instead of two sleeping dogs, Michael's going to have to deal with one dead dog and one very angry dog.

It should take about forty-five minutes for the tranquilizers to go into effect. Michael is supposed to sit in the woods and listen for the dogs to go quiet. It's ten o'clock. He should be making his way toward the house now. The top of the fence is lined with barbed wire, so Michael is planning on cutting a hole in the fence with some wire clippers. Then he'll crawl through the hole and tie up each dog. He has two long lengths of rope so that he can tie the dogs to different parts of the fence.

Once he's taken care of the two dogs outside, Michael is going to have to break into the house through one of the basement windows. He'll cut the phone lines and the power. Even though the fat man is in his own house, Michael claims that having a flashlight in the darkness will give him an advantage. Michael will also have to deal with the dog inside the house. He brought a hood with him with a cinch at the bottom. The hood is similar to the ones Clara made me and Michael wear when they drove us back to D.C. in the van. Michael's plan is to get the hood on the third dog and to lock it in a separate room downstairs.

The night air has gotten cooler, but it's still hot. I have the fan in the window, trying to pull the cool air in from outside. Michael should be tying up the dogs now. The whole job is only supposed to take another hour to an hour and a half at most. The fat man's life was forty-seven years in the making and is about to be unraveled by three and a half hours of work, and I'm sitting here. Michael is the only person in the world who knows where I am, and he's wandering through the darkness over two hours away. I wonder how many jobs he's going to have to do before Jared contacts him. Two? Ten? Every job is one more person that will die because I convinced Michael to help me.

What is that? Somebody's knocking on my door. How is that possible? Nobody's supposed to know I'm here.

Nineteen

I put the journal down. The last time I'd heard an unexpected knock like that, strangers came into my home, killed your father, and stole you from me. I wasn't about to let something horrible like that happen again. I stopped writing. My eyes scanned the apartment to gauge how quickly I could run. I had barely bothered to unpack my bag. It was sitting on top of the bed in the other room. I looked over at the fan buzzing in the window. The fire escape was on the other side of the window. I stood up, trying to move fast without making any noise. I took four quick steps into the bedroom. I put my foot on the bottom rung of the ladder leading up to the bed and pulled my duffel bag off the mattress. I threw the journal into the bag. Anything else not in the bag, I was prepared to leave behind. I heard another knock as I pulled my duffel bag off the bed. This one was louder. I felt sweat rising on my skin due to the heat and the adrenaline. I took a quick look around the bedroom to see if there was any other way out. The window in the bedroom had locked bars on it. Even if I could get through the bars, it was a four-story drop to the street.

I moved quickly, stepping back into the kitchen. I had opened the window to pry the fan out so that I could get to the fire escape. It was an old, squeaky window and it was no more than ten feet from the apartment door. I put my palm on the bottom of the window, getting ready to push. I heard a third louder, more forceful knock. Whoever was out there was less than ten feet away from me and was losing their patience. I pushed up on the window and it screeched like fingernails scratching a chalkboard. The banging on the door grew louder and more intense. The door shook. I grabbed the fan and moved it out of my way. I threw my duffel bag onto the fire escape and swung a leg over the window ledge. I looked down. I could climb down three stories and then jump from there. The city was buzzing beneath me. Lights were shining everywhere. I had forgotten all about Michael. I had forgotten about the fat man. If people found out who I was, none of that would matter. I was about to swing my other leg over and run when I heard a voice shouting through the door.

"Maria," the voice yelled. "I know you're in there. You don't have to be afraid." It was a woman's voice. I recognized the voice from somewhere. She knocked again. Then she shouted, "It's safer to stay than to run, Maria." I stopped. The voice didn't scare me. I straddled the window and tried to think of what to do. I tried to imagine what your father would have done, but your father wasn't there. Michael wasn't there either. I was alone.

"I'll be right there," I yelled toward the door. I pulled myself back into the apartment, leaving my duffel bag on the fire escape in case I had to jump for it. Then I walked toward the apartment door. I left the chain lock strung across the door and opened it the two inches the chain lock would allow. Then I looked outside.

A woman was standing outside the door. She was bigger than me but not by much. She was wearing cargo pants and a black tank top. She had a bulge in the pocket of her cargo pants that I was sure was a weapon. I recognized the woman. It wasn't so long ago that this woman had brought me breakfast when I was hungry. "Dorothy?" The woman nodded. What was she doing outside my door? It had been only a week since I was never going to see her again. "Are you alone?" I asked her.

"I'm the only one standing here right now," she answered.

"Okay," I said. Then I closed the door and unhooked the chain.

Dorothy stepped inside. Without asking, she began a silent examination of the apartment. Despite the heat, she closed the bedroom window as she passed it. Then she came back into the kitchen and looked out the window leading to the fire escape. She grabbed my duffel bag from outside and handed it to me. "You probably want this," she said. Then she closed the kitchen window too. With the windows closed, the apartment heated up like a greenhouse and the sounds from the city were muffled into little more than white noise.

The way Dorothy was moving made me nervous. She caught the look I was giving her. "You can't be too careful," she responded.

"Am I in danger?" I asked.

"Not that I know of," she replied. I wasn't going to second-guess her. She helped people hide for a living.

"What are you doing here?"

"We'll get to that," she replied. She looked over at me. "How are you?" she asked. I think she was trying to stop me from asking more questions. It didn't work.

"How did you know I was here?" I remember thinking how innocent Dorothy looked when I first met her. She didn't seem so innocent now.

"We've been following the two of you. It's standard protocol when people leave us without accepting our help. We need to make sure that they aren't turning us in."

"So you've been following us the whole time?"

"Not me," Dorothy said, "but someone." I felt a chill run down my spine. We had tried to be careful. No matter how careful we were, it wasn't enough.

"Why are you here?" I asked Dorothy again. I hadn't expected to see her again, ever. I hadn't expected to see any of them again. Once they said they couldn't help me, I believed that was the end of it.

She was looking out the windows of the apartment into the windows of the adjacent buildings. Satisfied with what she saw outside the window, Dorothy sat down at the kitchen table. "We want your help."

"My help?" I asked, too confused to be offended yet.

"We want you to help us hide someone." Before I had a chance to respond, she continued. "He's nineteen years old. He's your age, Maria. He doesn't want to become a killer, so we've reached out to him." I tried to think of something to say, some way to object. "We need a way station," she said. "Six days at most."

"Why me?" I asked.

"Neither side knows where you are. You're off the radar. Besides, we thought you might be sympathetic given your situation. This kid is basically Christopher in eighteen years. Wouldn't you want someone to help him?"

I looked at the clock on the stove. It said eleven thirty. If everything went according to plan, the fat man was dead. "Do you smoke?" I asked Dorothy.

"No," she answered.

"I haven't had a cigarette since you guys found us in D.C. It was one of Michael's conditions for agreeing to help me. I still carry a pack wherever I go, though." Dorothy's features softened. She looked more like the woman who brought me breakfast a week ago. "I never smoked before they kidnapped my son."

"If you need a cigarette, I'm not going to judge," Dorothy said.

I shook my head. "I'm saving them."

"For what?" Dorothy asked.

"I don't know," I answered honestly. The still, hot air in the apartment was stifling. "What does it mean to help you hide someone? What would you need me to do?"

"The kid needs a place to stay. We need to find him someplace in the city that's safe so that we can make a plan for him. The process of cleaning someone isn't simple. We've just made contact with the kid. It takes time. We knew you were here. It seemed to make sense. All you have to do is let him crash here."

"That's it?" I asked.

"That's all. When we're ready to take him to his next stop, we'll come get him."

"How do I know I can trust him? How do I know that I can trust you? You guys wouldn't even help me."

"You don't. I will tell you this, though. If you help us here, we may be able to help you in the future." I paused at this last statement. I nearly forgot everything else that she'd said.

"Are you telling me that if I do this, you'll help me find my son?"

Dorothy shook her head. "I can't make any promises, but I do have some influence with Clara."

I looked at the clock as I thought about it. Hopefully, Michael was on the road, driving home. "What side is the kid on?" I asked.

"Does that matter to you?" Dorothy asked.

"It's going to matter to Michael," I said. Dorothy looked disappointed. I didn't care. She wasn't the one putting her life on the line for me. "If it matters to Michael, it matters to me." I thought about the photo of your father that Michael had given me.

"He grew up on Michael's side, but hopefully he won't have to worry about sides ever again." Dorothy watched me think. "His name is Joe. You'll be saving his life."

I already had the fat man's death weighing on my conscience and I wasn't even sure he was dead yet. There would be more too, more bodies left in the wake of my mission to find you. I liked the idea of saving someone to balance out the karmic scales. But what about Michael? "If I agree, how do we do this? How do I find the kid?" I asked.

"The day after tomorrow," Dorothy said. "Meet me at noon in Tompkins Square Park. Do you know where that is? It's close to here."

"I can figure it out," I said, agreeing to help her before I even realized I'd consented.

"I'll have Joe with me," Dorothy finished.

I took a long breath, the same type of breath you take before diving into deep water. I looked at the clock again. It was almost midnight. "Okay," I said. I wasn't being naive. I understand the risks, but everything has risks. I simply have to hope that they're worth the reward. "But don't forget that you guys owe me."

Dorothy smiled a genuine smile. "I knew you were a good person when I met you. I knew that we'd be able to count on you."

She had an enthusiasm in her voice that I didn't share. "I didn't expect anything like this," I said to Dorothy as she stood up from the table.

"What did you expect?"

"I don't know," I said. "I just want to find my son."

"Things rarely happen the way we expect them to, but they happen anyway," Dorothy said before turning and walking toward the door.

"Dorothy." I stopped her before she let herself out. She turned back to me. "When this is done, after I've found my son, will you try to convince Michael to leave the War again?"

"We were already planning on it." Dorothy opened the door just wide enough to slip out. "See you at noon on Tuesday," she said, and then she was gone. Everything is happening so quickly now. I re-hooked the chain lock after Dorothy left. Michael is supposed to be back at his hotel in less than two hours. What am I getting myself into?

Twenty

I ran through the dark city streets as fast as my legs would carry me. It was four in the morning. The city was almost quiet. I wondered if I was still being followed. I questioned every movement that I saw around me and the motive of every person who was out at this hour. I knew my motive. I needed to know that Michael was okay. I had waited until three in the morning to call the first time. I just wanted to hear his voice. He should have been back at the hotel for hours by then. He didn't answer. I called again and again. Still no answer. Then I'd decided that I'd had enough waiting.

I'd never run so fast. I could feel the blood pumping to muscles in my legs; new muscles that I'd developed from my new exercising regimen. I could feel the extra air in my lungs. It took me less than twenty minutes to get to Michael's hotel. I didn't see anyone following, but I knew how little that meant. I knew that what I was doing was dangerous, but I felt compelled to do it anyway. I couldn't take losing another person that I cared about. The hotel lobby was quiet. One man was working the lobby. He looked up at me as I walked through the door. I put my head down and walked like I belonged there. The man buried his head back in his newspaper and didn't say anything to me. I knew where Michael's room was. I took the stairs. They seemed safer, less conspicuous. I bounded up the stairs, skipping a stair with every few steps, stopping at the door with the number 3 on it. The door was solid. It had no window to look through. I had no way to tell what lurked on the other side. I put my hand on the door handle and pushed the door open a crack. The hallway was empty. I could see the door to Michael's room. It looked exactly like every other door in the long hallway: closed and quiet. I stepped into the hallway. I stepped as softly as I could, trying to avoid making any noise. When I got to Michael's room, I knocked. I tapped lightly at first. Each knock was answered with silence. He had to be there. I knocked louder. He had to be inside. I spoke Michael's name into the door. I reached down to the doorknob and tried to turn it to see if the door would open. "Michael, are you in there?" I spoke into the door. The words felt too soft and too loud at the same time. "Michael," I almost shouted. I'd reached my limit. I couldn't risk waking up the people in the other rooms.

Then I heard a noise. It wasn't coming from behind the door. It was coming from the far end of the hallway. It was almost five in the morning now. My first instinct was to run. It's what I'd been taught to do. I was somewhere I wasn't supposed to be and I was going to be caught. I tried to stay calm. I took my hand away from the door and turned, ready to walk away, to run if I had to. I could hear footsteps behind me, coming toward me. They were loud and strange, like whoever was behind me was dragging one foot across the ground. I made it about halfway from the door to the stairwell when the voice stopped me.

"Maria?" it said, somehow finding that soft-versus-loud balance that had eluded me. "What the fuck are you doing here?"

I turned back around. Michael was standing in the hallway. He had his key in his hand and a duffel bag over his shoulder. I could see dark maroon specks on his hands. He wasn't putting any weight on his right leg. "I couldn't wait anymore. I was worried," I answered.

"You shouldn't be here."

"I know."

"Get inside," he said. He slipped the key in his door. I stepped into his room. I could see out the window. It was still dark outside, but the light would be coming soon. Even if I couldn't see it, I could feel it. Michael followed me inside, limping badly.

"What happened?" I asked. "You were supposed to be here three hours ago."

"Things didn't go exactly as planned," he answered.

"What happened to your leg?"

"You shouldn't be here," Michael said again. "What if they come and check up on me? What then?"

I had no answers to his questions. "We need to get you cleaned up and you need to tell me what happened," I said instead.

"Why do you need to know what happened?"

"Because the details are important," I said. I looked down at Michael's injured leg. His pants were taped to his leg with duct tape. Beneath the tape, his pant leg was torn to shreds.

"Why are the details important?"

"Because I need to learn. Joe tried to shield me from things and, when he and Christopher needed me, I was useless. I need you to teach me what Joe wouldn't so that I can protect Christopher next time. I need you to teach me so that I can help to protect you. I need to know everything."

"Okay," Michael said, "but not here. There's a first aid kit in the bathroom. Grab it. We'll go to the roof."

The first aid kit was on the counter in the bathroom. It was brand-new. Maybe Michael was more prepared than I gave him credit for. I stepped back out of the bathroom. "Let's go," I said. "You can lean on me on the way up." We took the elevator up to the top floor and then walked the one flight of stairs to the roof. A Do Not Enter sign hung across the door to the roof, but Michael assured me that the door wasn't locked. I pushed it open. We were alone, eight stories above downtown Manhattan. The city was quiet. The sky was a deep purple.

We found a spot where Michael could sit down. I knelt in front of him and started pulling the tape off his leg. I could see the blood. It was caked into his pants. "Whenever you're ready," I said. I opened up the first aid kit and took out the alcohol to clean out his wounds. "Tell me what happened."

"I pulled my car into the woods about a mile from the mark's house," Michael began with a nod, "so that no one driving by would see it. Then I took out the flashlight and headed into the woods. The woods were dark. The flashlight gave off just enough light for me to dodge tree branches. I pointed the light toward the ground in front of me, trying to make sure I didn't walk off a cliff. Every once in a while I heard something, leaves rustling or twigs snapping, but I could tell that the sounds weren't being made by people. Still, I held my knife in my right hand in case whatever was in the darkness attacked me.

"Eventually, I could make out the jingling of the dogs' collars above all the other sounds, so I knelt down and opened my backpack. I took out the meat and the drugs and molded two big meatballs full of roofies. Then I turned off the flashlight and started following the sounds of the dogs. Everything was on schedule. When I got near the fence, the dogs started going ape shit, barking and jumping. I knew I had only a few seconds before the fat man realized they weren't barking at squirrels, so I ran up to the fence and threw one of the drug meatballs over the fence. Both dogs ran for it, but once the first one got to it, the other one ran back at me. When he did, I threw the other meatball over the fence near him. Then I hightailed it back into the woods to wait for the drugs to kick in. I got a good hundred yards away and I listened. At first, everything sounded the same. I could still hear the dogs' collars through the darkness, but I could hear their movements start to drag as the drugs kicked in. I took the wire clippers and the rope out of my bag and I waited. When I was sure that the dogs were out, I walked back to the fence.

"There wasn't a lot of light in the back of the house, but there was enough for me to see the dogs. They were unconscious, lying about ten feet from each other, breathing deep, hard breaths. I took out the wire clippers and cut a hole in the fence just big enough for me to crawl through without catching my clothes. I was inside. So far, so good."

I had gotten all of the tape off of Michael's leg. Most of the blood was dripping down from around his knee. I lifted what was left of his pant leg up so that I could see the wounds. The sky was still too dark for me to get a good look. It was getting lighter, though. The city was waking up. I could hear it. We were running out of time. I wanted to hear the rest of Michael's story. I dabbed the alcohol on Michael's leg. I expected him to flinch when the alcohol hit his wounds. He didn't.

"So I go over to the first dog and I poke him with my foot to make sure that he's really out. The dog doesn't budge, so I figure I'm safe. I scoop the dog up in my arms and carry him away from the hole that I cut in the fence. I lie the dog back down on the ground and tie one end of the rope to the dog's collar and the other end to the fence. Then I go back for the second dog and do the same thing. This one makes a little noise when I nudge him, kind of a low growl, but other than that, he doesn't budge either. I carry him to the fence but on the other side of the hole, far away from the first dog. I could feel the dogs' body heat as I carried them. I could feel their hearts beating. They seemed so harmless, knocked out like that. I don't know how you teach a dog like that to be that vicious.

"Then I walk up to the house. I take that little crowbar out of my bag and I head to the basement window that we talked about, the one with the rotting wood in the frame. I start digging into the rotten wood with the crowbar. It was even more rotten than we thought from the pictures. Digging around the window frame was like digging a hole in soft dirt. It took only about ten minutes before I had dug out enough of the rotten wood to be able to pull the whole window frame out with my hands. So I take the window out and I slip quietly into the basement, trying not to rouse the other dog. I turn the flashlight back on. I take the hood for the dog out of my backpack. Then I walk over to the power box and I find the wires for the power and the phone. The power's the big deal, but I cut the phone line too because, what the hell?

"Then I tuck my knife into my belt and head for the stairs. I've got the flashlight in one hand and the hood in the other and, for the first time, I start thinking that we didn't think this through enough. I had felt the muscles on those dogs outside. There was no way I was going to be able to wrestle that dog into the hood. Every job has one of those moments where you suddenly feel like you're in over your head—even the easy jobs. It was too late to turn back, though. So I walk up to the top of the stairs and I put my ear against the basement door, trying to see if I can hear the dog. Nothing. I don't hear a sound. I turn off the flashlight and put it in my backpack so I can get two hands on the hood and still get to my knife quickly if I need to.

"Slowly, I start to push the door open and look around. The basement door opens into the kitchen. From there I can look to my right into the living room or to my left into the dining room. Both rooms look empty. I figure that the dog must be upstairs. Then I hear a low rumbling sound right in front of me. It sounds like a truck. So I look straight ahead of me into the kitchen for the first time and realize that the fucking dog is standing right in front of me. I can see its eyes shining in the darkness. The growl's so deep that I can almost feel it in the floorboards. The dog couldn't have been more than five feet from my face. I froze. I had the hood in my hands, but I had no idea how I was going get the hood on the dog's head. The dog's growl kept getting louder and louder, and I could see its teeth now. Then it leapt straight for my face. I moved about a foot to one side and put both my hands up to block the dog from ripping my face off. My hands hit the dog in the chest, and I just kind of push him with everything I've got." I looked up at Michael. He was enjoying telling the story now. It had been a long time since Michael had someone to tell his stories to. He kept going, pretending not to notice that I was watching him.

"I get lucky. I push the dog through the open basement door. The dog flies through the air and down the steps. Before I even hear his body hit the ground, I get out and close the door behind me. The dog rolls all the way down to the stairs to the bottom of the steps but it doesn't even faze him. In a second, the fucker was back up the stairs, scratching against the other side of the basement door like he's trying to dig his way through. So I grab a chair and prop it up against the door to make sure the dog's trapped. The dog is barking like crazy now, so I know that my cover is blown."

"Were you nervous?" I asked, wondering what it felt like to be on the verge like that, to be hunting.

"It's always safest to surprise people, but I wasn't nervous. I wasn't afraid of the fat man. I knew I could take him. So I run up the stairs as fast I can. I know that the quicker that I can get to his room, the less time the fat man has to calm himself down. As I'm running up the stairs, I pull the flashlight out of my backpack so that I'm holding the mask that I meant to use on the dog and the flashlight in the same hand. I can see the mark's door now. It's closed, so I know he's still inside, and I have to assume he's aiming a gun at the door." Michael caught me watching him. He held my eyes, watching me back, testing to see how I reacted to the rest of his story.

"So I start running, as low to the ground as possible in case the fat man shoots randomly through the door. When I get to the door, I don't stop. I reach up, grab the doorknob, and open the door without even standing up straight. Once the door is open, I dive into his room, getting as far from the door as I can in one leap. I hear the first gunshot while I'm rolling across the floor. The bullet pierces the wall about a foot from the door. Then there's another shot. It's nowhere near me. This one hits above the door. Even in the darkness, I can see the wood splinter. I pull the flashlight out in my left hand. My mark, finally getting his shit together enough to realize that I'm not by the door, turns toward me. When he does, I shine the flashlight right in his eyes, blinding him."

Michael stopped. He must have seen something in my face. "Do you want me to keep going?" he asked. "I don't have to. I don't know what you're going to learn from the rest of the story."

"Keep going. I need to hear it all," I said. Maybe there wasn't anything else to learn, but I wanted to know what things were being done on my behalf.

"Okay," Michael said. The city was alive beneath us now. Michael was talking over the din of the cabs and garbage trucks on the street. "The fat man flinches when I hit him with the light, so I drop the flashlight and I leap toward him. It takes only a second. In that second, I get the hood over his head. He drops the gun and I push him. I meant to push him just enough to get him away from the gun, but when I push him he stumbles backward and falls to the ground. He reaches up and tries to pull the hood off, and I wait. If he wants to see the man who's going to kill him, I'll give him that. But I move close to him. By the time he gets the hood off, I'm right there. I can see the fear in his eyes. I always expect them to say something like 'Please.' They almost never do. Then I plunge the knife into his neck, right below his jawline. I pull the knife across his neck, creating a gash from one side of his neck to the other. The blood comes now, pouring out. I take a step back. He never said a word. I waited until I was sure he was dead. It took only a couple minutes. Then I left."

I couldn't believe that was the whole story. "So how did you hurt your leg?"

"On the way out, I decided to go back through the hole I cut in the fence, since I knew the way from there. One of the dogs that I drugged had woken up. He must have chewed his way through the rope. As I climbed back through the hole in the fence, the dog grabbed me by the back of the leg. The damn thing's jaw was like a vise."

"What did you do?"

"Well, he was still pretty stoned, so I kicked him in the face with my other leg and finished climbing through the fence. He must have been too drugged up to figure out how to jump through the hole. Then I walked back to the car, but it was a slow walk because of the new holes in my leg. When I got back to the car, I knew that I had to clean myself up a little bit before walking through the hotel lobby, so I taped my pants to the wounds in my leg."

"And that's why you were late?"

"Yeah." Michael let out a small laugh. "You look disappointed."

"I thought there would be more to it," I admitted.

"I'm not a beginner at this, Maria. I'm good at killing people. Sometimes these jobs just aren't that hard."

I don't know what I was expecting. "I should go home," I said to Michael. I'd finished doing what I could to clean his wounds. Then I remembered Dorothy. I still needed to tell Michael about the promises I'd made while he was away. I walked halfway across the roof. I didn't want to tell him—not yet—but I knew that there wasn't enough time to wait. "That woman from the Underground found me," I said, turning back toward Michael.

"Who? Clara?" I could hear the surprise in Michael's voice.

"No. The younger one. Dorothy. They've been following us." Michael looked down at the ground, trying to process this information. "I told them that I would help them to hide someone," I said.

"You what?" Michael asked, sounding even more surprised. "I thought we were on the same page, Maria. I thought we had a plan."

"We are," I said. "We do." I shook my head, trying to think of something to say. "One of the kids they're trying to help needs a place to stay for a few days. They asked me to help. I said okay. It's nothing."

Michael looked away from me. "I need to get some sleep. Let's talk about this later. I'll come to see you later."

"Okay," I said. "Can you make it back to your room on your own?"

"I think I'll manage," Michael answered.

I wanted to say something else to him, *thank you* or *I'm sorry*. I didn't have the guts to say either. "I'll see you later?" was what I said instead.

"Go home," Michael answered, staring past me at the city. So I left.

Twenty-one

"So are you going to tell me about your decision to become a hero?" Michael asked. It was late in the afternoon. I was still awake when Michael knocked on the door. I tried to sleep but it didn't come. I could smell liquor on Michael's breath when he came inside.

"I'm not trying to be a hero," I told Michael. I just want to be decent, I thought to myself. "It's going to be six days at most," I assured him. "We're not even going to have to do anything." I made the same promises to Michael that Dorothy had promised me, even though I had no business doing so. I told Michael how Dorothy had promised to try to help us if we helped them.

"And you believe that?" Michael asked.

"I don't know. I think it's worth the gamble." Michael's leg didn't appear to be any better. His limp was noticeable. I felt guilty. I wanted to give him something. "The kid is on your side," I told him. Michael didn't say anything. He just nodded. "I wouldn't have agreed to it if he was on the other side," I assured him.

"You do realize that he might lead Them right to us?" Michael asked.

"Honestly, Michael, I don't even know who *Them* is anymore," I answered with a chuckle.

"Hopefully, no one ever reminds you," Michael said. He let the words sink in for a minute. He didn't sound angry. Instead he sounded disappointed. In that moment, I would have preferred anger. "When do we pick this kid up?"

"You don't have to help me."

Michael looked me in the eyes. His buzz was wearing off. "I don't have to do any of this," he reminded me.

"Noon tomorrow."

"Okay," he said. "I'll be here before ten. We'll need time to get ready." Then he stood up from the couch. "By the way, they gave me my next job," he told me. "It's in Philadelphia. They gave me two weeks."

"That's not enough time. Your leg—"

"It'll have to be enough time," he cut me off. "If you want them to trust me again, then I can't go asking for a breather after my first job." He walked toward the door. I didn't want him to leave—not like this. The only thing I wanted less was to ask him to stay. I didn't say anything, he walked out the door, and I was alone.

I slept that night. It wasn't a deep or an easy sleep, but it was something. In the morning, I woke up early to exercise. I did push-ups, sit-ups, and dips on one of the kitchen chairs. Everything is getting easier. I can feel the muscles in my body changing. I don't think it's visible, but I'm getting stronger. I went for a run. I was only planning on running for forty minutes, but I had excess energy to burn so I kept going and ended up running for over an hour. As I ran, I thought about your father. He used to go on long runs in the morning five or six times a week. Sometimes he'd be gone for two hours at a time. I used to ask him what he thought about when he ran. He told me that most of the time he wasn't thinking about anything—he was just putting one foot in front of the other and going. "And the other times?" I asked.

"I think about you," he'd say, smiling at me, "and Christopher and how lucky I am."

"What do you think about when you think about us?" I would tease him, fishing for details.

"I think about the three of us living in a small house in a small town somewhere. I think about going to Christopher's Little League games. I think about taking him fishing. I think about us growing old together, watching Christopher become a man. I think about me getting a potbelly and taking long naps on the couch on Sunday afternoons. I think about how beautiful you're going to look when your hair turns gray. I think about meeting Christopher's first girlfriend. I imagine she'll be a lot like you. I think about watching him fall in love."

"I guess it's a good thing your runs are so long," I'd say to him, and he would kiss me. They took so much away from me.

Twenty-two

Michael knocked on my door at almost exactly ten o'clock. He knocked once and waited. That's how I knew it was him. He was too proud to knock twice. I undid the chain lock and opened the door just wide enough for Michael to slip through. "How did you know it was me?" Michael asked.

"I recognized your knock."

Michael walked past me into the apartment without responding. I closed the door, and Michael began asking questions. He wanted to know everything that I knew about the kid: what he looked like, why he was running, where he was going next. He wanted to know where in the park we were supposed to meet. All Michael's questions made me I realize how little I knew. I said *I don't know* so often, the words lost their meaning. "What's with all the questions?" I asked. Dorothy had made it seem so simple.

"The kid's running, right?" I nodded. "That means somebody is chasing him." Michael walked over to the window and looked out. "And another thing, the next time someone asks you to meet them somewhere, you pick the place. Don't let them do it. Now we need to go to the park early to be able to scope it out. There's a lot we need to know. We need to get a feel for the sight lines. We need to understand our escape routes. If anyone sees me helping this kid, we can kiss Jared good-bye."

I hadn't even thought of that. "I can do this on my own," I said again. This time, after the torrent of questions I couldn't answer, I was worried that Michael would agree with me.

"You don't believe that," Michael said, "and if you don't believe it, then it's not true." His eyes were cold.

"What can I do to make this better?" I asked him. I wanted things to go back to the way they were. Michael ignored my question.

Michael made us walk around the park twice before we even went inside. First, we did one loop a full block away from the park, walking the streets surrounding the streets that surrounded the park. Michael explained that if we had to run, we'd want to know where we were running. We'd want to avoid the unexpected. Next we circled the streets directly surrounding the park. Michael kept looking up at the buildings around us, trying to determine what parts of the park were visible from the buildings and what parts were hidden beneath the trees. "If they try to pull us out into the open, you'll have to go and bring them back to me. We can't risk me being seen."

The park was full of young people of every shape, size, and color. I could hear children playing at the playground. No matter what they looked like, nobody would stand out in the park; nobody would look out of place. Maybe that's why Dorothy picked it. Once inside the park, Michael made us look for every place where someone could hide both in case we had to run and hide and in case someone might use one of the hiding places to try to ambush us. Then Michael had us study potential bottlenecks, exit routes that led to nowhere. By the time we were finished, it was close to noon. We went to the spot Michael had identified for us to wait, a shady spot under a tree on the grassy hill in the middle of the park.

"Now what?" I asked.

"Now we wait for them," Michael replied. "We're doing them the favor. They can come and find us."

So we waited, watching the faces of the people who walked by. Noon came. Michael had me so on edge that I expected the park to erupt into chaos as soon as the clock struck twelve. Nothing happened. Noon went. "How long are you willing to wait?" Michael asked. I hadn't thought about it. I hadn't thought I'd need to. Then I saw them. Dorothy was wearing the same baggy cargo pants. She had a white tank top on now instead of the black one. I could see the muscles in her arms flex as she walked. It was the first time I'd noticed them. I had fooled myself into thinking that she was sweet and innocent. She wasn't. She was a fighter like Michael. They just chose different battles.

"There they are," I said to Michael. Michael recognized Dorothy. She was walking with a young black man. I had grown accustomed to thinking of other people my age as younger than me because of everything I'd been through. The kid didn't look young, though. He had been through a lot too. The War isn't easy on anybody.

Dorothy was doing her best to casually scan the park as she walked, but she didn't see us. They walked past us. The kid walked next to her, staring straight ahead of him as if in a daze. He was tall and lanky, but he looked like an athlete. "Should we go get them?" I asked Michael.

"They're too exposed. It's too risky for me. You'll have to go get them."

I stood up and dusted myself off. "Okay," I said. I took one quick look around me before walking toward the path. I had to walk quickly to catch up to Dorothy and the kid. "Dorothy," I said in a whisper when I was only a few steps behind them.

She turned toward me when I said it. So did Joseph. I looked at him first. He looked more muscular up close, but his muscles were long. He looked tired. He had bags under his eyes. Then I noticed his eyes. They were a dark emerald green, unlike any eyes I'd ever seen before. I looked at Dorothy. She looked nervous. "Maria," she said in a single exhaled breath. "I almost thought you weren't going to show."

"We're under the trees," I said to her. "Michael thought it was safer there." Joe didn't say a word. He just gave me the same intense once-over that I'd given him. Then they followed me to the spot where Michael was waiting.

"How did you guys get here?" Dorothy asked. "We've been looking for you."

"We came early," Michael answered her. "We thought it would be safer if no one saw us. I didn't want to get Tased again." It dawned on me then why Michael had made us go through all that preparation. He was taking back some of the control he'd lost in the park in Washington, D.C. Even if they could follow us, Michael wasn't going to let them get the jump on him again. The park. The middle of the day. I hadn't even seen the parallels. Michael had.

Dorothy looked at Michael. She knew who she was dealing with. That's why she looked nervous. That's why she didn't think that I was going to show up. "You don't have to worry," Dorothy said. "It's only me this time. For jobs like this, where we believe we're working with people we know we can trust, we send only one person." Dorothy was alone. She was so brave. I wondered why she didn't run away like the people she helps. She looked over at me. "Maria," Dorothy said, "this is Joe." Joe stuck his hand out for me and I shook it. He had a firm handshake.

Michael interrupted the introductions. "What's the plan here, Dorothy?"

"It's exactly what I told Maria. Joe needs a place to stay for a few days while we prep his next stop. We'll come get him when it's ready."

Michael shook his head. "We've had enough of your surprises. We need to know when he's leaving. We need to make arrangements for the drop-off now." I hadn't expected this, but I wasn't going to argue. Still, it felt strange, standing there while Dorothy and Michael debated Joe's future right in front of him.

"Fine," Dorothy said. "How about ten o'clock on Sunday night? We can meet here again."

Michael shook his head again. "Maria's going to decide where we meet."

Everyone looked at me. I knew Michael was testing me. I didn't feel ready but I had to say something. I thought about the different routes I'd run over the past few days. "On the footpath beneath the FDR," I said, "in between the Brooklyn and Manhattan bridges."

"Okay. We can do that," Dorothy said. She turned to Joe. "Stay safe," she said. She reached out and hugged him. "I'll see you in three days." Joe just nodded. I couldn't tell if he was being quiet because he didn't have anything to say or if he was too emotional to speak.

As Michael, Joe, and I walked away, Dorothy called out to me. "Thank you, Maria," she said. "I know this isn't your battle."

I turned back to her for a second. "Just remember your promise," I said. She nodded. Then she walked away in the other direction.

I couldn't call the kid Joe. The name hurt too much. On the way back to the apartment, I asked him if I could call him something else, a nickname or a middle name.

"Everyone calls me Joe," he said. "My middle name is Reginald, but I hate it."

"How about Reggie? Do you hate that?" I asked. I didn't wait for him to answer. "Can I call you Reggie?"

He seemed dubious. "Whatever you need," he answered anyway. Michael took to the name change immediately. Apparently, he wasn't ready to call the kid Joe either.

Before Michael left me and Reggie alone, he suggested that we lay out some ground rules for Reggie. Reggie said okay. "Rule number one," Michael began. I wished that he didn't number the rules, but I stayed quiet. "No leaving the apartment without one of us with you. Rule number two: don't abuse your situation here. Listen to every word Maria says. No games. Rule number three," Michael said, because there always seemed to be three rules, "you never speak a word to anyone about who Maria is or who I am or what we did for you. Not now. Not ever."

"That's fair," Reggie said.

"Don't break the rules. Break any of those rules and you'll be lucky if I just kick you out on the street."

"Understood. I'm not here to play games. I just want to thank you guys for your help."

"Don't thank me," Michael said. "I had nothing to do with this. Thank her." Michael pointed at me. Reggie looked back at me again. I held his stare a little longer this time. When I broke it off, Reggie turned back to Michael.

"Thanks anyway," Reggie said to Michael.

Before leaving, Michael came up to me. Reggie had wandered into the other room. "Are you sure you're okay with this?" he asked me in a whisper.

"Yes," I said without hesitating.

"You're okay being alone with him?"

"I'm not afraid," I assured him.

"Maybe you should be," Michael answered.

"Why don't you trust him?"

Michael looked into the other room. I could see Reggie sitting on the couch. "Because he's willing to let other people risk their lives for him. I don't understand what type of person would do that."

I felt my skin go flush. "Maybe he's just"—I searched my brain for the right word—"desperate," I finished. I reached out to hug Michael before he left. It was awkward. I clutched him and he stood limply, barely touching my back.

Twenty-three

"What's his deal?" Reggie asked after Michael left. What he meant was, *Why is that guy such an asshole?*

"This whole thing makes him nervous," I answered.

"Are you and him an item?"

"No," I answered. "He's just a friend of a friend," I said, wondering at that moment if that's all Michael was. Reggie nodded again.

Reggie was sitting on the sofa, which I'd pushed up against the wall opposite the bed. I sat down on the floor across the room from him. "Can I ask you why you're running from the War?" I'd been waiting for Michael to leave so I could ask the question. I wanted to know what made Reggie different from all the others who didn't run. I knew why your father ran. He ran to try to protect you. Your father had his doubts about the War, but without you, he never would have run. I know that. I stared at Reggie. What made him so different? Why was he running when Michael refused to?

He got off the couch and sat down on the floor so that we were sitting across from each other but at the same level. "Have you ever heard of tithing?" Reggie asked me.

"Like with a religion?" I asked. I wasn't sure I understood his question. He gave me a quizzical look. "Like in the Bible. It says that you're supposed to give a certain amount of everything you have to the Church."

"I didn't know that."

"So what were you talking about?"

"We've got tithing too. Dorothy and her people told me about it. There are all these people who are part of the War that never fight. They have regular jobs. All those people, they're supposed to give twenty-five percent of everything they make to the War. Instead of blood, they pay for the War with cash." For some reason, I'd never thought about where all the money came from to fund the War or what people might do to control that type of money. I started thinking about the office that Michael had visited above Grand Central Station and how much money that must cost.

"How many people are there like that?" I asked. "How many people live normal lives and donate money?"

Reggie shrugged. "I haven't got a clue," he said. "Somebody's got to know, though. Somebody's collecting all that money."

"Is that why you ran?" I asked, confused.

Reggie shook his head. "No. I didn't know anything about tithing until Dorothy and her people told me about it. I'm just trying to figure things out."

"So why did you run?" I asked again.

"They wanted me to kill a woman."

Your father had killed women. Michael had too. "Had you killed men before?" I asked.

Reggie nodded slowly, solemnly. "Two," he said. "They told me that the first one helped plan my father's murder, so that didn't even feel like killing. I almost enjoyed it. Then there was the second man. Then they asked me to kill a woman."

"So you ran?" I thought the story was over.

Reggie was leaning against the wall. His feet were on the floor and his knees were up in the air in front of him. His wrists rested on his knees and his hands dangled loosely in front of them. The window was open. We could hear the traffic from outside. A breeze blew in through the window. "No," Reggie said. "I told them that I couldn't do it. Apparently, they thought I just needed more training, so they took me to the woman's house and they made me watch them kill her."

"And then you ran?"

He nodded. "She had two kids. They killed her because she was some type of engineer working on some sort of retinal identification technology."

"So, you ran because you think it's wrong to kill women?" I wanted to understand.

"No. I ran because I knew I couldn't hack the job."

I shook my head at him. He wasn't a coward. A coward wouldn't be brave enough to run. A coward would have killed that woman. "So do you still believe in the War?" I asked Reggie.

"The guys in the Underground are trying to convince me not to. They told me about tithing, about other things, but it's hard," he answered.

"Why is it so hard?" I asked, exasperated. I felt like I was talking to your father.

Reggie shrugged without saying anything. A car horn blared outside. Reggie flinched and shot a look toward the open window.

"You answered my questions," I said to Reggie after the silence went on for a few minutes. "Is there anything you want to know about me?" I expected him to want to know something.

"No," he said to my disbelief. I didn't know how much Dorothy had told Reggie about me, but I expected him to have at least some questions. "I already know all about you. We all do." The room went quiet. Even the noise from outside seemed to stop.

"What do you mean?"

"I mean the younger people in the War. We all know your story." I sat for a moment, letting what Reggie said sink in. He must have read the expression on my face. "I've heard that they even teach about you as part of the initiation sessions now."

"What?" I wasn't ready for this.

"They talk about you and Joe and your son. They tell the class how Joe died—how he was killed by his best friend. They teach about how your son was given to the other side. It's supposed to scare the kids straight. You're a legend." My throat got dry as Reggie spoke. My tongue swelled in my mouth. I squirmed. Reggie licked his lips nervously. "Are you okay?" he asked.

Nearly unable to speak, I asked Reggie if he could get me a glass of water. He went into the kitchen and filled a glass up with tap water. I drank it, hoping it would help get my body and brain functioning again.

Reggie sat back down on the floor again. "I didn't mean to upset you."

"No," I said, shaking my head. "It's good to know. I need to know these things."

"If it's any consolation," Reggie said, "a lot of people think that what they did to you and Joe was wrong. They don't say it out loud, but they think it. I think what they did is horrible."

"Thank you," I said. "That means something, I guess." I could talk now, but my head was still swimming. I think I was in shock. "Do they ever talk about where they took my son?" I asked.

He shook his head. "No, just that he's one of Them now."

I wanted to stand up, but my legs were too heavy. I felt used—

first violated and now used. It isn't enough that they killed your father. It isn't enough that they took you from me so that they can turn you into a murderer. Now they're telling children about us and trying to make us look like the bad guys.

I'm sitting at the kitchen table. Reggie is sleeping in the other room. I think it's been a while since he's slept in a bed. I can hear him breathing into his pillow as I write this. I'm glad that I decided to help him—to try to help him. Hopefully, Michael will come around too. Some things in this world are worth fighting for, Christopher. Always remember that. No matter how bleak things seem, there are always things worth fighting for. Once you've decided to fight, you can't hold back.

Twenty-four

Michael showed up that first evening with a case of beer and enough Chinese food to feed a family. He didn't call first. He simply came. It was good that he brought so much food, because Reggie ate almost half of it. God knows what type of meals Reggie'd been eating on the streets.

It was dark outside. I could see the black sky surrounding us through the window. When Michael showed up, it felt eerily like the grown-up had finally arrived. He had a now familiar manila envelope under his right arm—the details of the next job. He didn't say anything about it to me.

Michael sat on the kitchen counter. Reggie and I sat across from each other at the table. All three of us ate. Reggie was an expert with chopsticks. I asked where he learned. "The Happy Wonton in Prospect Heights," he said. "Mom always said it was healthier than McDonald's." Michael ate his food out of the box with a fork. We didn't talk much. We each had a few beers.

"Do you know about tithing?" I asked Michael after I'd finished eating. The two of them were still stuffing themselves.

Michael took his time chewing and swallowing the food in his mouth. "What do you mean?"

"I mean, do you know about tithing?" I didn't think it was a trick question.

"Yeah," he answered. He took a swig of his beer. "What about it?"

"How come nobody told me about it?"

Michael glared at me. He looked at me like he didn't even know me. "How did you think this thing worked?" he answered. "Somebody's got to pay for my hotel room and your apartment and the car we rented to get up here. None of this shit is free."

"It just seems like a lot of money," I said. Michael seemed on the verge of exploding. I tried to figure out how to proceed without stepping on a land mine. "Have you ever killed someone who was tithing?" I asked, inching closer to my real question.

Michael looked down at me over a forkful of fried rice. I thought for a second that he was going to stand up and leave. He didn't. "You think the War is all about the money," he said to me instead, figuring out where I was headed before I'd figured out how to get there.

"You don't think that's possible?" I asked. Doesn't he want to know the truth?

"Anything is possible. Some things are just really un*fucking* likely." He stood up from the counter and walked over to the refrigerator to get another beer. "You really want this to be simple, don't you?"

"Sometimes the simple answers are the right answers."

Michael turned back to me. His eyes were dark and bottomless, mirroring the sky outside the window behind him. Reggie sat at the table with his head down, trying to stay out of trouble. "Why can't you let it go, Maria," Michael said. It was an order, not a question.

"If you really want me to let it go," I said to Michael, "I'll let it go."

"That's what I really want."

Reggie spoke, trying to make peace, trying to change the subject. "So, how many people have you killed?" Reggie asked Michael.

"I don't keep track," Michael said, still glaring at me while shrugging off the question.

Reggie didn't let it die. "Come on," Reggie replied. "Everyone keeps track. Everyone says they don't keep track, but everyone keeps track." I watched Michael, hoping he wouldn't blow up. Something was wrong. I worried that Reggie was letting the beer talk for him.

"Why do you want to know?" Michael asked. I began to get claustrophobic. The apartment suddenly felt very small. The walls felt like they were inching closer together. "Are you going to judge me based on my number? Would it be better if I had a high number or a low number?" Michael didn't try to hide the condescension in his voice. He thought that, by running, Reggie'd lost his right to ask this question.

"I was just interested," Reggie said, taken aback by Michael's rebuke.

"I really don't keep track," Michael repeated, his eyes as hard as steel. Even I started to believe him.

"Why not?" Reggie asked. I looked back and forth between the two men. I wondered what these two men would be like if the War didn't exist. What would they do? Would they be good people? Would they be happy? Would they at least be happier? Then I thought about people from my former life. What would those people be like if they were part of the War? Would they be killers too? Would they be less happy? Happier? I thought about my father. What would he have done if he were a part of the War? I picked up a can of beer and drank half of it in one pull. I wanted to stop thinking.

"I don't keep track because I've got a big enough dick that I don't have to," Michael said. His voice was flat and emotionless. He stared at Reggie as he spoke. Reggie held Michael's gaze. Neither was going to be the first to look away. None of it mattered. Even if Michael didn't keep track, he still had a number. It existed, and there was nothing he could do to make that number go down. As long as he was helping me, that number was only going to go up. Did I have a number? Were the people that Michael killed to help me part of my number too? I finished the beer in my hand.

I wanted to break the tension. I didn't know what I could say to Michael anymore that wouldn't anger him. Instead, I asked Reggie where Dorothy was sending him next.

"I don't know," Reggie answered. "They won't tell me. They say it's safer for me and the people helping me if I don't know." His voice was shaky. "I won't know where I'm going next until I'm there."

"And then what?" I asked.

"I don't know," Reggie said. "All I know is that I don't get to go home again."

"I know the feeling," I told him. I thought of my house, the house I grew up in. It was merely a dream now, slowly fading from my memory. I kept my eyes open, not wanting to look at whatever I would see if I closed them.

"Trust the old man in the room," Michael chimed in, his voice bereft of anger for the first time all night, "going home is overrated." He just sounded sad now. "It's never the same place that you re-member anyway."

Before Michael left that evening he told me that he was going to Philadelphia. "What? Why?" I stammered in response.

"We only have two weeks to do the next job. I need to go down and do some reconnaissance."

"When will you be back?"

"When I know enough to come back."

"I should be coming with you," I told him.

He shot me a cold look. "Apparently, you've got things to do here. I'll leave you and your new friend alone." Was he jealous? Was that why he was acting so strangely?

"How can I get in touch with you if I need you?"

"You can't get in touch with me, so don't need to."

I didn't know what else to say. "Be careful," I muttered. Michael nodded in response and walked out the door.

Twenty-five

Reggie and I didn't leave the apartment the day after Michael left. "I wish you had a TV or something," Reggie said as he sat on the couch and stared out the window. It was still sweltering. I wondered when the heat was going to break.

"It would be nice to have something to pass the time," I agreed.

"Do you play cards?" Reggie asked.

I never really played cards growing up, but I was as eager as Reggie to kill the time. "I don't know a lot of games," I answered, "but if you have a deck, I'll play." Reggie walked over to his backpack. Everything he owned was in that backpack. He carried less around with him than I did. He reached deep into the backpack and pulled out a deck of red playing cards.

"So, what do you know how to play?" he asked. I shrugged. I knew how to play chess. I knew how to play backgammon. When it came to cards, I didn't even know enough to know what I knew. "Hearts?" Reggie asked. I shook my head. "Rummy 500?"

"I'm sorry," I said. I could feel what Reggie was going through, the angst. I knew what it was like to want to think about something else. I wanted to be able to give that to him.

Reggie mentioned another two or three games. I shook my head each time. "War?" he asked.

"Seriously?" I answered, but I knew how to play War. I remembered playing it when I was a child. Reggie dealt out half the deck to me and half the deck to himself. Then he counted to three and, when he said the word *three*, we both flipped over the top card in our hands. Reggie flipped over a jack. I flipped over a queen and swept both cards into my pile. He counted to three again. This time, I flipped over a three and Reggie flipped over an ace. He took the cards. On about the fifth or sixth flip, we turned over matching cards.

"War," Reggie said with relish. So we laid additional cards facedown on the table, additional casualties to a war whose outcome they had no say in. I lost the first war. Reggie took all five of my cards, including a king. We played game after game until it started to get dark outside. Both of us lost our fair share.

I didn't find the manila envelope until the second day after Michael left. It was sitting on the counter next to the microwave. At first, I wondered if it was a mistake. I wondered if Michael left it here by accident, if he was wandering around Philadelphia blind. I knew better than that, though. He left it here on purpose. He wanted me to read it. I'm sure of it. Michael had already opened the envelope. A jagged tear ran across the top where Michael had ripped open the envelope with his finger. I reached into the envelope and pulled out its contents, careful to make sure that Reggie didn't see what I was doing.

Superficially, the envelope's contents weren't any different than that of the fat man. Rummaging through it, I found a number of pictures showing various stages of our target's life. He was white. He looked athletic. He was handsome. In one picture, he was running.

In another, he was boxing. Each picture had a date and location written on the back. The earliest photos were taken in Chicago. Some were from Los Angeles. Only the most recent pictures were taken in Philadelphia. The Philadelphia pictures had all been taken within the last three months. In a few of the pictures, our target was standing in front of a classroom full of teenagers. I figured he was teaching initiation sessions for the War, like your father had. I figured wrong.

I spent most of the day looking through the material. I wouldn't let Reggie look at it. He asked to. He only wanted something to do. I reminded him that he was leaving the War, that he didn't need to look at these things anymore. "But you do?" he asked with more than a touch of sarcasm.

"Yes, I do," I told him without any notes of sarcasm or irony in my voice.

Our target is six feet, four inches tall. He weighs roughly 220 pounds. He'd been an amateur boxer when he lived in Chicago. I wondered if Michael left the envelope so that I'd know what I was getting him into. I kept reading. Our target was a civilian high school math teacher. He'd taught for over seven years in inner-city high schools in Chicago, Los Angeles, and now Philadelphia. He had won teaching awards. The pictures of him standing with a bunch of teenagers weren't of him indoctrinating children into the War. The pictures were of him teaching math to poor kids. I took out the two pictures of him in front of the class again and looked at them. The first one was from Chicago. Every student in the picture was staring at our target. The second photo was taken only a few weeks ago in Philadelphia. He demanded no less attention in the recent picture. On the surface, he looked like a good person. You can never let your guard down, Christopher. Even the best of them are killers.

I turned the page. The top of the next page contained the words

Thirty-one confirmed kills. I kept reading. The next thirteen pages described twenty-eight of the thirty-one kills. I counted each one as I read. Six were done in Chicago. Eight were done in Los Angeles. Two were done in Philadelphia in the two and a half years that he'd lived here. It seemed that they were cutting back on his local work. The other thirteen kills were executed while our target traveled during the summer, leaving a trail of blood wherever he went.

I noted that I still had three more killings to read about.

The next page began a whole new section titled *Prior Attempts*. This section felt unique and ominous. First was Chicago. The first person sent to kill our target had more than two dozen kills under his belt. He had all the advantages of training and experience. He tried to ambush our target as our target walked home to his apartment one evening. The details of what happened were sketchy. The only thing that anyone knew definitively was that the hit man's body was found in a Dumpster in an alley two days later. His skull was fractured. No one found the murder weapon, but from the size and shape of the wounds, it appeared to be an ordinary brick. Our target had killed a professional hit man with what he'd found lying on the ground around him.

They moved our target to Los Angeles shortly after he was ambushed the first time. He began teaching again. It was over a year before he was found. They sent another professional to try to finish him. Their plan was basically the same. So were the results. The body of the hit man was found four days later in an abandoned building. He died of traumatic head wounds, but this time he'd been electrocuted first. Our target played with him before he killed him.

Our target didn't leave Los Angeles right away. Instead he changed neighborhoods, hoping to get lost inside the city. The third attempt was a total debacle. It took place only three months after the second attempt. Even I could tell that it was poorly planned. They sent an eighteen-year-old kid after him. It was the kid's first solo job. He was the younger brother of one of our target's Chicago victims. The kid's death was quick and clean. There were no signs of struggle. His death appeared to be an afterthought.

After the third attempt, our target moved to Philadelphia. That was over two years ago. He was only recently positively identified. They were sending Michael to kill him this time. I had no way of knowing if it was because Michael had experience being ambushed and ambushing others or because Michael's failings made him expendable. Probably both. I wondered where Michael was and if he was safe. I wondered when he'd be coming back. I worried that he wouldn't be coming back at all.

I repacked the envelope early that evening. I had learned everything that I could from those papers. I slipped the envelope into one of the kitchen drawers. "Are you finally finished?" Reggie asked me. He was leaning against the doorframe leading into the kitchen. He must have been waiting for me to finish.

"For now," I told him. We ordered a pizza and sat at the kitchen table together, waiting for it to be delivered.

"I've been thinking about things," Reggie said to me as we waited. "I was thinking that maybe I shouldn't run. Maybe I should stay and help you and Michael find your son."

"You're just going stir-crazy from being cooped up here," I joked.

"I'm serious," Reggie said. "Running sometimes seems so cowardly when there's more that I could be doing."

"Dorothy promised me that they'll help me find my son if I help you to run. So running is what you can do for me. After that, you can be whatever type of hero you want to be."

"Okay," Reggie conceded, "but I'm going to repay you for what you're doing for me one day."

"Stay alive. Get away. If one day you decide that you want to fight, make sure that it's your decision and not somebody else's. That's favor enough for me for now."

I lay in bed that night, thinking about our next target and worrying about Michael. Even with Reggie there, I felt an emptiness without Michael around me. Maybe it was because we were trapped in that apartment. Two more days, I thought to myself. Three if you count Sunday.

On Friday morning, Reggie asked me if I would go with him to Brooklyn. He wanted to see his old neighborhood one more time and he knew that he'd have no chance once Michael came back. "No," I told him. "It's not safe."

"Nothing I do is safe," Reggie shot back. "Nothing I ever do again will be safe. You don't have to come with me, but I'm going to go crazy if I stay in here for another day."

"People will see you. People you know."

"I'll be safe. No one will be looking for me there. They can't think that I'm that stupid."

I thought about it, barely able to believe that I was considering letting Reggie do something colossally dangerous and stupid based on the logic that it was so stupid that it wouldn't be that dangerous. "Okay," I finally agreed. I didn't have the heart to stop him. Reggie and I were too much alike. I would've done almost anything for one chance to go back home before running away forever with your father, even if it was only for a few minutes. No one had offered that chance to me. No one even tried. I imagined what Michael would say to me. He'd probably tell me that sympathy is a dangerous emotion in this game. It didn't matter, though. Michael wasn't there to stop us. But it should have mattered. I should have made it matter. I still had a lot to learn.

"Thank you," Reggie said, towering over me as he stood up. "I won't forget this."

"Hopefully, I will," I said to him. I made Reggie wait while I went for a run before we left. As I ran, I felt people's eyes on me and wondered which ones were looking for Reggie. I looked into their faces, trying to read them. Everyone looked the same to me. I had a desire to keep running, to run for hours, to waste the entire day so that I wouldn't have to go back and make what I was sure was going to be a big mistake.

We rode the subway into Brooklyn. It was a short ride. My heart started pounding when we stepped off the train, before we walked up the stairs into the sunlight. I could hear people's voices out in the street as we climbed the stairs. We wouldn't have anywhere to hide. When we emerged from underground, I looked down the long street. People were sitting on stoops. Kids were playing games on the chalk-strewn street. Two old men were standing on the street corner, talking. Everything looked frighteningly normal. "This is a mistake," I said to Reggie.

"Stop worrying," Reggie said. "I know this neighborhood. If anything is out of place, I'll know it. Trust me." I wanted to trust him.

Reggie led me through more side streets to a pizza place where he knew we could get lunch. "I don't know where I'm going, but wherever I'm going, there won't be pizza like this," he said, smiling like a child in a candy store.

We sat at the back of the pizza place. I sat facing the entrance. I made Reggie sit with his back to the door. Even with his back to the door, people still recognized him. They came up from behind him to say hello. They grabbed him before he even knew they were behind him. Each time someone grabbed him, an image of the person's hands choking Reggie flashed across my mind. What would I do then? Run? Reggie returned each of their embraces.

"We should go home," I said, when Reggie finished his second slice of pizza.

"I am home." Reggie smiled. That's when I realized that the mistake I'd made wasn't letting Reggie risk getting us ambushed, although that was possible. The mistake was giving Reggie that tiny taste of home that could destroy his resolve. Now I knew why your father didn't let me go home one last time. When you're trying to run away, memories are like quicksand. They can suck you up forever. "Let me take one last look at the basketball courts before we go." I said okay. The damage already appeared to be done.

The basketball bouncing against the asphalt sounded like a drum or an excited heartbeat. I could hear it from two blocks away. "We're only looking," I reminded Reggie. He didn't acknowledge me. The men playing basketball recognized him as soon as we turned the corner. Three of the players were shirtless. The other three were wearing shirts that clung to their skin because of their sweat. "Joe," one of the men called out. Reggie lifted a hand in a wave—so much for staying anonymous. "Where you been?" the man yelled. "We need you. Little C here can't shoot for shit." He pointed to one of his teammates, who lifted his middle finger in response.

"I can't stay," Reggie called back to them. I wondered if I was the only one who could hear the sadness in his voice.

"One shot," the man said. "Show Little C how it's done."

Reggie looked at me. "One shot," he said, and ran toward the courts before I could object. I stood frozen, watching him run. I was sure each step was going to be his last. I was sure I was going to hear gunshots or the sound of approaching feet banging against the pavement. I remembered what it felt like in the park in Washington, D.C., when they'd kidnapped Michael and I'd stood there, unable to help. Reggie stepped onto the court. Someone passed him the ball. He caught it, dribbled once between his legs and then jumped. At the height of his jump, he shot, releasing the ball off the fingertips of his long, outstretched arm. He was halfway between the midcourt line and the three-point line. Five of the men on the court almost simultaneously yelled, "Oh!" as the ball went through the hoop. Two of the men high-fived. Little C looked at the hoop, wondering why he lacked what some men had. Reggie's smile grew even broader. For a few seconds, I thought that maybe the trip had been worth it.

"Can we go now?" I asked.

"Yeah," he said. "Now we can go."

That evening after Reggie and I had dinner, the phone in the apartment rang. I hadn't heard it ring before. It took me a second to realize what it was. At first, I thought it was some sort of alarm. When I finally picked up, I heard Michael's voice. "I wanted to check in and make sure that you guys were okay."

"We're okay," I told him. "Are you?"

"I'm fine," he said. Neither of us said anything for a few moments.

"I found the envelope," I told him, breaking the awkward silence.

"Yeah? What did you think?"

"I want you to be careful. I think our mark is dangerous."

"Dangerous is a relative concept," Michael responded.

"When are you coming back, Michael?"

"When do you want me to come back?"

"Soon. Now. Yesterday."

Michael let himself laugh. The sound of his laughter made me feel better than I'd felt in days. I looked over at Reggie sitting on the couch. He looked pensive. I didn't like that look. "I should be done with my recon soon," Michael said.

"We need you here," I said into the phone.

"Do you?" Michael asked.

"Yes."

"Good," he said, and then he hung up.

I woke up in the middle of the night. It wasn't unusual for me anymore. Usually there's no reason for it, only nightmares and bad memories disturbing my sleep. That night, there was a reason. I heard sounds coming from the apartment door. It sounded like someone was trying to get inside.

The lights were all off. The dark clouds outside covered the sky. The apartment was dark. I rolled over and tried to peer through the darkness. Reggie had been spending the nights sleeping on the floor on the other side of the room. I searched for him, wondering if he was already awake, wondering if he'd heard what I heard. His sleeping bag was still in the corner of the room but it was empty. My mind raced. They couldn't have come in and gotten him while I was sleeping, could they?

I slipped out of the bed, careful to step quietly onto the floor. I heard another rattling sound at the door. I stepped into the kitchen. Someone was standing in the darkness. The figure turned toward me. "Maria," he said.

"What are you doing, Reggie?" I asked. I reached over and turned on the lights.

Reggie had his backpack over his shoulder. The chain lock was still hanging across the door. Reggie had been blindly fumbling with it. That was the sound I'd heard. "I'm going home," Reggie said. "I'm not ready to run."

My mind immediately jumped to Dorothy's promise. *If you help us here, we may be able to help you in the future.* "You can't go home," I said to Reggie.

"I can. You saw me. We were there today. That's where I belong."

I shook my head. "That's not home, Reggie. That's a fiction. That's two hours. What about the rest of the time? Nothing's changed." Michael would have told me not to let Reggie go back to Brooklyn. He would have been right. He would have been right for all the wrong reasons, but what difference did that make? "They'll try to turn you into something you're not."

"I don't know if that's true. Maybe the person they want me to become is actually who I am. Maybe this really is in my blood."

I took a step closer to him. "No. It's not. It's not who any of you really are." I thought about your father and you and Michael. "You know that. I know you know it." Suddenly it wasn't about Dorothy's promise. It was about trying to help this lost, frightened kid get away. If I could save him, then maybe I could save you.

Michael's emerald green eyes began to glisten in the light, covered by a thin film of tears. "I want to say good-bye to my mother," Reggie pleaded. "I never said good-bye to her."

"You don't have to," I assured him. "She's your mother. She'll understand."

"Understand what?" Reggie pleaded.

"She'll understand that you had to leave her to be safe. She'll understand that you're safer without her, that you're better off without her. If she doesn't understand that, then she doesn't know what it means to be a mother."

"And you do? What were you a mother for, like, a month?" Reggie stared at me.

Reggie's words stung. He knew he'd hurt me. He started to apologize, but I cut him off before he had a chance. I didn't want his sympathy. I wanted him to understand. "Do you really doubt that I know what it means to be a mother? I watched them carry my baby away screaming, and haven't had a moment go by where I haven't heard those screams since. I would lay down my life in a second if it meant that my baby would be safe. And if I were your mother, I would want you to run and never look back."

"Are you sure?"

I took another step closer to Reggie. I reached out and held one of his hands. "It's the only thing in this world that I'm sure about." I needed to convince him. I needed him to understand. First him, then Michael. Then I could move forward and get back to searching for you. "You're not running from your mother," I assured him. "You're running *for* her—her and any other real friend you've got."

Twenty-six

Michael still hadn't come back. I hadn't heard from him since his one and only phone call. I didn't exercise on the morning of the drop-off. Michael had taught me that you don't exercise on the day of a job. You save everything—everything you have—in case you need it. If Michael wasn't going to show, I figured I should be doubly ready. It was the first day in weeks that I hadn't exercised. The lack of that release made me antsy. My body was begging me to burn off energy. Instead I sat in the apartment with Reggie, doing nothing. Reggie was in worse shape than I was. At least I'd gotten out of the apartment for my run the day before. Looking at Reggie was like looking at a coiled spring.

The air had grown cooler. At some point in the afternoon, the heat broke. It wasn't cold, just cooler. I kept the windows open. We could hear the city outside. I watched Reggie, trying to determine if he was enjoying hearing the city one last time or if the sounds were painful for him. He didn't let on one way or the other.

It was the middle of the afternoon when we heard a knock at the door. It was s single knock and then silence. "What the fuck was that?" Reggie asked, looking at me, growing more nervous with each moment.

"It's Michael." I was so excited to hear his knock that I'd almost forgotten how strange Michael was acting when he left, how disappointed he'd seemed to be with me. I nearly ran to the door. I unhooked the chain lock to let Michael in. I nearly hugged him, but stopped when I remembered how cool Michael had been to me. Michael stood in the doorway for a second. Somehow he looked bigger than I remembered. He was carrying a large brown paper bag in one of his hands.

"Hey, you two," Michael said as he stepped inside. He glanced over at Reggie. "Did I miss anything?"

"Almost," I answered him, referring to the fact that he'd finally shown up only hours before we were supposed to be meeting with Dorothy. "But I guess you have a few hours to spare."

"*Almost* is a word for people with too much time on their hands," Michael replied. He walked over to the cabinet to get a glass. His limp hadn't improved. He filled up his glass with water and drank the whole thing in two enormous gulps. Then he turned back toward us. He looked at Reggie. "You ready?" Michael asked.

"As I'll ever be," Reggie answered flatly. I wondered if I should tell Michael about Reggie's cold feet.

"I got something for you," Michael said to Reggie, reaching into the brown paper bag and pulling out a small silver gun. I saw Michael kill the two men in St. Martin. I listened to him describe killing the fat man. But a gun was something new. Reggie stared at the piece of metal in Michael's hand. "Do you know how to use it?" Michael asked Reggie. I remembered the crash course your father had given me in how to use a gun. *All you have to do is point it at anything scary and pull the trigger.*

"I think so," Reggie answered. He didn't question why he needed a gun. "Is there anything tricky that I need to know?"

Michael showed Reggie the gun. "There's no safety on this one,"

Michael said. "It's a double action, so all you have to do to fire it is pull the trigger. So when it's loaded, be careful with it. It's loaded now. You've got twelve bullets. Then you need to reload. Twelve shots go quicker than you'd think. Remember that."

"Okay. Anything else?" Reggie asked Michael.

"Yeah," Michael said. "It's a small gun. Small guns aren't very accurate from a distance. If you're going to use it, be close." Michael handed Reggie the gun. Reggie lifted it in front of him so he could feel the weight of it in his hand.

"Why did you get him the gun?" I asked. I didn't appreciate how Michael waltzed in here after five days and acted like he'd never left.

"Because he might need it," Michael said without looking at me. "Because I know what it's like to be out there with no one protecting you."

"He's got people protecting him," I said to Michael. I didn't want to believe that Reggie would need a gun. I wanted to believe that he would run away to a normal life and live happily ever after.

"Do you carry one?" Reggie asked Michael.

Michael shook his head. "I'm still part of the War. We were taught not to use guns unless we needed them. My knife has kept me alive this long."

"But the gun is okay for me?" Reggie asked Michael.

"Unless you tell me otherwise," Michael said, giving Reggie one last chance to back out before we hooked up with Dorothy again. Reggie put the gun in his pocket. A long silence filled the room.

"So, are you going to tell me how things went in Philly?" I asked Michael, killing the silence.

"Maybe," Michael answered. "Once he's gone. If you still want to know."

"What the fuck is that supposed to mean?" I nearly shouted. "Of course I want to know."

"This can wait," Michael said to me after glancing at Reggie.

"No," I told him. "It can't. I don't care if Reggie hears this. Hell, maybe Reggie should hear this. Listen, I know I should have asked you about working with Dorothy before agreeing to do it, but you've got to drop it. It happened. We need to move on."

"I'm not mad at you for agreeing to do this without asking me. You can make decisions. I'm not your babysitter."

"Then why are you mad at me?"

"I'm mad at you because you made a bad decision without really thinking about it," Michael said, pointing at Reggie. "You were careless. You can't be careless like that. You risked everything we're working for. You put yourself in danger. You put me in danger. Hell, you put your own son in danger."

"You're going to lecture me about being careless? Don't forget that I know a lot more about you than you know about me." Maybe it wasn't a fair thing to say, referring to all the stories that your father had told me about Michael before Michael even knew that I existed.

Michael shook his head. "I may be reckless, but I am never careless."

"You think there's a difference?"

Michael's voice lowered. "You're naive enough to think there's not? Carelessness is doing something without thinking about the risks and ramifications first. Recklessness is knowing the risks and ramifications and rolling the dice anyway. Recklessness can be a choice. I may choose to be reckless sometimes. I may choose to take risks. But it's always my choice. I am never careless. My recklessness is never a mistake."

"Why do you choose it, then?" I asked.

"To prove that I can," Michael said. "To prove that I'm in control. If I wasn't willing to be reckless sometimes, I would have dropped you the moment we got out of St. Martin."

I felt a chill run down my spine when Michael said those words, but I knew they were a lie. "That's the biggest heap of bullshit I've ever heard."

"You don't think that there's a difference between being reckless and being careless?"

"It's not that. I just don't think that's why you're mad at me. I think you're mad at me because you're worried that I'm going to leave you. You're worried that I found a different cause and that we're not on the same team anymore." I looked at Reggie. Even though I was the one doing the talking, he was watching Michael. "You think that Joe left you because of me and that I'm going to leave you because of Reggie, and nobody tells you shit and it makes you feel stupid and used." I could tell from the way that he looked at me that I was right. That look gave me strength. "I should have recognized it before, but I wasn't used to seeing you look scared. Stop me if I'm wrong."

Michael didn't say a word. He simply stared into my eyes. I have known all along why I needed Michael. I was only beginning to realize why he needed me back.

"Okay, then. Let's get a few things straight. First, Joe didn't leave you. He left the War because he figured out it was shit. He didn't tell you because he wanted to protect you. It's not more complicated than that. Second, I'm not going to leave you until we find my son, and even then it's going to be your call. I'm not just using you. Sadly for me, you're my best friend. So don't fuck that up, because I'm pretty sure that I'm your only friend." I gave Michael a moment to say something, but I didn't expect him to. It wasn't his style. I looked over at Reggie. He was sitting silently, absorbing everything. All these men, they're so physically strong but emotionally fragile.

"Okay, Michael. We've got, like, four hours before we have to meet Dorothy and send Reggie on his way. Are you going to tell us what we need to do or not?"

"Well, if you're done with your speech"—Michael feigned coolness—"I can probably help us work on a plan." I could already hear the sound of the old Michael seeping back into his voice. Nobody is fearless, Christopher. It helps to understand your friends' fears as much as your enemies'.

Twenty-seven

When we left the apartment, I felt naked knowing that I was the only one who wasn't armed. The sun was sinking behind the buildings as the three of us surveyed the point where the drop-off was supposed to take place in only a few more hours. The sky was an amber color. "So, where are we supposed to do this?" Michael asked.

"Between the bridges," I said. I was eager to get this done. I was eager to move forward. I could feel the same emotions coming from Michael and Reggie. Still, I knew what Michael was thinking as he eyeballed the area. Some park benches were bolted into the ground facing the water. A number of giant stone columns held up the highway above us. We could hear the cars rumbling by overhead. The columns were our best bet for cover. There was no place to hide.

"We're sitting ducks," Michael said.

"We're not blocked in," Reggie said in my defense, pointing toward the Brooklyn Bridge. "There's three escape points: north, south, and west. Maria's right. If anyone comes after us, we'll see them coming. If we go west, we head right into the thick of lower Manhattan. If we go north or south, we can eventually turn into Manhattan, or we climb up onto either the Brooklyn Bridge or the Manhattan Bridge and head into Brooklyn."

We moved in closer, walking under the Manhattan Bridge. For a moment, the sound of traffic from the bridge and the sound of the traffic from the FDR merged. It was beginning to get dark, but people were still on the path, jogging or riding their bikes. We stopped walking, standing along the path as people passed us; runners, young kids on bikes, old Asian men pushing giant black carts filled with God knows what, street vendors heading away from the South Street Seaport for the night.

"How much time do we have?" Michael asked me.

I looked at my watch. "Just over an hour," I answered.

"Let's get off the path, then," Michael said. "We'll make them wait. We'll come to them. They can take the risk of standing out here in the open." We began walking away. I looked back once as we walked. The bikers and the runners were beginning to thin out. It got darker earlier beneath the shadow of the highway. The lights draping the bridges were on, lighting up the sky and reflecting off the turbulent black water beneath them. As I looked, I saw one of the street vendors, a small Middle Eastern man, standing still, watching us. He had been pushing a giant metal street vendor's cart. The metal slats pulled up on the sides covered the cart's windows. When the man realized that I was watching him watch us, he put his head back down, leaned into the cart, and kept pushing. The cart moved.

We went to a bar nearby to kill the hour we had before the action started. We ordered sodas and pretended we were carefree. If the drop-off went down like it was supposed to, the whole exchange should have taken five minutes, ten tops. I have no idea how long the bloody mess that occurred actually took. It felt like an eternity. While we were in the bar it had grown dark and quiet. When we left, the only sound we could hear was the drone of traffic whizzing by above us. As we neared the water, I looked down the footpath running beneath the two bridges.

At first, I didn't see anyone. Then I noticed a figure sitting alone on one of the benches, facing the water.

"Is that her?" I asked Michael, pointing to the bench. The figure didn't move.

"There's only one way to find out," Michael said. We crossed the street toward the footpath. A boat floated by on the river, sending light flashing over the figure on the bench for only a second. It was a woman, her hair hanging down to her shoulders. Shadows flitted over her like smoke drifting from a fire.

"I think it's her," I said to Michael. A single biker rode by us, a small white light flashing on his handlebars. The bridges were like giant beacons of light now, pointing in different directions and both pointing away from where we were. Michael walked up to the railing overlooking the black water and turned so that he could get a good look at the woman on the bench. We were only fifty feet from her now. She still hadn't moved. I stepped close behind Michael so that I could see her. Reggie stayed a few feet behind us.

"Dorothy," I whispered into the darkness, hoping that she could hear me, hoping that she would turn her head and we'd be able to see her face. I was sure that once we saw her face, everything would be okay.

She did turn toward us. Everything wasn't okay. The light from the bridges reflected off the tears on Dorothy's cheeks. I followed her tears down her face to her mouth. Then I saw the tape covering her mouth. I looked up for a split second, following the sudden sound of wheels rolling over concrete, and saw a metal pushcart. It was coming toward us and gaining speed. I turned back to Dorothy, looking down at her hands. They were tied together and fastened to her lap as if she were praying. Her feet were tied together too and lashed to one leg of the bench. I remembered her telling us that she was working alone, since she was dealing with people she trusted. I remember thinking how dangerous that sounded. Even if she could trust us, there were so many people she couldn't trust.

Even over the sounds of the cars roaring on the highway overhead and the sound of the pushcart rolling toward us, I could hear a muffled sound coming from Dorothy's direction. She was trying to scream to us. She was trying to tell us to run. Michael ran—only instead of running away from Dorothy, he ran toward her. He cleared about half the distance between us and Dorothy before I saw Dorothy's head jerk forward. Her head bounced back up. For that split second, I could see the hole where the bullet had come out of the front of her head. Finally, her head came to rest, dangling loosely in front of her like the head of a marionette without a puppeteer.

I thought in a flash of each of the times I'd met Dorothy—the breakfast in the compound outside of D.C., the late-night visit to my apartment, the meeting in the park. Her death seemed too quick, like she deserved more drama. We all deserve more drama. Few of us get it. Reggie, I thought suddenly. What is going to happen to Reggie? I turned to him. "Run," I shouted at him as loudly as I could. From where he was standing, he couldn't see everything that was happening. Maybe he heard the gunshot. Maybe he saw the fear in my face. Whatever it was, he turned and ran. He was already past the first stone column when I turned back to Michael and Dorothy.

Michael almost made it to Dorothy before the second gunshot. For some reason, I hadn't heard the first shot. I hadn't been listening. Not for that. I was listening now. I turned in time to see the splash of water where the bullet entered the East River after whizzing past Michael. Michael heard the shot too. He dove down to the ground. I don't know if he knew how close the bullet had come to him. I looked over at the pushcart. Two men were stepping out of the back of the cart. They both had guns in their hands. As they stepped out, the small Middle Eastern man hurried from behind the cart. I could see the sweat on his forehead glistening in the dim, shadowy light. He was breathing heavy from pushing the massive cart. He had a gun in his hand too. Whatever rule Michael and your father had about guns, they didn't share it.

The first man was holding his gun in front of him, his arm out-stretched. He was ready to aim, ready to fire. He only needed a target. The man behind him had a rifle with a scope. He must have been the one that shot Dorothy. The pushcart must have been rigged for this. The men were moving quickly, having lost the el-ement of surprise. The man in the front was aiming his handgun at Michael. He pulled the trigger. I heard the crack. I looked over. Mi-chael was on the ground. He was about three feet from the bench where Dorothy's body was tied. He was crawling for the cover of the bench. The bullet missed him, but I saw dust from the concrete kick up as the bullet entered the ground only a foot or two from his legs. Another bullet came, one that Michael couldn't avoid. It hit his right calf. I saw his leg jerk and saw blood begin to seep from the wound.

I stood there, confused and frightened. The bench, Dorothy's body, even, would give Michael a little cover, but the men with their guns were no more than thirty feet from him. In no more than seconds, they would be able to walk up to him and shoot him at point-blank range. Michael was trapped. He had nowhere to run. I couldn't do anything to save him. The only thing that could save him now was a gun on our team. Michael reached Dorothy's body. His hands clambered up her legs, up to the pockets of her pants. I remembered seeing the bulge in her pocket the night she first came to visit me in New York. Was there any chance she had a gun, that they'd tied her up without having the time to search her? Maybe they'd just been lazy. I thought it was Michael's only hope. I tried to think of something I could do to distract the men with the guns to buy Michael time, but it was useless. I was useless.

I turned my head and looked south. I should have still been able to see Reggie running but I saw nothing. I turned my head quickly back to Michael. They were closer to him now. My eyes passed by the column closest to me. I saw him standing behind the column. Reggie hadn't run away. He hadn't deserted us. He stood with his back pressed against the column, trying to control his breathing. He was holding his gun in his hand. In the growing darkness, I could still see the shining color of his eyes looking to me for guidance.

"Reggie, now!" I shouted, still not bothering to hide myself. He gave me a small nod and stepped past the edge of the column. He aimed his gun toward the men as they closed in on Michael. He pulled the trigger. One shot. Then another. Reggie missed them with both shots, but he got their attention. I remembered how Michael said that the small gun wasn't accurate from a distance. We weren't close enough. Reggie kept pulling the trigger. He pulled the trigger, took a breath, aimed, and then pulled it again.

In between shots, I heard one of the strange men shout, "That's him." They were shouting loud enough that they could be heard over the sound of the traffic and the bullets. They were crouching down now, moving away from each other to try to keep from giving Reggie too large a target. I could see dust swirl up as the bullets hit the ground around them. "Let's get him," said the man with the rifle. They had come for Reggie. Reggie kept firing, but none of his shots hit anything but the ground.

"You guys get him," the Middle Eastern man said, "I'll finish this one and catch up." He motioned toward Michael. I could see Michael still rummaging through Dorothy's pockets. He'd found something but I couldn't see what it was.

The man with the handgun aimed it at Reggie. His gun was bigger than Reggie's and had to be more accurate. He pulled the trigger. Concrete from the column above Reggie's head crumbled and fell. Reggie didn't move. He aimed his gun again but he wasn't aiming at the men coming for him. Reggie was aiming his gun at the man going for Michael. The man was only five steps from the bench now. He hadn't bothered to shoot his gun. It wasn't necessary. He could walk right up to Michael and execute him. Reggie inhaled deeply and held his breath. He squeezed the trigger again. This time, he hit his target. It wasn't a perfect shot. It didn't even knock the Middle Eastern man off his feet, but Reggie hit him somewhere above his waist. The man grunted and stumbled for a second but didn't fall. It would have to be enough. The other two men were closing in on Reggie. Reggie turned and aimed his gun at them. He pulled the trigger again. Another bullet whizzed by their heads. Then Reggie ducked behind the column as the men returned a blaze of fire. I stood out in the open, in the middle of the madness, feeling like a spectator in the world's most awful game. No one even looked at me. It was like I didn't exist.

I looked over at Michael. The man Reggie had shot seemed to be regaining his balance. I saw a flash of light reflect off something in Michael's hand. He had his knife out. Michael shifted Dorothy's lifeless legs and rolled under the bench. Now he was only two steps away from his would-be executioner. The Middle Eastern man didn't even notice Michael until Michael stood up. By then, it was too late. He tried to swing around so that he could fire one last shot at Michael, but Michael was already too close to him. Michael put all his weight on his good leg, the one without the bite wounds or bullet hole. He reached up with his left hand and grabbed the Middle Eastern man by his shoulder, near his neck. Michael was holding whatever it was that he'd found in Dorothy's pocket in his left hand, but it didn't stop him from getting a good grip on the man's shoulder. Then Michael took his right hand and plunged it up toward the little man's chin. The knife entered below the Middle Eastern man's jaw and shot up, cutting through any skin, bone, or tendon that got in its way. Michael's knife wasn't a small knife, but all I could see of it now was the handle jutting out from below the man's jaw. The rest of the blade had found its mark. The little man's body seized for a moment, but it put up no more fight than that.

Everything with Michael happened so quickly that, for a second, I'd forgotten about Reggie and the other two men with guns. Then I heard a popping sound near my feet. I looked down. I could see the spot on the ground, only three feet from me, where a bullet had hit. I looked up. I was still standing out in the open, not bothering to hide or duck while the men shot guns at each other around me. The gunfire had slowed down. Reggie had taken cover behind the column and, every few seconds, would turn and shoot wildly at one of the other men. Without the time to aim, his shots inevitably missed their mark. The two men had hunkered down, taking what cover they could find, hiding from Reggie's bullets. They fired too. Their shots were more accurate, but Reggie moved too fast and they couldn't master the timing.

I felt helpless. I was only twenty feet from Reggie but I couldn't think of anything to do that wasn't suicidal. Reggie turned the corner and fired again. He was merely trying to keep the men at bay. He couldn't hold them off forever. Reggie had only twelve bullets. He'd be lucky if he had three left. I hoped he'd been keeping track. I looked at Reggie. He was bouncing up and down on his toes. He looked back at me. Then I heard my name.

"Maria." The voice came out of the darkness. I looked over and saw Michael kneeling over the body of the Middle Eastern man. Michael placed something on the ground and flung it toward me with all his weight. I could hear whatever it was he had pushed toward me scraping along the concrete. It stopped about five feet in front of me. I stepped forward and looked down. I could barely make out its shape through the shadows. A gun. I bent down and picked it up. I remembered how scared I was the only other time in my life I'd held a gun. I wasn't scared anymore.

I looked at the gun in my hand. It wasn't so different than the one Michael had given to Reggie. It was just bigger. I remembered what Michael had said to Reggie. *There's no safety on this one. It's a double action, so all you have to do to fire it is pull the trigger.* I turned and aimed the gun at the closer of the two men, the one with the rifle. He was crouched down on the ground, doing his best to squat behind an orange traffic cone. I began to squeeze the trigger. Before I finished, I heard a click. I don't know how I heard it. I think maybe it was because the sound was so different from all the other sounds that night. It was so small and hollow. I looked at Reggie. He was still holding his gun but now he had a look of panic on his face. He was out of bullets. "Get him!" yelled the man lying on the ground. Both men stood up. They ran toward Reggie. To get to Reggie, the man with the rifle was going to have to run no more than five feet from me.

I aimed the gun at him again. I held it in two hands. I'd have to hit a moving target now, but he was going to be so close. I aimed for the widest part of him. I waited until he was only about five feet in front of me and I pulled the trigger. The gun jerked in my hand. If I hadn't been so nervous, if I hadn't been holding on to the gun with both hands for dear life, it would have jumped from my grip. But I held on. I felt the gun's heat. I wasn't sure where I'd hit the man, but he fell to the ground, his body writhing. I walked over and looked down at him. He looked back up at me in shock, as if he didn't understand where I'd come from. His shock only lasted for a second. Once it wore off, he reached for his rifle. If he'd had a handgun, he might have moved quickly enough to surprise me, but the rifle was cumbersome. I took aim again. I felt powerful. I felt like I was finally in control. I don't know where I hit him the first time, but the second time I shot him in the head. His head jerked back and his body stopped moving. He was dead. I killed him.

I took a breath and remembered that we still had to deal with the last man. I looked up. Reggie was running now, sprinting into the darkness down the long path. The last of the men was chasing him. Every chance Reggie could, he ran behind something that might absorb a bullet. The last man held his gun in his right hand as he chased after Reggie. Every few steps he reached forward and fired, but he couldn't really aim while running. I lifted my gun again and aimed it at the man's back. I fired once but missed. He and Reggie were getting farther and farther away. I started to chase after them. We'd become a strange chain of violence. I pulled the trigger two more times, trying to hit the man chasing Reggie. It was no use. They were too fast. It was too dark. I was too lightheaded. The bullets simply disappeared into the night.

The last I saw of Reggie, he had turned and was running up the hill toward the Brooklyn Bridge. The last man chased him, but Reggie was faster. The distance between them seemed to be growing. The Brooklyn Bridge—if Reggie could get over it, he'd be on his home turf. If he could make it to Brooklyn, I was sure that he'd be safe for tonight. After that, who knows? Dorothy was Reggie's ticket out of this mess, and now she was dead.

I finally stopped running. I put my hands on my knees and tried to catch my breath. Then I heard the sirens. I pulled myself together and ran back to Michael. I could still help Michael. Reggie was gone.

Michael was sitting on the ground when I got back to him. His legs were splayed out in front of him and he was leaning against the fence separating the sidewalk from the river. A pool of blood was collecting under his left leg. I took a quick look at the carnage around us. The body of the man I'd shot lay facedown on the concrete. The body of the man Michael stabbed sat hunched on the sidewalk, his shirt covered in his own blood. Then there was Dorothy, still sitting on the bench, her head dangling loosely in front of her. The sirens were getting louder. "We need to get out of here," I said to Michael.

"Where's Reggie?" he asked.

"I couldn't keep up with them. He was too fast. He was heading for the bridge."

"And the guy chasing him?"

"He was still chasing him, but I think Reggie is faster."

Michael nodded. "Okay, let's move." He looked up at me. For the first time that I could remember, he didn't try to hide his pain. "I need you to help me up," he said. I walked over to him and squatted down, throwing one of his arms over my shoulder. "You've been exercising, right?" he asked. I stood up, lifting his body with me.

"You can lean on me the whole way," I said. We walked together, heading north. A park was in front of us, full of trees and shadows. It would provide us with some cover. From there, it wasn't far to my apartment. "Do you think those sirens are for us?" I asked Michael as he limped beside me.

"Maybe," he answered. "Maybe not. We're probably not the only reason this city has for sirens." I kept moving us forward. We made it to the shadows of the park and kept going. We made it back to the apartment before midnight. The apartment felt still and empty. Michael didn't have the strength to make it back to his hotel. We were lucky that he made it as far as he did. Before we went to sleep, I had him take off his pants so that I could look at his wounds. The holes around his knee from the dog bite weren't healing. They were still open, still leaking an ugly pus. "Your dog bite is infected," I told him.

"I'm not really worried about that right now," he said, grimacing.

I looked farther down his leg for the bullet wound. I found the entry and exit wound. That was good. It meant that there probably wasn't any bullet left in Michael's leg. I had purchased a virtual pharmacy after Michael had come back that first night with the burns on his back. I stacked the medical supplies on the couch next to where we sat on the floor. Michael looked over the pile of supplies with his eyes but he didn't move any closer to them. I bought the supplies in case he ever stayed over and I needed to attend to his injuries. I always thought I'd be attending to old wounds, not new ones. "You weren't pre-med at your college, were you?" he asked.

"No," I answered. "Nothing that practical." I picked up some cotton swabs and the alcohol. I thought about how much time I'd already spent cleaning Michael's wounds. I dabbed the alcohol on the bullet holes. He didn't flinch at the burn from the alcohol. This time, I hadn't expected him to. I took two pieces of gauze and held them against Michael's leg. "Can you hold them in place while I wrap?" I asked. Michael didn't say anything. He reached down and placed one hand on each piece of white gauze. The gauze wouldn't be white for much longer. When I finished wrapping his calf, Michael took his hands away and leaned back, lying flat on the floor. His chest rose and fell with deep, deliberate breaths. I didn't ask Michael if it hurt. I could feel his pain just by watching him.

I looked at the clock. It was nearing one in the morning. "We're going to have to get out of here, Michael. After what happened, we can't stay here. They knew about Dorothy and Reggie. We're going to have to go to Philadelphia."

"I know," Michael said. "We'll leave tomorrow night."

"Do you think we'll be safe there?"

"We'll be *safer* there," Michael said through gritted teeth. "The plan I had for the job—that's out the window, though." He looked down at his new injuries. "I can't do it on this leg." The blood was seeping through the bandages on Michael's leg. It would stop eventually. It might lead to another scar. I was almost jealous of Michael's wounds, jealous of the way his skin burned and the flesh tore away from his body. At least he had something to show for his pain.

"That's okay. I can help you this time." I shot a man dead, I thought. I'm not useless.

Michael shrugged. "If that's what you want." He didn't say any more. He didn't need to. The innocence had been leaking out of me for some time—maybe since the day I met your father—like the slow evaporation of perfume from a bottle. It had to. I know that. I don't regret it. When I shot that man, I took the perfume bottle and smashed it. Now the stink was everywhere.

Twenty-eight

Evan and Addy kept moving. They kept running. They kept hiding. They found more moments alone in the darkness. Evan had more questions for Addy. Sometimes Addy had answers.

"How do you know where we're going?" Evan asked Addy. "How do you know where to find the people who are supposed to help us?"

"When I was with the Underground," Addy answered, "I used to work at a compound in Florida. I'm just trying to get us back there. I know people there. We just have to hope that the compound wasn't raided like the houses in L.A."

"Has there been any more news?" Evan asked Addy. Addy checked her phone frequently. Evan watched her every time she did. Each time, he could feel his stomach churning.

Addy shook her head. "Only more cryptic messages about the revolution still being alive, but the Underground was never part of the revolution anyway. They were too timid. We have to hope that's what kept them safe."

"Nothing else?" Evan asked.

"Nothing about any raids in Florida," Addy answered, intentionally evading Evan's question, intentionally neglecting to tell him about the rash of stories about the nationwide manhunt for the eighteen-year-old home-grown terrorist from Maine; intentionally neglecting to tell him about the

interviews with people that knew Evan growing up. Evan's old neighbors said that he was generally a good kid. He was good at sports and well liked, but he and his best friend—his ever-present, mysteriously unnamed best friend—were kind of loners. Addy also neglected to tell Evan about the man who was all over the news, claiming that he saw Evan somewhere in New Mexico. He claimed that he'd given Evan and a young woman a ride. The man said that he didn't realize who Evan was until he saw Evan's picture on the news later that day. Addy kept all that information to herself. It was a burden she was willing to carry on her own for Evan's sake.

"Even if we find the people you used to work for, how do you know that they're going to help us?" Evan asked Addy. "I'm not even part of the War."

"Because Reggie doesn't leave people behind," Addy said, willing to leave it at that.

But Evan wouldn't let her. "Who's Reggie?" he asked.

"He's in charge of the group I used to work for. He's been with the Underground forever, ever since they pulled him out of the War almost twenty years ago, right around the time when things first started going crazy. Reggie's always kept his head. He's saved a lot of people during all the madness. He acts like he owes it to the world, for some reason."

"But how do you know you can trust him?"

"Because he's the person that recruited me," Addy said. "He's the one who pulled me out of War. He's the one who taught me to hate the War to begin with."

"Why did he pull you out? I mean, why you?" Evan had thought about this for some time now, imagining that Addy had been someone important before she left the War. "Who were you when you were part of the War?"

"I was nobody," Addy confessed.

"I don't believe that."

"Believe it," Addy said, shooting him a look to try to prepare him for disappointment. "I was in the intelligence group. I was on a team responsible for researching hospital records and birth announcements to try to connect lineage so that we could identify people on the other side. I was the youngest person on our team, which meant that I spent a lot of time fetching other people's coffee."

"I don't understand," Evan said. "If you were a nobody who had to be taught to hate the War, why did this Reggie person bother to recruit you?"

"I asked him the same question. He told me that he had spies working inside the assignment bureau in intelligence. They're the guys who determine whether you're going to be a soldier or a planner or an educator or a nobody. One of Reggie's spies saw my profile."

"What did it say?" Evan looked at Addy. He had no idea what to expect. He had no idea what he was going to learn about her.

"According to Reggie, my scores indicated that I had the aptitude and disposition that would have made me an excellent soldier. He said my scores in those areas were very near the top of the charts. That's one of the main reasons why he recruited me."

Evan still didn't understand. "He recruited you to the Underground because your test scores said you would have been good at killing people?"

Addy shrugged. "According to Reggie, killing people and saving people require the same basic skill set. The only difference is perspective."

"If you would have made such a good killer, why didn't they turn you into a soldier in the first place? Aren't there a lot of woman soldiers?"

"Yeah, there are tons of woman soldiers, but my test said something else too. My test scores also indicated that I had what they called an inclination toward independence."

"An inclination toward independence?" Evan repeated, feeling the hollow, clinical sound of the words as he said them.

"Yeah," Addy confirmed. "And, apparently, that's not something that's looked on very highly when handing weapons to eighteen-year-olds and ordering them to go out and kill."

"But Reggie was okay with it?"

Addy nodded. "Reggie wasn't just okay with it. Reggie told me that it was as much a reason why he recruited me as my other scores. He valued independence. I think he had high hopes for me. I'm pretty sure I let him down."

"Because the same independent streak that made him recruit you ended up turning you into a rebel?"

"Because I got sick of sitting around doing little things when big things were happening all around me."

Evan knew how Addy felt. He knew what it felt like to feel destined for bigger things. "Have they always screened soldiers like that? Have they always tried to avoid independent thinkers?" Evan asked.

"I don't know," Addy answered. "I don't know if they always screened them or if they started because of something that happened or something that someone did," she added without elaborating.

Evan thought about it for a minute. "It doesn't say much for the soldiers, does it? I mean, it means that the soldiers are basically chosen to be human drones with a predilection for violence."

Addy shrugged. She knew better. She'd met a lot of former soldiers during her two years working with the Underground. "Either that," Addy answered Evan, "or the tests are a bunch of crap." It was obvious to Evan which of the two options Addy believed. "I try not to put too much weight into psychological tests given to sixteen-year-olds. Even if they're accurate at the time, people change."

"But Reggie believed in the tests?"

"He thought that they were better than nothing. Reggie was looking for people who weren't afraid to break the rules. That's how he found me. That's why we can trust him."

Twenty-nine

The city blew by the windows of the cab as we drove toward China-town. I watched the buildings go by in a blur. We were leaving New York. I wondered if I'd ever come back. Michael put his hand on top of mine like he had that day on the airplane leaving St. Martin. It felt good, the touch of another person, Michael's touch. I looked in the direction of the Brooklyn Bridge and wondered about Reggie again. Michael and I'd spent the day sitting in the apartment, listening for a knock on the door, dreading we might be discovered in the few hours before we left. A couple times, I hoped for a knock though. I hoped it would be Reggie so that I'd know he was okay. Maybe someday I'll hear a knock on my door and it will be Reggie. Maybe Reggie made it to Brooklyn and Brooklyn protected him. Maybe Reggie outran the bullets in the last man's gun. Maybe, maybe, maybe.

Reggie had saved Michael's life. He could have run away as soon as he saw what they did to Dorothy. I told him to run, but he didn't. I wonder if what I did saved Reggie's life. It all depends on whether or not Reggie is still alive. If he's dead, then my killing didn't serve any purpose. "I've got something to show you when we get on the bus," Michael said as the cab wove through traffic.

"What is it?" I asked.

"You'll see," he said.

The cabbie let us out on Canal Street. We walked the half block to a bus stop near the entrance to the Manhattan Bridge, across from some sort of Chinese clinic. Other people, mostly Asian, were already waiting on the sidewalk for the bus, standing with their suitcases. The Chinatown buses were cheap buses that ran from one Chinatown to the next, up and down the Eastern seaboard, stopping in D.C., Philly, New York, and Boston. We walked over and got in the back of the line.

The bus left at midnight. We'd be riding under the cover of darkness. After everything that had happened, I wasn't sure if I believed that darkness helped. By the time the bus pulled up, it was five minutes to midnight and we were standing at about the midpoint of the line. We shuffled onto the bus, paying the driver our fare as we got on. Michael and I made our way to the back. "I don't like having people sit behind me," Michael said. I went to put my bag up on the overhead rack. Michael put his hand on my bag. "Do you still have that thing you found the other night?" he asked. I knew that he was referring to the gun. I nodded. "Is it in the bag?" he asked. I nodded again. "Then let's keep the bag in our laps."

The bus was only a third full. None of the other passengers sat too close to us. Everyone tried to keep their distance from everyone else. I could feel the rumble under my feet when the engine started. The driver turned the interior lights off, making it dark inside so people could sleep. He pulled the bus into traffic and we were moving. We drove west. I watched the city out the window for as long as I could, up until the moment the bus entered the tunnel to New Jersey. We drove under the water and New York was gone.

The sky over New Jersey was dark. Only intermittent flashes of light flared over us as we drove past streetlights or well-lit buildings. Michael turned to me. "I thought you'd want to see this," Michael said as he reached into his duffel bag. He pulled a postcard out of his bag. He handed it to me. I flipped it over in my hands and waited for a flash of light so that I could see it better. When the next flash of light came I saw that it was another postcard from Washington, D.C., but it wasn't one that I'd ever seen before. It had a picture of the Jefferson Memorial surrounded by cherry blossoms on it. "I found it in Dorothy's pocket," Michael said.

"Is this what you were looking for?" I asked.

"No. It was more of a consolation prize. But I saved it for you." I flipped it over. Even in the darkness, I could see that there was something written on it, but I couldn't make out the words. I reached up to turn on my reading light, but Michael stopped me. "Let's not draw attention to ourselves," he said. So I waited for another flash of light. While I waited, I tried to imagine what the postcard might say. My imagination nearly drowned in the possibilities. The words were there, right in front of me, but I couldn't read them. Another flash of light came. I saw only the first few words. The postcard was addressed to me.

Dear Maria, it started. I was so startled when I saw my name that I couldn't read any more before the light disappeared again. I held the postcard closer to my face, hoping I could read it in the darkness, but the words were hidden in the shadows. *Dear Maria*. I wondered if Dorothy wrote the postcard herself. The bus hurtled down the turnpike. We were coming up on an oil refinery that was lit up like a vigil. I'd have time to read the whole card. I looked down and waited for the light to come. When it did, I read,

> *Dear Maria,*
> *Every picture is a picture of a picture*
> *Of a picture of a picture of a scene.*
> *Every memory is a memory of a memory*

Of a memory of a memory of a dream.
On the sixth day, you can find your reward under a rock in the
creek in the park.

I didn't need any time to solve the riddle this time. I knew what it meant right away. I knew to ignore the poem and concentrate only on the words that came after it. The sixth day was Saturday. My reward was my prize for helping Reggie: Dorothy's promise that she'd help me find you. Under a rock in the creek in the park had to refer to Rock Creek Park. I suddenly felt a chill run down my back. I turned to Michael. "Do you think they'll still help me after what happened?" I asked, holding the postcard tightly between my fingers.

"They better," Michael answered.

"But Dorothy's dead, and we don't know what happened to Reggie."

"People die," Michael said with a shrug. "It's no excuse to welsh on a promise."

I looked out the window. We were already far from the city. All I could see were empty fields and trees zipping by us in the night. "You never trusted them in the first place," I said to Michael.

"Yeah, but you did," he answered. "I don't see any benefit to stopping now." The moon hung low over the trees. "Sometimes you just have to believe whatever helps you get through the day. There's no point in truth if it has no utility." He took a shirt out of his duffel bag and balled it so that he could use it as a pillow. He took the balled-up shirt, placed it on my shoulder, and rested his head on it.

I don't want to sleep. I want time to go faster. I want to physically push it forward. Michael fell asleep in minutes. It's too dark to read, barely light enough to write. Instead I've been staring out the window, wondering where you are right now, wondering if something inside you misses me.

Thirty

"What was he like?" Addy finally asked Evan during one of the moments when they were alone and everything was quiet. She'd been holding back the question for so long, over so many miles. She was afraid of how Evan would react to it. She was afraid he would be jealous of her interest in his old friend. She was afraid of what she'd have to reveal to Evan once they started talking about him. But even Addy's endurance had its limits. She simply couldn't wait any longer.

"Who? Christopher?" Evan asked, as if it were possible that Addy was asking about someone else. Who else could she be asking about? It was Christopher who brought the two of them together. Before the night of the fire, Christopher was all they had in common.

"Yeah, Christopher," Addy answered, trying to sound as insouciant as possible, trying to pretend that her interest was merely casual. "Growing up, I mean. What was he like?"

Addy shouldn't have been worried about asking Evan about Christopher. Evan had spent the past two weeks asking himself questions about Christopher. The questions in Evan's head only doubled after Addy told him that Christopher was gone. What was Christopher like growing up? Evan thought about how much different his answer would have been if someone asked him the question only two months ago. It was strange how so much of *what happened over the past few weeks—all things that should have had nothing to do with his and Christopher's childhood together—seemed to have everything to do with their childhood. "He was quiet," Evan said, "and intense. People thought that he was so different from everybody else because he was kind of a loner and because he didn't give a shit what people thought or said about him. He really wasn't that different from everyone else, though. He was like a lot of other kids we grew up with, just more—" Evan took a breath, searching for the word. "Focused" was all he could come up with.*

Addy gave Evan a searching look, begging with her eyes for him to continue. Evan obliged. "It's hard to describe what someone you grew up with was like while you were growing up with him. He was my best friend since we were less than three years old. It's the same as if I asked you what you were like growing up. You are who you were. What's there to explain?"

"But Christopher must have been different from the other kids," Addy said, not bothering to explain to Evan why she was so sure that he had to have been different.

"I guess," Evan began with a shrug. "In the beginning, when we were really young, he really was just like everyone else. Maybe he was a little quieter. Oh, and he had nightmares," Evan remembered. "He had these vicious nightmares. I remember the first night he slept over my house. His parents warned my parents about his night terrors—that's what they called them—but we had no idea how bad they would be. That first time, my mother stayed up with him until morning. Chris and I were sleeping on the floor in my bedroom in sleeping bags. Every time Chris screamed, I woke up and I looked down and saw my mother, sitting on the edge of my bed, leaning over Chris, running her hands over his forehead and whispering to him that everything was okay. It was like no matter how many times my mother said everything was going to be okay, Chris knew it wasn't true. My mother was superstitious, so she didn't dare wake him up. Instead she simply sat there next to him, trying to soothe him. There were lulls, mo-

ments when the screaming would stop, but it always came back. My parents didn't let me ask Chris to sleep over again for years after that night. My mother didn't have the stomach for it. The next time I was allowed to have Chris sleep over again was after he promised me that the nightmares were gone."

"What were the nightmares about?" Addy asked, searching for meaning in every word.

"I don't know. I don't think Chris knew. I don't think he remembered them when he woke up."

"What was he screaming? Could you understand any of it?"

Evan shook his head. "He just screamed these terrible, high-pitched screams. A few times I heard him shout the word no over and over again. He called out for his mom and his dad a few times too, but he never said anything that made any sense."

"How old was he when the nightmares stopped?" Addy asked.

Evan began to feel like he was being interrogated, but that didn't stop him from talking. He wanted answers almost as much as Addy did. He thought that maybe together, they could find them. "I don't know. We had to be in the fifth grade when I had him sleep over again. What is that—ten years old? Eleven?"

"Do you know why the nightmares stopped?"

"It's hard to say," Evan said. "It's not like his parents medicated him or anything. But now that I think about it, other things started to change around then too. I never really put the two together before. Right around that time, Chris made me start taking karate lessons with him. He became obsessed with it—it was his first obsession. He also got this pull-up bar in his house that his father mounted on the frame of the door leading into their laundry room. I'd go over to his house and we'd spend half our time just doing pull-ups. Most of the kids in our class could only do, like, four pull-ups. A bunch of kids couldn't do any. Chris could do over twenty when we were only twelve years old."

"How many could you do?" Addy asked, figuring that Evan couldn't have been that far behind his best friend.

"Twenty-three," Evan answered with a proud grin. Addy knew that Evan would remember the exact number. She would have remembered if it had been her. "Chris had the school record at twenty-five."

"You said that things started to change. What else changed?" Addy asked. She wanted to know more. She wanted to know everything. "It had to be more than him making you take karate lessons and the two of you doing pull-ups."

"There was more," Evan answered, trying to figure out how to explain what he'd simply known growing up: that something was happening to Christopher. It was like a lever had been pulled inside of Christopher's head. "It was more than that. He became more withdrawn around other people around then too. I think that for a while I was the only person he really talked to. And that changed only when we were in high school, because he made me set him up on dates with a few of my girlfriend's friends. Those dates were a disaster." Evan laughed.

"How was he withdrawn?" Addy asked, focusing on the details that seemed important to her.

"He became even quieter. When you were with him, he'd be intensely focused on something one minute, and the next he'd seem totally distracted. But when he was focused, I've never seen anything like it before."

"When he was focused, what was he focused on?"

"He had us play these survival games in the woods, like we were training for the end of the world. We'd run, climb rocks, wade through rivers. He started getting his hands on whatever weapons he could find and we'd take those into the woods too. We'd practice throwing knives into trees from twenty feet away and sometimes even farther. Then he got other things. Hatchets. Bows and arrows—there were a lot of bow hunters where we grew up. I don't know where he got any of the stuff. I didn't ask because I

didn't want to know. Eventually, he got his hands on some guns. We prac-
ticed shooting cans off fallen trees."

"Did you ever shoot anything else?"

"No. I wanted us to practice on squirrels or deer, but Chris was against
it. Instead one of us would throw a rock or a tennis ball as high into the air
as we could and the other one would try to shoot it out of the sky. Chris
almost never missed."

"What did you think of all of this?" Addy asked.

"I thought it was awesome," Evan answered. "It was so much fucking
fun. What fourteen-year-old boy wouldn't like doing that shit? Hell, it
sounds like fun now."

"But it wasn't fun for Chris?" Addy guessed.

Evan shrugged. "Fun for Chris was different from fun for everyone
else. Even when we weren't out in the woods, Chris spent all of his free time
reading these crazy books about aliens and secret societies and conspiracy
theories. If I didn't know him, I might have thought that he was a weirdo
too. We quit karate after two years because a tae kwon do studio opened up
in town. Chris made me start taking tae kwon do with him. When I asked
Chris why we were switching, he told me that he didn't think we were
learning fast enough in our karate classes. Fast enough for what? I had no
idea. I mean, no one in that class learned anything half as fast as Chris. I
didn't question him, though. I did what Chris wanted me to, because Chris
was the only thing in my life that made the world seem big. But he did
things because—" Evan stopped midsentence, staring down at the floor,
trying for the first time that he could remember to figure out what had
been driving his best friend. Evan began to wonder how much Christopher
might have known back when the two of them were playing in the woods.
He wondered how much Christopher had kept from him.

"Because why?" Addy asked.

Evan lifted his head. "Because when Chris turned eleven, he suddenly became paranoid or something. It was like his nightmares escaped his sleep and started following him around while he was awake."

"But you never asked him what he was paranoid about?"

"I used to tease him about it sometimes, and he would laugh. But I never asked him about it, because I was his friend. If he wanted to tell me, he would have told me. I think one of the reasons why he didn't run away from me like he ran from everyone else was because I was willing to accept all of his weirdo shit without asking questions."

"Did the paranoia ever go away?" Addy asked.

"No," Evan answered, shaking his head for emphasis. "It just got more intense. After two years of tae kwon do, he made us quit that so we could drive two towns over to start taking boxing classes. It was the same as before. Chris didn't think he was learning fast enough in tae kwon do. He never thought he was learning anything fast enough. I tried to help him relax. I tried setting him up on those dates—some of the girls we went to high school with were into his brooding, like they thought he was a char- acter from a teen romance or something—but the dates never went any- where. The girls thought the brooding was cool. They weren't ready for everything that went with it."

"It sounds lonely."

"I think he was lonely, but I think he was too caught up in everything else to even notice how lonely he was."

"He's lucky he had you," Addy pointed out.

"Maybe I should have done more for him." Evan's heart thumped in his chest. He began to feel guilty that he didn't try harder to understand his friend. "But what could I have done? No matter how old I was, Chris always seemed older than me. He'd become a grown-up when we were twelve. By the time we were seventeen, it was like he was twice my age."

"Did you ever wonder if he was crazy?" Addy asked.

"No," Evan answered. "I was always sure that he was the sanest person I knew. Even then, if someone asked me if he was crazy or the rest of the

world was crazy, I would have told you that the rest of the world was crazy every day of the week and twice on Sunday." Evan thought about everything that had happened to him over the past couple weeks. "I just never would have guessed how crazy."

"Did other people think he was crazy?"

"I don't know," Evan answered with a shrug. "I never gave a shit what other people thought about him."

"What do you think now? Now that you know the story about Christopher's real parents? Now that you know about the War? Now that you know everything?"

Evan shook his head in protest. "I don't know everything," Evan answered. "All I know now that I didn't know then was that Chris actually had reasons to be paranoid, and now he's gone."

Silence engulfed the two of them. Addy let it fester. "He's not dead, Evan," Addy suddenly blurted out. She'd been keeping her secret long enough.

"What?" Evan shot Addy a confused look. "You said—"

"I said he was gone. That was the truth. I never said that he was dead."

"What the fuck does that mean?"

"He came to me the night before our compound was raided. He told me he was leaving. He wouldn't tell me where he was going. He asked me to try to convince you to go home. He said he knew that if he told you he was leaving, you'd try to follow him. He didn't want that for you."

"So he just left us?"

"I don't think he knew what was going to happen, but yeah, he just left us," Addy said, sounding as despondent as Evan. "I tried to get him to explain."

"I can't believe that he didn't say good-bye. I can't believe he would abandon us like that. There has to be more to it. What happened to him?"

Every time Addy looked at her phone, she was hoping she would see some news about Christopher, but no news ever came. Even though she knew that he left before the raid, she wondered if he was even still alive. "I don't know," Addy said, "and it doesn't matter anyway. The two of us still have to move on. We still have to get to Florida and find help." Addy finally spoke the words that she'd been saying to herself over and over again for the past five days.

"It does matter," Evan said to Addy, a tinge of anger at being kept in the dark this long sneaking into his voice, "and you know it."

It did matter—to Evan, to Addy, and to the uprising. Addy knew that it mattered, but ever since the night that Christopher told her that he was running away, she'd been trying to convince herself otherwise.

Thirty-one

It took me almost the full two days before I was comfortable with my part in the plan. At the end of our second day in the hotel in Philadelphia, Michael told me that he had something for me. I remembered the picture he'd given me and the gun he'd given to Reggie and wondered what type of gift he had for me now and what the gift would mean. He handed me an unwrapped white paper box. I opened it. Inside was a black knife in a sheath.

"What's this for?" I asked as I slid the knife out of the sheath. The knife was thin but solid. It had a black handle and a black blade. The blade was symmetric, sharp on both edges, and came to a point at its tip.

"Protection," Michael said. "It's called a boot knife, but you can hide it almost anywhere. You don't need a lot of practice to use it. You pull it out and stab or cut. It'll work."

"But I already have the gun," I reminded him.

"That's fine," Michael answered. "Keep the gun. Carry it. But guns are loud and difficult to use at extremely close range." I didn't like the sounds of those words—*extremely close range*. "Hopefully, you won't need it," Michael continued. "But you should have it."

"Okay," I said. He gave Reggie a gun, but he gave me a knife.

"I'd hide the sheath on the inside of your waistline with the handle sticking out beneath your shirt. You can access it quickly there, but it will be well concealed." I nodded to Michael. I planned on listening to him. Michael knew knives. I'd seen enough to know that.

"So, do you think you're ready for this?" Michael asked me.

"Yes," I answered. I slid the knife slowly back in its sheath and quickly pulled it out again for practice. I hadn't been ready. That morning, Michael gave me our target's file. He told me to take the day to look it over. He knew that I didn't feel ready yet. He thought rereading our target's profile might help me to overcome my hesitation. I knew that I was being a hypocrite, letting other people do my dirty work for me but suddenly developing a conscience when I had to do it myself. I was ashamed. I thought I'd be ready after what I'd done under the highway in New York. I wasn't. It was different when it was planned. It was another step. I took the file to the public library to study the material. I found a nearly empty spot at the back of the reading room on one end of a long table. The table was broken up into reading cubicles with high wooden walls on each side for privacy. I sat down at the table and dropped the manila envelope in front of me. I read and reread the file. I read about the people that our target killed, the people that he tortured. I also read about the kids that he taught. I wanted to be sure that by following through on my part of the plan, I'd be doing something positive for the world and not just something positive for you and for me. I couldn't. Our target was too full of contradictions to be sure about anything.

After a few hours of rereading the file without finding the magic potion that would make me okay with my part in this man's execution, I stood up. I needed to try to get my bearings. I felt dizzy. I grabbed the papers and slipped them back inside the envelope. I put the envelope under my arm and walked. I needed a moment. I walked out of the reading room and headed for the front door. I thought the fresh air might do me some good. Before I got to the door, however, I noticed a computer lab to my right. Seven of the ten computers were taken. Three of the computers were free. I decided that the fresh air could wait. I had to check something first.

I sat down in front of one of the computers. I pulled up the Web site for one of the local New York newspapers. I knew what section I wanted to read. I'd read that newspaper every day when I was in New York, searching for a way back into the War, searching for murders, trying to figure out which ones were related to the War and which ones were truly random. I could never tell. I don't suppose anyone could unless they knew something.

This time, I knew something. I clicked the link to the local crime section. The story was already a couple of days old, but I found ancillary stories from that day that linked back to the original. The original story was about a nighttime shooting that took place beneath the FDR, along the East River, just north of the South Street Seaport. It was a story about a botched robbery. According to the story, a white man and a white woman ambushed an Iranian street vendor as he was pushing his food cart back to his storage location, hoping that he would be flush with cash after a full workday. The perpetrators were said to be carrying a large knife. When they approached the street vendor, he pulled out a gun to try to defend himself. During the ensuing chaos, shots were fired. The shots were reported by the cars driving by on the highway. The event came to a tragic conclusion when both perpetrators were shot and the street vendor was stabbed. All three died at the scene before the police or ambulances arrived. In the story, they identified Dorothy using a name that I'd never heard. I suppose it was probably her given name. I wonder if her family knew where she was or if they only found out when they saw their dead daughter's picture in the newspaper.

I searched the Web site for a bit, looking for information about another incident, perhaps another shooting. I looked in the local Brooklyn section. I didn't find anything. The paper didn't have any record of any other murders or any other shootings over the past three days. That meant one of two things: either Reggie had gotten away or they were able to completely bury Reggie's murder. I flipped back to the story about the street vendor. I scrolled to the bottom of the page. At the bottom of the page, they had pictures of all three of the dead. On one side of the page was a picture of Dorothy next to the picture of the man that I had shot. On the other side of the page was the picture of the Middle Eastern man. In Dorothy's final image to the world, her face floated next to the faces of her enemies, next to the faces of the men she'd spent her life trying to save people from, next to the faces of the men she'd died trying to save Reggie from. It wasn't right. Dorothy was better than them. She deserved better.

I went back to the reading room. I threw the envelope back down on the table. I took the contents out. I didn't need fresh air anymore. That need had been subsumed by an internal fire. I flipped to the pages describing the mark's thirty-one confirmed kills. I skipped the rest. I ignored the contradictions. The mark was one of Them. He was the bad guy. It didn't matter which side he was on. They were all bad guys. Dorothy was the good guy.

The plan is simple. I'll pose as a student. I'll approach our mark, pretending to have an interest in next year's track team. With all the expulsions, suspensions, transfers and truancy, the school has enough students coming in and out of its halls that it shouldn't be unusual for our target to meet a student he's never seen before. All I have to do is pass for a high school student. That shouldn't be a problem. When I look at myself, I see all of the weariness and worry, but I'm still only eighteen years old. I'm still only five feet, two inches tall. It's only my eyes that worry me. My eyes have aged beyond their years. I'm counting on being able to cover up the wrinkles and bags around my eyes with makeup. I'll approach our target inside the school after he's coached track practice and ask him about the track team. The goal is to lure him into a specific classroom to talk. Michael will be waiting outside, with a clear view of the classroom's windows. If Michael sees me enter the classroom with the mark, he'll know that everything is going as planned. That'll be his cue to move. If I feel like something is wrong, I'm not supposed to go into the classroom. If I feel like anything is wrong, I'm supposed to walk away. Once Michael comes into the room, all I have to do is leave, locking the door behind me. The classroom doors have keys that lock only from the outside, presumably so that students can't lock themselves in. Whatever their intended purpose, it makes for an ideal trap. My only job is to act as the bait.

"You have the key to the door?" Michael asked.

I held it in my hand. "I stole a copy from the janitor's closet."

"And you're confident that you can make sure that our mark is unarmed?" Michael asked.

"I'll take care of it," I told him. I saw the skepticism in his face. "I won't go into the room if I'm not sure," I assured him. "If you see me walk into that room, you're good to go. I won't do anything that puts you in more danger than you're ready for. Trust me."

"Okay," Michael said, "I trust you."

Thirty-two

I leaned closer to the mirror and began to apply my makeup. I tried to be subtle at first, applying a base to hide the wrinkles developing around my eyes. Once that was done, I added color. Subtlety was no longer important. I wanted to look like a sixteen-year-old girl. I used eye shadow that matched my dress and dark eyeliner to surround my eyes. I lingered, enjoying feeling like a girl again. Then I puckered my lips and applied dark red lipstick to them. I had gone to a mall near our hotel to buy clothes with money Michael gave me. I bought a blue skirt and a loose-fitting white top that tied up the neckline in the front. The top was cut lower and the skirt shorter than I was used to. Still, I'd look conservative compared to most of the other girls in the school. I put the outfit on and looked at myself in the mirror. I was in the best shape of my life. I could see the outline of the muscles in my shoulders through my blouse. I could see the clefts in my calf muscles. I stared at the woman in the mirror. My eyes looked gray. Your father used to tell me how much he loved my deep blue eyes. I had been beautiful for him, but he's not around to be beautiful for anymore. Instead I have to be strong for you.

I stepped out of the bathroom. I wanted Michael to see me before I left. I wanted to make sure that he knew exactly what I looked like, so that he would be sure it was me walking into the classroom and not somebody else. When I stepped out of the bathroom, he was sitting on the floor, stretching, his legs spread apart, his torso bent all the way down to the ground between his legs. He looked up only when he heard the bathroom door click closed behind me. He stared for what seemed like minutes. I felt more naked than if I'd been naked. I could feel my cheeks begin to grow flush.

"How do I look?" I asked.

"Like jailbait," he answered.

"I suppose that's a good thing?"

I waited for an answer that didn't come. "Five thirty?" Michael asked instead, confirming the time.

"Five thirty," I repeated.

"Lift up your shirt," Michael said out of the blue.

"What?" I responded, the blush on my cheeks intensifying.

Michael looked at me like I was a fool. "Lift up your shirt," he repeated. "Just a little." I finally realized what he was asking. I lifted my blouse a few inches above the waist of my skirt. When I did, Michael could see the hilt of the knife he'd given me sticking out of the waistline. He nodded in approval. "And the gun?"

"It's in my purse," I said.

"Good."

I didn't know what else to say. I didn't know the pre-assassination customs, so I simply turned to walk out of the room.

"Maria?" Michael said as I walked away from him.

"Yes?" I didn't turn around.

"Be safe," Michael said. "If anything happens, if anything feels wrong—*anything*—bail out."

I couldn't turn to face him. I wanted to but couldn't. "That doesn't sound like you, Michael," I said. "You've never been the bail-out type."

"That doesn't mean you don't have to be," Michael said, his voice deep and resonant. I could feel its bass in my joints. "We're not the same. I've always had more to fight for than to live for."

Our target was unwaveringly punctual. It was a trait I imagined he developed due to the War. We knew his daily patterns. Michael had studied them while Reggie and I were in New York. We knew where he would be almost by the minute. The timing was important. I had to approach him after track practice but before he had a chance to get back to his classroom to change. He wore sneakers, short socks, athletic shorts, and the type of T-shirt that is supposed to wick away the sweat from your body during track practice. It was an outfit that left very few places to hide a weapon, and all I had to do was get him into that classroom without a weapon.

We chose the classroom where I was supposed to lead our target for a number of reasons. First and foremost, it was along the route that he took from the track to his classroom. It was also around a corner from the most crowded part of the school. In the early evening, the foot traffic in front of this classroom would be nearly nonexistent. According to Michael, our target was often the only person walking those halls after five o'clock. Finally, it was the classroom whose door could be most clearly seen from the street where Michael would be waiting. Michael would see us as soon as we entered. Then he would make his move.

I snuck into the school and waited in the hallway near the classroom. I leaned up against a set of lockers, trying to play the part of an ordinary teenage girl. I was beginning to feel more comfortable in the outfit. I didn't get any strange looks from the other students as I walked down the hall. They didn't see who I really am: a widow, a mother, a killer. I took a deep breath, trying to focus on the job. I looked down at the hem of my skirt. It fell about an inch above my knee. I reached down and grabbed the skirt's waist. I lifted it another half inch so that the skirt rode even higher up my leg, careful not to drop the knife. I looked at my watch. The mark was supposed to walk by any minute.

I heard his footsteps coming down the hallway before I saw him. I could tell it was him by the purpose in his steps. I held my breath and counted my heartbeats to try to gauge my heart rate. It was beating too quickly to count. I could back out. If it felt wrong, I could abort the whole plan, but my time for that was running short. I took another deep breath. How would I know if something felt wrong? Everything in my life felt wrong. Right didn't exist anymore, only gradients of wrong.

I heard one set of footsteps. The mark was alone. I had been afraid that he would be walking down the hall with one of his students. I put that fear aside. I stepped away from the lockers as I heard the footsteps round the corner toward me. I stood up straight. I put one hand on my purse and grabbed the wrist of that hand with my other hand. I arched my back slightly. I wanted to get his attention.

I saw the mark turn the corner. Michael was already supposed to be waiting outside, staring through the classroom window, waiting for our entrance. "Mr. Ford," I called out to the mark, using the name that he'd given himself as a teacher in this city, even though I knew it wasn't his real name. He heard my voice and looked at me for the first time. Until then he had been walking with his head down. He hadn't expected to see anyone—not then anyway. He knew, like I did, that this hallway was usually empty at this time of day. "Can I help you?" he asked, looking me over, trying to find me in his memory.

"I wanted to talk to you about the track team," I said, trying to follow my script as much as the mark would let me.

"Are you a student here?" the mark asked. I stepped closer to him, hoping he would do the same. I knew I wasn't going to be able to simply talk him into following me into that classroom. I needed to entice him somehow. He didn't move closer, but he didn't move away either.

"I'm new," I said. I looked into his eyes to see if they might tell me something. All I saw was confusion. "I've seen you coaching the other students," I said, taking another small step toward him. We were close now, close enough that if he turned away from me, we were bound to touch. Would he be so pure that he wouldn't even consider what I was offering him? I'd read his file. I couldn't believe that would be the case.

"What would you like to know?" the mark asked. His voice didn't waver.

I had thought about this part of the conversation in my head. I had tried to think of what to say to him, but everything that I thought of sounded like a line from a bad romance novel. None of them sounded real. I needed this to seem real. We were so close that I could feel his breath on my neck. He'd been sweating, and I could smell him. It wasn't an appealing smell, though if it were someone else in a different situation, I might have thought differently. Not knowing what to say that wouldn't sound ridiculous, I simply reached down and ran my hands along the waist of his shorts. Then I reached down farther and cupped his crotch with my hand. It was forward, but I didn't have time for subtlety. I moved my hand and immediately felt a twitch and a growth beneath it. The mark's instinctive response to my hand on his crotch gave me the courage to continue. That response wasn't the only reason that I'd chosen this approach, though. Dressed for track practice, the mark had only one place where he could hide a weapon. His shirt was tight enough to see his muscle definition in his upper body beneath his clothes. If a weapon were under his shirt, I'd see it. His socks were too short to hide anything of any real danger. That left his shorts: the waist and the crotch. I felt everything. He was unarmed. I left my hand there for a second. Then I looked up at him. The look on his face surprised me. I could still see confusion on it, but now it was confusion tinged with anger. I pressed on, hoping that he was simply angry with himself, knowing that he wasn't going to be able to resist, that he was going to cross this line like he'd already crossed so many in his life.

"Do you want to talk about it in the classroom?" I said, motioning to the door behind us. He looked back over his shoulder at the closed door. Then he turned and looked back at me. My hand was still resting on his crotch. The blood hadn't receded. If anything, it had grown.

"Okay," he said in a voice that was only half convincing. He was beginning to make me nervous, but I decided that I couldn't go back now. I'd compromised too much already. I walked toward the door to the classroom. I didn't want to turn my back on the mark, so I took my hand off his crotch and placed it on the small of his back, leading him toward the door, making sure that he was walking next to me and not behind me. I kept telling myself that all I had to do was open the door and walk inside, and Michael would come. That was the plan.

I opened the door. It opened outward into the hallway. We stepped together into the classroom. I heard the mark close the door behind us. I glanced out the window for a second to see if I could see Michael. I didn't see anybody. I had to hope that he'd moved so quickly, I didn't have a chance to see him, that he was already on his way. I turned back to the mark, unsure of how far I would have to take this charade before Michael arrived.

I felt the sting on my face before I saw or heard anything. It wasn't until I was tumbling, already halfway to the ground, that I realized what had happened. The hand had swung from seemingly out of nowhere. I'd heard the sound as his open palm connected with my cheek. My purse, with my gun in it and the key to the door, flew off my shoulder and slid away from me across the floor. I thought about trying to crawl for the purse, but worried that the hand would strike me again. I could still feel the tingling on my cheek and began to feel the soreness in my jaw as I rolled over to face him again. He was standing above me, his face flushed with anger. I could see his chest moving up and down with labored breaths. He was struggling to contain his rage. He took a step toward me and I flinched reflexively.

"Who are you?" he yelled.

"I'm a new student," I said, almost choking on the words.

"Fuck you," he responded to my lie. "I know you from somewhere. Who are you?"

I struggled to get to my feet. I grabbed the desk next to me and pulled myself up. The mark stepped around me, placing himself in between me and my purse, knowing that I could have a weapon in there. Slowly I stood up. He'd hit me hard. I'd never been hit that hard before. My vision was still blurry. My head throbbed. Where was Michael?

"Are you going to hit me again?" I asked. I felt weak and small. Even after all of the exercising and all of the planning, he still made me feel weak. He was sweating. I could see his forehead glistening. My vision was beginning to focus again.

"If you tell me who you are, if you tell me the truth and I like the answer, then I won't hit you again."

"That's a lot of ifs," I said, not meaning to sound smart.

He raised his hand again and stepped toward me. This time, his hand wasn't open; it was balled into a tight fist. If he punched me as hard as he'd slapped me, I might never wake up. As he stepped toward me, I remembered. I reached down with my left hand, lifted up my shirt, and pulled my knife from its sheath. The mark was coming toward me so quickly he almost ran into the blade. He stopped short, and I lifted the blade of the knife so that it was inches from his face.

"You don't have the stones," he said, looking me up and down.

"I don't need them," I said. "If you scare me enough, I won't need courage for this—just fear." He took another step toward me anyway. I slashed at his face, opening up a gash on the closest thing to me, his nose. I hadn't been aiming. I hadn't had time to practice with the knife, other than quickly pulling it from its hiding place along my waist. The mark stopped again. He reached up and touched his nose with his hands. Then he held his fingers in front of his face, staring at his own blood.

"Who are you?" he asked again. "I know you're not one of Them. If you were, I would have killed you already." I believed him. What was left of my innocence saved my life. "Why do I recognize you?"

"How do you know I'm not one of Them?" I asked, trying to buy time.

"I can smell Them," he said, his facing turning mean and cold. He was talking about Michael. He was talking about your father.

I knew why he recognized me. "You teach initiation classes for the War?" He nodded. "Then you've seen my picture." I watched him, waiting to see the recognition in his eyes. Until that moment, I didn't know that both sides taught their people about us.

"You're the one with the baby?" That's what he called you: *the baby*. They all knew. They all talked about us. "What do you want with me? I didn't have anything to do with your kid."

He was wrong. He was so wrong. "You know about my son," I said. I felt brave, filling up with righteous anger. "And you fight in this War. And you still don't do anything about it. That means that you have everything to do with my kid." I looked down at the purse on the ground. By positioning himself between me and the purse, he had left open the path to the door. I could have run for it, but I couldn't risk leaving the purse. The mark was quiet, trying to digest the situation. Over the silence, I heard a shuffling noise of a man with a limp walking from out in the hallway. Michael was moving slowly but he was coming. My gun was in the purse. I promised Michael that I wouldn't signal him to come unless the mark was unarmed. The last thing I wanted to do was to arm him with my own gun.

I walked in a circle around the mark, keeping the tip of my knife pointed toward his face. His eyes didn't show fear. Instead they showed cunning. He was trying to plan his next move. He didn't want to hurt me, but he would if he had to. I took one small step after another toward the purse on the ground. His eyes flashed toward the purse for a split second, deciphering my plan in an instant. He moved quickly, lunging forward. I took a stab at him again, plunging the knife about a quarter inch into his chest and pulling it out again. I fell back for a second and I reached down and grabbed the purse. The mark looked down at the wound in his chest. Then he looked up at me again. I could see that all the hesitation that he'd had about hurting me was gone. I was his enemy now. I'd read about what he did to his enemies.

Michael had to be right outside the door by now. I ran for it, knowing that I didn't have time to reach into the purse and pull out the gun. The mark was right behind me. He took two steps after me and then stopped. When I reached the door, it was already open. Michael had opened it. He was standing there, his knife drawn.

"What the fuck is this?" the mark said out loud to me, as if I'd betrayed some sort of trust. Then to Michael: "You can't use her to trap me. You can't use an innocent as bait. That's against the rules."

Michael looked at the mark. The mark was already bleeding in two places. He looked down at me standing almost next to him. Michael's eyes moved to the cheek where the mark had struck me. Michael must have seen something there, a bruise or a reddened handprint. "I'm not a big fan of the rules," Michael said. His voice was quiet but loud enough for the mark to hear him. Michael wasn't being witty. He was stating a fact. The rules had killed his best friend. The rules had kept him from living a new life. Michael wasn't a fan of the rules.

"You can leave, Maria," Michael said as he stared at the mark. "Get the door on your way out."

I stepped outside the door and closed it behind me. I leaned my back against it and rifled through the purse for the key. My hands were shaking. I heard some commotion coming from inside the room, desks screeching along the floor. I heard a loud banging sound. I turned for a second and looked through the small rectangular window in the door. I saw the mark. He was coming toward me. Michael was behind him, but the mark was faster. I didn't have time to keep looking for the key. Instead, I turned. I leaned my back against the door with all my strength and will. I reached down and grabbed the doorknob with both hands, trying to keep it from turning. A split second later, I felt the doorknob begin to twist beneath my grip. I felt every muscle in my body, all those muscles that I'd been training over the past months, tighten as I tried to keep the doorknob from turning. It turned anyway. All I could do was slow it down as it slipped beneath my fingers. Then I felt a push against the door. I braced my feet on the ground and pushed into the door with everything I had. The mark was less than two inches behind me, separated from me by two inches of cheap wood. I pushed against the door with all of the strength I had, with more strength than I had ever had before.

The mark was trying to escape certain death, and I was using my new muscles to stop him. I didn't want to think about what would happen if he got out. I didn't hear Michael stab him. I remembered the sound from that night in St. Martin, how I heard the stabbing sound from much farther away, but this time I didn't hear it. I was too tired. The door was too thick. All I heard was the mark's grunt as the blade entered his body. The pressure on the door weakened. The mark was still pushing but not as hard anymore. Finally, I heard a higher-pitched, whimpering sound, like the sound of a dog who'd been disciplined by its master. Then the pressure on the door let up completely. The muscles in my legs gave way and I crumpled to the ground.

Michael was able to push the door open enough to slip through it. When he opened the door, a trickle of blood seeped out into the hallway. "I thought you said you had the key," Michael said, as I sat there on the ground, spent.

"I couldn't get to it in time," I answered. He looked down at me and almost laughed.

"No matter," he said. "The job's done. We need to get out of here." I couldn't stand up. My strength was gone. Michael leaned down and grabbed me under one of my armpits. He lifted me to my feet, ignoring the pain in his leg. "You did good," he said as he slung one of my arms over his shoulders to help me walk.

I didn't look back at the door, at the blood or at the body. "What took you so long to get here?" I asked Michael.

He didn't answer me and we limped away together.

Thirty-three

That night, Michael wanted to go out to celebrate. I didn't believe that we had anything to celebrate. "You have to celebrate," Michael said to me, without much joy in his voice. It made me remember the Michael that your father had described in his journal. If felt like Michael was trying to remember that Michael too.

"This is ridiculous," I said to Michael as we walked to South Street. "We should be hiding."

"You sound like Joe," Michael said.

I refused to be insulted. "Joe was smart."

Michael stopped walking. He turned to me so that we were facing each other on the sidewalk. "He was," Michael agreed. "Joe was always more disciplined than me, and look where that got him." He paused long enough for the silence to confirm that I had no response. "Just a few drinks," Michael promised. "It's important." I didn't understand how it could be important, but if it was important to Michael, it was important to me too.

Michael picked the darkest, dingiest bar we could find. He let me pick our seats, so we went to the table farthest from the door in the back. The jukebox was blaring loud enough that neither of us could hear anyone in the bar but each other. Michael went to the bar and ordered our first two drinks. He returned with four glasses in his hands: two pint glasses half-full of Guinness and two shot glasses with a mix of Baileys and Irish whiskey. He put the glasses down on the table, a pint glass and a shot glass in front of me and a set in front of him. He sat down on the graffiti-riddled bench and picked up his pint glass. He lifted the pint glass and held it halfway across the table. "To a job well done," he said with all the enthusiasm of a man delivering a eulogy. I lifted my pint glass and clinked it against his. I made the only toast that I could think of.

"To not drinking alone," I said. Michael smiled. He put the pint glass back on the table, picked up the shot glass, dropped it in the pint glass, and chugged. "I still can't believe I'm doing this," I said before following suit. The taste of the drink hit me right away. The effects of the alcohol didn't take much longer. Michael got up and got us more drinks.

"How does it feel?" he asked me.

"How does what feel?" I asked, assuming he must mean more than the effects of the alcohol.

"Your first job," he said.

I looked down at the drink in my hand. I swirled the thick liquid around the glass. "It wasn't my job," I said to Michael without looking up at him. "I just wanted to make sure you were okay," I finished, knowing that I was trying to convince myself as much as Michael.

"Whatever gets you through the day." Michael laughed.

"How do you do it?" I asked Michael, throwing it back at him.

"How do I get through the day?" Michael laughed again, more genuinely this time.

The bar was filling up. The music was still loud enough to cover our voices. Even so, I lowered my voice into a new whisper. "How do you kill people and then move on like nothing ever happened?"

Michael took a sip of his scotch and shrugged. "I'm a child of paranoia," he said. "It's what we do."

I shook my head. It wasn't true. "Joe struggled with it," I said. "Even before he met me, Joe struggled with it."

"Does that make it better?"

"Yes. It does."

Michael finished the drink in his hand. "You're right, Maria. Joe struggled with it. Even in the beginning, when revenge is enough for most people, it wasn't enough for Joe. So he bought all that good-and-evil crap they feed us. He had to, or he would have snapped. He had to believe that everything he did was righteous." My mind flashed back to the kid that your father killed in the field in Ohio. It was the last thing that boy ever said: *I'm not like you. I'm righteous.* Then your father shot him in the head. "But if that's how you get by, you're going to struggle with doubt." Michael's voice got weak for a moment. "I loved Joe for that. I loved Joe because he wanted to be good."

"What about the people who don't buy into the good-and-evil stuff?"

"Some people get off on the power. They like to play the game, whether they believe it or not."

"Jared?" I guessed. Michael didn't respond.

"But what about you? How do you get by?"

Michael shrugged. "I never thought I had a choice. This is the life I was born into. This is what I have to do."

"That's it?"

Michael's eyes glanced across the faces of the people in the bar. I tensed up, ready to react if he saw something. His eyes landed back on me. "I tell myself that everyone that I kill is playing the same game as me." Then he added, as if it was an afterthought, "And I hope that there's a good reason for all of it. I hope that I'm the good guy." I couldn't help but think that he was more like your father than he let on.

"You could have run like Reggie did."

Michael shook his head. "You know that's not my style."

"You seemed pretty confident that there were good reasons for the War when we spoke to Clara."

"No. I never said there was a good reason. Just a reason."

"What if you find out the reason and it turns out you're the bad guy?"

Michael shrugged again. "Then I was born to be a bad guy." After a pause, he said, "Tell me something about yourself."

"What do you mean?"

"Tell me something that I don't know about what your life was like before this."

I honestly considered it for about a second. Then I shook my head. "No."

"I just want a better feel for who you really are."

All I could think of was that I'd helped kill a man today. "Who I am now and who I was then have nothing to do with each other. If I was going to tell you stories about what I was like when I was a little girl, I might as well tell you stories that I read in a book." Michael looked at me and waited. I had nothing more to say. Maybe a time will come when I can tell you stories, but I need to get some of the girl I used to be back first.

Michael was right about the drinking. Already the memories of that afternoon were beginning to fade in my head. Soon the only memories that were left were those of the mark's blood trickling through the crack in the door as Michael slipped out, and the relief I felt when the pressure on that door from the mark's pushing subsided. Those memories weren't going to go away, no matter how much I drank.

"And you?" Michael asked after we were silent for some time. I didn't know what he meant. He saw my confusion and clarified. "How do you plan on getting by?"

I wasn't ready for the question. It struck me like a bat to the head. My eyes welled up with tears. I blame some of it on the alcohol. "I do it all for Christopher." I clenched my jaw, trying to stop the emotion. "I don't care if that makes me the bad guy either." I picked a napkin up off the table and wiped the tears away from my eyes.

"You were good today," Michael said, trying to cheer me up.

"I felt weak," I told him.

"You messed his face up pretty good before I got there. That didn't look weak to me." Michael leaned in closer to me, putting his elbows on the table. "Listen, there's always going to be someone stronger than you. That's true if you're five-feet-nothing like you or if you're Jared. In your case, you're always going to be physically weaker than most men. Your job isn't to become stronger than them, because you can't. Your job is to become as strong as you can. It's to become stronger tomorrow than you were yesterday. It's to remember that everything you do is practice for the next thing you do. That's it. He hit you hard in the face. I saw the mark. But you got back up. Two months ago, you never would have gotten up off the floor. And you held the door closed when the mark was pushing on it."

"Barely," I said, but the pep talk was working. I was feeling stronger.

"Doors are either opened or they're closed, Maria."

A slow song came on the jukebox. Michael's eyes scanned the bar again. My body didn't tense up this time. I was too tired. "Do you want to dance?" he asked, staring at the empty space in the middle of the bar.

"Here?" I asked. "People will see us."

Michael shrugged. He didn't care. I imagined what it would be like. Michael would stand up, pulling my hand, pulling me up off the bench and leading me to the empty space in front of the jukebox. He'd put his arms around my waist, and I would reach up around his neck and place my hands on his shoulders. I'd run my hands over the raised skin on his back where the letters had been burned forever. I'd rest my head on his chest and we would simply sway there, our feet hardly moving. Then I would close my eyes and imagine that I was dancing with your father. I wondered who Michael would imagine he was dancing with. It didn't matter. The only people we had to dance with was each other.

The song ended before I could respond. I looked up at Michael and told him that I thought we should go. He agreed. When we got back to the hotel room, Michael climbed into his bed and I climbed into mine. We both slept. If it weren't for the alcohol, I'm not sure if I ever would have gotten to sleep that night. Before we went to sleep, Michael told me that he was going to call in tomorrow to find out what his next job was. He asked if I wanted to listen. I said yes.

Thirty-four

Evan and Addy might not have made it out of the convenience store in Louisiana if Addy hadn't reacted so quickly to the screaming. They were that close to being caught or worse. The convenience store was small and quiet, the exact type of place that Evan and Addy had been trying to get their supplies from. Only this time, one of the store's customers recognized Evan from his pictures on the news. She was a seventy-year-old woman making her once-daily trip to the store. She never bought more than a day's worth of supplies, not wanting to waste anything in case she didn't make it to tomorrow. She saw Evan and she screamed. That was the first scream. The little old lady never expected any of the monsters that she saw on her television to actually crawl out of her TV into real life, but there Evan was, walking down the aisle toward her. He was carrying a box of generic cereal and a quart of milk in his arms. He wasn't looking at the lady when he first turned into the aisle. He was looking down at the price tag on the box of cereal, doing the math in his head, trying to figure out if Addy would think it was too expensive. Addy was already at the cash register, waiting for Evan to get back with the rest of their makeshift breakfast. She made him go back for the generic cereal after he'd first grabbed a pricey name brand.

The old lady saw Evan turn the corner toward her but didn't recognize him at first. She couldn't get a good look at him while his head was down, staring at his cereal box. It was his dark, messy hair that first got her attention. Her lips began to curl even before she saw Evan's face. She hated how the young people neglected to comb their hair. She thought it showed a lack of respect for the rest of the world. Then Evan lifted his head. When she saw his face, she recognized him immediately. She'd seen his face dozens of times. It took her a few seconds before she started screaming, though. She knew that she was staring at the terrorist, but it took her a few seconds to decide whether he was real or merely a figment of her aging mind. The spell was broken when Evan said "Excuse me" as he stepped around the harmless-looking old lady in the soup aisle. When she heard him speak, she knew he was real. The imaginary monsters didn't speak. Only the real ones had voices.

Before she screamed, the little old lady pulled a can of condensed soup off of the shelf and threw it at Evan's back. He was close enough to her that the lilting throw managed to hit him on the back of the leg. Evan turned around. When he did, she picked another can off the shelf. "What the hell?" Evan shouted when he realized that she'd thrown the first can at him on purpose and was about to throw another. He didn't understand what was going on. He didn't put it together. She was sure then that the terrorist was going to attack her. In her head, she saw images of being thrown to the ground and torn to pieces by his sharp terrorist teeth and claws. She screamed.

"IT'S HIM!" she shouted, as if she'd been saving her breath for the past ten years for this moment. It was louder than she'd yelled since she was a girl.

"What the hell?" Evan muttered again, utterly confused by the old lady screaming at him.

"THE TERRORIST!" the little old lady shouted, this time using every molecule of remaining air in her lungs. Until that moment, until Addy heard that word shouted into the air, Addy hadn't realized the power of the

label they branded on Evan. In the world Addy came from, the word didn't carry any weight. Terror was a part of life. Not in this world, Addy suddenly realized. The little old lady wasn't brave. It was that word, that label. The little old lady was doing what any of them would do when faced with a terrorist or a werewolf or a zombie. She was doing her civic duty. When no more sound would come out of the little old lady's mouth, she hunched over, gasping for air.

Once Addy realized the power of that word, she jumped right into action. She knew she didn't have much time. She leapt over the counter toward the burly man manning the register. She moved before he had a chance to recognize the words that the old lady had released into the air. Addy planted a hand on the counter and swung her feet over it like a gymnast clearing a vault. The man behind the counter didn't see Addy coming toward him. He was too busy watching the old lady and the kid in the soup aisle. At first, the man behind the counter thought that maybe the kid had tried to steal the crazy old bag's purse or something. Then the kid turned toward him. Maybe it was because the word was already floating in the air, but that's when the man behind the counter recognized Evan's face too. Over the past three days, the man behind the counter had seen Evan's face more times than he'd seen his own. The terrorist was in his store. The man behind the counter realized that he was finally going to get his chance to be a hero. He reached beneath the counter and grabbed the pump-action shotgun that he kept there to scare away the meth addicts trolling for easy robbery targets. Then there was another scream.

Evan's eyes drifted across the aisles toward the sound of the second scream. It was a younger woman, maybe in her late twenties or early thirties. She had a little boy with her who couldn't have been more than three years old. The kid had dark skin and curly black hair. The woman screamed and charged toward Evan. She wouldn't have recognized him on her own either. Like the man behind the counter, it was the word TER-RORIST hanging in the air like a scent that made her remember Evan's *face and allowed her to make the mental jump from what she'd seen on the news to her own reality. No one doubted for even a moment that Evan was the bad guy. He was everything that had ever gone wrong in their lives. His very existence was unfair.*

The man behind the counter started to lift the shotgun up toward his shoulder, but somehow it stopped before he could get the barrel any higher than his waist. The man behind the counter didn't realize that Addy was already standing next to him. All he knew was that despite how he moved his arms, the shotgun wasn't pointing in the direction he wanted it to. He tried to lift it up again but it was stuck, pointing down to the floor. Then he saw the hand holding on to the muzzle. His eyes followed the hand up to a wrist and then up the arm to the face of the woman standing next to him. He tugged at the gun, trying to pull it from the woman's grip. Instead of holding on to it tightly, Addy let the barrel slip a few inches through her fingers. The man kept pulling upward, and the gun slipped up toward his face. After a second, Addy retightened her grip on the nozzle of the gun and now pushed upward in the same direction the man was pulling, until the butt of the shotgun slammed into his nose, blinding him with pain. Then Addy yanked the shotgun from the man's hands.

"Evan!" Addy shouted. Evan turned toward Addy's voice. The second woman was still charging at him from the other side of the convenience store, leaving her child standing alone and scared in the corner. Addy threw the shotgun to Evan. She knew that he knew how to use it, that he'd practiced shooting shotguns with Christopher in the woods as a kid. Evan caught the shotgun with one hand. Then he turned toward the woman charging at him while wailing out that wicked, raw scream. Evan aimed the gun at the woman's chest. She saw the gun and tried to stop running. Her feet skidded across the floor only a few feet in front of Evan. She stopped. The sight of the gun aimed at her chest had instantaneously brought the woman back to reality. Evan squeezed the trigger. He pulled it just enough to feel the tension in the trigger pushing back against the skin on his finger. If he had

pulled the trigger any farther, he would have blown a hole clear through the woman's chest.

"Everybody calm down!" Evan heard Addy shout as she leapt back over the counter. The chaos stopped. It had lasted only seconds. The motion and the screaming stopped too. As if in a dream, Evan could hear the warbling country music coming out of the store's speakers again.

"Go back to your kid," Evan whispered to the woman standing in front of him. The rage in her face had been replaced by fear. She began to back away from Evan, backing toward the now-crying child. Evan looked back at the old woman who had started it all. She was holding herself up on one of the store shelves, now too weak to stay on her feet on her own.

"Does anyone else have any weapons?" Addy yelled. She was answered with a less-than-totally-convincing silence. "If you do have a weapon that you're not telling me about," Addy shouted, "just remember, it's not as big as ours." Addy eyed the shotgun in Evan's hands.

Even as Addy did the yelling, all eyes stayed on Evan. Not only was he the one holding the gun, but he was also the television nightmare come to life. "I want everyone to take their cell phones out," Addy shouted, not lowering the volume of her voice even though the chaos had died down and she needed just three people to hear her. "I want you to give me your cell phones." They all did as they were ordered; they all handed their cell phones over to Addy, who took them and put them in her backpack. Then she went back to the counter and yanked the landline out of its jack.

"I don't want any bullshit," Addy shouted. "You." She turned toward the woman with the kid. "That's your car?" Addy pointed to the only car in the parking lot with a car seat in the back. The woman nodded. "Give me your keys," Addy ordered. Evan did his part too, pointing the gun back at the woman as Addy made her demands. The woman fished a set of keys out of her purse and handed them to Addy. Addy walked back toward Evan. "Let's get out of here," she whispered to him. She was in no mood to press their luck.

"Not yet," Evan answered her. He swung the gun around and pointed it at the man behind the counter. The man's hands were up near his face, trying to stop the blood from pouring out of his nose. The blood was already beginning to dry. "Open the register," Evan ordered the man. The man followed Evan's orders. He opened the register. "Give her the money," Evan said to the man, motioning toward Addy.

They got eighty-three dollars out of the cash register.

Addy pulled the car seat out of the car before they drove off, abandoning it on the sidewalk in front of the store.

Evan left rubber marks from the car's tires on the pavement as they sped away.

Thirty-five

Michael went through the code: three random names followed by three transfers. After the third name, a man picked up. "Hello, Michael," the voice said. The voice was deep and sonorous, like a voice you might hear on the radio. I was listening on the second handset that we'd requested from the front desk for a conference call. Before letting me listen in, Michael made me promise that I wouldn't make a sound. I didn't expect it to be a difficult promise to keep.

"Hello, Allen," Michael said. I remembered what your father told me. Allen wasn't a name. It was a rank. From what I knew, they assigned Allens to soldiers who were either problematic or who showed particular promise. I had little doubt that Michael was both.

"Nice work with the Philadelphia job," Allen said. They already knew. It had to be in the news by now. I tried to imagine how they would cover this one up. Suicide? A disgruntled student? "Are you still in Philadelphia?" the voice asked.

"Yeah," Michael answered.

"Okay, you're going to have to leave right after this call." My heart raced for a second. Michael looked calm.

"Why?" Michael asked.

"Nothing to worry about, but Their network is buzzing."

"They don't know anything, right?"

"Nothing dangerous."

"Okay," Michael said. "Where should I go? Where's the next job? I can go now."

"I don't think that's going to work. You're just going to have to get out of Philly." Michael and I looked at each other. We were both thinking the same thing, that they'd found us out, that they somehow knew I'd helped him kill the teacher and that he was helping me.

"Is there something wrong?" Michael asked. His voice was calm.

"No," the voice said. "The opposite—that's why the next job might take a little while."

I could see on Michael's face that this wasn't normal. "I'm shitty at riddles, Allen," Michael said.

"I'm going to patch you through to someone who can explain," the voice said. "He'll debrief you on your next job."

The line went silent. "Okay," Michael said. Then we heard a click as the call was transferred. My stomach churned. I looked at Michael for some assurance. He looked at me and shrugged.

A new voice came through the phone. "Michael?" I recognized the voice right away. I recognized it in my bones. My joints went numb. Michael recognized the voice too. I saw it in his face.

"Jared?" Michael asked. I fought the urge to scream into the phone. I wanted to yell at him, *What did you do to my son, you bastard?* Michael, sensing my reaction, reached down to unplug my handset. When he reached down, I did too. I grabbed his wrist. He looked at me. I shook my head and placed my index finger across my lips, promising to be quiet. I wanted to hear this. I wanted to hear every word. As much as I hated Jared, he was the one we were looking for, the one that might be able to lead me back to you.

"It's good to hear your voice, Michael," Jared said. "It's been too long." He was using his friendly voice. I've heard his friendly voice before. I've heard his angry voice too, and his heartless one. "Are you glad to hear from me?"

Michael smiled before he answered, as if Jared could see him through the telephone line. "Of course I'm glad to hear from you. Finding you is one of the main reasons I came back."

"Good," Jared said. "I wasn't sure if you would be." The sentence sat heavily in the air, loaded with so many unspoken words and thoughts.

"What's this all about, Jared?" Michael finally asked, breaking the silence.

"You know that I've been promoted. Right, Michael?" Jared asked. I knew that Michael knew, but that he only knew because he read your father's journal.

"I've been a bit out of the loop," Michael lied. "But I'm not surprised."

"I'm in charge of a lot of people now," Jared said. "I make decisions for a lot of people now." He'd been promoted again. I wondered if killing your father helped with that promotion.

"That's great, Jared," Michael said. "But what does that have to do with me?"

Jared's voice got light. He sounded almost excited. "You're on my team," he said to Michael. "I've been following your work since you came back. I was worried that you might have changed, but you haven't, so I asked to have you transferred to my team." I had the urge to remind Michael what Jared had said about him—that Michael was a fuckup whose one skill, killing, was a savant's gift. I wanted to tell Michael that he couldn't trust Jared. But I kept my word. I stayed quiet.

"Does that mean that we get to work together?" Michael asked.

"Not yet," Jared said. "I've got one more job for you first. It's a big job. I picked it myself. You do this, and you don't have to worry about people questioning you anymore."

"Great. What's the job?"

"It's an international job," Jared said. "It's in Istanbul. It's a team job. You'll be working with a local."

"Team job?" Michael said, looking at me over the phone. "You know that's not my style, Jared." I immediately knew what it meant. If Michael had to team up with someone else, there was no place for me.

"We all have to adjust, Michael," Jared said. "I need you to do this. Too many people still think that you're a loose cannon. A team job was the only way I could think of to get you to lose that reputation."

"There's no other way?" Michael asked. He didn't wait for Jared to answer. "Why are you sending someone from here over to do a job in Turkey? Why don't you just have a local do it?"

"You're an instinctive killer, Michael. I want your partner to learn something from you."

"He's a kid. Isn't he?" Michael asked after a pause.

"This'll be his first job," Jared answered. It was an initiation job. Michael wasn't just killing now. He was supposed to teach this kid how to kill too.

"When do I leave?" Michael asked, his voice lacking in enthusiasm.

"The international jobs take some time to arrange," Jared answered. "You leave from New York in four days. You'll have to lie low in Turkey for a few days before you come back. All told, it should take about three weeks."

"And when I'm done, do I get to see you?" Michael asked. I felt a shiver run down my back.

"Yes," Jared said, his tone somber. "I guess we have a lot to talk about." I loathed him. I wished him dead. I wished it had been him that I shot. I wished it had been him that I lured to his death in that classroom.

"Yeah, we do," Michael answered.

"Get out of Philly and lie low for a couple of days," Jared said. "In three days, check into a hotel in New York. We'll find you once you check in."

"Got it," Michael answered.

"Feels kind of like old times. Doesn't it, Michael?" Jared said. He was smiling as he said it. I could feel his smile through the phone.

"Just like old times," Michael answered without any of Jared's joy. "I'll see you in three weeks."

"You got it, friend," Jared said. Then he hung up.

Thirty-six

We spent two days together here at the Jersey shore before Michael left for Istanbul. Michael wanted to show me all of his and your father's old stomping grounds. He wanted to show me the exact spot where he'd saved your father's life. In all of Michael's stories, I felt the weighty absence of a third character. Michael told the stories as if Jared never existed. After two days, Michael left for New York. I still haven't figured out what I'm supposed to do.

I went to the Internet café and checked my e-mail at least eight times in the first two days after Michael left. Michael and I created new e-mail accounts. We were the only people in the world who knew those e-mail addresses. Each time I logged on, my in-box was empty. It was supposed to be empty. We agreed to use the e-mail addresses only in cases of emergencies and so Michael could tell me when he was coming home. I wasn't supposed to get a message for three weeks. The first time I logged on, I logged into my old e-mail address too—the one that I used before I met your father. I hadn't logged into that account in over a year and a half. I was curious. I had more than ten thousand unopened e-mails and a message telling me that my account was over capacity. I thought for a second about looking at the names of the people who sent me e-mails and at the subject lines of the messages. I didn't. Nothing I saw there was going to help me. I logged out and haven't logged back into that account since.

I'm still at the Jersey shore. I decided to stay after Michael left. Your father loved it here. Being here makes me feel closer to him. I've gone to the southern tip of the island a few times and looked out over the water. Your father fought for his life in that water, killing in order to survive. I used to not understand. Now, staring out into the turbulent, dark water, I only hope that I can be as strong as your father was. I listen to the crash of the waves and I imagine that he's whispering to me beneath the ocean's roar. The problem is that I can never understand what he's trying to say.

I can't keep checking an e-mail address for a message that I know isn't going to come. I can't sit here and wait for ghosts to whisper secrets to me. I need to figure things out for myself. Michael won't be back for three weeks. I can't afford to waste that time.

I've increased my exercise program. I've been running on the beach. It's different from running on pavement. It works different muscles. I've been going for long swims in the ocean. I've been doing push-ups, sit-ups, pull-ups, everything I know how to do to get stronger. Michael was right. My job is to be stronger tomorrow than I was yesterday. I can feel myself getting stronger. Still, I know that I can do more.

I can't get Jared's voice out of my head. I always knew that I was going to hear it again if we made it this far. For some reason, I expected it to be different. I expected killing your father to change him. He sounded the same. He still sounded like a man without any doubts. I hated him for how he sounded almost as much as I hated him for what he did. At the same time, I wish I could sound like that. To be free of doubts is to be unstoppable.

I finally figured out what I need to do. It's been more than a week since Michael left. I packed up my duffel bag again, shoving my whole life into that bag. I have a few changes of clothes, your father's journal, this journal, and my baby-development book. I have the un-opened pack of cigarettes that I've been carrying around since Michael made me quit. I have my knife and my gun. Finally, I have the postcard that Michael found in Dorothy's pocket. Before I left, I went back to the southern tip of the island one more time. I let your father whisper to me again. I still couldn't understand what he was saying. Then I said good-bye.

> *Dear Maria,*
> *Every picture is a picture of a picture*
> *Of a picture of a picture of a scene.*
> *Every memory is a memory of a memory*
> *Of a memory of a memory of a dream.*
> *On the sixth day, you can find your reward under a rock in the*
>   *creek in the park.*

I read the postcard over and over again on the train to D.C. Michael had received a series of postcards. I had one postcard. Only one. Even so, Dorothy had made a promise. I had no doubt that she would have kept it if she were alive. She wasn't. I had no intention of going to Rock Creek Park. I wasn't going to walk in there and stand around, waiting for someone to come to me, someone who might not even be there. I'd been doing enough standing and waiting. I remember that first night when I made contact with Michael. I remember standing there in the darkness, not moving even when someone pointed a gun at me. I remember waiting for Michael to come to me. Even in the face of the death, I stood there and waited. Not anymore. You deserve better. Lucky for me, while trying to decipher Michael's postcards as we drove up from Florida to Washington, D.C., I had basically memorized them. I knew where they would be tomorrow and the next day and the day after that. I wasn't going to wait for them to come to me. I was going to go to them.

Thirty-seven

It's Tuesday night. I'm staying at a hotel in Crystal City in Arlington, Virginia. It's cheaper than anything that I could find in Washington, D.C. It's a quick walk over the bridge into Georgetown. From there, I can walk to Foggy Bottom and catch the metro to anywhere. The Einstein Memorial is only a short walk from the bridge too. I spent this morning there, scoping it out. It took a couple hours to sweep the area. The statue is in an elm-and-holly grove south of the Academy of Sciences. The statue is surrounded by trees on three sides. The fourth side opens up onto Constitution Avenue. In the statue, Einstein is sitting on a set of steps with a paper full of mathematical formulas in his lap. If you touch the statue, you can feel how the stone has been worn away by years of children sitting on Einstein's lap. On the ground by the statue's feet is a map of the planets and the stars. Legend is that if you stand in front of the statue and whisper to it, it will whisper back to you. I didn't dare try.

I came back to Virginia in the afternoon. I wanted to buy more ammunition for my gun. After all, what good is having the gun if you don't have enough bullets?

The hotel has a business center. After spending an hour and a half at the hotel gym, I went in and logged onto a computer to check for an e-mail from Michael. My in-box was empty. I thought about sending Michael a quick message, asking him if he was okay, if everything was going as planned, to tell him that I missed him. I didn't. I wonder if Michael is doing the same thing on his end, checking his e-mail every day to see if I've written to him. I wonder if he is disappointed every time he opens his e-mail and sees that I hadn't.

I woke up early. I didn't know how early Clara's men would arrive, but I wanted to get to the statue before them. I couldn't imagine that they would get there too early. They wouldn't want to be the first people there. They wouldn't want to do anything that made them stand out. I remembered Malcolm X Park. They came out of nowhere, first the ones that grabbed Michael and then the ones that grabbed me. If I got there first, I might be able to see them come in. I had to be sure it was them. I simply had to do everything right. I had to avoid mistakes. I had one chance. If I blew it, things would get very dangerous very quickly.

I packed my backpack. I put the gun in the outside pocket, where it would be easy to reach. I tucked the knife into the waistband of my pants, with the handle hidden beneath my shirt, the way Michael taught me. The knife already saved my life once. I felt more comfortable with it pressed against my thigh now than I felt without it. I put two bottles of water in my bag, along with an apple and a couple of granola bars that I'd picked up the day before. I threw in the old, unopened packet of cigarettes that had somehow become my personal rabbit's foot. Finally, I threw in the journals. That was enough.

The sun wasn't up yet when I walked out of the hotel but the sky was already turning a lighter shade of blue. The sun was up somewhere and its light was catching up to me. I walked out through Crystal City toward the bridge to Georgetown. I decided to walk the whole way. I wanted to loosen up my muscles. The sky grew lighter as I walked. A mist was rising up off the Potomac as I crossed the bridge. I felt for a moment like I was walking through a fog into another world. I crossed the bridge and took a right-hand turn toward the neighborhood of Foggy Bottom.

I didn't head straight for the statue or the trees behind the statue, where I planned on making my stakeout. I knew not to do that. I'd learned. Instead, I looped around the area. As I circled, I looked for anything that might be suspicious. When that loop was finished and I felt that everything was safe, I made a smaller loop inside the first. I rechecked everything that I had checked the day before. No mistakes. I made four smaller, concentric loops before I closed in on the statue. By the time I was finished, the dawn had turned to morning and the sun hung low in the sky. I could see people walking along the river across the street, but no one had come to visit the Einstein statue yet. I did one pass by the statue, gliding my hand over Einstein's lap, feeling the effects of all those happy children. Maybe one day I can take you there. Maybe one day I can sit you on Einstein's lap, and you can whisper to him and he'll whisper back to you.

I didn't linger at the statue. I had to get to my hiding place before any visitors arrived. I needed to be able to watch the people come and go without being seen. The mistake I'd made when Michael and I were kidnapped in Malcolm X Park was that I'd kept my head down, looking for something that didn't exist. That's the purpose of the riddles. The riddles distract you so that they can monitor you. I had been looking for clues, and Michael had been looking at me. Neither of us was watching what we should have been watching. I wouldn't make that mistake again.

I slipped into the trees. I knew exactly where I wanted to go. It was a small spot nuzzled among three trees. The trees wouldn't hide me completely but they would provide enough cover so that Clara's men wouldn't be able to get a good look at me. From a distance, I imagined I appeared to be a regular college girl enjoying the weather, relaxing with a book. They would have to get a lot closer to me to realize that I wasn't a college girl, that I wasn't enjoying the weather, and that I wasn't relaxing. I wasn't going to let that happen.

I settled down on the small incline, high enough to have a clear view of the statue and the area around it. I could see people come and go. I would see anyone who came looking for clues to unanswerable riddles. More importantly, I would see the people watching those people.

It was another hour before the statue had its first visitors, two slightly overweight parents and their two children, a boy and a girl. The girl was older and wore glasses. She ran up to the statue and began reading the equations carved onto Einstein's lap. The boy stopped at the map of the night sky on the ground and jumped from one star to the next, crossing universes in giant leaps. The father took pictures. After about fifteen minutes, they walked on. After that family, no one came for another half an hour. I looked at my watch. It was ten o'clock. If they were going to come, Clara's men would come soon. Even if they didn't want to be the first visitors, they wouldn't be so late that they'd risk losing a convert. Another family came and went. I ate one of the granola bars and drank some water. After the second family left, the visitors came in steadier streams. I marked each visitor on the pages of this journal. By eleven o'clock, twenty-seven people had come and gone. None stayed very long. The day was getting hotter and brighter. I hadn't seen any stragglers. I didn't see anyone watching anyone else.

By noon, forty-five people had come and gone. At twenty minutes after noon, another group came. It appeared to be two families, one young couple and one loner. I looked at the loner's face. I thought I recognized him from somewhere but I wasn't sure where. I tried to remember the faces of the people that I'd seen at the compound when they kidnapped me, but that wasn't it. Then it hit me. He'd already been there. He'd come in an earlier group, at around eleven o'clock. I watched him. He stood there, staring at the statue for a few minutes. Then he walked on. He'd done the same thing that last time. I studied the man's face. I saw him again a little more than a half hour later. He wasn't the only one. All in all, I determined that three different people were making repeated trips to the statue and moving on without talking to anyone.

I knew that there had to be a fourth person with them. It took four of them—two pairs—to kidnap me and Michael. It made sense to work that way. It was a classic buddy system. I kept watching, unsure of how or when to make a move. I couldn't do anything until I saw the fourth. Until then, making a move would be too risky.

At close to three o'clock in the afternoon, the first man came again. More than eighty people had come to visit the statue. This guy had already come at least five times. I was missing something. I stood up and walked away from the trees that were protecting me. I had to get closer to see what I was missing. I watched the man walk up to the statue. Carefully, I walked in close enough to see the expression on his face, close enough to see everything he saw. He stood in front of the statue for two or three minutes, but he barely looked at it. Instead he stared down at his feet. He moved his right foot over the map carved into the stone beneath him, tapping it as if drawing a picture with his toe. Then he lifted his head and looked directly at me. I froze. I thought I'd blown it. Then I realized that he wasn't looking at me. He was looking at something behind me. I had an urge to turn around to see what he was looking at, but I fought it. They would have noticed me and—and what? Run? I didn't want to risk it. Instead, I walked away, heading toward another clump of trees. When I thought I had gotten far enough away, I turned and looked back. Someone was standing at the top of the hill. I watched. The man at the top of the hill nodded to the man at the statue. Then they both disappeared simultaneously.

I repositioned myself. I had been concentrating so hard on what was in front of me that I missed the man standing behind me. I found another tree to hide behind where I could watch both the statue and the top of the hill. Twenty minutes later, another of the repeat visitors walked up to the statue. It was his sixth visit. I looked up at the top of the hill. The man there reappeared at almost the same time. Repeating the pattern, the man near the statue made a few seemingly random taps on the ground with his toe before walking away. They were signals. Everything was coordinated nearly down to the minute. I should have assumed as much. These people weren't amateurs. They wouldn't survive if they were. I couldn't be sure what the messages were about but I wasn't about to wait to find out that they were about me.

I waited until the man on the hill disappeared again. Then I walked out from under the cover of the trees. I quickly made my way up toward the top of the hill. I found a spot not more than fifteen feet from the place where I'd seen the fourth man appear and I hid again. I unzipped the outside pocket of my backpack.

Eight minutes after I got to my new hiding spot, the man reappeared again. He stood at the top of the hill for five minutes. I watched as he nodded toward the statue. Then the man on the hill turned around and started walking away. He wasn't alone this time. I followed him. I carried my backpack at my side, my hand jammed in the outside pocket. I walked carefully, aware that I was following someone who had no choice but to spend his life paranoid that someone was following him. I don't think he ever would have guessed that the person following him was me.

I made up some of the distance between us with each step. He was taller than me, at least five-foot-ten, so I had to make almost two steps for each one of his to catch up to him. I wanted to see where he was walking before I gave myself away. He walked up to the street behind the Academy of Sciences and took a left toward Twenty-third Street. He looked at his watch as he walked. Everything was coordinated. I wondered how much time he had before he was supposed to be back to his post on the hill. The street wasn't crowded, but we weren't alone. The strangers gave me cover—I could hide among them—but they were also potential witnesses to be wary of when I pulled out my gun.

I was only a few feet from him when we neared Twenty-third Street. He hadn't turned around, hadn't looked back or even glanced behind him. It made me nervous. I saw him reach into his pocket. My stomach knotted up and I squeezed the handle of my gun. I watched his hand. He pulled a set of car keys from his pocket. He was walking back to a car. It was a fortunate fact—fortunate for me, not for him.

I closed to only a step or two behind him. He still didn't look back. He was in too much of a hurry to look back. For some reason, he hadn't given himself enough time get to the car and back to the top of the hill without rushing. Whatever the reason, he wasn't as aware of his surroundings as he should have been. Nobody's perfect. He walked around the back of the sedan to the driver's-side door. I was right behind him, walking silently.

I could see only two other people on the streets by the time he opened his car door. They had kidnapped me in front of a park full of people and no one reacted. I had to take the chance that the two people on the street weren't heroes. Few people are. It's hard to be a hero, and it's not because people aren't brave. Many are. They're simply not taught how to be heroes. They lack the instincts and reaction time. He turned toward the car. He leaned down and grabbed the door handle. I was only four feet away from him. As he turned, he noticed me for the first time.

He knew right away that something was wrong. He simply didn't know what it was yet. In his world, so much could go wrong. I could have been one of any of a long list of potential enemies. I'm sure that he didn't even know that I was a member of that list. "Can I help you?" he muttered to me. I could hear the fear in his voice. I wasn't used to having people fear me. In one quick, practiced motion I pulled the gun out of the front pocket of my backpack and then slung the backpack back over my shoulder. The man looked down at the gun and froze.

"Unlock the doors," I ordered. The man leaned down with the key toward the car door. Every movement made me nervous. "With the button on your key chain," I said. "Unlock them with that." I was holding the gun low, trying to hide it from the rest of the world. I didn't have a lot of time. The others at the statue would realize something was amiss in less than ten minutes.

The man clicked the button on his car keys twice. I heard the doors unlock. I opened the back door, still pointing the gun at the man. "If you want the car, you can have the car," he said. His voice was calmer now. I hadn't shot him yet. Most of the people on his list of enemies would have shot him by now.

"Get in the car," I ordered. "In the driver's seat." He nodded. He moved slowly, trying not to scare me into shooting him in the back. As he lowered himself into the driver's seat, I climbed into the backseat directly behind him, matching him movement for movement. I kept the gun pointed at him, not pulling it away for even a moment. When he couldn't see it, I'm certain he could still feel it.

"Now what?" he asked as he sat in the driver's seat.

"Close the door and start the car," I ordered. I felt powerful. He reached out and closed the driver's-side door. I watched his hand, careful to make sure that he wasn't trying to grab anything from the pocket in the door. Once his door was closed, I closed mine. He put the key in the ignition and started the car. An open laptop sat on the passenger's seat. He had to come back to the car to input or check something on his computer. It was the only thing that made sense. The Underground was using technology that the two sides in the War were afraid to use. They needed to stay a step ahead.

"Now what?" the man asked again. He hadn't begged or cried. He reacted the way only someone who had been expecting something like this to happen would react. Even so, I could see the beads of sweat on his forehead through the rearview mirror.

"Turn the air-conditioning on," I answered, "and drive."

"Where to?"

"First, away from here. And then to Clara."

He looked at me in the rearview mirror. For the first time since the moment he first noticed me, he looked scared. He didn't move. I lifted the gun and jammed it into the back of his neck. "Drive," I said. "Now. Don't try anything funny." He reached down with his right hand and put the car into gear. I peeked at my watch. The next visit to the statue would be in less than four minutes. "Go north."

He pulled out onto Twenty-third Street and began driving. I looked behind us to see if anyone saw anything. Everything seemed normal. I felt a sudden rush of adrenaline. I almost smiled. I eased the pressure of the nozzle of my gun off the man's neck and leaned back, all the while keeping the gun aimed at the back of his head. I made sure that he could see where I was aiming the gun when he glanced at me in the rearview mirror.

We drove straight up Twenty-third Street. I watched the street in front of us. It was full of ordinary traffic. We were part of it now, driving away. I wanted to get more distance between us and the Einstein statue. I wanted to make sure that they couldn't find us, even if they tried following us. "Take your next left," I said. "Drive into Virginia."

The man did as he was ordered. When he turned the car, he looked at me in the rearview mirror. "Who are you?" he asked. What he was really asking me was, Why are you pointing a gun at me? In his world, they were the same question.

"My name is Maria," I answered. "You've heard of me. You've all heard of me." I looked into his eyes in the mirror as I spoke. "They kidnapped my son and killed his father. I met Clara a few months ago and asked her for help. She refused. Then someone else promised me that you guys would help me. That person is dead now. I'm here to make sure that Clara honors that person's promise."

"Dorothy," the man said. I could hear the sadness in his voice. I nodded.

"Once we get into Virginia, take me to Clara." He didn't answer. He simply kept driving.

We crossed into Virginia only a few minutes later. I felt safer. The last time I made this drive, I was locked in the trunk of a car for two hours. I couldn't hold the gun in front of me like I was for two hours. I looked at the driver in the rearview mirror. "I'm putting my arm down," I said. "You might not be able see the gun, but, trust me, you don't want to try anything. Keep driving. It would only take me a second to pull the trigger."

"I can't take you to where you want to go," the driver said. His eyes met mine in the mirror.

"What do you mean, *you can't take me*? You have to. You don't have a choice." I could still see fear in his eyes, but I suddenly realized that he wasn't afraid of me. He was afraid of Clara.

"We're not allowed to bring anyone to the compound unless Clara targeted them for recruitment."

"But I've already been there," I told him. I could see the surprise on his face.

"Not like this," he said, shaking his head.

"No. The last time I went to see Clara, two of your friends threw me in the trunk of a car."

"I can't bring you there," he repeated.

I lifted the gun again. I leaned forward and pressed the nozzle of the gun into the back of his neck so that he could feel the metal. "You people don't know when to let go. You're willing to die for this?" I couldn't believe his stubbornness. He didn't answer me. He knew I wouldn't appreciate his answer. "Didn't you leave the War to stop this foolishness?"

He lifted his head and stared at me in the mirror. It was a cold, hard stare. "I left the War because I was tired of the killing."

We rode for another five minutes in silence. I had no idea where we were headed. We were probably getting farther from Clara's with each passing minute. "Do you have a cell phone in the car?" I asked the driver. I knew that your father and Michael didn't carry cell phones, but they didn't travel with laptops either.

"Yes," the driver answered.

"Then call Clara."

"I don't know her number."

"Then call the compound. Call anyone. When they answer, ask for Clara. Say that Maria wants to talk to her about Dorothy. Do it now."

"The phone is in the glove compartment," the driver said.

"You can get it. Just move slowly." He reached over with his free hand and opened the glove compartment. I could see inside. I could see the phone. I could see the Taser. "Don't touch anything but the phone," I ordered.

"I won't." I believed him. He wanted a way out. He picked up the phone. He dialed it, taking his eyes off the road as little as possible. He put the phone to his ear.

"Put it on speaker," I ordered. The driver hit a button and the sound of ringing filled the car.

It rang three times. "Hello?" someone picked up and said after the third ring. It was a man's voice.

"Robert?" the driver asked.

"Roman," the man on the other end of the line said. The driver's name was Roman. At least that's what he'd named himself. "Where are you? We got word that you disappeared. We thought something might have happened to you."

"I need to talk to Clara," Roman said, his voice cracking slightly as he made the request.

"What's going on? Why do you sound like you're calling from underwater?"

"You're on speakerphone," Roman answered. "I need to talk to Clara. Is there any way you can get her?" Roman looked at me in the mirror. I nodded. "Tell her that Maria wants to talk to her about Dorothy." Silence. It sounded like Robert had put the phone on mute. The name Dorothy meant something to all of them.

I could hear when Robert unmuted the phone. "Give me five minutes," he said. "Do you have five minutes, Roman?" Roman looked at me again. I nodded again.

"Yeah," Roman answered. We were put on mute again. Two minutes later a new voice, one that I recognized, came over the phone.

"Are you okay, Roman?" Clara's voice was crisp and authoritative.

"He's okay," I answered for him, "for now. I need to see you, Clara."

"Is this Maria?" Clara asked. I wanted her to recognize my voice the way I recognized hers. She didn't. Our meeting didn't mean as much to her as it had to me.

"Yes." I swallowed and continued. "I've politely asked Roman to bring me to you, and he refused. I don't want to become less than polite. Will you give him permission to bring me to you?"

It took a moment for Clara to answer. "Bring her in," she finally said. "When will you be here, Roman?"

"Two and a half hours," Roman replied, stepping on the gas. He was eager to get out.

"Okay," Clara answered. "See the two of you soon."

Roman and I didn't speak for the rest of the ride. I took Dorothy's postcard out of my backpack, folded it in half, and slipped it into my pocket. I rested my hand in my lap but I didn't let go of the gun.

They were waiting for us when Roman pulled the car into the compound. At least a dozen of them were standing, with guns drawn, in front of the building. Four were women; the rest were men. Clara wasn't among them. One of the men gave Roman a hand signal to roll down the windows. Roman did. All four of the car's windows slid down, letting in the smell of the forest air. It smelled rich and alive.

"Get out of the car!" the man yelled. "If you have any weapons, hold them out in front of you so that we can see them!"

I did as I was told, not because I was afraid of them but because I knew that all of this was because they were afraid of me. Roman didn't move. I opened my car door. I held both of my hands out in front of me. One had the gun in it. The other was empty. All twelve of their guns were pointed at me. "Place the gun on the ground," the leader yelled. I knelt down and placed my gun on the dirt road beneath us.

"I'd like to get that back when I leave," I said as I stood up with my hands in the air. One of the women ran in front of me and grabbed my gun.

The leader walked up to me. "Is that your only weapon?" he

asked, close enough to me now to stop shouting. I nodded. He looked to Roman, still sitting in the car, for confirmation. Roman nodded too. The leader turned me around and made me place my hands on the car. He motioned toward one of the other women, who came over and frisked me from my neckline down to my shoes. She felt the knife, hidden beneath my shirt. I had gotten so used to it that I forgot it was there.

"I forgot about that," I said. The woman took the knife away. "I'd like that back when I leave too," I said to the leader. He gave me a frustrated look. He took his gun and put it in its holster on his belt. When he did, the others relaxed their weapons. "I just want to talk to Clara," I said.

"You have a funny way of asking," he said.

"You guys don't make it easy," I answered.

Four of them escorted me into the building. Two walked in front of me, two behind me. They led me down the same hallway that I'd been led down only a few unbelievably long weeks before. It looked smaller now. We passed the stairs that led down to the room where I'd spent the night. The staircase was dark. They pushed me forward, toward Clara's room. I'd put so much hope into my last visit to this place. I was so disappointed when I left. I didn't come with the same expectations. I knew now that no one else was going to find the answers for me, but they made a promise. I planned on holding them to it.

Clara's door at the end of the hall was open. I could see her sitting behind the desk. I was led through the door. Clara didn't look up from her papers until I was inside the room. When she did look up, she looked at my escorts. "You can leave us," Clara said, and they walked out of the room. Clara seemed tired. I heard the door close behind me. Clara finally looked at me. "You can sit down if you'd like," she said. I walked around to the chair that Michael had sat in last time I was there. "I wouldn't have expected this from you, Maria," Clara said, as I lowered myself into the chair.

"You have no idea who I am," I answered her. "How would you know what to expect?" The leaves on the trees outside the window were still. "I'm sorry about Dorothy," I said. Clara looked down at her hands. "Do you know what happened to Reggie?" I asked.

Clara looked up at me. "Who's Reggie?"

For a second I thought that Dorothy had been working on her own, that Clara didn't know anything about Reggie. Then I remembered. "Joseph," I said. "The boy Dorothy was helping to escape. I called him Reggie."

"He's safe," Clara answered. "We found him three days after the shooting. He wasn't hurt. We've moved him to a safe place." Reggie was safe. I saved him. I took a life, but I saved a life too. I kept the balance. "Why are you here?" Clara asked. "You're not here just to check up on that boy, are you?"

I had the postcard folded in my pocket. They hadn't taken it when they frisked me. I unfolded it and placed it on Clara's desk. "Dorothy had promised me that if I helped her hide Reggie she or you would help me find my son." Clara picked up the postcard. She read it slowly. I said the poem to myself as I watched Clara read. *Every picture is a picture of a picture of a picture of a picture of a scene. Every memory is a memory of a memory of a memory of a memory of a dream.*

"Dorothy was always so clever with her poems," Clara said when she was finished reading. "I don't know what we're going to do without her."

"Michael found that on Dorothy's body after they shot her," I said, pointing to the postcard. "I never got another one." There was an uncomfortable moment of silence. "We tried to save her," I added.

"I know," Clara answered. "Joseph told us what happened." She sighed a weary, exhausted sigh. "Where's Michael now?"

"He's in Turkey," I answered.

"Are you two not together anymore?"

"No. We are. He's doing a job in Turkey and then we're meeting up again."

"So, he's fighting again?" Clara asked. She sounded disappointed.

"He never stopped," I told her, using his line.

Clara laughed a joyless, unflattering laugh. Did she think that her cause was the only just cause? "What do you want from me?" Clara asked, dropping the postcard on the desk.

"I want you to honor the promise that Dorothy made to me."

"I already told you I can't do that. I don't know where your son is. I don't know where they're keeping that information. I can't afford to have agents rifling through documents to find a child who won't be a part of the War for another seventeen years."

"Dorothy promised me."

"I never told Dorothy to make that promise." I felt sick to my stomach. "Maybe she was going to try to convince me to help you after she got back. Maybe she was going to try to help you herself. Dorothy was very independent and your story—" She paused. "A lot of women sympathize with your story."

"But you don't?" My voice was angry now.

"I can't afford sympathy. You have no idea how dangerous it would be to have my men digging around for information that might not even be kept at their location. If one of them got caught, it could destroy everything I've worked for."

"What if I find out where the information is? What if Michael and I gave you that much?"

Clara paused for a second, thinking. She shook her head. "I still couldn't afford to have an agent rooting around in delicate information like that. Every agent I have on the inside is crucial. They each save dozens of lives. I can't let them take unnecessary chances."

Unnecessary. I stared at the ceiling for a moment, trying to think. "What if we didn't ask them to root around for the information? What if all we asked was for them to help us get inside so that we could get the information ourselves?"

"You'll never make it into one of those buildings and out alive," Clara said, "even with our help."

"I'm not asking for your predictions." I flattened the postcard on the desk and pushed it back toward Clara. "You can have this," I said. "It's probably the last thing that Dorothy ever wrote."

Clara reached for the postcard. She touched it. "What if I say okay? How do you propose that we do this?"

"You give me a phone number or an e-mail address. I'll reach out to you when we find out where they're keeping the information. Then you can tell me what you can do to help. I'm not asking for much."

"How are you going to find out where the information is?" Clara asked.

"That's not your problem."

Clara lifted the postcard and read it again. "Okay," she said when she was finished. "I'll give you an e-mail address, not a phone number."

"Thank you," I said. My heart swelled, happy to get any concession. It was better than nothing.

"Don't thank me," Clara said, waving the postcard in her hand. "Thank Dorothy."

"One more thing," I said before standing up from the chair.

Clara looked up at me without hiding her frustration. "What?"

"Michael won't be back for another week or week and a half. I want to stay here during that time," I said.

"Why?" Clara sounded honestly surprised by my request.

"I want someone to teach me how to defend myself, how to fight."

"In a week?"

"As much as can be taught in a week," I said.

Clara chuckled. "You'll have to be kept away from any confidential information," Clara said. "We'll have to lock you in at night. You'll be chaperoned at all times. No cameras. No weapons, except when you're training. No writing material. We'll give you your things back when you leave."

"You don't trust me?" I asked.

Clara laughed. "You kidnapped one of my men. You work with someone who thinks we're a cult. I can't afford to trust you."

I trained for seven days: two with the gun, two with the knife, three with my hands. Everything they taught me was geared toward my shortcomings, not my strengths. "The only strength that matters," I was told, "is a lack of weaknesses. Everything else is just for show." Everyone who trained me, everyone I met, they're all rooting for us, Christopher. They're all rooting for you. After my seven days of training, I left and went back to Washington, D.C., not knowing where else to go.

Thirty-eight

"Why is he so important to you?" Evan asked Addy a day or two after Evan had told Addy everything he knew about Christopher. They'd taken the eighty-three dollars they'd stolen from the cash register at the convenience store in Louisiana and driven north. Addy knew enough not to continue moving in a straight line once they'd been spotted. She didn't even need to be taught that; she had been, but the lesson wasn't necessary. Their ultimate destination still hadn't changed. All the diversion did was add a day or two to their journey. After agreeing to take their money and splurge on a dinner instead of a hotel room they were settling down for the night in the woods somewhere off the side of the road.

Addy didn't bother pretending that Evan could be asking about someone other than Christopher. Addy shook her head. "It's not just me, Evan. Christopher is important to all of us."

"Okay," Evan responded, "but why? Nobody's told me why he's so important."

"It's not even him, really," Addy said, trying not to trip over her own words. She'd never had to explain it before. Everyone fighting against the War and everyone in the War already knew why Christopher was so important. They didn't just know it; they felt it. "It's what he represents. It's what they all represent."

"Who are 'they all'?" Evan asked.

"Christopher and his parents—Christopher, Joseph, and Maria," Addy said. "His parents by blood. The parents that you knew, the couple that raised Christopher, they weren't Christopher's birth parents. You knew that, right?"

"Yeah," Evan answered her. "Chris told me what he found out. He told me what happened to his father—that his father was killed by his best friend because his dad wasn't willing to turn Christopher over to the other side. Chris didn't know what happened to his mother." Evan paused. "Do you know what happened to his mother?"

Addy nodded. "I didn't know that no one told Christopher what happened to her." She paused for a moment, wondering if she should have said something to him. "They killed her too. It just took them a little longer. They made martyrs out of both of them."

"You call them martyrs, but I still don't understand why people think they're so important."

"That's only because you didn't grow up with the War. You don't understand what it's like. When you turned sixteen, you weren't taught that you were going to have to spend the rest of your life taking orders from some strangers and being afraid of every other stranger that you walk past on the street. It's not only what we were taught, though. We learned to be afraid well before we were taught why. I don't remember a time in my life when I wasn't afraid."

"Kind of like Christopher," Evan suggested.

"Kind of," Addy agreed. "Maybe it was in Christopher's blood. Maybe we've all got paranoia in our veins."

"Like some sort of disease," Evan finished for her.

"Yeah," Addy agreed, never having thought about it that way before. "So you have to try to understand what it was like, Evan. You have to try to put yourself in my shoes. I grew up being afraid and not even knowing what I was afraid of. Then, when I was barely more than a kid, some strangers

came in with a sort of PowerPoint presentation from hell, meant to teach me that I'm not nearly afraid enough. Not only do they tell me that I need to be more afraid, but that I need to be angry, too. They tell me that monsters are real and that I have to spend the rest of my life—however long or short that might be—fighting the monsters without even knowing who they are. And the only people who can tell me the difference between the monsters and my friends are more strangers—but these are strangers that I'm just going to have to trust." Addy's voice quickened with each word until she had to stop to take a breath. "So, I have to do my part to help fight these monsters, but I can't just go out and do it, because I need to rely on some faceless voice to tell me how and when. Even then, that faceless voice will only tell me who some of the monsters are, but not all of them. They won't tell me who all of the monsters are because they don't even know. And the fear isn't even the worst part," Addy went on. "Maybe it is for some people, but it wasn't for me. I could live with the paranoia, but they tell me all of this and then they give me a fucking desk job. Some people are afraid of the monsters. Some of us just can't get used to the powerlessness." Addy felt tears rush to her face, but she fought them off. She despised crying.

Evan didn't interrupt. He didn't say a word. He didn't even move, afraid any distraction might make Addy stop talking. "I heard whispers about Christopher before I even knew about the War," she continued. "I remember hearing my mother talking to her sister. They would whisper about the Boy. For a long time I thought they were whispering about a brother I had that died. So many other people around me had died these secret, barely spoken-about deaths that it made sense to me that I'd have a brother I'd never met. I should have known better, because when my mother and my aunt whispered to each other about the Boy, they always seemed excited, almost happy, in a way that they never seemed when they talked about my dead uncle or my father.

"So, when I turned sixteen, my mother drove me two hours, and I sat in the garage of a house of a girl I'd never met, and some guy in a suit taught

me about the War for the first time. The guy in the suit didn't say anything to us about Christopher. They actually did teach Christopher's story during the initiation sessions for a few years. It was supposed to scare people, to make them think twice before breaking the rules. I heard that they even showed pictures of Christopher's dad's dead body. Instead of teaching people what happened when you broke the rules, it taught people how heartless and cruel the War was. Neither side of the War looked good. The only sympathetic figures in the whole story were the corpse, the mother, and the baby. So instead of scaring people, Christopher's story inspired them. The story taught us that some people were brave enough to stop following blindly. It taught us that some people were brave enough to fight back. It taught us that we could rebel, that we could be brave, that we could try to be a part of the world. It taught us that we could stand up on our own and, if we failed, we'd merely end up in the same place we were likely to end up if we fought in the War anyway. Nobody escapes the War alive. They tried to make an example of Christopher's father, and we turned him into a martyr. Then Maria did what she did. After that, the War machine went into damage control. They stopped teaching about Christopher. They tried to quiet the story, but it was too late. The story had already spread too far. By the time I was initiated, they hadn't officially taught Christopher's story in more than a decade."

"So how did you find out about him?" Evan asked.

"He was everywhere. After our initiations, they tried to keep the newly initiated from contacting each other. They wanted to be able to mold us, but we found each other anyway through Internet groups and e-mail chains. At first, I thought everyone in the Internet groups or on the e-mail chains was another kid like me, but eventually I learned that there were adults on there too. Everything always led to talk about the Boy. I learned that his name was Christopher. I learned that he wasn't my dead brother like I'd thought. He was more than that. A lot of what people said was just rumors, but if you paid enough attention, you could piece together the truth. Do you understand now?" Addy asked Evan.

"I think so," Evan said, but thinking it wasn't enough for Addy anymore. She wanted Evan to feel it like she did.

"It's not just Christopher," Addy told Evan. "It's what his parents tried to do for him. It's what they represent to all of us. We're all so scared and powerless. We're so isolated from the rest of the world. And then we hear this story about a man who falls in love with an innocent girl from outside the War, and he is brave enough to run from the War to try to save his unborn child from this wretched life, even though he knows that he probably won't make it. And the innocent girl is brave enough to run with him. And the girl loves him even though he's from the War and she's not. And when they come and kill her man and steal her baby, that innocent girl finds the courage to fight against the War, even though she could walk away. She dives into the War so she can save her son, so she can do what Christopher's dad couldn't. Even though she's not part of the War, she's the one brave enough to fight the people that the rest of us are afraid to fight, no matter what the cost." Addy lost her fight with the tears. They began to roll down her face as she remembered what it felt like to feel hope for the first time in her life. "People were inspired, Evan. Even before I learned the story, people had been inspired by Maria and Joseph. More people were running from the War. It's like I told you: so many people heard about Christopher's story and decided to run from the War that the Underground couldn't keep up. People were killed. Once that happened, talk changed from running to fighting. You can only run until you've run yourself into a corner. Then you have to actually turn and fight, even if it's a fight you're probably going to lose."

"So, people started to actively rebel against the War?"

"No," Addy said. "For a long time, it was all just talk. Everyone was waiting for something."

"What were they waiting for?"

Addy wiped the tears from her cheeks. "Something—or someone—real that they could rally around."

"Christopher?" Evan asked.

Addy nodded. "People needed to know that he was alive and that he hadn't joined the War. They needed something to have faith in."

"So he's some sort of hero to all of you?" Evan asked.

"No," Addy answered, her voice firm. "I don't believe in heroes. I stopped believing in them when I stopped believing in fairies."

"Then what is he?"

"Christopher is a symbol. He's a living symbol of everything his parents did for him and the courage it took for them to do it. As long as Christopher's alive and not part of the War, he's living proof that his parents—in their own way—beat the War, living proof that the War can be beaten." The tears stopped. Addy was done.

"So, what happens now that Christopher's run away?" Evan asked.

"I don't want to think about it," Addy replied.

Thirty-nine

I barely slept last night.

Yesterday, for the first time since I created the account, I had an e-mail in my in-box. It was from Michael. To my dismay, the message was short and lacking in substance. All it said was, *where are you? i'm coming home.* It seemed wrong to me, after so long, to send such a brief message. I was still in D.C. It seemed silly to leave, since I had no idea where they would send Michael when he got back anyway. I hit the Reply button. *I'm in Washington, D.C. Where are you? Are you okay? When are you coming back? Is everything okay?* I thought about typing, *Have you spoken to Jared?* I decided not to. Michael would tell me soon enough. I had to be patient. I hit Send. I sat at the computer for another two hours, waiting for a response. I looked at my watch. It was two in the morning in Istanbul, but I had no way of knowing if Michael was still there. For all I knew, they'd sent him to Asia or California or back to New York. Wherever he was, I couldn't sit in the hotel's office center forever, so I called it a day.

I got out of bed at six this morning and went back to the office center. I had another message. Michael had replied. *how did you know about dc? where can we meet tomorrow?* I read the message over and over again, trying to decipher what it meant. Did it mean that Michael was already in Washington, D.C., too? All I could do was respond to the second question. I thought for a long time, trying to think of a landmark that hadn't already been co-opted by the Underground. I thought about Michael's other rules. Reckless but never careless. I felt like I had to prove to Michael that I hadn't forgotten everything that he had taught me. I needed to think of a place where we would be difficult to monitor and that had sufficient escape routes in case we were ambushed. I started typing at least eight times, each time thinking of some reason to nix my idea before deleting everything I'd written. Then I wrote, *On the steps in front of the amphitheater at Arlington National Cemetery. Do you know how to get there? What time do you want to meet?* Before hitting the Send button, I added, *Do you have news for me?*

This time, I got a reply in only forty minutes. I still hadn't gotten up from my chair. All his response said was, *i'll find it. between noon and three o'clock.* I cursed Michael again for being so terse and so vague. Then I went for a fifteen-mile run to try to burn off some energy. Hopefully, I'll be able to get some sleep tonight.

Forty

Michael's back. He's talked to Jared. They're going to meet.

I got to Arlington National Cemetery two hours before I was supposed to meet Michael. I didn't have the patience to sit around my hotel room and wait. I spent the time walking the cemetery, weaving between fields dimpled with grave markers. They go on forever. It would be easy to visit the cemetery in the morning and believe that more people were buried there than had ever lived. For most of the morning, I didn't see another living visitor. I avoided eye contact with the few visitors that I did see. They were happy to reciprocate. That didn't stop me from wishing that every headstone was surrounded by mourners. I stepped off the path and read the inscription on one of the headstones. On the top of the headstone was a cross. Beneath the cross was a name. Beneath the name was a rank. For those who fought in wars, beneath the rank was the war's name. Beneath the name of the war was the date on which the person was born and, beneath that, that date he died. Beneath the date the soldier died was grass. Beneath the grass was earth. The names were different. The dates were different. Even the wars were often different. The grass and the earth were always the same. Where are the visitors? I thought to myself, reading another tombstone, this one with a Star of David on the top. I knew where the visitors were. They were busy living.

After two hours of wandering, I headed for the steps in front of the amphitheater. I followed the procedure that I learned from Michael again. I circled the amphitheater, checking for hiding places and escape routes, looking for anything suspicious. Finished, I found a spot on the steps where I could wait with a clear view of my surroundings. It didn't matter. Michael snuck up on me anyway. One minute I was sitting alone, and the next Michael was sitting beside me. He did it on purpose. "Why did you make us meet here?" Michael asked me before I even realized that he was there. "Cemeteries give me the creeps."

"I thought it was a good spot. We've got solid escape routes and clear views in all directions."

Michael smiled at me. "Yeah," he said, "but it still creeps me out."

I smiled too. I didn't even have to force it. "It's nice to have you back, Michael. How did your job go?"

"It's done," Michael said without elaborating.

"How was your partner?" I asked.

Michael shrugged uncomfortably. "He was a kid."

"Did he do the job?" I asked, knowing that this *kid* was basically my age—the age Michael and your father were when they first learned to kill.

Michael shook his head.

"But I thought you said the job was done?" I blurted out before realizing what Michael was telling me. Michael had done the job himself. I could see it in his eyes. "Won't they find out?" I asked.

Michael laughed. "Who's going to tell them? I'm not telling anybody, and the kid sure as hell isn't going to blab that he didn't finish the first job that they ever gave him."

"Was he afraid?"

"No. He was eager."

"Then why didn't he do the job?"

Michael looked out over the fields dotted with rows of white, his eyes squinting against the bright sun. From here, all the headstones looked the same. "I didn't let him."

"Why not?"

"Because he didn't understand how it will change him," was all Michael said. "If I tell you something you want to hear, can we leave this place?" My heart started racing. Michael didn't wait for me to respond. "I'm meeting Jared tomorrow night. He got in touch with me after the Istanbul job was finished."

My skin tingled. "What? Where?" I asked.

"At a bar in Georgetown," Michael answered. An image flashed in my head, one that I hadn't seen but had imagined hundreds of times. It was an image of your father and Jared sitting across a table from each other in a dark bar, speaking as friends for the last time. I wondered if Jared picked the same bar to meet Michael, if he and Michael would end up sitting in the same booth. "That's why I wanted to know how you knew to come to D.C."

"I didn't," I said. "I was already here." I didn't bother to tell Michael why. We had more important things to talk about. "Let's walk to the Mall," I said. "We can talk while we're walking."

"Finally," Michael said, standing up and wiping the dust off his jeans.

We walked over the bridge, crossing the Potomac and heading into D.C. Michael was still limping, but his limp was less pronounced now. I could tell by the way he walked that his leg hadn't gotten better. Michael had merely learned how to disguise his limp better. I grilled Michael as we walked. He told me what he could, which wasn't much. Michael requested the meeting. Jared selected the time and place. Michael let him, breaking his own rule.

When I stopped questioning him for a few minutes, Michael looked me up and down. "You look good," he said. It wasn't flattery. The Michael that I knew didn't do flattery. It was an observation. He thought I looked stronger.

"I'm going with you when you meet with Jared," I said to Michael.

"That's not possible," Michael answered. "He'll recognize you. I recognized you in St. Martin, and I'd only seen pictures. You tend to remember the faces of the people who fuck up your life."

"I'll make sure he doesn't see me," I answered. "I need to be there." I don't know why the need is so strong. I trust Michael, but I don't know how he's going to react to seeing Jared again. Michael could walk up to Jared and hug him, or he could walk up to him and stab him in the throat. Nothing would surprise me. I want to make sure that Michael remembers what we're trying to achieve here. We have a goal.

"I'll tell you everything he says," Michael tried assuring me.

"What are you going to say to him?" I asked. He could at least make me feel comfortable that he had a plan. So many variables were in play. How was Michael going to get him to tell us what we needed to know? Would Jared even know anything that could help us? We'd put so much emphasis on this one plan, on this one horrible person.

"I don't know," Michael said. "I haven't thought about it." He was lying to me. I didn't know why he was lying to me or what exactly he was lying about, but I could tell that he was lying. We were gambling everything on one conversation, and Michael wouldn't even tell me what he was planning on saying. That's when I realized that Michael came up with this plan to use Jared not because it was a brilliant plan, but because it was the only thing that popped into his head. For most of his life, asking Jared for help was the only thing that had worked for Michael. I needed to make sure that we didn't blow it.

"Okay," I said, agreeing to let Michael go alone. If he could lie to me, then I could lie to him too. Nothing is keeping me out of that bar.

Michael didn't have his own place to stay, so he stayed with me. I liked having him sleep so close to me again. I liked hearing him breathe as he slept.

Forty-one

Michael told me where he was meeting Jared. He told me when. That's all I needed to know.

I left the hotel room early in the morning. When Michael asked me where I was going, I told him that I was simply too anxious to sit still all day. It wasn't a lie. It just wasn't the whole truth. "Are you mad at me because I don't want you to be there?" Michael asked me as I headed out the door. It almost felt like a lover's quarrel.

"No," I told him. "I've got some things to take care of—that's all."

"What sort of things?" he asked.

"Don't worry about me," I answered. "I'll make myself busy." I stepped through the door.

"Aren't you going to wish me good luck?" Michael asked.

I held the door open for a moment. I didn't look back at Michael. "No," I told him. "I'm hoping you don't need it."

I took my backpack and my last four hundred dollars in cash with me. Michael would be able to pay the hotel bills now. I walked into Georgetown. I knew a hotel not far from the bar where Michael and Jared were going to meet where you could get a room for less than two hundred dollars a night. I'd researched it when I first got to D.C. Check-in wasn't until one in the afternoon. It was only ten in the morning when I got there. It didn't matter. I didn't plan on actually checking in anyway.

A pimply-faced boy was working the front desk. He was probably a student at one of the local colleges. Is he older than me? I can't even tell anymore. "Listen," I said to him after walking up to the front desk. "I need a room for the day—just the day. I'll be out by seven p.m. I'll give you a hundred dollars in cash if you can get me in a room now." The boy looked confused for a second. "No one else even needs to know that I was ever in the room. You'll still have time to fill the room with a late check-in. For you, it's a free hundred dollars."

The boy nervously eyed the five twenties in my hand. He looked around to see if anyone was watching him. "Just you?" he asked, with all the tawdriness that the question implied. I had no right to be insulted. I nodded. He punched a few buttons on the computer in front of him. Then he reached out and snatched the cash from my hand. He spoke in a whisper. "Here's the key," he said. "The room's on the second floor." His excitement barely covered the fear in his voice. "What do I do if someone asks questions?" he asked.

"Play dumb," I answered. I assumed he could handle that.

"Okay," he said, giving me a conspirator's smile. I didn't return it. I took the stairs to the second floor and found the room. It was small but it would do. I didn't need luxury. I looked in the bathroom. One wall was covered with a mirror above the sink. The other side of the bathroom had a small bathtub with a shower. I put my backpack down on the counter next to the sink. I unzipped it and looked inside, trying to decide if I should leave anything behind. I eyed the gun, the knife, the journals, the unopened pack of cigarettes, the cash. I took it all with me. I reminded myself that Jared was walking the same streets that I was. If I met him, I wanted to be ready.

I walked back down the stairs and out a side door. I didn't trust the poker face on the kid behind the counter. When I got to the street, I kept my head down as much as possible. When I was on the run with your father, I eyed everyone with suspicion. Now I was only on the lookout for one person. If Jared saw me on the street, everything could be ruined. After walking a few blocks, I hailed a cab. I didn't have a lot of money left, but I didn't have time to walk all the way to Old Town Alexandria, either.

I told the cabdriver to take me back across the river to Crown Wigs, a small specialty store that advertises more than six hundred models of wigs and claims to employ experts in medical-related hair loss. It wasn't selling novelty wigs as sex toys or Halloween costumes. It sold wigs to people who didn't want to look like they were wearing wigs. I went inside. I was in the store for over an hour. My wig is called the Camilla. It was made from real, blond, straight hair. The bangs cover enough of my face to conceal it. The wig cost more than the hotel room, and I still wasn't done spending. On my way to the metro back to the hotel, I bought new clothes: black pants that hung loose enough to move in and a thin gray sweater that was tight at the top but loose enough at the bottom to conceal any items I might want to hide along my waistline. I was going for stylish but practical in a way I'd never in my life imagined I'd have to worry about.

It was the middle of the afternoon when I got back to the hotel. I went inside the same way I'd left—through the side door and up the stairs. I slid my key card into the door and, to my relief, the little green light came on and the door handle gave way. Once back inside the room, I spread my new clothes out on the bed. Then I took out the wig and walked into the bathroom. I tried on the wig in front of the mirror. It was a fight to fit the wig over my own unruly hair. I tried pulling my hair back, but I still couldn't get the wig to look natural. I opened drawers in the vanity beneath the sink. All I found was a shower cap and a miniature sewing kit. I walked back out of the bathroom and grabbed my backpack. I pulled out the knife. I knew how sharp it was. I took it out of its sheath and walked back into the bathroom. I looked at myself in the mirror and grabbed a thick chunk of curls. I raised the knife and cut. If I moved the knife in a sawing motion against the hair, it sliced through without much pain. Clumps of hair came off in my hand. With each cut, I felt a small tug against my scalp, and then I'd cut with the knife and the pain would be gone. Strand by strand, my dark hair fell to the floor.

I tried the wig on three more times as I cut. Each time, I realized that it would look more realistic if I kept cutting. The knife was a blunt tool, not built for style. By the time I was done, my longest curl in front was no more than two inches, maybe four when pulled straight. The back was even shorter. It had been harder to control the knife when cutting the back. I slid the wig on for the last trial. I lifted my head and looked at myself in the mirror. I rustled the blond hair of the wig, letting it pitch shadows on my face. Maria was gone. I still wasn't quite Camilla yet. I still had makeup to apply and clothes to put on and a gun and a knife to hide among their folds.

Camilla left the hotel room at half past six, even earlier than I'd promised the kid at the front desk. I left the key card on the top of the television. I took one last look at myself in the full-length mirror in the bathroom. Only a few people in the world could have recognized me in the disguise. Your father would have. My mother might have, if she would recognize me at all. Maybe my father. I didn't know the whole list, only that it was short. I left the gun in the backpack. I had tried to hide it beneath my sweater by tucking it in the hem of my pants, like I'd seen the men do, but it was too obvious. The knife, however, was in its now customary position, with the blade pressed against my upper thigh.

It was before seven o'clock when I got to the bar. The sky outside wasn't even dark, but the inside of the bar was. The bar oozed darkness. I looked around. Two men sat at the bar, and a small group sat in the booth closest to the front door. The booths ran along the right wall, opposite the bar. All the booths but the first one were empty, including the one farthest back, the one I knew Jared would pick. I felt like I'd been in that bar before. I walked over to the jukebox. I flipped through five pages of albums. Frank Sinatra. Otis Redding. This was definitely the place where Jared and your father met. I went to the bar and ordered a club soda with lime. The bartender asked if that was it, and I answered, "For now. I'm meeting someone here later."

The bartender served me my drink. I took a sip and walked toward the booth in the back. I didn't have too much time to waste. Jared might come early. He might do the same thing that Michael did whenever meeting someone, circling and observing and taking mental notes. I stopped at the booth. I looked at the dark wood of the table and the black leather of the benches. Your father sat in that booth. They tried to erase the memory of your father from the world, but I knew better. He sat right there, less than a year ago, and had a conversation with his killer. In less than an hour, that same man would be here again, sitting in the same booth, talking to Michael.

I took a seat at the bar, near the back and where I could pretend to be watching television. From that seat, I could watch Michael and Jared without looking like I was watching them. I thought that I might even be able to hear them if I concentrated and drowned out every other sound. I thought that maybe I could at least catch a few words. I faced the door. I ordered a red wine. I wasn't planning on drinking the wine, just spilling a little bit every so often so that the bartender would think that I was drinking. I glanced over at the empty booth. I had a clear view of it from my seat. I could see both benches. I tried concentrating my hearing, trying to drown out everything but the silence emanating from the booth. The problem is, it's hard to tell your silence from someone else's.

I was on my second glass of wine when Jared walked through the door. A small pool of the red liquid was gathering near my feet. I recognized him immediately. I felt a tremor run through my body. It felt like free-falling without a parachute. I recognized him even before I saw his face, when he was merely a silhouette against the light from outside. I recognized his shape, his walk, his posture. He closed the door and walked into the darkness. My eyes focused. His face hadn't changed. How could it not? It should have grown older or weaker. I lifted my glass, further concealing my face, as he walked toward the back booth. He passed only a few feet away from me. I remembered the burning hatred with which he had once looked at you. I must have been looking at him the same way.

For a moment, Jared's eyes moved over me, but only barely. I was a stranger to him. I was half-relieved and half-angry. How dared he forget me? Then I remembered that I was in disguise. Jared sat down in the booth, facing the door. A few seconds later, the waitress came up to him. She seemed to know him. They spoke normally and I could hear them. I could hear almost every word. Only whispers were my enemy now.

I looked at my watch. It was ten of eight. Michael wasn't planning on leaving the hotel until eight o'clock. I sat at the bar for twenty minutes and watched Jared sip his Manhattan alone. His face betrayed nothing; no nervousness, no anger, no remorse, no happiness. His face was a mask worn for no one, seen only by me. Then Michael walked through the door.

It was darker outside when Michael entered. I didn't recognize him at first, framed by the gray night air. Then I recognized his limp, slight enough now that most people wouldn't notice it, disguised as a simple hitch in his gate. Michael took a few steps into the bar and then looked around. His eyes brushed over each booth until he came to the last one and saw Jared. His mouth broke into a smile. I'd so rarely seen Michael smile that it was almost disconcerting. Michael walked toward the back of the bar. I put my head down, staring into my half-empty glass of wine, letting my blond bangs droop over my face. Michael didn't glance in my direction.

When Michael was only a few steps from the back booth, Jared stood and extended his hand toward Michael. Michael brushed it aside and pulled Jared into a hug. "It's good to see you, Michael," Jared said as the two men pushed away from each other's grasp.

"It's good to see you too," Michael replied. I could hear a tinge of sadness in his voice. "It's been a long time."

"Sit down," Jared told him, motioning toward the vacant bench across from his own. "We've got a lot of catching up to do." Michael turned and took a quick glance around the bar. He scanned the whole place in two turns of his head. His eyes rolled over me as I turned and pretended to watch the television. Then he sat down. Jared motioned for the waitress. My head began to throb. The entire bar was pulsating around me.

When the waitress came back to their booth, Jared ordered another Manhattan. I half expected Michael to order an Irish Car Bomb. He ordered a regular bottled beer instead. The bar was about a third full now, but if I focused all my energy, I could still hear Michael and Jared talk. I tried not to do anything but listen. My vision went fuzzy; the world around me dissolved.

"How have you been?" Michael asked Jared, as if he were making ordinary small talk.

"Good," Jared answered, a smile crossing his lips. "I've been good."

"So, you're a big, important man now, huh?" Michael asked.

Jared laughed. "It's all relative, I guess."

Michael matched Jared's laugh, almost parodying it. "So you're saying you're just a big, important man compared to me?"

"Yeah," Jared answered, the sarcasm scarcely evident in his voice. "That's what I'm saying." The laughter died slowly. "You know that's not true, Michael. You've been doing some pretty good work too. Even when you were in St. Martin, everyone was following along. You've got to know how happy we all are to have you back." Jared tipped his martini glass toward Michael. Michael clinked it with the edge of his beer bottle. "Now tell me it feels good to be back," Jared said. It almost sounded like an order.

"You know I love doing this," Michael said. "It just took me a while to get my head on straight after . . ." Michael's voice trailed off. He stared at his beer.

"After what happened to Joe," Jared finished for him after a pregnant pause.

"Yeah," Michael answered. He gave Jared a cold, hard stare. So much for small talk. I hated seeing Michael act friendly to Jared, but I also didn't want him to blow it. We need this, I thought to myself, trying to send signals to Michael over the sounds coming from the jukebox.

Jared placed his elbows on the table. He leaned forward, toward Michael, and spoke again, his voice lower now. He wasn't whispering, but he was speaking softly enough that I couldn't hear him anymore. I saw Michael nod without knowing what he was nodding about. I needed to know. Michael said something back to Jared. I couldn't hear him either. The most important moment in my life was happening right next to me, and I had been reduced to less than a spectator. I looked around the bar to see if there was anywhere I could go where I might be able to hear them again. The booth next to theirs was still open. I could move there. I could tell the bartender that my friend was coming soon, and I could sit only inches from Michael and listen, but if I sat there, they'd stop talking. I knew that much. I looked over at their booth, risking looking almost directly at them. Behind the booth was a thick, black velvet curtain separating the bar from the bathroom doors. I was sure that I would be able to hear them from behind the curtain. They kept talking, and I was missing every vital word they spoke. I decided to go for it. I stood up, straightened my pant legs, and turned. I took the four or five steps past their booth toward the bathrooms as casually as I knew how. Then I slipped behind the curtain. Once behind the curtain, I opened and closed one of the bathroom doors so that it would sound like I'd gone inside. Instead of going inside, I backed into the curtain, almost pushing myself up against the back of Jared's seat. An inch of velvet curtain separated me from the man who killed your father. I had my knife secured in the waistband of my pants and a gun in my purse. Revenge would have been easy.

I could hear Michael's voice again. "So, you think you did him a favor?" Michael asked. He sounded skeptical or confused—I couldn't tell which. I stopped breathing and listened through the black curtain.

"No," Jared answered, his voice a decibel quieter than Michael's. "You're twisting my words. All I said was that if he was going to run, he might be better off. I don't know." Jared's voice got even quieter now but I could still hear him. "I hate what I did to Joe, but I'm glad that it was me that did it and not some punk trying to make a name for himself. Either way, Joe was never going to make it."

Michael didn't say anything. I wanted to peek around the curtain to see the expression on Michael's face. Instead I stood as still as death. After a few minutes went past, I heard Jared's voice again. "You have changed a bit, Michael," Jared said. "You seem older. You've matured." More uncomfortable silence came from Michael's side of the table. "Can we change the subject?" Jared finally asked.

"We should be celebrating. I'm all for talking about Joe, but let's talk about the good things. Joe wouldn't want us to be fighting, Michael."

"To Joe," Michael's voice said after a moment's hesitation.

"To Joe," Jared's voice echoed. I heard glass clink against glass, then more awkward silence. Every silent moment seemed an eternity. "Listen, Michael," Jared said. "I'm buying tonight. I hope you're up for another round or two."

I heard Michael's laugh again, deep and bellowing. "I haven't changed that much, Jared. I still don't turn down free beer."

"Good to hear," Jared said. "Order us another round. I'm going to hit the head."

It took me a second to realize what Jared meant. A second was almost all the time I had. Both of the bathroom doors were directly behind me. I was standing in, at most, fifteen square feet of space. I didn't have time to lunge for one of the bathroom doors, open it, and slip inside before Jared saw me. Jared would have seen the door swing closed and would have known that someone had been standing behind the curtain, listening to him. I'd be trapped inside. I had only one option. As Jared pulled the curtain back to step through it, I backed into the folds of the curtain, pulling as much of the blackness around me as I could without being too obvious. The bar was already dark, and as I pulled the curtain around me, I was nearly swallowed by the darkness. I felt like I was swimming in it. I cursed my new-found blond hair, knowing it might give me away. I reached down and grabbed the handle of my knife. I couldn't use the gun here. It would be too loud. We were too close. Clara's people taught me how to use the knife, though. Two motions. First, slice the throat clean to prevent your victim from screaming. Then make a clean upward stab under the ribs and into the lungs. I almost couldn't see anything through the slit in the curtain in front of me, but I saw Jared. He walked through the opening in the curtain. He looked nervous. Michael was making him nervous. I held my breath and didn't move. Jared didn't look up. My heart was beating in my chest so intensely that I worried that Jared would be able to hear it. He seemed to be walking in slow motion. If he lifted his head, if he even looked in my direction, I was ready to cut him. If it came down to him or me, it was not going to be me. I squeezed the handle of my knife. Jared reached for the doorknob to the bathroom. I pulled the knife up two inches from the lip of its sheath. Jared opened the bathroom door. He paused. Then he walked inside. He closed the door behind him, and I heard the water from the faucet begin to run.

I exhaled silently. I had to get out. I didn't have time to think about what I should do. I stepped out from the creases in the curtain and walked back to the bar. I didn't look toward Michael. I didn't dare. I went straight to the bar. I paid my tab and walked out the door.

I felt the muscles in my chest relax when I stepped outside and breathed in the cool night air. I knew that I would miss the rest of their conversation. I knew that I would miss everything else that they said about Joe, about you, about who might know where you were. I had to live with that. I had to trust Michael. I had no choice. I had almost blown it. I walked out of the bar and across the street. Trusting Michael didn't mean that I had to trust Jared. That was a step too far. I'd seen what Jared was capable of. I spotted a small alley between the buildings on the other side of the street. I slipped into the darkness and waited for Jared and Michael to come out.

I didn't know how long I would have to wait. I assumed it would be a while, that they would have at least two or three more rounds, toasting to more things that I didn't believe in, discussing how righteous ruining my life had been. So I was surprised when I saw Michael walk out of the bar only half an hour later with Jared in tow. When they first stepped out of the bar, I backed into the shadows. Jared took stock of the now-empty street around him. For the second time that night, he failed to see me hiding in front of him. Michael didn't bother to look around. He came through the door and started walking. He was heading down toward the river. Jared caught up to him with a few quick strides and the two of them began walking together. They were still talking, leaning in toward each other like conspiring thieves. I waited until they were a full block away before stepping out of the darkness. Then I followed them. I stayed on the other side of the street so that I wouldn't arouse their suspicions, but I made sure that I could always see them.

They kept walking downhill toward the river. When I was sure that they couldn't see me, I jogged across the street. I knew that there was a park there. It would be empty at this time of night. I didn't understand why they were going there. It wasn't safe. It would be a perfect place for Jared to turn on Michael. I wasn't going to let that happen again. I pulled the gun out of my backpack and slipped my finger over the trigger. Everything was becoming darker. I kept following them, careful not to make a sound. As the air grew darker, I closed the distance between us so that I could watch Jared's hands as he walked. Fortunately for him, he didn't make any suspicious moves. His first suspicious move would have been his last.

I was close enough to them now, dipping in and out of shadows as I walked, that I could have heard them talk, but they were quiet. The park in front of us was empty, free of witnesses. It was just Jared and Michael and me. When they got into the park, I heard Jared's voice. When he started speaking, I slipped behind a tree and stopped moving. I was less than twenty feet from them. I tried to position myself behind Jared so that he would have to turn to see me.

"We couldn't talk in there—not about this," Jared said to Michael, his voice slightly louder than a whisper.

"I don't get it," Michael said. "We can sit there and talk about killing, talk about the War, but we can't talk about this?"

"*You don't understand.*" I recognized Jared's patronizing tone. That's how he talked to your father before he killed him. I tightened the grip on my gun. "You think I picked that bar at random? They know me there. They know what I do. They're part of it."

"So, you're worried that if they hear you talking about this, they'll start questioning your motives? They'll start questioning your loyalty?" Michael asked.

"No, dipshit," Jared said. "I'm worried they'll start questioning yours. There are people in this game that still aren't ready to accept you back. I'm working on that, but it's not a simple play. And, frankly, this conversation isn't helping your case."

"Are you questioning my loyalty now?" Michael asked Jared.

"Look, Michael. There was no way for me to know how you were going to react to the whole thing with Joe, and now you're asking me where the kid is?" My mind flashed back to something Jared had said the night he stole you from me about what he'd do to you once you grew up. *I'll kill the evil little fucker myself.* He'd meant those words. I know he meant them.

"Just tell me where Joe's kid is," Michael demanded. I wanted to run through the darkness and kiss him.

"Why?" Jared asked.

Michael didn't hesitate. "Because he's all we have left of Joe. Don't tell me that doesn't mean something to you. I know you're not a monster."

Jared lifted his hands in the air. I moved the gun in front of me, holding it there until I could see that his hands were empty. "But he's one of *Them* now," Jared said. "He's on the other side."

"I don't even know what that means," Michael said. "If you can tell me what the fuck that means, then I'll go home right now, and I will keep on killing without saying another word."

"Joe believed," Jared said into the darkness. "That's why he ran."

"I believe," Michael replied, shaking his head. "Trust me, I believe. That's part of the problem, I believe without understanding what I believe in." Then there was silence. The only noise was the sound of the river. The dark water rolled past us, shimmering in the moonlight. I stood as still as possible, only partially hidden by the tree. No one spoke for three or four minutes.

"I don't know where he is," Jared finally said, breaking the silence.

"Don't give me that shit." It was Michael's conversation now. He had all the power.

"I can't afford to lose another friend, Michael," Jared said. "I don't want to give you the tools to do something that you'll regret."

"You think that I don't already regret everything I've done since I was eighteen years old?"

"Don't say that," Jared said.

"Just tell me where the kid is. Give me this one thing, and when I'm done, I'll play the good soldier until somebody puts me in a hole in the ground. I'll stack the bodies so high, you won't be able to see over them."

Jared shook his head. "I really don't know where he is."

"Then who does?" Michael asked, the words coming out almost before Jared finished speaking. "I know you, Jared. I know how the game is played. I know that we don't give people away to the other side without keeping track of where they are."

Jared laughed. "I keep telling them you're not as dumb as they think you are," he said. Jared breathed in a deep breath. "Even if you don't end up regretting whatever it is you're going to do, I'm pretty sure I will." Jared reached down toward the belt of his jeans. I lifted my gun and aimed it at the back of Jared's head. We were so close. I started to squeeze the trigger. Jared pulled a piece of paper out of his pocket. It looked like a business card. I loosened my grip on the gun.

"Do you have a pen?" Jared asked Michael. Michael was quick, handing Jared something as if he'd been ready for the question. "I don't know what you're going to do with this information. I don't want to know. If anything happens, I'm saving myself and selling you out as a traitor."

"Fair enough," Michael answered.

"There's a building in Tribeca, in New York. It's not our building. It's one of Theirs. I'm not going to tell you where we keep our information." Jared wrote something down on the back of the business card. "You want to know where Joe's kid is, take the information from Them." He handed the card to Michael. Michael looked at it.

"That's the best you can do?" Michael asked.

"That's the best I'm going to do," Jared answered, "and more than I should."

"What now?" Michael asked, holding the card in his hand.

"I've got another assignment for you. Call in tomorrow when you're sober and I'll give you the details."

"You're the one giving me my assignments now?" Michael asked.

"Yeah," Jared answered, "until they don't consider you a special case anymore."

"When will that be?" Michael asked.

"At this pace?" Jared laughed. I could hear the anger in Jared's laugh. He stopped short of answering Michael's question. "I wish I could stop you," he said instead.

"You can't," Michael cut him off. Michael held up the piece of paper in his hand. I could see the whiteness of the paper reflected in the moonlight. My whole life was on that piece of paper. "Thank you, Jared," Michael said. "I needed this." He'd gotten what we'd come for. We didn't need Jared anymore.

"I'm getting soft in my old age," Jared said. "Go home."

Michael didn't bother to say good-bye. When Jared spoke, Michael turned away from him and started walking along the river toward the bridge to Virginia. I waited in the shadows, watching Jared. I knew he wasn't above shooting his friends in the back. Jared didn't move. He watched Michael walk away until his silhouette disappeared in the darkness.

"Fuck," I heard Jared whisper beneath his breath. "What did you just do, Jared?" he asked himself. Then he turned and started walking away. He'd taken only about ten steps before I decided what I was going to do. Michael was gone. I followed Jared. Even after everything I'd heard, the only words that kept echoing through my head were *I'll kill the evil little fucker myself.*

I kept the gun in my hand, holding it down near my waist. The path that Jared was walking down was empty except for him. I didn't worry about hiding myself anymore. I started walking faster, making up the distance between the two of us. Jared started moving quickly now too. I don't think he saw me, but he must have felt something behind him. I had to double my pace. Soon I closed the gap between us to little more than ten feet. Clara's people taught me how to use the gun. Lesson number one was never aim a gun at someone you weren't willing to shoot.

It was clear now that he knew that I was following him. I kept watching his hand, watching to see if he would go for a weapon. If he did, I would have to move more quickly than I wanted to. I was worried that speed could lead to mistakes. I had to trust my training. Strips of moonlight shone through the trees. Jared stepped quickly between darkness and light. I wanted to reach him before he got out of the park, before he got somewhere where someone might try to help him. I kept my strides long and even and was able to close the gap between us until I was almost touching him.

"Jared," I said, loud enough for him to hear me. I wondered if he would recognize my voice. He stopped and turned toward me. I lifted my gun and aimed it at his head. I was face-to-face with the man who had taken you from me and killed your father. For one brief moment, I would make sure he got a clear look at my face in the moonlight. For that moment, I regretted the wig and the makeup. I wanted Jared to know it was me.

I squeezed the trigger.

Before the gun fired, something like a train hit me from behind. The gun slipped out of my hand and fell to the ground. I heard a shout. "Run, Jared!" I was confused, trying to piece together what was going on. I could barely see. Jared must have had people protecting him. He hadn't trusted Michael after all. Maybe it was one of those thugs that helped him take you from me. I tried to remember what I'd learned at Clara's about hand-to-hand combat. I wheeled around to orient myself. Before I could get my bearings, someone leapt on top of me, pinning me to the ground with his knees. I slipped an arm out from under one of the legs pressing down on top of me and punched up at my attacker. My fist connected with a nose. I heard a crunching noise and felt the gush of blood on my hand. "Run," the man said again, this time his voice muted by his own blood. "I'll take care of her." I didn't know what that meant. I didn't want to find out.

I heard footsteps running away from me in the darkness. Jared was getting away. I could see the gun shimmering in the moonlight to my right. The body lifted off of me for a moment, and I rolled to the side as quickly as I could to grab the gun. My survival instincts had kicked in. Still, as soon as my hand felt the handle of the gun, a foot came down on top of it, pressing my wrist into the ground. I rolled over again, remembering my training, preparing to kick into the person's groin.

"Fuck," the voice said, "I think you broke my nose." I stopped. I recognized the voice now. I didn't recognize it earlier because I'd never heard Michael yell before. I held my foot in the air above me for a second, trying to decide whether or not I should still kick him in the balls. I didn't. "What the hell are you doing here?" Michael asked me. I could see him reaching up, trying to slow the stream of blood coming from his nose by pinching its bridge with his fingers. I hesitated, caught between answering his question and asking a million questions of my own, the most immediate being, *Why did you stop me?* Michael didn't wait for me to answer. "We've got to get out of here in case he comes back." Michael looked around us, searching for the best escape route.

He reached down and helped me to my feet. Once I got up, we started running together. I knew where we could go. I'd run there before—the C&O towpath. It ran for miles through the woods and would be empty at night. We ran the first mile and stopped. The lights of the city were already lost behind us. Michael was breathing heavily. He was out of shape, his injured leg clearly impacting his training. I let him catch his breath. He had to suck in air through his mouth since his nose was clogged with blood. He wheezed as he breathed.

While he caught his breath, I reached up and pulled the wig off of my head and put it in my backpack. I was embarrassed for him to see me in it. Then I reached for the makeup around my eyes and on my cheeks. I felt it with my fingertips and smeared it across my face. I knew I couldn't take off the makeup yet, but I could change it. I could distort it. I had that power. I didn't want to look pretty.

Once Michael caught his breath, he told me that he saw me at the bar the moment he walked in. He recognized me through my disguise. He always recognized me. He'd known that I was standing behind the curtain listening to them. He'd known how close Jared had been to finding me.

"I wanted to shoot him," I said to Michael.

"I know, but we still need him. We still need his help to get inside."

"We don't need his help. I can get us inside," I told Michael. He looked at me with a mixture of confusion and doubt. "I'll explain later." I wondered if Michael would have saved Jared even if he knew the deal I'd cut with Clara. I tried not to dwell on it. We had too much to do.

I was worried that Jared might have recognized me. "No chance," Michael assured me. "Not the way you looked tonight."

"How did I look?" I asked, expecting him to say something snide about my disguise or the makeup smeared on my face.

"You look like a fighter. That's not the way you looked the last time Jared met you." Even so, we agreed that we needed a new place to stay until Michael could call Jared and get his next assignment. We were getting too close to take any chances.

On our way back toward the city, I asked Michael what he would say when Jared asked about the woman who attacked him. "That you were one of Them," Michael said, "and that I took care of it." After Michael talked to Jared, it would be my turn to reach out to Clara with the information Jared had given us.

Forty-two

Addy and Evan stopped in Georgia, about two hours outside of Atlanta, for the night. They could have kept driving. It would have only been another ten hours or so from where they stopped to their destination in Florida. After all they'd been through, it would have been an easy ten hours. Addy wanted to wait one more night, though. It was Sunday. She said that she didn't want to get to the compound on a Sunday, that she was worried that too many people would be off. She told Evan that she wanted to make sure she would recognize a lot of people when she and Evan arrived. Evan didn't doubt any of what Addy said, but he knew that Addy had other reasons for wanting to stop, for wanting to wait one more day. She was afraid. Evan could tell. She could hide her fear from most people, but she couldn't hide it from Evan anymore. He could see it in her. Evan had spent the better part of the past two weeks amazed by Addy's utter lack of fear. Fire didn't scare her. Guns didn't scare her. Being chased by the entire world didn't scare her. She was afraid now, though.

Evan figured out part of the reason why Addy was afraid. He figured out that she was afraid that her old friends wouldn't take her back. She was afraid that they wouldn't accept her after she'd run off on them, and that she and Evan would have nowhere to go. She was afraid that she'd dragged Evan all the way across the country only to get them stranded on the wrong side of a burned bridge. Evan wanted to tell her that he didn't care. He didn't care if people he'd never met refused to accept him. What was the Underground good for anyway? It seemed to Evan that all they could do was help them run and hide. He and Addy seemed to be doing a pretty good job of that themselves. He didn't say any of this to Addy, though. Being accepted back by her old friends seemed important to her. Evan didn't want to ruin that. Instead, he memorized what he was going to say to Addy if it all went badly—how they were better off alone, how her old friends didn't deserve her, how she was too strong and too brave for them anyway. In many ways, Evan was more prepared for rejection than acceptance.

Evan figured out only part of what Addy was afraid of, though. He didn't realize that her fear of rejection paled in comparison to her fear that her old friends would simply be gone. What if they'd been smoked out and hunted down too? What if she and the other rebels had pushed too hard too quickly and had destroyed everything in the process, including the Underground? Addy could live with being shunned. She was ready for that. She'd prepared herself for that possibility before she ran off to join the rebels in the first place. Addy had never been afraid of being an outsider. On the contrary, nearly every decision she'd made throughout her entire life pushed her in that direction. But after what happened in Los Angeles, Addy felt a need to know that her old friends were still there struggling, even if she didn't think they were struggling hard enough, even if she wished that they'd stop running and start fighting. It was the struggle—any struggle—that would at least give Addy some hope that the world could still be changed. More than anything else, Addy wanted to feel that hope that Christopher had once given her. As much as Evan could give her, he couldn't give her that.

"Why do you think Christopher left us?" Addy asked Evan as they waited together for the time to pass.

Evan shrugged. He didn't feel like Christopher had deserted him. In Evan's mind, Christopher merely deserted the War and this absurd fight against the War. Evan couldn't blame him for that. "This isn't his fight.

Maybe you guys expected too much from him. Maybe he felt like he was being used."

Addy shook her head. "He knew that he wasn't being used. We gave him a chance to run in the beginning. We gave him a chance to get away. He said that he wanted to fight."

"Yeah, but how could he understand what it meant to fight? He didn't know about any of this growing up. I know. I was there." Evan's voice didn't sound as certain as he wanted it to. "He was paranoid, but he would have told me if he knew about all this, right?"

"Christopher didn't know about any of this growing up," Addy assured Evan. "But we told him everything as soon as we found him."

"How? How can you possibly tell someone all of this and have it make any sense?"

"His parents kept journals." The words came out of Addy as if she were making a confession. Evan had no idea how much Addy knew. "His mother put them in a safe-deposit box, hoping that Christopher would never need them. Before she died, she arranged to have the key to the safe-deposit box sent to Christopher when he turned sixteen."

"So, he's known about the War since he was sixteen?" Evan asked, still trying to fit all the pieces together.

Addy's shook her head. "No. He ignored the letter his mother had sent to him. He put the key to the safe-deposit box in a desk drawer and pretended he never got it. By that time, Christopher was already so paranoid that he was more afraid of the truth than the paranoia."

"What was the truth?"

"The truth was that the whole time the two of you were growing up together, people were following Christopher. The truth was that he had a reason to be afraid. People had been following him since he was eleven years old. His mother had done everything she could to hide him before she was killed, but it didn't work. He'd become too important to stay hidden. That's why he was paranoid."

"So, when did you guys finally tell him about all of this?"

"As soon as we found him, we made sure he read his parents' journals, and we told him everything. We gave him a chance to run then too. I swear. He told me that he didn't want to run."

"When did you tell him about the War?" Evan asked again. He needed to know that Christopher had never kept anything from him. He needed to know that his friend was true.

"As soon as we could."

"When was that?" Evan pressed.

"We found him right after he turned eighteen." Addy paused for a moment, almost too ashamed to continue. *"We found him right after the people who had been following him tried to kill him for the first time."*

The men in the woods, Evan thought. *"That was only four weeks ago,"* Evan said. *"Christopher turned eighteen four weeks ago. Can you blame him for running away? How did you expect him to become a war hero in four weeks?"*

"Somebody has to be the leader," Addy said to him. *"He was the only one that could bring everyone together. He understood that."*

"And if he died for your cause, would anybody remember who he was? Would anybody care? Or would his death be just another symbol?"

Addy's voice softened. *"If I die, is anyone going to remember who I was? If you die, will anyone remember you? At least Christopher has the chance to be a symbol."*

Evan stopped. He didn't agree with Addy, but he didn't want to hurt her either. He could let her have her symbols, and he could keep his friend. He knew that there would be enough fights for them in the future without them fighting each other. Evan sensed Addy's need for something, even if it was something that he knew he couldn't give her, and walked over to her. He took a stray lock of Addy's dark red hair and tucked it behind her ear. Then he kissed her. He didn't hesitate anymore. Evan's fear of Addy had deserted him somewhere along the road, hundreds of miles ago.

Addy felt the rough hair on Evan's face brush against her skin when he placed his lips on hers. She kissed him back, grabbing the back of his neck and pulling him closer into her. As they kissed, she reached up and began unbuttoning her blouse. Evan and Addy didn't say another word to each other that night. Neither wanted any more words. They enjoyed the silence. They both knew that after tomorrow, they either wouldn't be alone anymore or they'd likely be alone together forever. Secretly, neither one of them was sure which one they were hoping for.

Forty-three

It's been days since I last wrote to you, Christopher. I'm sorry. Things are moving so quickly now. Everything seems to go either too slow or too fast. I haven't had any time to write. I've barely had any time to think other than about the plan. Michael and I are breaking into the information cell tomorrow. Your information is inside. We're in Tribeca, not far from the building. Your file is on the third floor. It has the names of the people who have been raising you and their address. I think we're ready. I hope we're ready.

Clara was true to her word. I sent her all the information that Jared had given Michael, hoping it would be enough. I told Clara where they were keeping your information. Then I wrote, *According to our agreement, it's your turn.* She responded three hours later. Michael and I were holed up in a dingy hotel in northeast D.C. when she responded. The hotel was cheap and felt safe. It's amazing what feels safe to me now. I read her answer in a nearby Kinko's a few hours after she sent it. My fingers trembled on the keyboard. *We have a mole in an intelligence cell in Tribeca. I want to cross-reference it first to make sure we're talking about the same place. I only know of one cell in that area. I will write again in the next twenty-four hours with details if possible.*

Clara wrote again twelve hours later. Michael and I found an all-night Internet café and I sat there for almost the entire twelve hours, hitting Refresh, waiting for Clara to respond. Jared told Michael that his next job was in Cleveland. Michael had four days to rest and then he was supposed to check in with his safe house. They were letting Michael stay in a safe house again. Michael was supposed to have checked in yesterday. He didn't. I don't suppose they'll give him another chance. When we're finished, maybe I can still convince Michael to go work with Clara.

The second e-mail I received from Clara said, *Can confirm that they have only one intelligence cell in Tribeca.* She confirmed the address. Even that was enough for me. Knowing that the key to finding you was in an actual place was enough. I would have stormed in by myself. I don't think anyone could have stopped me. The problem is that I need to get out too. After the address, Clara wrote, *Will set up meeting between you and the mole. Be careful. I don't want him getting hurt or blowing his cover. He can help with information, but then you're on your own. Go to New York. Check your e-mail again in two days.*

We took the train to New York. Michael used his ATM card to take out as much cash as he could without immediately arousing suspicion. It was enough to last us a week or two on cash alone. He gave me most of it, telling me that he still had the credit cards that he could use. I didn't argue. I took the cash. We were on the same team. He wasn't being gallant or noble. He was being practical.

We got to New York a day after I'd received the second e-mail from Clara. I wanted to go right to the building in Tribeca. I wanted to see it, to scope it out. I thought that if I was closer to that information, closer to the truth, I'd be closer to you. Michael wouldn't let me go. "Let's talk to the mole first," he said. "There's nothing to see now that we can't see after we know what we're dealing with." I remembered his lecture to me about recklessness versus carelessness.

When Michael first gave me the lecture, I thought that carelessness was akin to not caring. I was wrong. It's not being able to control how much you care.

We were in New York for less than twenty-four hours when I got the third and final e-mail from Clara. It was short and simple. *Tomorrow (Sunday) at noon. Brighton Beach. Second Street gazebo on the boardwalk by the chessboards. He'll answer to the name Palti. This will be my last e-mail. I am shutting down this account. Godspeed, Maria. We're rooting for you.* That was it. My only connection to the Underground was burned again. At least I had gotten something this time before the bridges were razed.

Michael and I decided to take the subway from Tribeca to Coney Island. From there it was a short walk to Brighton Beach. It was a cool, foggy morning. It felt more like autumn than summer. The air was thick and heavy with moisture that snuck into your clothing if you didn't hold it close against your skin. It was a long train ride to Coney Island, over an hour. Once we were out of Manhattan and in Brooklyn, the subway emerged from beneath the ground and we rode the rest of the way on elevated tracks above the surrounding neighborhoods. Michael and I didn't speak much. We listened to the sound of the subway rumbling over the city. For the most part, our subway car was empty. Every few stops someone would get on or someone would get off, but only the two of us made the trip from start to finish. Coney Island was the train's last stop.

The low fog hung over the city streets as we sped over them. Close up, I could see the endless rows of buildings, row after row, stretching out until they disappeared into the fog. The last time I had been in Brooklyn, I was with Reggie. Reggie was okay. Looking out over the fog-covered buildings brimming with quiet, endless humanity, I wondered why I even doubted that he'd survive. He had all this to hide in, all of this to melt into and disappear. It's there for you too, Christopher. It's there for us. We can be safe. I know it. The subway car lurched forward.

Our train ride stopped a block from the ocean. We got off the subway and walked to the boardwalk. A cold wind blew in from over the water. The beach was wide and flat. I could see the waves churning in the sea. The sky was gray. I looked to our right. A motionless Ferris wheel, its gondolas blowing in the wind, dominated the skyline. The beach was empty except for a straggler or two walking near the water. Even they wore pants and jackets. "This way," Michael said, motioning down the boardwalk, away from the still-empty Ferris wheel.

Our footsteps echoed on the wooden slabs of the boardwalk as we walked. In my head, each echo announced to everyone around us that we didn't belong there. Only a few people walked past us on the boardwalk. Those that did pulled their collars up around their chins, battling the wind. The people we passed looked old and hard, like they'd survived something. Some people eyed us suspiciously. Others walked by us without giving us a second glance. I'd learned to be more worried about those that didn't look at us than those that did. Paranoia is your friend. Your father taught me that.

We were walking for about fifteen minutes before we could see the Second Street gazebo. It jutted out onto the beach in front of us. Under the gazebo, I could see the old men staring down at chessboards on tables built into the boardwalk. Most of the tables were empty. Three were occupied. The two tables closest to the boardwalk, farthest from the water, had men sitting at either side of the table, facing each other. They were all old men with white hair and deep wrinkles in their faces. They hunched over the chessboards, contemplating their next moves.

As we got closer, I could see the tiny chess pieces, like little black and white toy soldiers, standing on the tables between the men.

Farther from the boardwalk, closer to the ocean, sat a solitary man at one of the tables, his back to us, facing the sea. We stepped into the gazebo and began walking toward him. If he wasn't alone, he would have looked like all the other old, hunched men Michael nodded to as we passed them. Michael didn't like walking past them and leaving our backs open to an ambush. Michael didn't trust the old men. Michael didn't trust anyone. "We must be mad," he whispered under his breath to me as we stepped closer to the man sitting alone at the end of the gazebo.

When we neared the lone man, he stood up with a jerk. He hadn't even looked back at us. For a moment, I thought Michael was right. The whole thing was a trap. My heart pounded and my hand reached down toward my knife. It was reflex now. Fight or flight weren't mutually exclusive anymore. Luckily, the lone man simply stood up, turned, and walked around to the other side of the table. He looked up at us for a second and then, without even acknowledging our presence, sat down facing us this time, his back to the ocean. He immediately began studying the pieces again. He was playing both sides of the game, first black, then white. Michael and I slowed our walk. I took a glance behind us. The four other old men were still engrossed in their games. The lone figure's hair was dark and curly. His eyebrows were unruly and wild. He could have passed for the son of any of the other four men at the tables. Michael and I stepped up to him. We were early. It wasn't even eleven thirty yet. The man didn't look up at us. Michael glanced at me. "Palti?" I asked.

Without answering me, the man continued to stare down at the pieces on the chessboard. I looked down at the game. If someone who knew nothing about chess looked at this board, they would never be able to guess the positions of the pieces when the game started. Each side had lost about a third of its pieces. From what I could tell, however, the game looked even. After a few minutes of silence, the man reached down. He pushed one of the remaining white pawns farther into black's territory. "You're Maria," he said to us, looking up at me after making his move. "You're early." He didn't sound excited to see me.

"We're sorry," I said. "We can come back if you'd like."

"No," the man said, "we might as well get this over with." He looked down at the board again, as if trying to remember the position of all the pieces in case the wind blew them away. "We can sit at one of the empty tables." I could hear the waves crashing on the beach behind us. "I didn't know that there would be two of you," he said, sitting down on the bench at the empty table next to his.

"This is Michael," I said. "He's working with me. I hope it's okay that he's here."

Palti looked Michael up and down. "It's fine. I was actually nervous that you were going to try to pull this craziness off by yourself. Are you one of Clara's people?" Palti asked Michael.

Michael shook his head. "No."

"Michael was friends with the boy's father," I said to Palti, filling in the blanks that Michael did not, "the boy we are trying to find. I thought Clara would have told you about him."

"Clara doesn't tell me much," Palti said, taking a loose cigarette out of his jacket pocket and lighting it. "I don't think she trusts me." He smiled a humorless smile. "Smoke?" he asked, pulling another loose butt out of his jacket.

"No, thank you," I answered. Michael shook his head. Palti put the cigarette back in his pocket. "What did Clara tell you?" I asked.

"She told me who you were. She didn't need to go into too many details. I already knew all about you—the legendary Maria." The way he said it made me uncomfortable, but I tried not to show it. "She asked if we had information about your son. I told her that we did." My heart sped up. "She asked if I could help you get into the building, if I could tell you where the information was." He flicked the ash of his cigarette down onto the wooden floorboards beneath us. "And I said no. I told her that I had no interest in getting you killed, that you'd been through enough already." He stopped speaking then, as if that was the end of the story.

"What made you change your mind?" I asked, prodding him to continue, hoping that the story didn't actually end there.

"Clara told me not to underestimate you, that she'd made that mistake." I heard Michael chuckle under his breath. "Clara never told me exactly what you want, though."

"I want to find out where my son is so that I can find him and save him," I said. I had practiced being as concise as possible.

"Save him from what?" Palti asked.

"The War," I answered quickly.

Palti laughed. "I was afraid of that," he said without elaborating. "I can tell you where the information about your son is. I can help you get into the building. I can disarm the back-door alarm. I can get you a key to the door and tell you the guards' schedules. But I can't be there when you go in. I give you the information. I give you the key, and then you forget I exist."

"Why?" Michael asked, sounding more curious than confrontational.

"Clara gave me strict orders." Palti smashed the end of his cigarette butt into the empty stone table between us.

"And why do you listen to Clara's orders?" Michael asked.

"I've given up on the War," Palti said to Michael, not insulted by his question. "I haven't given up on order. I'm not an anarchist."

"Just a spy," Michael said, finishing Palti's sentence.

Palti smiled again, showing his crooked teeth. "Just a spy," he echoed.

"Okay," I said to Palti, interrupting the back-and-forth. "What can you tell us?"

Palti looked away from Michael and back at me. "The building has five stories," he said. "Each one is guarded separately. The first floor is primarily storage. It's full of office supplies, computers, and furniture. There's nothing of interest. It's designed that way on purpose. If anyone accidentally comes inside the building, they'll see nothing of value. The second floor has the nonproprietary information," Palti said.

"What does that mean?" Michael asked.

"It has the information that we've collected about the other side," Palti said. "Information from spies, information that we've stolen, information that we've been given through negotiation, information that we've gotten from our own research—it's all there on paper, at least the piece of it that's stored in our building. We keep only paper files. Nothing gets stored electronically. No matter how good your security is, once you put things on networks, you're begging to be hacked." I could almost feel Michael's muscles tighten as Palti spoke. The information on floor two might have been the information that got Michael's family killed. It was all there, blandly, coolly, on paper.

"What about backups?" Michael asked out of the blue.

"Other buildings," Palti said. "I don't know where. No single bit of information is kept exclusively in one building. Everything is duplicated and spread out. I don't know exactly where any of the other buildings are. I know only this one."

"How long have you been at this one?" I asked.

"Twenty-four years," Palti answered. He couldn't have been older than his midforties. He must have started there when he was close to my age.

"That's a long time," I said without thinking.

"Thanks for reminding me," Palti answered with another wan

smile. He took another cigarette out of his jacket pocket and lit it. "Anyway," he continued, "the third floor and half of the fourth floor contain proprietary information." Palti looked at Michael. "Information about our side, information that we've kept and modified and expanded over the years. When someone on our side has children or gets married or gets promoted, if their file is assigned to us, that information goes on either the third or the fourth floor. The files are kept more or less alphabetically."

"What do you mean *more or less*?" I asked.

"Well, sometimes people change their names," Palti answered. "We don't reassign them if they do. Instead, each person is assigned a ten-digit number when their file is created. That number never changes."

"Do people know their own numbers?" Michael asked. I knew he was trying to figure out if his side did it the same way, if he had a number, if your father had a number.

"No," Palti answered. "We don't even know our own numbers. Our files, the files about me and the people I work with, are kept at other sites. We could probably come pretty close to guessing our numbers based on the files we have, but we don't know."

"Who knows?" Michael asked.

"The numbers are assigned in one of the three central units. Those units have the keys needed to figure out which information cell has any specific piece of information. Without those units, it's like a library with no card catalogue, the Internet with no search engines. But we're getting off track."

"So, my son. He's going to be in the *W*s," I said to Palti, picking the first letter in your father's last name.

Palti shook his head. "No," he said. "That's not your son's name. Not in the system. Your son's file was created when he was given to his current parents."

"So where's his information?" I asked. "What's his name?"

Palti told me the name they gave you. It's a name I'll never use and I hope you forget. Some things you're better off not knowing.

"His file is on the third floor?" I asked.

"Yes," Palti said. "It's on the third floor." I'd heard enough. I was ready to talk about how we were going to get inside. Michael kept asking questions.

"What's on the fifth floor?" Michael asked.

Palti looked at Michael as if he'd been waiting for Michael to ask him the question. "The fifth floor," Palti said, "and a growing portion of the fourth floor, has the historical information. The information here is kept chronologically, not alphabetically like the rest of the building."

"What do you mean, historical information?" Michael said breathlessly.

"It's the information that we've kept about the War, going back hundreds of years, at least the portion of it that's stored in our location. The newer information is stored on the fourth floor. The older information is on the fifth."

"Have you been up there?" Michael asked, staring at Palti now. "Have you been to the fifth floor? Have you looked at the files?"

"I don't go to the historical information often," Palti said. "We're not supposed to dig where we're not needed. They call me a Historian. That's the job title they've given me, like they call men like you soldiers. But I'm a file clerk. I don't pretend otherwise."

"You said you don't go often. That means that sometimes you do go. What have you seen?" I was surprised by Michael's sudden interest. Of course, Michael probably never thought he'd be sitting in front of a strange little man who had the ability to do something Michael could never do. He had the ability to peek behind the curtain.

"Nothing," Palti said, shaking his head. Michael's shoulders slumped. Palti continued, "I go to the historical records because sometimes current records become historical and need to be filed. You don't know how many times I've been asked to pull a nonproprietary file. They never tell me why. Then, a few weeks later, they ask me to refile it in the historical information section. Or sometimes, out of the blue, I'll be asked to file a file whose last entry was a wedding or the birth of a child in the historical information section. I'll date it and I'll file it. When I started, our historical information section was exclusively on the fifth floor. Every day it grows."

"So, how do we get inside?" I asked, hoping Michael was ready to move on.

Palti reached into his jacket pocket, the one opposite the one he'd been pulling his cigarettes from. He took out a large key with a square head. He placed it on the table in front of him.

"That's it?" Michael asked.

Palti nodded. "That's a copy of the key to the back door. I'll disable the exterior alarms. I can make it look like a system failure. You'll still have to avoid tripping the interior alarms. I can tell you how to get to the third floor without tripping them. Then there are the guards. They work in shifts. There are gaps in those shifts. No one has ever tried to break into our cell before, so the guards aren't very diligent, but that doesn't mean that this will be easy."

"You say that no one has ever tried to break into your cell before. What about other cells?" I asked.

"There was a building in San Diego about twelve years ago. Five men attempted a breach. The building was razed, burned to the ground."

"The men who broke in burned it down?" I asked.

"No," Palti said. "We burned it down. The information was compromised. We couldn't trust it in that state anymore. We had the redundancy we needed to re-create all the information we lost and the intelligence to change the information we had to."

"What happened to the five men?" I asked.

"They were still in the building when we lit it on fire," Palti answered. "I updated two of their files myself. No matter what I do for you," Palti said, staring straight at me, "the odds of you making it out of the building with the information you want and without bloodshed is almost zero. Someone's blood will be spilled. If you're lucky, you'll be the one who gets to decide whose."

"Then why don't you just get the information and give it to us?" Michael asked.

"If you want to act on the information," Palti answered, "you need to steal it, or they'll figure out that there's a spy. When are you planning on breaking in?"

"As soon as possible," I answered, not wanting to waste another moment. He told us that he needed two days to figure out the best way to disable the exterior alarm. He also advised us to attempt the break-in at night. It would be simpler. The streets would be empty. There would be fewer guards and they would be tired. Then Palti diagrammed the guard schedule, pointing out the gaps. I studied the paper. Michael studied Palti's face.

When Palti was done telling us everything he knew about the guard's movements, Michael ask him one final question: "Why should we trust you?"

"I'm a liar, a thief, and a traitor," Palti answered him, "but some people have found me useful. The call is yours to make."

We sat with Palti in the cold wind beside the gray ocean for another two hours, going over details of the building and descriptions of the employees who would be working there at night. We had to trust him. We had no choice. Michael and I have spent nearly every waking moment since we met with Palti going over the plan and scoping out the building. We make our move tomorrow night. We've practiced our parts, rehearsed them like dancers practicing for opening night. It's going to work, Christopher. It has to. Sitting in a building only a few blocks from where I am right now is a file with a piece of paper that is going to lead me to you. Iron doors and walls of fire couldn't stop me now.

Forty-four

I'm staring out the window of a train, heading west. I'm coming for you, Christopher. I'm alone now, but I'm coming.

You need to know what happened that night. You need to know what Michael did for you. We waited until a little after one in the morning before heading to the intelligence cell. We knew that the plan, even if successful, could take hours. Palti told us that the night shifts start at ten o'clock. By the time we got inside, the security team would have already been on duty for almost four hours. They'd be tired and bored. Michael doubted it at first. These people were guarding the most important weapon either side had: information.

Palti questioned Michael. "You are a soldier, correct?" Michael nodded. "Do you know why you were selected to be a soldier?" Michael shrugged, unwilling to tell this spy that he believed that he was selected to be a soldier because someone saw something special in him. "You were selected because they knew that they could train you. You were born to follow. Even if you lead, you lead people to follow the orders of others. That's why all of you are chosen. The people working in these intelligence cells—we weren't selected to be soldiers. We were selected to be glorified security guards and file clerks—even if they call us Facility Patrolmen and Historians. Most of us have worked at this site for more than ten years and nothing has ever happened. Can you imagine what it would be like to work at a job where nothing happens for ten years? If you are going to have any success, it's because my colleagues think of you as the bogeyman, and everyone knows that the bogeyman doesn't exist."

The street behind the intelligence cell was dark and skinny, not much more than an alleyway. The buildings on the dark, skinny street had high walls with large doors that closed up like giant drawbridges. They were the buildings' back doors, used mostly for deliveries. At one in the morning, the street had no more motion than a painting. Even so, Michael and I hid in the shadows near the buildings. We had spent more than one night watching this street and never saw another person on it. The street had nothing to offer—no bars, no restaurants, no music, no prostitutes, no drug dealers. Only locked doors.

It was twenty after one when we reached the building. I had the key in my pocket. I had my backpack on my back. Inside the backpack I had my gun, a change of clothes, the wig, a roll of duct tape, some charcoal we had purchased from an art store, a small tool kit we had purchased from a hardware store, and my lucky, unopened pack of cigarettes. I had my knife strapped to the outside of my thigh with a Velcro strap. I didn't need to hide the knife for this job. To be seen was to be caught. To be caught was to fight. Michael had two knives and two guns. I asked him why he needed two guns. "One to aim," he said, "and one to create cover."

We stood outside the back door of the building. I took the charcoal out of my backpack. Michael nodded. I rubbed a thick layer of charcoal on my fingers. Michael leaned toward me. I took my darkened fingers and reached out, touching his face. I rubbed the charcoal into his cheeks, his forehead, and his chin. Streaks of gray ran across his pale face. I wasn't trying to cover his whole face. I was simply helping him to blend in with the shadows. When I was done, I handed Michael the charcoal and he did the same to me. I closed my eyes as he rubbed his fingers over my cheeks, down the bridge of my nose, and around my eyes. When he was done, I took the key out of my pocket. We stepped closer to the building. According to Palti, only six people would be working in the building at this time of night. Michael and I had surveyed the comings and goings the previous night to confirm this. Everything Palti had said to us about the building had checked out. The six employees included five Facility Patrolmen, one guarding each floor, and one Historian. It was a requirement to have at least one Historian on site at all times in case of emergencies. When I asked Palti how often emergencies pop up in the middle of the night, he smirked and said, "You'd be surprised." During the day, anywhere between four and eight Historians would be there. One or two of them would be stationed on each floor, and each Historian was supposed to stay in the archives on the floor he was assigned to that day. During the day, their key cards wouldn't even get them into the archives on other floors. The guards' key cards never gave them access to the archives. They spent years doing nothing but patrolling the hallways and corridors linking the archives. At night, when only one Historian was on duty, that Historian could go anywhere. His key unlocked every door.

The back door was large and thick. It had no handle, being fashioned primarily to be opened from the inside. It was painted black like the walls around it, so it wasn't easy to find. The night guard on the first floor was stationed at the front of the building. He usually stayed at his station, with no reason to walk the halls. Nothing on the first floor had any value. Besides, if anyone broke in through the back, the alarm would go off—the alarm that Palti was supposed to have already disconnected for us. After feeling my way through the darkness, I found the keyhole. I took the key out of my pocket, aligned it with the keyhole, and pushed. The key stopped when it had gotten only about halfway into the lock. I cursed Palti. He'd failed us already. Michael glared at me. His face told me that he had never trusted Palti to begin with. But it was an old lock. I jiggled the key. It moved. The key slid in the rest of the way.

Palti had given us the right key. We still needed him to have disabled the alarm for the plan to work, though. I twisted my wrist. The key turned in the lock. "Gentle," Michael whispered. Without a handle, I had to pull the key toward me while it was still in the lock to open the door. I held my breath, waiting for the unholy blaring of an alarm. Palti assured us we'd hear it if it went off. "The whole neighborhood will hear it," he said. It was a regular alarm, set up for vagrants and common thieves. The more sophisticated alarms were farther inside. The door creaked slightly as I pulled it open and then—silence. He may have been a liar, a thief, and a traitor, but Palti got us into the building.

We stepped inside. No lights were on in the back half of the building. The only light was the gray light leaking in from the front where the guard was stationed. Palti had drawn us a map of each of the five floors of the building. Michael and I had studied them, memorizing them so that we could move effortlessly through the darkness. Once we had committed the maps to memory, we shredded them. The first floor was little more than a long, snaking hallway. At different points in the hallway, doors on either side opened into large storage rooms. These doors were unlocked. There was no need to lock them. If thieves got that far, the storage rooms showed the thieves that there was nothing to steal here but old office furniture. Immediately in front of us, on the left side of the hallway, was the freight elevator. According to Palti, no one ever used the freight elevator. He wasn't even sure if it worked. Plus, it had its own separate locks and no one had a key. Michael carefully closed the back door behind us. The hall became even darker. We stood in silence, waiting for our eyes to adjust.

Once we could see well enough, we started walking silently down the hallway. The hallway ran all the way from the back to the front of the building, but there was a door halfway through the hallway, dividing the building in two. We were in the back half. The guard was in the front. Still, we knew we couldn't take any chances. The door dividing the hallway in two was adjacent to the door to the staircase. The passenger elevator was on the guard's side of the door. The stairs were on our side. That was okay. We weren't going to use the elevator anyway. We just had to be careful not to make any noises that the guard might hear through the hallway door and, if we did, we had to be ready to remedy the situation quickly. When we got to the door to the staircase, I took the gun out of my backpack and held it at shoulder height—the way I'd been taught— scanning the darkness for danger, ready to aim and shoot. Michael dropped to his knees in front of the door to the staircase, looking at the lock. I reached into my backpack and took out the tiny tool kit and handed it to Michael. After Palti described it to him, Michael was sure that he could pick the lock. I never doubted that picking locks was one of his skills. Picking the lock was only one of the hurdles, though. The door was also equipped with an alarm that was set to go off as soon as the door was opened. Michael couldn't disable the alarm from this side of the door. That's where the elevators came into play.

The elevators in the building were old and, according to Palti, painfully slow. The employees didn't trust them, even in the daytime. No one wanted to get trapped in one of the rickety elevators in the middle of the night. Besides, waiting for and riding the elevator from one floor to the next could take up to five minutes, when it would take only thirty seconds to take the stairs. The guards had hourly shift changes. Each hour on the hour, they would change floors. It was supposed to keep them fresh and alert, never letting anyone get too comfortable or too bored. It was also a check against napping. Each hour, the person on the fifth floor would go down to relieve the person on the fourth floor, who would go down to relieve the person on the third floor, and so on until the person on the first floor was relieved and sent all the way up to guard the fifth floor. The guards weren't supposed to take the stairs because the alarm on the stairs was supposed to be armed at all times. The guards were supposed to take the elevators. The guard whose shift changed from the first floor to the fifth floor almost always did. Everyone else weighed the risk of getting in trouble for the seemingly minor infraction of taking the stairs against waiting for an old, slow elevator that they didn't trust anyway. So they frequently bent the rules and took the stairs. Palti had worked plenty of night shifts. He'd seen them all do it. They'd disable the alarm, walk down a flight of stairs, leave the stairwell, and then reactivate the alarm. The stairway alarm was a single-alarm system, triggered by any of the doors leading to the stairwell from one of the five floors. When the alarm was disabled, anyone could open any door without fear of the alarm going off. So the plan was to listen to the stairwell. Listen for the rule breakers. We'd open doors only when someone else was in the stairwell, and even then only when we knew that they were far away.

"Five guards? That doesn't sound like enough," Michael had said to Palti as we went over the plan again. Michael believed he could take out all five guards on his own. He'd faced down as many as three professional killers at once, and Palti had described these guards as little more than card punchers.

"Five armed Facility Patrolmen guarding a building that no one is supposed to know exists, a building that hasn't had one attempted break-in for the twenty-plus years it's been in use." Palti looked up at

Michael. "But yes, there are only five guards at night. But each of those five has a gun and, even more dangerous than that, each carries with them a small yellow box with a red button on it. The button has a clear plastic cover that needs to be flipped up for the button to be pushed. But if someone pushes that button"—Palti shook his head— "hell will rain down on that building. If one of those buttons is pushed, you've got ten, fifteen minutes at most before the building is surrounded."

Kneeling in the darkness, Michael took two small metal tools out of his tool kit. They looked almost like dentists' picks. I stood over him, gun at the ready, listening for any sound, looking for any movement. No one was going to press that button on my watch.

Michael inserted the end of both tools into the lock on the stairwell door and twisted them. Michael held his ear close to the door. He worked the tools back and forth for what felt like two or three minutes. Then he replaced one of the tools with a different one from his kit. He did the same thing with those two for another minute or two. Then he stopped. I hadn't heard anything. Michael looked up at me, smiling. "I got it," he whispered, holding the picks in place. "It's an auto lock, though. As soon as I take out the picks, it will lock again."

"Don't open the door yet," I whispered back to him, "not until we know that the alarm's been disabled." Michael nodded. We didn't have to worry about the guard on the second floor taking the stairs, not yet. The guard on the fifth floor would move first. Without taking his tools from the lock, Michael placed his ear against the door and listened. I checked my watch. It was two minutes before two a.m. Our timing was close to perfect.

We waited, as still as stone. Michael was frozen with his ear against the door and his hands holding his tools in position in the lock. I stood over him, trying not to get distracted by the silence, trying to concentrate on making sure that we weren't discovered. The best-case scenario was that the guard on the fifth floor would use the stairs and that Michael would hear him. If Michael didn't hear him, then the guard on the fourth floor moving to the third floor would do. We only wanted to make it to the second floor on this shot. That was the plan.

I tried watching the darkness for anything suspicious, but I couldn't help but watch Michael's face too. One minute after two a.m., Michael's eyes lit up, and then he closed them tightly. "What is it?" I asked.

"Shhh!" he said without moving his hands from the lock. "I don't know. I don't know if I heard anything."

"We have to be sure," I whispered.

"I know," Michael said, pushing his ear harder against the door, closing his eyes to try to shun all his other senses. His hands started to move. "It's them," he said in a rushed, breathless voice. "They're on the stairs."

"You're sure?" I asked.

He nodded. "Pull the door," he ordered. "Quick." I reached forward and grabbed the metal handle on the door. I pulled and listened. At first there was no sound—no alarm, no nothing. Then, out of that nothingness, I heard footsteps. I couldn't tell how high above us the footsteps were. All I could tell was that they were coming down the stairs, inevitably getting closer to us. "Let's go," Michael said.

I stepped inside the stairwell. No light leaked through the cracks around the doors to the stairwell. It was pitch-black inside. Michael followed me and, as gently as he could, closed the door behind us. When the door closed, I saw the first flicker of light. It was a single flash like a silent bolt of lightning from over the horizon. Then it vanished. A second later, it flashed on and off again. Michael saw it too. We looked up the dark stairwell. Each flight of stairs between floors snaked around and ascended in the direction opposite from the flight below it, so the stairs leading from the second floor to the third floor were directly above our heads. This created a small platform at each floor where the stairs changed direction. The door to each floor was on this platform. We looked up. We could still hear the footsteps on the stairs. Whoever was walking down the stairs was carrying a flashlight and swinging it as he walked, creating the flashes of light and making the shadows in the stairwell dance. The footsteps were getting louder. "He has to be at least two stories up," I whispered to Michael. Michael nodded. I could barely make out the movement of his head in the darkness. The plan was an intricately timed dance. For it to work, we had to silently get to the top of the first flight of stairs, near the door to the second floor, before the guard from the third floor reached the second floor.

We moved up the stairs, side by side in the darkness, as fast as we could without making any noise. I could almost feel the weight of Michael's injured leg as we made our way up. He couldn't limp silently, so he refused to limp, gritting his teeth and ignoring the pain. I moved in front of him. We made it to the top of the first flight of stairs. We stopped only three or four steps below the second-floor platform. As practiced, we leaned our backs against the wall to the stairwell. I looked down at Michael. He was standing two stairs below me. I could see his shadowy silhouette in the darkness. He had one of his knives in his hand. I held my gun in front of me. We didn't want to be seen, but we were ready in case we were.

The footsteps that we'd heard were the footsteps of the guard on the fourth floor moving down to the third. Once we stopped moving, we heard the sound of the door on the third floor being opened. As it opened, light flooded the stairwell. I looked down at Michael again. He looked ridiculous in the light, standing with his back against the wall, hiding in plain sight like a toddler who doesn't yet understand the game of hide-and-seek. In the light, we were the most obvious things in the world. The only chance we had was that no one would look at us in the light and no one would notice us in the darkness. Michael had questioned this part of the plan when we mapped it out with Palti. "So, we're just supposed to stand there and hope no one looks at us?" he asked. Palti nodded, explaining the shape of the staircase again, explaining that there would never be any reason for anyone to look in our direction. "It's not that you have to hope that they don't look at you," Palti told us. "They won't look at you. They won't look at you because they don't want you to be there. To look is to suppose you might exist." The door to the third floor closed again, swallowing the light. Then the third-floor door opened one more time, this time so that the relieved guard on the third floor could come down to the second. We heard his footsteps. We saw the beam of his flashlight hit the second-floor platform above us. The guard was whistling. I recognized the song. It was a song that my father used to play for me on the jukebox at my favorite diner when I was a kid. I squeezed the handle of my gun with both my hands, trying to stay focused.

The guard reached the second-floor platform. He was so close to us. If I reached out, I could touch him. As Palti predicted, he didn't turn toward us. He didn't shine his flashlight in our direction. The guard reached out and pulled open the door to the second floor. Once again, light flooded the stairwell, this time shining directly on Michael and me. If the guard had turned around, it would have all been over. Instead he walked through the second-floor door, letting it close behind him.

"Now," I whispered to Michael. We had to move fast. We had to get out of the way before the guard on the second floor walked down to the first. As quickly and quietly as we could, we climbed up to the second-floor platform, past it, and then up three or four more steps. If the guard took the stairs, he'd have no more reason to look up at us than the other guard had to look down. Plus, as long as he was on the stairwell, we'd know that the alarm was disabled. We could watch him walk down toward the first floor and, when he walked through the first-floor door, we could slip through the door to the second floor before he had time to reactivate the alarm. Then we could end our little ballet, for an hour at least, and get down to work.

After only a minute or two, I saw the door open and the final guard step onto the stairwell. Though we'd already heard the footsteps of three of the five guards, this was the first one that I saw. It was a woman. She wasn't large but she wasn't small either. Her shoulders were broad compared to her waist. She let the door close behind her without looking up toward us. She stood there, waiting for the darkness before she flicked on her flashlight. Then she began walking down the stairs toward the first floor, chasing the beam of light in front of her.

Michael and I waited again, not saying a word, not needing to. So far the plan had worked perfectly. It worked exactly like Palti, Michael, and I had diagrammed it, exactly like Michael and I had practiced it. Unknowns stood in front of us, though. We had to walk through that door to the second floor with no way of knowing where the guard patrolling the second floor might be. We had to be ready to attack. We hadn't found any other way. We looked. Believe me, we looked. Violence was simply inevitable. Then, after dealing with the guard, we would have to start our search for the Historian. He was the only one who could get us inside the archives where your information was. The Historian literally held the key.

The female guard stopped halfway down the stairs leading to the first floor and turned back toward us. Had she heard something? She flicked the beam of the flashlight around the empty stairwell. I readied my gun. We were on the next flight of stairs. She couldn't see us from where she was standing, but if she came back up, we'd have to do something. I listened for the footsteps. Michael took a step closer to me. I reached back and put my hand on his chest, stopping him. The light turned away from us again. The guard began walking back down the stairs like she was supposed to.

Michael relaxed. We waited for the sound of the door. We knew the procedure. The female guard would relieve the guard on the first floor, who would take the elevator up to the fifth. In an hour, the whole thing would start all over again. Palti had shown us how to disable the stairwell alarms once we got onto the second floor. So that gave us an hour—one hour before the guards began switching places again, one hour before they'd realize something was wrong. We had one hour to find the Historian, get his key, and find your file. It would all be over soon, for better or worse. The female guard pushed open the door on the first floor, the door that Michael and I had entered through only minutes earlier. We saw the flash of light caused by the opening of the door and then the subsequent darkness. We had only a minute, maybe two, before the alarm was enabled again. Michael stepped down the stairs, pulling the door to the second floor open, holding his knife out in front of him like a hunter. I followed behind him, holding my gun in front of me. We walked through the door, nearly in unison, careful not to make a sound. The guard could be almost anywhere. If he saw us, we'd have to get to him before he could press his alarm or reach for his gun. Once through the door, I turned right and Michael turned left exactly like we'd practiced. We scanned the hallway. The element of surprise would buy us only a few seconds.

The hallway was empty. Either the guard was around the corner by the elevator bay or he was in the bathroom. Either way, we had a moment to position ourselves for our ambush. It was better this way, better with even a minute to prepare. Maybe we wouldn't have to kill him. We made our way down the hallway toward the elevators, walking in the same direction, communicating silently through looks and hand signals. If the guard was in this direction, we'd surprise him. If he was in the other direction, we'd set a trap for him. Either way, we were ready and unafraid. According to Palti, the guards were lazy. But they weren't really lazy. I knew that. Michael knew that. They simply didn't care—not about this. They cared about this only as much as other people made them care. Outside these walls, they had families to care about, lives to care about. I wonder how many people in this War are like Michael or Jared or your father, and how many people are like those guards.

We made it to the corner at the end of the hallway. Around the corner were the elevator bay and the second-floor archives. I let myself get excited for a moment, thinking that the Historian might be on this floor, might be right around the corner. We stopped before turning the corner and listened. Silence. Then I heard something, the rustling sound of movement. It wasn't coming from around the corner. It was coming from behind us. I reached out and tapped Michael on the shoulder. "He's in the bathroom," I whispered to Michael. "Should we go around the corner and wait for him?"

"No," Michael answered. "Let's jump him when comes out. He'll be more vulnerable then." I followed him as he jogged back past the stairwell door toward the bathroom. When we got closer, Michael motioned for me to stand on the other side of the bathroom door. I nodded and positioned myself. We had the door surrounded, each of us on one side with our backs pressed against the walls. We'd wait until he was outside the bathroom and then we'd take him. I knew my job. I'd block the door to the bathroom so that he would have no escape route.

We stood there for what seemed like a very long time. My internal clock kept reminding me that we had only an hour. I wanted to look at my watch to see how much time had passed, but I didn't dare sacrifice any of my concentration. Then we heard it: the sound of water running from a faucet. He was washing his hands. My body tensed. The door began to open. The hinge was on my side, so my view of the guard was blocked by the door as he stepped out into the hallway. I heard a sound like a gasp or a grunt. Then the door swung closed again and I could see. Michael had grabbed the man, pulling him forward, out of the doorway. By the time the door was closed, the guard was already down on his knees in front of Michael. Michael was holding his knife near the guard's chin. The guard's hands were held out, both pleading and showing Michael that he wasn't holding a weapon or the button. No one said a word. No one needed to. Everyone knew what was going on.

When the door closed, Michael looked up at me for a split second. The guard didn't move. He was too busy looking at the blade on Michael's knife. "Where's the Historian?" Michael asked, somehow shouting in a whisper.

"What?" the guard said, looking in my direction for a second, hoping I might have an answer that would chase away his terror and confusion. I could see his chest heaving up and down.

"The belt," I reminded Michael. "Don't forget the belt."

Michael nodded and turned back to the guard. "Give us your belt," he ordered. "Now!" Minutes were passing too quickly.

The guard reached down and unclipped his belt. Both the holster of his gun and the red button were clipped onto it. The button was exactly as Palti had described it: a small red button on a yellow, radio-enabled box with a clear plastic cover over it. I looked at the button and remembered Palti's warning. "Hand it to me," I said to the guard. I reached one hand out for the belt, aiming my gun at the guard's forehead with the other hand. I wanted him to see where I was pointing the gun. If he made a move toward the button, I would pull the trigger. He handed me the belt.

"Okay," Michael said. "Now where's the Historian? What floor is he on?"

"I don't know," the guard said. All the blood had run out of his face.

"I don't think you want to play games here," Michael told him, pushing the knife closer to his face. "You answer a few questions for us, and I promise you that you'll get to go home in one piece. Is the Historian on this floor?"

"No," the guard said quickly, somehow stammering over a single syllable. "He's not here."

"Then where is he?" I asked lowering the gun and looking into the guard's eyes.

"He was on the fifth floor when I was up there, but that was hours ago. He could have moved since then. I really don't know." The words were an apology, spilling out of the guard's mouth uncontrollably.

"Does he normally switch floors?" Michael asked.

The guard thought about the question for a minute. Then he shook his head. "Not this guy. He usually stays on one floor. He only moves when he's ordered to."

"Fifth floor?" Michael asked again. The guard nodded. "Get the tape," Michael said to me. I reached inside my backpack for the duct tape.

"What are you doing?" the guard asked.

"Keeping you safe," Michael answered.

"Put your hands behind your back," I ordered. Michael taught me how to tie a person's hands and feet with the duct tape so that escape was nearly impossible in any less than a few hours. I wrapped the tape tightly around the guard's hands, taping them together behind his back, twisting the tape so that it tied from multiple directions. Then I taped the man's legs together. He didn't say a word. He simply stared at Michael's knife. Finally, I pulled the man's hands down and taped his hands and feet together behind his back.

"What are you going to do with me?" the guard asked when I finished.

"We're going to put you in the bathroom," Michael said, "and you're not going to try to get out until someone comes and gets you." I don't think he believed us. I think he thought we were going to kill him. People in his War didn't leave survivors. He didn't know we weren't part of his War.

"Your mouth," I said to the man.

"Huh?" the man looked at me as if he'd forgotten that I was there.

"Close your mouth," I ordered him. Without asking any more questions, he closed his mouth and I wrapped tape twice around his head, covering his closed lips.

"Done?" Michael asked when I cut the last piece of tape.

"Done," I answered. I looked down at my handiwork. All that the guard could move was his eyes, which darted back and forth between me and Michael. Michael reached down and grabbed the man by the collar. Michael dragged him into the bathroom, pulling him into the stall farthest from the door. When Michael got back from the bathroom, he holstered his knife. "We need to disable the stairwell alarm," he said.

"And then the fifth floor," I said.

"And then the fifth floor," Michael echoed. We made our way to the box next to the stairwell door. Michael took his knife back out and popped open the box. A time existed when disabling the alarm would have been difficult. When it was originally installed, the control box contained numerous trip lines so that even the slightest mistake would have triggered the alarm. It would have taken hours to disarm the alarm if the trip lines were still in place. Lucky for us, the guards had more than hours. They'd had days, weeks, even years. They had already done the hard work for us, jerry-rigging the alarm so that they could easily disarm it before entering the stairwell. They had set up a system of switches that could be flipped on or off from any floor. Palti showed us how we could use their handiwork to easily pull the whole thing apart. Michael peered inside the box. I looked over his shoulder. I could see the two wires connected at the top. Michael reached out, still careful not to touch any other part of the box. He grabbed the wires and twisted their connector counter-clockwise. The connector came off after only three turns. Michael pulled the wires apart. Everything was quiet. We wouldn't have to worry about the door alarms anymore. Michael, still holding the separated wires in his hand, looked at me and smiled. "You ready?" he asked.

"Let's go," I said, walking past him to the door. I stopped at the door for a second, took a deep breath, and pulled open the door. It swung easily. The stairwell was silent. The alarm was dead. Michael followed me into the stairwell. We stood together in the darkness for a minute, letting our eyes readjust. Then we started up the stairs in unison.

We ran past the door to the third floor. I could feel it pulling me toward it like a magnet. The answer to everything that mattered in my life was on that floor, but we couldn't get it without getting the key first. We kept running. We ran past the fourth floor and kept running. I figured that we had only forty minutes before the next shift change. In forty minutes we had to get to the fifth floor, disable the guard, get the Historian's key, get back to the third floor, disable the guard on the third floor, find the information, and escape. It wasn't a lot of time. It was going to be close. I put my head down and ran faster, taking the dark steps two at a time, jumping ahead of Michael and his lame leg.

I made it up to the door leading to the fifth floor and waited for Michael to catch up. I counted in my head, once second, two seconds, three seconds. He was standing next to me in three seconds. Even so, it felt like wasted time. I gave Michael a quick look to make sure he was ready and not too winded. He nodded to me before we jumped through the door, much like we had done the last time. *Everything you do is practice for the next thing you do.* Like before, the hallway in front of us was empty. We didn't have to guess at the guard's location this time. We heard someone laughing at the other end of the hallway, around the corner from us, in front of the archives. We moved toward the sound, each of us holding our weapons in front of us, trying not to make any noise. We didn't have time to think about a plan. We knew what we had to do. Move more quickly than the guard does. Don't hesitate. Don't doubt. Just go.

We rounded the corner, still in unison. The moment we rounded the corner, I keyed in on the guard. He didn't suspect anything. He was facing away from us, looking into the archives, breaking protocol by talking on his cell phone. We didn't worry about what he was looking at. Despite his leg, Michael moved instinctively. He knew that the guard was in a vulnerable position. He got to the guard before the guard had a chance to turn around. He beat me there by two steps. By the time I reached the guard, Michael was already clutching the guard's left wrist, twisting it. If the guard had been smart, if he had been properly trained, he would have reached for his gun with his free hand. Instead, he turned and tried throwing a punch. As the guard swung, Michael grabbed the guard's right wrist. Michael now had both of the man's wrists in his grasp. Michael was about to either kick or knee the man to try to get him to the ground. That wasn't necessary. Instead I walked up to the man and placed the nozzle of my gun against his temple. "Don't move," I said in a voice I hoped would keep the guard calm. The guard turned his eyes toward me without moving his head.

Michael took the man's cell phone. He hung up the phone and threw it across the room. Then Michael reached out and unbuckled the guard's belt, taking the guard's gun and the button all at once. Michael stepped away from the guard and dropped the guard's belt behind him. I took two steps backward as well, trying to move to a safe distance from the guard. A bullet to the head would be as effective from two feet as zero. The guard stayed still, not taking any chances with his own life.

"What do you want?" the guard asked Michael.

"Him," Michael said, pointing into the archives. I hadn't even looked toward the archives. The walls separating the hallway from the archives were glass. We could see into the archives. We could see shelf after shelf full of bound papers sitting on top of dozens, if not hundreds, of file cabinets. I looked through the glass. Standing no more than ten feet away from us behind the glass was a short man with gray hair and a pair of small, round eyeglasses. He wasn't moving. He was staring at us, a look of shock and fear on his face. We didn't worry about sneaking up on the Historian. The Historians weren't armed. They didn't carry buttons. He had no way to sound the alarm. The only things we had to fear from the Historian were stubbornness and loyalty.

"The Historian?" the guard asked, dumbfounded. Michael nodded. "I don't have a key to get inside. He's the only one with a key."

"Does he like you?" Michael asked the guard. His tone of voice scared even me.

The guard's confusion was growing now, being fed by his fear, like oxygen feeding a fire. "We don't talk. I don't know," the guard stammered. Michael thought for a second. He was trying to decide what card to play next. Michael pulled out his gun. He aimed it at the guard. Now both of us were pointing our guns at him.

"Get on your knees," Michael ordered the guard. I could feel my stomach churn, unsure of how far Michael would be willing to take this charade. The guard hesitated for a second. Then he got on his knees. "Face the glass," Michael ordered him. The guard moved so that he was facing the glass, facing the still-frozen Historian. "The fucker puts names on papers and files them in columns for the living and the dead. He studies this history but he doesn't see the blood," Michael muttered to himself, just loud enough for the guard to hear. I could see the words register in the guard's face. That was Michael's goal. We didn't merely need the guard to be afraid. We needed him to sell his fear. Ultimately, the guard was irrelevant, a means to an end. We needed to get to the Historian.

Michael turned and looked through the glass directly at the Historian. He held his gun out to his side, pointing it at the guard's temple. "Come out," Michael yelled to the Historian. "Come out and nobody gets hurt." The Historian's hands were shaking. He looked frail and old. I wondered if he and Palti were friends. They must have worked together. The Historian looked down at the guard as Michael spoke, leaving no doubt that he could hear Michael through the glass and understood what was happening.

The Historian didn't reply. He barely moved. His eyes drifted from the guard, over to me, and back to Michael. The charcoal smeared on Michael's cheeks made him look menacing and more than a little crazy. The Historian shook his head slowly from side to side. Michael yelled again. "If you come out, we won't hurt you but if you don't come out, we will kill him." Michael pushed the nozzle of his gun into the guard's forehead. "Ask him for help," Michael whispered to the guard.

The guard stared at the glass in front of him. "Please, Seymour," the guard said as loudly as he could muster.

"Come on, Seymour," Michael echoed. "Don't let this man die for no reason."

Seymour stepped closer to the glass. He put one hand on the glass in front of him and stared down at the guard. "What happens if I come out?" he asked. The words were barely audible through the glass.

"We just want your key," I said, stepping forward between the kneeling guard and the glass. "We need it. We don't want to hurt anyone." I felt the mistake in my words as soon as I spoke them. I didn't need to see the pained look on Michael's face, like someone punched him in the gut, to know it was a mistake. We needed the Historian to be afraid of us. If he wasn't afraid, he wasn't going to open the door. My telling him that we didn't want to hurt anyone made him less afraid.

"Now we have to scare him again," Michael whispered to me. Our clock was running. I stepped back again so that the only thing between Michael, who was standing with his gun pointed at the trembling guard, and the Historian was a one-inch-thick piece of bulletproof glass. "You have ten seconds to open the door," Michael called out. Then he started counting down. "Ten. Nine." I watched the Historian. Michael was right. He wasn't afraid anymore. "Eight. Seven." He didn't believe that we'd go through with it. "Six. Five."

"Please," I shouted to the Historian in between Michael calling out numbers. The Historian wouldn't look up at me. Instead he stared down at his hands. "Four. Three." It was over. I had ended this guard's life as surely as if I'd shot him myself. "Two. One." When Michael said the word *one*, the Historian looked up to see what happened as if watching the end of a magic trick. The word seemed to hang in the air. For a moment there was no other sound. I looked over at Michael. "Fuck," he said under his breath, shaking his head. Then he took the gun and tucked it back into the waistband of his pants. The guard saw Michael do this and exhaled. He was still on his knees. He thought it was over, that he was being spared. For a second, I thought it was over too. We were wrong. Michael simply realized that the gun would be too loud. He couldn't risk firing it. Somebody on another floor might hear. He needed something quieter. Michael pulled out his knife. He walked up behind the guard before the guard had a chance to look back, before he had a chance to realize that this was how his life was going to end. Then Michael slit his throat from ear to ear. I heard a gurgling sound, not unlike the sound of a recently unclogged drain. It was the only sound the guard's body made. He fell to the floor with hardly a twitch. Almost immediately, blood began to pool on the wooden floor beneath his neck.

I looked away from the guard's body. I looked through the glass at the Historian. He had come forward and was standing there, both his hands pressed against the glass, his face nearly touching it. He was staring down at the guard's body in shock. I saw his lips move. "Why?" he said too quietly to hear. I knew that he didn't expect an answer. He was the Historian. He was supposed to be the one with all the answers.

Michael stepped closer to the glass. He leaned toward it. Michael's face was only inches from the Historian's. "We have the guard on the second floor tied up in the bathroom. If you don't get out here right fucking now, we're going to drag him up here and make you watch us kill him too. There's a female guard on the first floor. We'll get to her eventually if we have to. How many people do you want to kill tonight, Seymour?"

Seymour stared at Michael. "Me?" Seymour asked. He stared at Michael through the glass like he was staring at some brutal animal at a zoo.

"How many, Seymour?" Michael shouted, throwing his reservations about noise to the wind. When Seymour didn't move, Michael turned to me. "Watch him," he said loud enough for Seymour to hear him. "I'm going to go get the next one." Michael started walking away, toward the stairs.

"Wait," Seymour yelled as Michael walked away. Michael stopped. "If I give you the key, no one else dies?" Seymour asked. I wanted to shout to him "Yes!" but I'd already said the wrong thing once tonight.

"That's what I've been saying, Seymour," Michael said and continued walking away.

"Okay," Seymour said. "I'm coming out." Seymour walked toward the glass door. He pushed a button and swung the door open. I looked over at Michael. Michael was staring through the open door, staring at the pages and books full of information, full of details, full of secrets about the War. He almost looked entranced. Seymour stepped through the archive doors.

"Where's the key?" I walked up to him and asked.

"It's around my neck," Seymour said. I reached out and grabbed the lanyard he had around his neck. A small electronic key card was dangling on the end. I took out my knife and cut the lanyard from around Seymour's neck so that I didn't have to pull it over his head. Like that, I was holding the key in my hand.

I stepped away from the Historian and slipped my backpack off my shoulder. "What are you doing?" Michael asked.

"I'm getting the tape out," I told him, "so that we can tape him up like we planned."

Michael shook his head. "There's no time for that. We're behind schedule. Besides, if we bring him with us, he can show you where to look. He can help you find it. Without him, it will take too long." Michael was right. We couldn't have more than twenty-five minutes left. We were still going to have to incapacitate the guard on the third floor and then find your file. I looked through the glass at the seemingly endless files in the archives. We'd never make it out if we had to find your file ourselves.

"You're right," I said, pulling my backpack back onto my shoulders. I aimed my gun at Seymour. "Don't try anything funny," I said. "We're going down—"

"—to the third floor," Seymour finished my sentence.

"How did you know?" I asked. I could feel Michael becoming impatient behind me.

"I recognize you," the little man said with no pride in his voice. "I know why you've come."

For the first time that I could remember, I was happy to be recognized. "You know where my son's file is?" I asked.

"Yes," he said.

"Then take me to it," I ordered him.

"Are you sure that's what you want?" the Historian asked. "Are you sure that's what's best for him?" Who was he to ask what is best for you? He was a nobody—a file clerk. I'm your mother.

"Let's go," I said, waving the gun toward the stairs. Seymour started walking. I walked behind him. Michael followed me. I kept the gun aimed at Seymour's back. We stepped into the dark stairwell. "Can you see enough to walk down?" I asked Seymour, speaking as quietly as I could.

"I think so," Seymour answered. We started descending through the darkness, praying we were alone. Seymour moved slowly, testing each step before moving.

"Fuck this," Michael whispered in my ear. I could just make out the outline of his face. "I'm going ahead. I'll take out the guard while you guys are coming down. Give me the key card. Once I finish with the guard, I'll start going through the files. We need every minute."

"Okay," I answered. I handed Michael the key card.

Michael slipped past Seymour. Seymour kept walking, slowly, carefully. The shadow that was Michael disappeared around the corner as he passed the entrance to the fourth floor. I kept the gun aimed at the old man. A second after Michael disappeared around the corner, the stairwell lit up for a moment, the light leaking through the doorway as Michael opened the door to the third floor. For a second, I saw us—the feeble man in front of me, me aiming a gun at him—and no one else. When the door closed, the darkness swallowed us up again.

The old man almost slipped once. I had to reach out to grab his arm to keep him steady, but eventually we made it. I ordered Seymour to open the door to the third floor. He hesitated and then he pushed it open. It was quiet on the other side. We stepped into the hallway. It was empty. I saw no sign of Michael or the guard. "Keep moving," I said to Seymour, pushing his shoulder with the nozzle of the gun. The old man turned down the hallway and began walking toward the archives.

We turned the corner. I still didn't see anyone. The doors to the archives were propped open. Someone had jammed books against the base of the doors, using them as doorstops. Seymour stopped walking for a second when he saw those books, as if he'd come upon another dead body. I pushed him forward.

After a few more steps, I could see inside the archives. I could see Michael. He was alone. Clearly, he had already disposed of the guard. Michael hadn't left a trace. Behind the glass, Michael was pulling file after file off the bookcases and rummaging through the file cabinets. He was glancing at them, looking at the names on the top, and then hurling the papers in the air behind him. The paper amassed on the floor like snow.

"What are you doing?" Seymour yelled. He broke out into a trot toward Michael. It was the fastest he'd moved all night. "You can't do that!" Seymour shouted as he ran.

Michael didn't even bother to look in Seymour's direction until the old man was only two or three feet away from him. Then Michael flicked out his knife, as if he'd been holding it up his sleeve, waiting for an opportunity to perform the trick. The Historian stopped, his nose only a centimeter from the tip of Michael's knife.

"I can do whatever I want," Michael said to the little old man. "There aren't any rules when you're not playing the game." Michael didn't tell the Historian what he was really doing. We had discussed this beforehand. This was part of the plan. We had to create a diversion. We had to make sure that they didn't know what information we'd actually come for. If they realized that we were looking for you, they'd move you before I ever got a chance to take you back. So instead we decided that we would take nothing from the building. We would leave every slip of paper. I would memorize your address. And we would wreak havoc with the information so that they would never know what we cared about and what was merely garbage on the floor.

The Historian looked at the papers strewn about his feet. He didn't cry when Michael killed the security guard on the fifth floor, but I thought he might cry now. "Where's my son's file?" I asked him.

He looked back at me, then turned and glared at Michael one last time. "This way," he said, motioning for me to follow him. We walked past row after row of files. I counted eight rows before Seymour stopped. Then he turned and started walking down one of the small corridors in between the bookshelves. He walked about two-thirds of the way to the end. I followed right behind him, still pointing the gun at him. We were in the middle of the floor, lost amid the records, lost amid the secrets. In each bookshelf were stacks of files, each full of somebody's story. "It's here," Seymour said, motioning toward one of the file cabinets on the floor.

"Get it out," I ordered him. I tried my best not to let him see that my hand was shaking. He bent down and pulled on the small handle on the top drawer of the file cabinet. The cabinet opened slowly but silently. Inside the drawer were dozens of hanging paper files, each with a typed label on the top. The Historian, with practiced hands, riffled through them. His eyes scanned the label on each file before he flipped to the next one. Then he stopped, his hands gripping a green folder containing only two or three papers.

"Ah," he said, "here it is." He sounded somewhat joyful, as if he forgot he had a gun pointing at him. He lifted the folder out of the cabinet.

"Give it to me," I ordered him, my heart beating so strongly that I could hear it like a metronome in my head. Seymour handed me the file. I opened it. It was only three pages long. The first page had a picture of your father on it and listed his defining characteristics— his height, estimated weight, eye color, and hair color. The next sheet of paper had a picture of me with the same list beneath it. The third page had a picture of you. It was taken after they'd stolen you from me. You were bigger in the picture. You'd grown. Beneath your picture was typed the name that they'd given you and your actual birth date (Jared must have known exactly when you were born). Beneath your birth date was the phrase, in all capital letters: *ADOPTED—ORPHAN OF WAR*. Another date was listed beneath that. The second date listed was roughly three weeks after they'd taken you from me. It must have taken them three weeks to settle you into a new home. Beneath that date was a man's name and a woman's name, tagged with the labels *Father* and *Mother*, respectively. I tried to control my breathing. I tried to remember where I was. Beneath those names was an address. You were in California, in a town called Mendocino. I stared at the address. I said it to myself over and over again to make sure that I wouldn't forget it, not as long as there was breath in my body. I handed the folder back to the

Historian. "Put it back in the cabinet," I said. He looked at me like I was crazy. "Put it back," I ordered him. He took the file from me, leaned back over the file cabinet, and put the file back in its place.

"Let's go," I said to the old man, motioning for him to walk in front of me, back to where Michael was. He gave me a confused look, like he was actually expecting us to let him go once he'd given us the information I was looking for. "Move," I ordered the man who had been free to look at your picture and your address every single day. He'd had everything I wanted. He'd had it for months.

Michael did a number on the archives. I soon found myself walking through nearly ankle-deep streams of paper. Michael was still busy dumping out files when we found him. He had an insane look of pleasure on his face, as if creating this chaos was one of the greatest things he'd ever done. Michael threw another set of files in the air and let the paper drift down around him. Then he noticed us coming toward him. "Did you get it?" he asked.

"Yes," I told him.

"Good," Michael said. I stepped closer to him, farther away from Seymour. Killing Seymour hadn't been part of the plan, but we both knew that we couldn't avoid it now. He knew too much. He knew why we were there. He could have ruined everything. I don't feel bad. Seymour wasn't innocent. Who's guiltier: the man who pulls the trigger or the man who tells him where to aim the gun?

Seymour figured it out too. "You promised me," he said, his voice shaking as he backed away from us.

"I'm sorry, Seymour," I said as he began to backpedal faster.

"You said that no one else would get hurt," Seymour stammered.

Michael shrugged. "Haven't you learned anything from all these papers, Seymour? More people always get hurt." Seymour turned and ran. He had to know that there was no escape, but he fled anyway. He used all the life he had left in him to run. Michael leapt after him, his knife drawn. Seymour ran between the shelves full of files. Michael was quickly catching up to him. When Seymour could feel Michael bearing down on him, he turned down one of the smaller corridors, reaching out and toppling one of the shelves behind him. The shelf fell with a crash, knocking into the shelf beside it. They both came tumbling down. The books on them flew into the air, their pages coming loose and drifting to the ground. Seymour kept running, finding energy that could come only from being chased by death. Michael put away his knife and pulled out his gun. We didn't have time for the chase. Seymour made it to the end of the stacks and turned down another corridor. Michael sidestepped the clutter and got one clear line of sight through the shelves. He barely had time to aim before pulling the trigger. As fast as Seymour had been going, it wasn't fast enough. He fell in a ball to the ground. Michael was blocked from walking to Seymour, but my path was clear. When I reached him, I heard him moaning. Michael had aimed for his chest, worrying more about stopping him than killing him. When I got to Seymour, he was still alive. I aimed my gun at Seymour's head and pulled the trigger. I didn't need to fire a second shot.

We had gotten what we came for. Now it was only a matter of getting out before the two remaining guards realized that no one was coming to relieve them from their posts. That's all that was supposed to be left anyway. I looked down at my watch. We had five minutes before the guards were supposed to change shifts. After that, we had an extra five minutes, tops, before the guards realized something was wrong.

"Let's go," I called across the room to Michael. I was standing over Seymour's body. "We're done. We don't have a lot of time." Michael was standing on top of pages and pages of paper. Years of secrets were strewn about his feet.

I expected Michael to look excited. We'd done it. The months we'd spent together running, planning, and fighting had finally paid off. His scars, his injuries, they weren't for nothing. Instead, Michael's face was drawn; his eyes were far away. "You go ahead," he said to me. "I'll catch up."

We had a plan. This wasn't it. "What do you mean? It's time to go," I yelled at him.

I looked at his hand. He was holding Seymour's key card. "I need to go upstairs," he said, "to the fifth floor. I've got the key. I can find the answers."

I should have known better than to give Michael the key. I should have realized that he wouldn't be able to help himself once he got this close to all those secrets. "You don't have time," I yelled to him.

"I'll meet you back at the hotel," he said, refusing to argue. Before I could say anything else, he turned and ran out of the archives, toward the stairwell. I tried running after him. He moved quickly, even on his wounded leg. I had to dodge a few fallen bookshelves and nearly slipped on the fallen papers on the ground. I ran around the corner and made it just in time to see the door leading into the darkness of the stairwell swing closed.

I didn't have time to follow him. I had what I'd come for, what I'd sacrificed so much for. Michael was on his own. I could only hope that he'd make it out okay. I took a deep breath and pulled open the door to the stairwell. I stepped into the darkness. I could hear footsteps on the stairs above me—Michael's footsteps. They were growing quieter as he got farther away. I started running down the stairs as quickly as I could without falling, heading away from Michael, heading for the exit. I'd be outside in a minute, breathing the fresh air, standing beneath the open night sky. I reached the platform between the first and second floors. I rounded the corner. I was almost free.

I saw the light before I heard the sound. It was a short, quick flash of light, little more than a spark in the darkness. Even that tiny spark made colors dance in my eyes. Was there a bang too? There must have been, but I didn't notice it. My brain must have been too confused by the light. I heard the bang after I saw the second flash, though. For a split second, the stairs around me were illuminated. I could see into the shadows. I was still alone on the stairwell. Michael wasn't. The gunshots were coming from different guns. I heard another shot echoing down the staircase like the sound of distant fireworks. I stopped. I was halfway down the last flight of stairs but I wasn't moving anymore. I was waiting for another gunshot. Everything was quiet. I looked down the stairwell. I could make out the outline of the door to the ground floor. I never would have gotten anywhere without Michael. What if one of those shots hit him? I couldn't abandon him like that. I turned around. Then I began running back up the stairs.

I ran past the door to the second floor, wondering if the guard was still tied up in the bathroom. I turned the corner and kept running. I passed the door to the third floor, picturing the utter chaos that we'd left inside. As I neared the platform in front of the fourth floor, I squinted, barely able to make out a shape slumped in the shadows in the corner. It wasn't moving. I climbed two steps closer to the platform. On my second step, I kicked something that was lying on the stairs. I bent down. It was a long metal flashlight. I held it in my hand for a second, unsure of what to do. I listened for noises, trying to make sure that no one else was in the stairwell. It was quiet. I pointed the flashlight at the ground and flicked it on. A cavern of light erupted through the darkness. I lifted the flashlight toward the platform, afraid of what I might see. Before I could even make out the outline of the shape in the corner, the light from the flashlight reflected back at me from a pair of eyes. It was a body but it wasn't Michael's body. It was a large man, slightly overweight. He had a uniform on. His head was hanging loosely on his neck, his lower jaw resting against his chest. I moved the flashlight toward his hands. He was still gripping a gun.

I stepped onto the fourth-floor platform and moved the flashlight beam up the stairs toward the fifth floor. The stairs were empty, but halfway up, their color changed. I began leaping up the stairs, skipping steps as I went, until the blood started. Then I kept running, moving to one side of the stairwell, trying to avoid slipping in Michael's blood.

I got to the top of the stairs and pushed the door open. Beneath the fluorescent lights, the blood on the floor took on a vibrant shade of red. It almost glowed. I dropped the flashlight and followed the trail of blood into the archives. The key card was lying on the floor in front of the glass doors. There was blood on it. I picked it up and used it to unlock the doors. I ran through them. "Michael!" I shouted, knowing that we barely had any time to get back down the stairs. The only response was the sound of shuffling papers. I followed the noise through the labyrinth of shelves. "Michael!" I shouted again. He still didn't answer. I ran to the end of the corridor, chasing the sound. That's where I found Michael. He was sitting on the floor, surrounded by pieces of white paper, half of which were now colored by his blood. I watched him grab another sheet, seemingly at random, and look at it. "Michael," I said, more softly now.

He looked up at me, his eyes wet. "Why are you here?" he asked me. "You weren't supposed to follow me. I told you to go."

"I heard the gunshots," I told him. "I couldn't desert you like that." I looked for the wound on Michael's body. I couldn't see anything. Then I saw the blood seeping through the back of his shirt. He'd been shot in the back. It was bad. "We have to get out of here," I ordered. "We have to get you to a hospital. We still have at least five minutes."

Michael shook his head. We didn't have five minutes. "He hit the button." I didn't understand what Michael was saying at first. "The guard on the fourth floor," Michael explained, "he must have heard us going down the stairs with the Historian. He was waiting for me when I came back up. He hit his button right before I shot him."

They were already on their way. Palti had warned us. *If someone pushes that button, hell will rain down on that building.* "Then we need to go now, before they get here." I stepped forward and grabbed Michael's arm, pulling him to his feet. It was like lifting deadweight.

"I won't make it. Even if I get outside, they'll find me." He looked down at the blood on everything around him. "I can't hide anymore." He looked up at me, his eyes on fire. "Go, Maria. Run."

I didn't hesitate. Michael was right. I couldn't save him. It was too late. If I moved quickly, I could still save you. So I ran. I ran out of the archives and toward the stairwell. I expected total darkness when I entered the stairwell, but it was full of light dancing along the walls. Then I heard footsteps—lots of footsteps. They were still at the bottom of the stairwell, but I could hear them. Hell was already raining.

I pushed open the door to the fifth floor again and ran back inside. I retraced my steps toward Michael. "They're already here!" I shouted. "They're in the stairwell!"

Michael answered me this time. "Are they close?" he shouted back to me, with a strength I didn't think he still had in him.

"Not yet," I yelled back, "but they're coming."

A second later, Michael was standing in front of me. His face was pale but he didn't look weak anymore. "We have to get you out of here," he said, shuffling past me, toward the elevators. He walked up to the elevator, aimed, and fired two shots into the elevator's buttons.

"Will that keep them from being able to ride the elevator up?" I asked, hoping Michael knew what he was doing.

"Probably not," Michael said, "but it's worth a shot." We walked past the passenger elevators and around the corner toward the stairwell. We saw the entrance to the freight elevator, the one that nobody used. There was a button next to it. Michael pushed the button to see what would happen. Nothing. He kicked the freight elevator doors. Then he stepped forward and tried to pry open the doors with his fingers. "If we can get it open, maybe you can climb down the cable," he said. I was standing near the door to the stairwell. I put my ear against it. I could hear them climbing, getting closer. "Fuck!" Michael shouted and kicked the freight elevator doors again. They wouldn't open, not without a crowbar.

"Easy, Michael," I said. "Those doors aren't opening. We have to stay calm." Even as I said the words, my heart was racing. Sweat was seeping out of my pores. We settled in, facing the stairwell doors, our guns at the ready, waiting for the deluge. For a moment, everything was quiet. I looked at Michael. I knew we didn't have much time, but I had to ask. "Did you find anything?"

Michael knew immediately what I was asking. He shook his head. "There was too much information. I couldn't make sense of any of it."

"Why did it suddenly matter?"

Michael shrugged. He didn't look at me when he spoke. "I'm a fighter, Maria. I need something to fight for. And this"—Michael waved his hand between the two of us—"was almost over." Then our conversation was interrupted by the sound of a ringing bell at the other end of the hall. Michael and I both heard it. We looked at each other, momentarily confused. "The elevator," Michael said.

I turned in time to see two of Them running toward us down the hallway. I lifted my gun, holding it in two hands and looking down the sights like Clara's people had taught me. I aimed, adjusting slightly for the first man's speed, and fired. Then, without hesitating, I moved the sights of the gun to the second man, aimed, and fired again. Both men fell to the ground almost simultaneously.

"Looks like the elevator still works," Michael said, not bothering to comment on my shooting. "That means that there will be more of them soon." I put my ear back against the door to the stairwell. They were moving slowly. Either they didn't know that there were only two of us or they didn't know what floor we were on. "Where are they?" Michael asked.

"Still at least two floors down," I said.

"The roof," Michael said. "The stairs keep going up. Maybe you can get on the roof. Maybe you can escape from there." It was an idea—the only one that had any chance of working.

"It's worth a shot," I said. "But we need to move now."

"No. We have a few seconds," Michael said, breathing heavily. I didn't understand why we would wait, but I trusted him. "You still have that pack of cigarettes?" Michael asked.

"My good-luck cigarettes?"

"Yeah," Michael said. "Give me one."

"What for?" I asked, thinking that there was some aspect to Michael's plan that I didn't understand. I should have known better. Michael never was much of a planner.

"I'm going to smoke it," he said. I reached into the backpack and grabbed the unopened pack of cigarettes. I pulled out a cigarette and handed it to him. Then I pulled out a lighter and lit it. I could hear the footsteps through the door now. They were getting closer. "Give me your gun too," Michael said, inhaling on the cigarette.

"What for?" I asked again.

"Because I'm going to need a lot of bullets," Michael answered.

"If we leave now, you can come with me. We can both make it." I knew it was a lie but felt compelled to say it anyway.

Michael laughed a pained laugh, the cigarette dangling from his lips. "Do me one favor, Maria," Michael said. I looked at the lines on his face. He looked tired. "When you find Christopher, tell him about me," Michael said while looking at each of his three guns, trying to figure out how many bullets were in each. Then he looked at me again for the last time. "Do what I was never able to do. Make my life mean something." I nodded. My throat was too dry to speak.

"Are they at the bottom of our staircase yet? We need them to be close so that the light will blind them, even if it's only for a second." That's why we were waiting. I knew Michael had a reason. I put my ear to the door. They were close. I nodded to Michael again to let him know that it was almost time. As I nodded, the bell from the elevator rang again. They were everywhere.

"When we go through, you go up," Michael said. "Don't look back." I heard footsteps coming toward us from the direction of the elevator. There was so much more to be said, but there wasn't any time. Unable to think of anything to say, I leaned forward and kissed Michael on his cheek. He stared down at his hands. Then he reached out for the door handle. His eyes were steel. He wasn't afraid. He didn't know how to be. Michael swung open the door to the stairwell and stepped through it. I followed him. Michael turned toward the stairwell below us, a gun in each hand and one more tucked into his belt. He started shooting before I even made it through the door, painting the stairwell with bullets. I didn't look back. I ran. I ran up the stairs, gunshots echoing behind me. At first it was only Michael, but before I reached the top of the stairs, the sound of his guns was joined by the sound of a whole orchestra of gunfire. I reached the door at the top of the stairs, threw all my weight against it, and burst through.

It felt like leaping into cold water. The air outside was cool and quiet. It was brighter on the roof, bright enough to see without a flashlight. I didn't know how much time I had. I ran to the edge of the roof. I ran toward the front of the building. There was no way down from there, no fire escape, nowhere to jump. The street in front of me was wide and lined with sidewalks. When I got to the lip of the roof, I glanced down. Four men in black uniforms were guarding the front door. I knew the back of the building wouldn't be any better as far as escape routes went. The street there was thinner but still too wide to jump across. I looked toward the sides of the building. The building to my right was taller than the one I was standing on. It towered over me like a brick wall. The building to my left was a full story shorter than the one I was on. My only chance was to jump over the edge, hoping to clear the distance between the buildings like I'd seen in so many movies. I ran to the edge and looked over. The space separating the buildings was about eight feet. A year ago, the gap would have been too wide. I wouldn't have had the courage or the strength to jump it.

I backed up to get a running start. I couldn't believe that Michael was still holding them off. They must not have known that I was there. They must not have been looking for me. I flexed my calves, readying myself to run.

"Stop!" a voice shouted from behind me. It was a woman's voice. She sounded armed. I had an urge to reach for my own gun, to turn and fire like I was in a duel. Then I remembered that I'd given my gun to Michael. I slowly turned around.

I could see the woman's face in the moonlight. It was the guard from downstairs. I could tell by her uniform. She wasn't one of the professional killers responding to the dead guard's alarm. I thought about running, hoping that she wouldn't have the courage to pull the trigger or the aim to make it matter. We made eye contact. Her gun was pointed directly at me. I didn't know if she knew how to shoot, but she definitely knew how to aim. She lowered the gun for a moment. She took a step closer to me. "I know you," she said with tangible surprise in her voice. "You're the woman with the baby," she said. *The woman with the baby*—the words echoed in my head. "What are you doing here?" she asked.

I steadied myself. "I'm trying to find my son." I hoped that she might have children of her own. "You guys keep the information about where he is here."

I could see the uneasiness in the woman's gaze. I could feel her doubt. "What are you going to do if you find him?" she asked, like so many people had asked me before.

"I'm going to save him," I said.

"From what?" She took another step closer to me, raising the gun so that it was aimed at my chest.

"From this," I answered her. We could hear the commotion going on inside the building as the summoned killers found the guard's body on the fifth floor. "Please let me go. No one needs to know you let me go. No one needs to know that I was here." She was close enough now that I could see the pity in her eyes. I had killed or helped kill four of her coworkers, but she was a woman, maybe a mother herself. She knew that there were things in this life more worthy of pity than death.

She lowered the gun. "Go," she said, whispering the word into the night. I didn't give her a chance to change her mind. I turned around and ran toward the side of the building. When I got to the edge, I leapt.

Forty-five

It was early afternoon when Addy and Evan finally turned off the highway toward the swamps. They'd left Atlanta in the dim light of the dawn. They were still driving the car they'd taken from the screaming woman with the child in Louisiana, though they'd replaced the Louisiana plates with Georgia plates. They spent most of the day's drive passing through flat, open land dimpled with billboards, strip malls, and golf courses. It was only during the last bit, miles from the main roads, that they were engulfed in dense thickets of trees and surrounded by swampland. It was here, hidden inside the dense swamps that were hidden inside the constructed sprawl of the Florida suburbs, where they hoped to find Addy's old friends. Reggie's compound was somewhere in these swamps. Addy had made this drive hundreds of times. Many of those times, like now with Evan, she was bringing someone with her for the first time, preparing to introduce him to his new life. Nothing was ever the same for the people Addy took to the swamps. They were abandoning their lives, their family, their friends, their purpose, and putting all of their faith in her and Reggie. Even with those hundreds of drives under her belt, Addy couldn't remember ever being as nervous as she was at that moment. Even the first time she made the drive, she'd been too naive to be truly frightened. She wasn't as naive anymore.

It was hot and humid, even hotter and more humid in the swamp than it had been on the open road. Addy rolled down her window and made Evan do the same. She turned off the air-conditioning in the car. She wanted to be able to hear everything. She was hoping to hear voices traveling over the swamp as they drove closer to the compound. With the windows down and the air-conditioning off, Evan could feel sweat starting to drip down his forehead. A mosquito flew into the car through the open window. Evan heard it buzz by his ear before landing on the back of his neck. He felt the pinch of the mosquito bite before his open hand flew up, crushing the bug against his skin. Evan pulled his hand back. The crushed bug stuck to his palm, surrounded by a ring of blood.

With the heat, the mosquitoes, and the silence, Evan felt like they'd already driven dozens of miles since they turned off the last paved road. At the speed Addy was driving, Evan knew that his mind was playing tricks on him. They'd be lucky if they'd driven a single mile. Speed wasn't an option anymore. Addy was leading the car over a slim, winding strip of solid ground elevated above the surrounding swamp. The strip wasn't much wider than the car. A wrong turn would drop them into thick mud that they would never be able to pull out of. Trees grew out of the swamp surrounding them, the roots plunging down into the murky water. Evan looked out the window, scanning the water for movement. All he saw were dragon-flies and mosquitoes. He didn't hear anything. There was nothing to hear. He wondered when that should start making him nervous. "How much farther?" he asked Addy.

"We're about halfway," Addy said without looking at him. He noticed the tension in her voice.

"You're sure this is safe?" Evan asked. Addy ignored the question and kept driving. Come on, Evan, she thought instead. You know better than to ask me that.

A few minutes later, Evan noticed the solid ground beneath their car growing wider. They were nearing some sort of island in the swamp. After the maze they'd just driven through, Evan wondered how anyone ever found this place. He decided not to annoy Addy with any more questions.

George saw Addy *and Evan's car coming slowly out of the swamp before Sam did. It was easier to see through George's binoculars than through the scope of Sam's rifle. When George saw the car, he nudged Sam on her shoulder and motioned toward the beat-up car. Sam immediately fixed her sights on it, focusing the scope of her rifle just above the driver's-side door. She aimed for the open window. She and George had already been sitting in the tree for eight hours without seeing a single thing worth noticing. They weren't surprised. It was their third shift staking out the compound in the past week, and they hadn't seen anything unexpected during the first two shifts either. No one did. Ever since the night of the raids, every-thing had been quiet. Each shift, Sam and George simply sat in the hunting nest nailed into one of the trees surrounding the compound and silently waited.*

George and Sam watched the car as it pulled to a stop. Two people got out. George eyed them both. He could switch focus with the binoculars quicker than Sam could with the scope of the rifle. George and Sam were trained. They knew their roles. George's job was to watch. Until she got the word, Sam's only job was to aim.

"There are two of them," George whispered to Sam. "A man and woman. They look young. The man is maybe five-eleven with short, dark hair. The woman is probably about five-four or five-five with long red hair." Sam kept the rifle pointed at the red hair on the woman. It was the easiest trait to follow against the thick green and brown background of the swamp. Through the rifle scope, it was impossible to get a good look at the woman's face. "They don't seem to suspect that they're being watched," George finished.

Evan knew something *was wrong before he even understood what he was looking at. The mass of black, charred wood in front of them had once been a building. He could see that now. The shape of the building's foundation covered most of the hard ground on the island in the swamp. From his seat in the car, it looked to Evan like the building's foundation was almost the only thing left. A few pieces of the wall were still standing, but even those looked like they were moments away from crumbling into a pile of ash, all charred black with unnatural cracks where light showed through. Before he could say anything, Addy got out of the car.*

Evan got out too, chasing Addy. "I don't know if this is safe," Evan called out to Addy, but she ignored him again. Instead Addy began to walk quickly toward the remains of the building, almost jogging. Evan ran after her. As he ran, he saw how much bigger the building was than it first appeared. Somehow, whoever built the building was able to build it downward into the earth, despite the surrounding swamp. When they reached the edge of the building's foundation, Evan looked down into the pit. Before it burned down, a whole story of the building had been buried underground. Most of the ground floor had collapsed into the floor below it, covering everything with broken, burnt wood. Looking into the pit, Evan could see partially burnt desks and singed metal cabinets with their empty drawers pulled out. "Jesus," Evan said, "how big was this place?"

"More than thirty of us worked here," Addy finally answered him, kicking a charred piece of wood over the lip of the building and sending it tumbling into the pit.

George and Sam *kept their sights on the targets, following the couple from the car to the remains of the building. Their orders couldn't have been clearer. They weren't there to simply watch and take notes. They had a mission. Part of that mission included orders to shoot and kill anyone suspicious who came to the compound. They were supposed to lose the bodies in the swamp. Without taking her eye away from the scope of the rifle, Sam began to stretch her fingers so that she could pull the trigger twice in quick succession. The faster she could get from the first target to the second, the easier it would be. The less time that the second person had to run, the better. "Give me the word," Sam whispered to George, and rested her index finger back on the trigger.*

"What do you *think happened?" Evan asked, unable to contain his questions. He thought he probably knew. He thought he'd lived through it. It looked like whoever had been here followed the same MO as the people who attacked them in Los Angeles. He looked down at the rubble. Whoever had burned the compound down had apparently cleaned the bodies out too. Evan saw no evidence of life in the pit, nothing but old furniture and crumbling walls.*

"Over there," Addy said, pointing toward the back corner of the compound, "that's where Reggie's office used to be. It didn't have windows. Reggie used to say that when they finally came for him, he didn't want to see them coming. It must have been a massacre."

George reached over *and placed a hand gently on Sam's shoulder. She tensed. It had been a long time since Sam killed someone, but she was ready to fire, shift her aim, and fire again. Killing isn't something that you forget how to do. "Wait," George whispered to her. He was still staring intently at the couple through his binoculars. "Don't fire," he said. "Don't shoot," he said, his voice growing louder.*

For the first time since the car pulled up, Sam took her eye away from the rifle's scope. "Come on, George," she whispered. "What's going on?"

George reached over and grabbed Sam's rifle, pulling it so that the barrel was aimed anywhere but at the targets. Sam shot George a look,

*wondering if he'd gone mad. George thrust the binoculars into Sam's hands.
"I think it's her," he said, barely containing his excitement.*

"Who, the redhead?" Sam asked.

*"Forget the hair. Look at her face. It's Addy," he said to Sam. "Holy shit,
I think it's Addy."*

*Sam took the binoculars from George and aimed them toward the
woman with the red hair. She twisted the knobs on the binoculars to focus
them better. The last time Sam had seen Addy, her hair was an ordinary
brown color. Sam and George didn't know that Addy dyed her hair red
when she joined the revolution. It didn't matter. Addy's face hadn't changed.
Sam waited a second until Addy turned toward them. That's when Sam
saw Addy's face. "It is," Sam said to George, not bothering to whisper anymore. "It's Addy."*

*They stood up. "Addy!" George shouted as loudly as he could, as if there
was nothing in the world to be afraid of. He leapt in the air. "Addy!" he
shouted again, waving his arms wildly.*

Addy heard the *shouting coming across the swamp from the trees. Even
though it was impossible, it sounded like someone was yelling her name. If
she hadn't been so numb from staring at the burnt corpse of the compound,
Addy would have been smart enough to be afraid. She would have grabbed
Evan and made a run for it, back to the car. Instead she lifted her head
toward the voice and scanned the trees for the sound. She half expected to
turn and have the tip of a bullet be the last thing she ever saw. Instead she
saw a figure in the distance, dressed in full camouflage, standing impossibly
on the branches of a tree, jumping up and down and waving his arms in
the air.*

"Addy!" George yelled again.

*Before even being sure she wasn't going insane, Addy started running
toward the edge of the island, toward the edge of solid ground, toward the*

person shouting out her name. Someone else was in the tree too. The two figures started to climb down from the tree. The first one jumped down while still about three feet above the muck, making a splash in the murky water. The second followed quickly after the first. Then the two figures started wading through the water, lifting their knees as high as they could so that they could move faster. "Sam," Addy said, as she stood at the edge of dry land. She meant to shout it, but it came out no louder than a whisper. "George," she said louder, but still not loud enough for the two of them to hear her over the sounds of their own splashing. "Sam!" she finally yelled loud enough for them to hear.

George had overtaken Sam in the water and reached dry land first. He pulled his boots out of the muck and grabbed Addy in a giant hug, lifting her feet off the ground. When Sam reached them, she plunged into the hug like she was diving in water, grabbing both George and Addy and pulling them closer together.

"We thought you were dead," George said to Addy when the three of them finally eased up on their grips of each other. He was answered with Addy's tears. She didn't even mind crying this time. Addy grabbed George and hugged him again, squeezing him like a scared child squeezing her teddy bear. Questions began to pile up in Addy's brain, so many questions. How did the two of them escape when the compound was raided? Who else escaped? Was Reggie okay? But Addy decided that those questions could wait a few more moments, at least until she was able to breathe again.

Forty-six

I'm not afraid of Them—not anymore—but I am afraid. I've missed so much. You're old enough to understand your own name now, but the name you know isn't the name I gave you. I've been fooling myself, telling myself that something deep inside you will remember me. You're everything to me and I'm nothing to you. I can make only one promise to you, Christopher. No matter what happens, I will always love you.

I've got two more days on this train, two more days to try to think of what I'm going to say to you when we meet again. Sometimes I take out the picture of your father that Michael gave me and I stare at it. Someday I'll worry about telling you about your father. Someday I'll worry about telling you about Michael and the sacrifice he made for you without asking for anything in return. Someday I'll tell you who you really are. Right now, I'm simply praying that you'll accept me.

Forty-seven

I saw you today. You're so big, more like a little boy than a baby. You've changed so much. I still recognized you right away. I recognized your father in you. It was unmistakable.

You crawl so fast. And you stand up and take steps while holding on to things! You haven't let go and taken any steps on your own yet. I could still be with you for that. I could still be there to cheer you on as you take those first brave steps.

You seem so happy. You laugh all the time. You seem healthy too. I shouldn't have expected anything different. I should have known that the people raising you would do a good job. They would raise you like any other normal child. They would try to shield you from the inevitable horror of your future all the way up until you turned sixteen. Then they'd stand aside as strangers taught you how to hate, like they did to your father and Michael and Dorothy and Reggie and Palti, and that kid your father and I killed in Ohio, and the security guards at the intelligence cell, and the teacher in Philadelphia. You'd turn sixteen and they'd give you tests and decide if you were going to be a killer or just another cog in the machine. I don't know which is worse. What did Michael say? *If you're going to be part of the knife, you might as well be the blade.* Either way, you have to spend your life looking over your shoulder, hoping that the person behind you isn't following you. When the woman who has raised you looks at you, I can see the love in her eyes. She's doing her best. But for you, her best isn't good enough.

They really did their best to hide you, putting you in this small corner of the world. I was still in the car when I first saw Mendocino rising out of the distance. The road jutted out over the rocky coastline and gave me a clear view north. The town of Mendocino was no more than a few dozen houses with a few stores and hotels sprinkled throughout it. Driving up to this little town surrounded by tall, yellow grass is strange, like driving up to a prairie town from a Laura Ingalls Wilder novel that had been plopped down on a cliff jutting impossibly into the Pacific Ocean. When I saw the town, I thought for a second that this whole thing had to be an elaborate trap or a cruel joke. If they wanted to get rid of me, this was a perfect place to do it. I tensed my fingers on the steering wheel and kept on driving. You were here. I could feel it.

It was late afternoon when I first pulled into the town. The sun was sinking toward the ocean. I parked my car by the gas station near the entrance to the town. Your address was burned into a special part of my brain where I only kept things that belonged to you: the image of your face the first time I saw you, the feel of your grip when you grabbed my fingers, the sound of your crying when they took you from me.

It wasn't hard to find you in such a little town. I was in the town for only forty-five minutes when I first saw you. You were in a small, fenced-in yard in front of a house near the headlands. You were playing on a blanket that someone had spread out on the grass. You had a few books and toys splayed out in front of you. A woman was in the yard too. She had frizzy blond hair and brown eyes. She was much older than me. She was hanging clothes from a wicker basket on a clothesline. Most of the clothes were yours, tiny little onesies with pictures of cartoon whales and owls on them. I stood on the street, a little gravel road, pretending to be walking to the headlands to watch the sunset. I forced myself to keep walking. I can't even describe for you how hard it was to fight the urge to run to you right then and there and take you in my arms and run away. The woman was alone. I would have gotten away with it. Getting away with it wasn't the only consideration, though. I can't simply snatch you up and take you away. I have a list of things I want to learn before I take you away: what foods you eat, what your favorite toys are, when you take your naps, what songs you like. I ordered myself to take three days. You've had enough pain in your life already. When I take you back, I want to do everything I can to lessen the trauma of being ripped from another family. I walked past you toward the ocean. You didn't even look up at me. You were too busy playing with a toy drum.

That night, I found a place where I could sit and look inside your house without being seen. I could see into the house's light-filled windows. I sat in the dark and watched you play until they put you to bed. I wish I'd been close enough to hear you laugh. When you laugh, your round head bounces up and down on top of your round belly, while your fat little legs stick out in front of you. I could have sat there watching you for the rest of my life if someone could have promised me that things would never change, that you'd always be that safe and happy. No one can promise me that, though. You're going to get older. That's why I need to save you.

You had a bottle of formula at a little after six in the morning today, right after you woke up. According to my book, I should wean you from the formula soon, but I'll wait. You had cold oatmeal three hours later. You had lunch at twelve thirty. You had a snack of apple-sauce at four thirty. Of all the things you ate, the applesauce was definitely your favorite. You screamed when they tried to take it away before you'd eaten every last morsel. At six o'clock, you had dinner, macaroni and cheese with chopped-up broccoli. You had an-other bottle of formula before going to bed. You were asleep by seven thirty. I'm writing everything down.

You took two naps during the day; each one lasted about an hour and a half. The first was at ten in the morning and the second was at three in the afternoon. You went through a lot of diapers. I need to buy diapers.

You clap when they play music for you. You smile. Your smile is so sweet, my heart nearly broke. They've made me miss almost a year of that smile.

On the way back to my hotel from watching you, I passed a store with a mannequin in the lit-up window. It was one of those headless mannequins. It was wearing a little black cocktail dress. I stared at it. I don't even know for how long. It was beautiful. I tried to imagine in what life someone might wear a dress like that. The only way I could imagine myself wearing a dress like that was as a disguise.

Two more days, Christopher. Two more days.

I'm drawing myself a bath. The water is hot. The whole bathroom is steaming up. I want it to be hot enough that it hurts when I climb in. I want it to be so hot that it takes a few minutes before I can even be comfortable immersed in the water. I almost want it to burn.

I think you waved to me today. It's hard to know for sure, since you wave at everything. I'm coming for you tomorrow. I'm going to take you during your morning nap. The husband should be at work. I don't have a car seat for the rental car, so I'm going to have to take their car. You'll be more comfortable that way anyway. Hopefully, you'll sleep in the car, and by the time you wake up, I will have found a safe place for us. I still have enough of Michael's money to hide us. If everything goes right, we'll be far away by the time they're able to report anything.

I've missed you so much, Christopher. I can't wait to hold you. I want to grab you in my arms and hug and kiss you. I can't wait to show you how much I can love you.

Forty-eight

When Addy was finally able to speak, nothing but questions poured out of her mouth. Evan had sidled up behind the three of them, Addy in her jeans and black shirt, and the two strangers decked out from head to toe in mud-covered camouflage. Despite being only a couple feet away, no one seemed to notice Evan. Addy kept asking the strangers how they survived the raid and if anyone else made it. When Addy was only about halfway through her questions, George cut her off. "We weren't raided, Addy," his voice, deep and resonant, said.

Addy stopped speaking and stared at him for a second, dumbfounded. She thought for a moment that maybe she'd misheard him. Addy looked over at Sam. Sam was nodding, confirming the words that Addy fought to believe. "Then what happened here?" Addy asked, motioning toward the charred wreckage of the compound.

"We burned it down ourselves," Sam answered her. "Reggie always planned it this way. He'd always planned on razing the whole place to protect the information if we had to abandon it. That way no one could get their hands on any of the information about any of the people we cleaned."

"So everyone is okay?" Addy asked. "Reggie is okay?"

Sam nodded her head. "Everybody's fine."

"Then what are you guys doing here?"

"*Reggie has us working here,*" *George answered.* "*We were looking for you. Reggie was sure that you'd come back. He wanted to make sure someone was waiting for you.*"

For a second, Addy was speechless. She felt like she was being teased. "*If you were looking for me, what's with the gun?*" *Addy asked, motioning toward the rifle slung over Sam's shoulder. She'd never seen anyone in the Underground carrying a gun like that before. Had that much changed in the weeks she'd been gone?*

"*If anyone but you showed up here, we were supposed to shoot to kill,*" *Sam told Addy.*

Addy felt a mosquito biting her arm. She didn't care. She ignored it. "*Who told you to do that?*" *Addy asked.*

"*Reggie's orders,*" *Sam answered her. So much had changed in the weeks that Addy'd been gone. Addy had never known Reggie to give an order like that. Sometimes pickups didn't go as planned and blood was shed, but it was never ordered. Addy wasn't sure if she should be proud or disgusted.* "*It's getting serious,*" *Sam assured her. Sam's voice was tense and determined.*

"*Everyone is joining forces, Addy,*" *George told her.* "*People would have found you and told you, but after we learned about the raids in Los Angeles, everybody but Reggie thought you were dead.*"

"*What do you mean, 'Everyone is joining forces'?*" *Addy asked George.*

"*Everybody,*" *George echoed, sounding more serious than Addy had ever heard him sound before.* "*The Underground. The rebels. Everybody. All the factions. Everywhere. It's global. People are coming out of the woodwork. It's the final push. We're finally going to try to end the War.*" *Addy's heart began to beat so strongly that she could feel her pulse in the tips of her fingers.*

"*You were right about fighting, Addy,*" *Sam said when George was done.* "*You were just a little off on the timing.*"

Addy kept looking back and forth between George and Sam, waiting for one of them to crack a smile or laugh so that she could be sure that this was all a twisted joke. Neither flinched. Neither even grinned. They were se-rious. "How is this all possible?" Addy asked. It was a pipe dream, getting everyone who was against the War to finally work together. It was impos-sible.

"Christopher," George said. "It's all Christopher. He's bringing everyone together."

"Christopher?" a voice broke in from outside the circle. It was Evan. He'd been listening in silence the whole time. "Do you know where Chris-topher is? Do you know if he's okay?"

The three of them—Addy, George, and Sam—looked up at Evan as he spoke, as if he'd suddenly materialized out of thin air. Addy felt guilty. She'd completely forgotten that Evan was even there. "Evan?" she said with sur-prise. Then she collected herself. "Evan, this is George and Sam," Addy in-troduced the three of them. "I used to work with them here. They're part of the Underground."

Evan reached his hand out, and George and Sam took turns shaking it. "You're the kid from the news," George said to Evan, recognizing his face from the pictures.

"He's with me," Addy said to them, stepping closer to Evan, touching his elbow with her hand. "Don't believe everything you see on the news."

"I never have," George laughed. Addy wondered if she should tell them who Evan was. She wondered if she should tell them that Evan had grown up as Christopher's closest friend. She decided not to. Evan was going to have a hard enough time adjusting without having to answer any more questions about Christopher.

"So, do you know where Christopher is?" Evan asked again.

"Yeah," George answered him, staring straight into Evan's eyes. "He's with Reggie." Addy's shock slipped out in an audible gasp. George turned toward Addy. He nodded to confirm to her that he was speaking the truth. "Reggie is helping Christopher. They're working together to make sure that everyone is ready for the uprising."

Forty-nine

It's over. For now, it's over. Maybe I should have simply grabbed you and ran.

I got to the house at a little after nine in the morning. I went to the same spot where I'd secretly been watching you for the past three days. It gave me a clear view into your house but kept me relatively hidden. I could see you, but no one in the house could see me. It was sunny. It would be hot later, even this close to the ocean. You'd go down for your morning nap in an hour. My plan was to get you out of the house shortly after you fell asleep so that you'd be too tired to understand what was happening. I hoped that you'd eventually wake up with me and think that the past eleven months had simply been a long nightmare.

I sat down and reached into my backpack for my lucky pack of cigarettes. It was opened now, one cigarette short of a full pack. I took a cigarette out of the pack and placed it between my lips. I lit it. It was the first cigarette I'd had in, what, seven months? Eight? I smoked it until the cigarette had burned about a quarter of the way down. Then I felt stupid, ridiculous even, so I threw the barely smoked butt on the ground and stamped it out with my foot. The world is already full of enough silly rituals. I don't need to create new ones.

You went down for your nap a little bit late. She didn't put you in your crib until almost half past ten. You cried at first, rocking yourself back and forth in your crib before falling asleep. I could see into your crib through the open window. I watched you as you stopped fussing and your breathing calmed, your tiny chest rising and falling at a slow, even pace. That's when I decided it was finally time to go and get you.

The front door of the house faced south, overlooking the rocks and, eventually, the ocean. The air was full of the constant smell of salt from the sea. I walked around the house and up to the front door. I knocked three firm, solid knocks. The irony wasn't lost on me, remembering the sound of the knocks on the door the day they stole you from me. This was different though. I was taking back what was rightfully mine.

I knocked. Then waited, listening. I heard a rustling sound on the other side of the door. The last I saw of the woman through the window, she had been in the kitchen, putting dishes away. She didn't answer the knocks at first, but I knew that she'd heard me. I didn't knock again. I didn't want to appear too eager. Instead, I waited. Eventually, I heard the woman put some dishes down on a counter. I heard her footsteps as she started walking toward the door. Her steps were slow and apprehensive. I saw her pull back the curtains next to the door and peek out the window. When she looked out, she saw only me—tiny, innocent me. When They came to take you from me, They came with five heavily armed men. The curtain dropped back in place. Seconds later, the woman opened the door.

"Can I help you?" she asked. She opened the door only a crack, barely wide enough for her to look out. She tried to block my view inside her house with her body. She was dressed in white linen pants and a breezy coral button-down blouse.

"I'm sorry," I said. "I was going for a walk out to the headlands and I was hoping that I could use your bathroom. I'll only be a minute."

The woman glanced back into the house without opening the door any wider. She was looking toward your room. She shook her head. "My baby is asleep," she said. "I really don't want to wake him." *My baby*, she'd said.

"I'll be really quiet," I said. "I promise." I bounced on my feet, trying to sell the lie.

The woman took a long look at me as if she were peering into a dark hole. "Do I know you?" she asked. "You look familiar."

I swallowed, trying to think of what to say besides *Of course you recognize me. You see me every day when you look at your son.* "I'm on vacation here in town," I told her. "Maybe you've seen me walking around."

She kept staring at my face. She knew that she recognized something else. She glanced again toward your room. I worried for a moment that she might be putting it all together. "I really need to use your bathroom," I said, trying to interrupt her train of thought. "Then I'll be out of your way."

She didn't want to open the door. She was nervous. I made her nervous. She looked past me down the street, toward the other houses, looking to see if anyone else was outside, to see if anyone would be there to save her if she screamed. The street was empty, but I was small and looked innocent enough. "Okay," she said, opening the door wider. "But please be quiet. The bathroom is at the end of that hallway," she said, pointing toward her husband's bathroom, the one at the other end of the house, away from you.

"Thank you," I said, and jogged past her, moving lightly on my feet. I didn't want you to wake up either. I may have wanted it less than she did. I ran inside the bathroom and closed the door behind me. Once inside the bathroom, I took off my backpack. I reached inside and took out what remained of the duct tape. My knife was strapped inside my waist. Before leaving the bathroom, I looked at myself in the mirror. A short-haired, tired-looking woman stared back at me with fierce eyes. I flushed the toilet. Then I turned on the faucet and splashed some cold water on my face. This was it. I steeled myself, taking deep breaths. Then I stepped back outside the door, holding the duct tape in my left hand.

She was waiting for me right outside the door. She should have had a weapon. If she were a soldier, she would have had a weapon. She wasn't a soldier, though. She was a tither. She and her husband paid for the War with a check every month. That's why they didn't have to fight. They paid their way out of it. She knew enough to be afraid, but not enough to do anything about it. When I stepped through the door, she glanced down at my hands. She saw the duct tape. Then she looked back up at my face. "What do you want?" she said, her voice quiet and shaky.

"I'm not one of Them," I said to her. It didn't matter if *Them* was your father's side or hers. I had gotten comfortable using the term *Them* interchangeably. To me, *Them* were the true believers, no matter what side they were on. "I'm not here to hurt you."

She started backing away from me, walking slowly backward toward the kitchen. "Then what are you here for?" she asked. She was going to run soon. I could tell. She was going to turn and run and I would have to chase her, catch her, subdue her, and silence her—all without waking you up.

"You still don't know why you recognize me?" I asked her, knowing full well that I was this woman's worst nightmare. She would have been happier if I was one of Them. If I was one of Them, she'd be as good as dead but *her baby* would be safe.

"No," she said, staring at my face, trying to put the pieces of the puzzle together.

"I'm here for Christopher," I said, trying to catch up to her, to walk toward her faster than she was backing away.

"Who?" she asked. They never told her your real name.

"My son," I said, looking over her shoulder toward your room.

Then she realized. The life seeped out of her face. "No." She began shaking her head. "You can't. You can't."

"I'm not going to hurt him either," I told her, feeling a sudden urge to console her. "I'm here to save him."

"Save him from what?" she asked, almost in a panic-induced falsetto.

I thought about how to answer the question this time. She deserved the painful truth. "You," I told her.

Before she could turn and run, I raised my voice, hoping to stop her. "There's no use running," I told her. "I'll catch you." I looked at her. Her skin sagged around her muscles. She wasn't prepared for this. "You've spent almost a year raising my son," I said to her. "You want to know what I've been doing all that time?" I didn't wait for her to answer. "I've been training." Everything you do is practice for the next thing that you do.

She ran anyway. She turned and sprinted toward the kitchen. They kept knives in the kitchen. Maybe there was a gun there too. I ran after her, pulling out my knife as I ran. When I got close enough to her, I kicked one of her feet out from under her. She fell to the floor. As she fell, I pulled out a large strip of duct tape and cut it with the knife. She hit the hard floor with a loud thud and immediately turned over to face me. I was on top of her before she had another moment to think, my knees jabbing into her chest. She saw the knife. I took the duct tape and pressed it across her face, covering her mouth before she had a chance to scream. She reached up with one hand to try to hit me, but I caught her hand in the air. Then I stood up and twisted her wrist, forcing her whole body to roll over. She began crying. She kept trying to scream through the duct tape. Her body was shuddering. Her screams came through the duct tape like low, quiet moans. Once she was on her stomach, I placed one knee into the small of her back and reached for her other hand. I was holding the knife and her wrist in the same hand, trying not to cut her. I pulled her hands together behind her back and taped them together, exactly like I'd taped up the security guard in the intelligence cell. Once her hands were taped together, I taped her feet. I couldn't afford to have her get up and run, not in this town, not with her hands taped behind her back and her mouth taped shut. Tying her up took me only a few seconds. I was fast and efficient. Once I was sure she was immobilized, I listened. The house was quiet. You were still asleep.

I rolled her over again and pushed her up against the wall. Her eyes were red. Tears were streaming down her face. I remembered what it felt like. I remembered lying on the ground and wishing that they'd shoot me and put me out of my misery so I wouldn't have to watch them take you away. I looked into the woman's eyes. "I know you love him," I said to her. "I appreciate that you've treated him well. But you were going to turn him into a killer. You were going to make him hate." She shook her head, trying to deny what she knew was the truth. "And he's my son," I said more forcefully. "You had no right to have him in the first place."

I stood up. I found a chair in the kitchen and dragged it next to her. Then I picked her up and sat her down on the chair. She tried to say something to me through the tape, but I ignored her. I wrapped more tape around her body, securing her to the chair. Then I went outside. I'd hidden a large duffel bag behind some shrubs outside the front door. I grabbed the duffel bag and came back inside. The woman was struggling against the tape but wasn't making any progress. Her chest kept heaving as she cried. I was worried she might hyperventilate, but there was little I could do. I wasn't going to undo the tape, and she didn't know enough to control her breathing. With the duffel bag in my hand, I began collecting things, things that they weren't going to need anymore. I knew where they kept your diapers, your clothes, your bottles, your pacifiers. I began taking everything that I'd seen them use with you over the past three days and throwing it in the duffel bag. I wanted to take enough to last me for two days. Then I could start to replenish the supplies on my own. To get your diapers, I had to walk into your room, right past your crib. You were sound asleep. You were the most peaceful thing I'd ever seen. The last thing that I grabbed was the car keys off the hook on the wall near the front door.

I ran out to the car. I opened the trunk and threw the duffel bag inside. Then I went back in the house for you. If I'd only been seconds faster. I made two steps toward your room. Then I heard a sound coming from outside. Screeching tires. I looked outside. A car fishtailed in front the house, pulling to a loud stop. He'd come back. The husband had come back. He was supposed to be at work. She must have called him while I was in the bathroom. She must have assumed that I was one of Them. But then why did she stay? She stayed to protect you. Even knowing the rules, even knowing that They weren't supposed to hurt you, even knowing that she didn't know how to fight, she stayed to protect you.

Through the white curtains on the front window, I saw him step out of the car. He had a gun in his hand. He slammed the car door behind him and started running toward the house. He didn't stop to think or to plan. He was running headlong into danger. I can only imagine what she'd said, speaking in a whisper in the seconds she had while I was in the bathroom. *One of Them is here. I'm going to protect our baby. I love you.* Time wouldn't have allowed for much more than that. He was running toward the door, hoping he'd made it in time to save his child and, only if he were lucky, his wife. It all would have been fine if it weren't for the goddamn gun. I wasn't afraid of him, but I was afraid of the gun. I still had the duct tape in one hand and the knife in the other. I hid behind a corner that he'd have to pass before he saw his wife tied to the chair. I could get a jump on him from there.

The front door swung open. The man shouted, "Maggie!" as he crossed over the threshold into the house. I could hear the panic in his voice. He should have been more careful, but how can you expect someone to be careful when they think that everything they care about in the world is already gone? I'm telling you now, Christopher, that in those moments when you fear the worst, you have to close your eyes to everything that you know is true and simply believe— believe that everything is going to work out for you, believe that your enemies deserve whatever comes to them, believe that you are unstoppable, believe that you are righteous. If you can't believe those things in those moments, you'll be torn to pieces.

From where she was taped to the chair, the woman could see me. She could see me standing with my back pressed against the wall and my knife in my hand. Her eyes flitted between me and the hallway. I would know when her husband came into view by the look in her eyes. She was trying to loosen the tape around her mouth. I could see her working her tongue furiously against the back of the tape. She wanted to warn her husband, but she was making no progress. I heard the footsteps coming toward us. Then I heard the man yell, "Maggie!" again. This time I could hear both the panic and the relief in his voice. As he yelled her name, the woman's eyes widened into giant orbs of fear. He didn't notice. He was too happy that she was alive. He stumbled toward her, falling to his knees in front of her. I took a silent step toward his back, readying the knife. He reached up for the tape covering his wife's mouth. I couldn't let him undo it. She would scream. I had to decide what to do. The man's hand caught the corner of the tape and, as it did, I kicked him hard in the kidney.

He fell forward and to the side, rolling onto his back as he fell. He didn't lose his grip on the gun. He staggered backward on his hands and feet, doing a type of crab walk toward the wall while trying to piece together what was happening. Finally, his eyes fell on me as I stepped toward him with my knife. I had a knife. He had a gun. It shouldn't have been a fight. He stood up and pointed the gun at me, and I still wasn't afraid. He was a tither. He killed people with his money, not his hands. I stepped closer to him. He stepped back. "Put the gun away," I ordered him.

At first he didn't answer. I repeated myself. "Put the gun away," I said, this time adding, "and no one gets hurt." I'd have to tie him up too. It was the only way to ensure that I'd get out of Mendocino.

He shook his head. The gun was shaking in his hand. "No," he said, as strongly as he could muster. But he wasn't strong. I was strong.

"I'm just here for my son," I said. "I don't want anything to do with you or your wife." He understood what I was telling him, putting it all together quicker than his wife had. He glanced over at his wife as if looking for instructions. Should he give in and save the two of them or should he fight? His wife shook her head vigorously. She was ready to die for you.

If I didn't act quickly, he would eventually build up the courage to fire the gun. I knew that. It was like a dam in a river. The more time that passed, the greater the pressure on the dam. Eventually it would overflow or crack. If he didn't put the gun down, I was going to have to kill him. I didn't want to kill him, Christopher, but I was going to do what I had to. Your father had died trying to save you. Michael, a man who didn't even know you—a man far braver than the man in front of me—had died trying to save you. Why shouldn't this man die too? Why should he get special dispensation? Michael's words echoed in my head: *Do what I was never able to do. Make my life mean something.* Nothing was going to stop me from saving you.

By the time the man's eyes shifted from his wife back to me, I was only inches from his gun hand. Before he had a chance to react, I grabbed the gun with my left hand and aimed it away from me. Then I took my knife and stabbed the man's wrist, trying to force him to let go of the gun. A low, guttural scream came out of him. Blood shot out of his wrist and he stared at it with the strange detachment of a man unaccustomed to seeing his own blood. Some of his blood got on my shirt. I didn't want any more of his blood on me. I didn't want to pick you up, covered in the blood of the people you thought were your parents. I'd seen you covered in blood before, mine when you were born and your father's when they took you away from me. I never wanted to see that again. Michael said that your father used to strangle people because it was neat. Done right, it was also quiet. Knives were bloody. I threw my knife off to one side. Guns were loud. I threw the gun off to the other side. I took the duct tape and unrolled a piece about three feet in length. It made a ripping sound. The roll was almost gone. I wouldn't have had enough tape to tie the man up anyway.

He was still staring at his blood when I stepped behind him, moving quickly, thought and action merging so that I moved the moment ideas entered my head. When I got behind him, I wrapped the ends of the strip of tape around my hands. Then I lifted the tape over his head, aiming the nonsticky side toward his neck, and pulled. The tape dug quickly into the man's neck, but it was broad and flat so it didn't begin choking him right away. He tried to run away from me but I held on, pinching the tape so that it would become thinner in its center and dig deeper into the man's flesh. He was bigger than me, so when he stepped forward, he pulled me with him. I lifted my feet off the ground and dug my knees into the man's back for leverage, pulling backward even harder. He was stumbling now, carrying me with him on his back, trying to spin me off of him like a rodeo bull. I held on tightly. I wasn't going to let go. Running out of air and ideas, he turned and ran backward into a wall as hard as he could. I could hear him gasping for air. I ignored the pain as he rammed me into the wall.

I dug my knees deeper into his back, pulling even harder on the tape. The room was painfully bright, full of the sunlight coming in through the windows and reflecting off the polished hardwood floors. The man backed into the wall again, harder this time. The whole wall shook when I hit it. Something fell off of a shelf. It came crashing to the ground and shattered into a million pieces. It felt like the loudest sound I'd ever heard, louder than fireworks, louder than gunshots. Seconds later, you began to cry.

You were awake. I pulled tighter. I could feel the man getting weaker. I could see the color of the back of his neck changing, turning purple. He started stumbling forward again, taking each step deliberately, trying to stay on his feet. At first I didn't know what he was doing. Then I realized. He was going for the gun. He took another step toward the gun lying in the corner, past the dining room table. The gun was only two or three steps away. When we got even with the dining room table, I took one knee off his back and kicked the table as hard as I could. The table moved, screeching across the floor. A corner of the table hit and broke through one of the dining room windows. You screamed louder, wondering why no one had come to comfort you yet. I wanted to be the one to comfort you. When I kicked the table, the man lost his balance. He took two weak steps to his left, nearly drained of energy. Then he fell to his knees. I pulled tighter. I could see blood coming out of the man's neck from beneath the tape. No more sound was coming from him. There were no more that he could make. I looked over at the man's wife. She was staring at us, crying again.

I felt the man you knew to be your father die. I felt the last shudder of life ripple through his body. Then nothing. I took my knees off of his back and put them on the floor. I let go of the tape and the man rolled onto his stomach, his arms caught beneath his body. The position looked uncomfortable. Comfort wasn't a concern anymore. You were screaming now, bordering on hysteria. I stood up and took a deep breath. I could go to you now.

I walked into your room. I wanted to pick you up, to soothe you. I wanted to comfort you and stop your crying. I thought back to when They took you from me and how I wasn't able to comfort you then, how I wasn't able to stop your screams. I recognized the sound of your crying. I heard it in my sleep nearly every night. You were standing up in your crib, holding on to the bars for balance. When I walked into your room, you looked up at me and cried even louder. I wasn't the one you wanted. I had tried to prepare myself for this. I knew that it would take time, but my heart ached all the same. You looked past me toward the open door and pointed. You bounced up and down on your feet. Real tears were rolling down your cheeks. You wanted her.

I ignored your pleas. I walked up to you and lifted you out of your crib. You kept crying. I pressed your body into mine, resting your head on my shoulder. Holding you was the most wonderful feeling I ever felt, even though you fought me. It was like they had stolen a piece of me, the only piece that mattered, and I was finally getting it back. I was whole again. I was different—the time had made me different—but I was whole. You dug your head into the crook in my neck, wiping the tears on my shoulder. I felt like a mother again.

We walked out of your room. We were only a few steps from the front door. We were about to walk out when the screaming began. I turned and looked back. The woman had gotten a corner of the tape free from her mouth. Her husband must have dislodged just enough of it for her to work it free. At first, her scream was just that—a meaningless, mournful wail. Then there were words. "You can't do this!" she screamed. "You can't take him from me!"

When she screamed, you began screaming again too. You screamed the first word I ever heard you speak. "Mama!" you shouted to someone who wasn't me, reaching your hand out toward the woman in the chair.

"Please," she screamed. "Please." I had to retape her mouth. Someone might hear her. I needed the time to get away. I had to put you down on the ground so that I could put the tape back on her mouth. I placed you on the floor on your hands and knees. I walked to the body of her husband first to get what was left of the tape. Then I went to the woman. As I neared her she began whispering to me in fits. "I'll take him away," she said. "I'll run. I won't make him a killer. I promise. I'll do anything. Please." She paused for a second, knowing that nothing she was saying to me was making a difference. Then she added, "I love him."

"So do I," I whispered to her, and then I stretched a length of tape around her head, covering her mouth. I turned to look for you. You were still crying. I could hear you, but you weren't where I'd left you. Instead you'd crawled from the place on the floor where I'd put you down. You crawled to the body of the man you thought was your father. He was lying there like I'd left him, his arms trapped beneath the deadweight of his body. Now you were sitting next to him, your face turned up toward the sky, your mouth open, your lower lip jutting out and trembling. You didn't understand. You were crying like there was no peace or justice in the world. We had to leave. I walked over to you and picked you up again. You clutched me this time, confused, frightened, and happy that someone, anyone, was holding you. That someone was finally me.

We made it outside and to the car. I buckled you into the car seat.

You were still crying. I went into the trunk. I took out a pacifier and a small blanket from the duffel bag. I put the pacifier in your mouth and handed you the blanket. You immediately began to suck on the pacifier and knead the blanket with your tiny hands. Then I got into the driver's seat, turned the key, and drove. You fell asleep eventually. You slept for almost three hours before waking up again. I hope that you dreamed pretty dreams, dreams that helped you to forget everything you'd seen and heard.

You seemed okay when we stopped for dinner. You ate. I fed you with a spoon, even though you wanted to hold it yourself. You adapt quickly. Maybe that's because you've already been through this before.

It took all my strength to keep from trying to teach you to call me Mama, to try to reclaim that word. In time, I guess—I hope.

Fifty

"There's something else, Addy," George said after giving Addy a moment to allow the news about Christopher and Reggie to sink in. Addy looked at George, unsure if she could handle any more news. All the assumptions she'd been making about the world were already turned on their head.

"What is it?" Addy asked, worried that he was going to give her some bad news to balance out all the good.

"We weren't sent here just to find you and welcome you back." George shot Sam a quick, nervous glance. "Reggie has a job for you."

"A job?" Addy asked. "Doing what?"

"We don't know," Sam answered Addy. "He gave us this." Sam pulled a sealed envelope out of her jacket. "Reggie ordered us not to open it. Even when we tried to convince him that you might be dead, he insisted that you were the only one who could do this job." Sam handed the envelope to Addy.

Addy's name was written on the outside of the envelope. Addy recognized Reggie's handwriting. She'd convinced herself she would never see that handwriting again. "Do you guys mind if I go read this?" Addy asked, motioning toward the wreckage of the compound, hinting that she wanted to read it alone.

"Go ahead," Sam said. George nodded in agreement.

Addy looked up at Evan. Addy didn't want to be completely alone. She wanted Evan to come with her. Evan understood, and the two of them walked toward the burnt remains of the building together. The staircase leading from the ground level of the compound's wreckage to the basement was still mostly intact. Addy and Evan descended the stairs together into the rubble, leaving George and Sam waiting above them. Addy felt strange walking through the remains of what had been her second home for more than two years. Even if no one died in this fire, it didn't mean there weren't any ghosts.

Evan peered into the empty cabinets and desk drawers as he walked, stepping around the burnt debris strewn about him. He didn't know what he was looking at or what he was looking for. He just stared at the charred remains, amazed at how many secrets had been hidden from him throughout his short life. He wondered how many more secrets were still floating out there for him to uncover.

The two of them found a place to sit, an old burnt desk that still appeared sturdy enough to hold their weight. They sat down. Addy reached her trembling hand for the envelope. She tore it open. She pulled the letter from inside and began to read it to herself. Evan said nothing. He gave Addy the moment to let her read the entire letter before asking any questions.

When Addy finished reading the letter, she looked up, a new wave of shock registering on her face. "What did it say?" Evan asked. "What does Reggie want you to do?"

Addy stared blankly into space. She didn't turn toward Evan when she spoke. "Reggie wants me to find Christopher's mother." No emotion slipped into Addy's voice. "He wants me to find her and bring her back to him. He said that he needs to explain something to her—a promise that he'd failed to keep."

"I thought you said that Christopher's mother was dead." The air was so still that, for a moment, it felt to Evan like time had stopped.

"I did. That's what I was told. That's what we all were told. But she's *not dead. It's all here in Reggie's letter. She started the rumor herself be-cause she thought it would help protect Christopher. She's alive. She's alive but she doesn't know that Christopher is working with Reggie."*

They sat in silence for a few moments while Addy waited for Evan to respond. "So, how do we find her?" Evan finally asked.

Addy was relieved to hear the word we *in Evan's question. She knew how crazy everything must seem to him, but she also knew how much crazier it could get. She wanted to be there for him. She wanted him to be there for her. "Reggie gave us some leads," Addy said, holding up the piece of paper. "From there, we improvise." Silence again. Addy broke it this time. "We should get out of here, Evan. It's probably not safe for us here."*

Evan stared at the wreckage around them. "Where is it safe for us, Addy?"

"Let's go," Addy said to Evan without answering his question. She reached one of her hands out toward Evan's. He took it. Their fingers inter-twined. Then the two of them walked out of the wreckage together to George and Sam.

Fifty-one

It's going to be hard to explain my decision to you. Even if I can explain it, you may never understand it. Don't think that I didn't agonize over this decision. I did. I have to do what I think will be the best for you. I've come to realize that I can't shield you from this War, Christopher. I'm eighteen years old and I'm a part of this War now too.

They would have chased us forever. They would have found us. People I've never met recognize me. They know who I am. They know things about me. I've become a face in the cautionary tales they tell their children. I violated their rules even though I was never supposed to be a part of their War. Now I'm marked. I've been branded almost as clearly as Michael was. Instead of the words *I fight because I remember* branded on my back, I have the words *I run because They won't forget* branded in the lines on my face. I could manage it. I could run. I could hide. I'd be better at it this time. But that's not the life I want for you. You deserve better. You're only beginning. You have so much to learn. I may be young, but I like to believe that there was a time when I could have taught you all the things you deserve to know. That time has passed. Now I can't even teach you the one thing that I most want you to learn—that the world is a beautiful and decent place.

Every day I pick you up and hold you, and I'm happy. That's why leaving you is going to be so hard. It's been three weeks already. You've grown accustomed to me. You smile and laugh when I pick you up in the morning. You clutch me and hug me, and all I can think the whole time is, Never let go, Christopher. Never let go. But I know that every day that I keep you only makes it crueler. You're going to cry when I leave you now. You're going to wonder when I'm coming back. When I don't come back, you're going to wonder why I left you, and you're not going to get any explanation—not for a long time, not until you read these words. So let me explain it to you now. I'm leaving you because I love you more than anything— more than my own happiness, more than life itself.

Your first birthday is in a week. It's selfish, but I am going to stay with you until then. So I've got one more week until my heart is ripped out again. It'll be different this time, though. This time I'll know that it's what's best for you. This time I'll be ripping out my own heart, something I'd gladly do for you over and over again if I had more than one heart to tear free. You'll understand someday.

I know a couple who I think will take you in. They used to babysit for me when I was a little girl. They were young then. They weren't able to have children of their own. I know that they always wanted to have a family. I remember overhearing her talk about it with my mother. They'll be good to you. They'll love you. They'll be able to give you everything that I can't. Hopefully, even as you read this, they're the faces that you think of when you hear the words *Mom* and *Dad*. They live in a house down the street from our old summer house in Maine. I haven't been there since I was thirteen years old. I called them yesterday to make sure that they still live there. I found their number on the Internet. I recognized the woman's voice when she answered the phone. It sounded kind. After all these years, it still sounded kind. I hung up. Hearing her voice was all I needed.

Maybe a time will come when things will have changed enough that it's safe for us to be together again. I hope it's true, but I'm skeptical that this War will ever change. I know what I'm going to do after I drop you off in Maine. I'm going to drive to Ohio. I know details about a boy who was murdered in a field in Ohio almost a year and a half ago. I know enough details that they'll believe me when I confess to shooting him in the head. That boy was the first person that I ever saw killed. It doesn't matter that I didn't pull the trigger. If I want to get my old self back, I need to start at the moment when that innocent girl that I was began to fade away. I'll accept whatever punishment they give me. None of it will hurt half as much as the punishment that I'm already giving myself.

In the meantime, it's a long drive from here to Maine. There are plenty of sites to see and places to stop on the way. I figure we can take our time. I don't think it will be a problem stretching the drive out a few more days.

Fifty-two

They were on a boat, skipping violently across the South China Sea. The long, thin wooden boat cut through the smaller waves but climbed and dove over the larger ones. A mist of briny water sprayed up over the boat as the hull smacked down against the surface of the water. Christopher could feel the pellets of mist on his skin and could taste the salt from the seawater on his tongue. He looked to his left and, in the distance, could see whole villages built along the edges of tiny green islands. Entire buildings stretched out over the water, held up by no more than bamboo rods jutting out of the sea. Brightly colored clothes hung along clotheslines running from one hut to the next. To his right, Christopher could see dozens of giant metal cargo ships, each one towering over them, some of them stretching at least ten stories over them, reaching impossibly high above the surface of the water. Smaller boats and giant cranes packed the ships with metal containers. Christopher had never in his life seen anything like it.

Another boat, one nearly identical to theirs, drove past them in the other direction. At least twenty people sat huddled together in the other boat as it bounced above the water's surface. Their boat held only the three of them: Christopher, Reggie, and the captain. The captain was a small, round-faced Asian man. His skin was wrinkled and leathery. He had welcomed Christopher and Reggie with better-than-adequate English and deep, reverent bows. It embarrassed Christopher to be treated with such unearned admi-

ration. "Accept it now," Reggie told him with each new person that they met, "because you're going to have to earn it later."

Christopher and Reggie had already been traveling for more than twenty-four hours. It took that long to make it halfway around the globe. The flight to Singapore took twenty hours by itself, including their short stopover in Frankfurt. It was the first time Christopher had ever been on an airplane. Once in Singapore, Christopher and Reggie boarded a packed commuter ferry to Indonesia. They met the captain of their little boat in a port near the ferry terminal in Indonesia. This was the final leg of the first part of the journey that Reggie had planned for them. First Indonesia, then Istanbul, then New York. Christopher had little idea what each stop would have in store for him.

Christopher looked up toward the bow of the boat. Reggie was sitting near the bow with his back to the sea ahead of them. Reggie's bright green eyes reflected the color of the water around them. His gray hair made him look ten years older than he was, but it gave him an air of wisdom. "How are you feeling?" Reggie shouted back to Christopher when he noticed Christopher staring at him. Reggie had to yell loud enough to be heard over the sound of the boat's engine and the incessant crashing of the waves against the boat's hull.

Christopher was tired. He'd been through so much in the past four weeks. He'd fought, killed, run, been saved, been worshipped, and been lied to. Yet he knew that his journey and his fight were only beginning. "I feel good," he shouted back to Reggie. He gripped a rope running along the side of the boat to avoid being heaved into the sea by the waves. "I feel ready." Ready for what? Christopher had no idea.

Trevor Shane lives in Brooklyn with his wife and son.

CONNECT ONLINE

www.childrenofparanoia.com

They waited until Christopher turned eighteen before they tried to kill him.

Ever since Christopher was a small child, he knew that someone was watching him. Even though he couldn't see them, he could feel their eyes burning into his skin. He could feel people lurking in the shadows, watching his every move. They were waiting but Christopher had no way of knowing what they were waiting for. He never told his parents that people were watching him. Christopher was trying to protect them. They knew that Christopher had problems. They knew that he wasn't a normal kid but they simply believed that everything related back to something that happened to Christopher when he was a baby, something that Christopher had no memory of. Christopher heard his parents whispering about it late at night when Christopher was supposed to be asleep. Whatever had happened to him when he was young didn't matter. Christopher wasn't afraid of his past. He was afraid of his future. Before he learned anything else, Christopher learned how to be paranoid. That was his birthright.

Since Christopher only knew that he was being watched and didn't know who was watching him or why, he did what he could to prepare for anything. He took karate lessons. He learned to box and to wrestle. He took tae kwon do classes. He took every fighting class the little town he grew up in had to offer, and then, when he got his driver's license, he took every class offered in the surrounding towns. He didn't stick to any one thing for very long. He never felt like he was learning fast enough. He'd get frustrated and quit and then try something new, each time hoping that, this time, he would learn fast enough. Even though he moved around, he learned. He integrated skills. He was a misfit but he wasn't afraid of bullies or jocks or any of the kids in his town. He had other things to be afraid of. Even among the outsiders, Christopher was an outsider. Christopher really only had one close friend. Even before Christopher had felt strangers' eyes watching him, Evan had been his friend. They were different. Christopher was practical. Evan was a dreamer. Evan saw something bigger in their future, something more than what their little town offered people. The other kids feared Christopher because he was different. Evan reveled in the fact that Christopher was different. That's what drew him to Christopher in the first place. He was more than this small-town high school life full of little more than jocks and nerds and cheerleaders.

Maybe everything would have turned out differently had Christopher remembered the key that he received on his sixteenth birthday or the note that came with the key that he never read. He'd hid them in the bottom of one of his draws and tried to forget them. As sure as Christopher was that he was being watched, he was just as certain that the key would unlock answers for him but he wasn't sure he wanted answers. As afraid as Christopher was of the people watching him, he was even more afraid of why. Sometimes Christopher did his best to pretend that he was simply imagining things. Maybe it would have been better that way. Maybe it would have been better if Christopher was crazy and the rest of the world was sane. But Christopher wasn't crazy. Someone was watching him. They were watching him and waiting for Christopher's eighteenth birthday.

It was the evening of Christopher's eighteenth birthday and he was driving home from Evan's house. He was in his own car, a beat-up, rusty heap of junk that he had bought for three thousand dollars the day he got his license. It was already dark. Christopher had gone to Evan's house to show Evan the gift that his parents had given him for his birthday. It was an autographed baseball bat, signed by David Ortiz. Big Papi. "The man who killed the ghost of the Bambino," Christopher's father, a die-hard Red Sox fan, used to tell Christopher when he was growing up. It meant little to Christopher. No matter how hard his father prodded him, Christopher couldn't find any interest in team sports. They seemed pointless to him. He had other things on his mind. Even so, Christopher's father supported the sports Christopher did play. Christopher's father went to Christopher's wrestling matches and karate matches and everything else. After every match, win or lose, Christopher's father always said the same thing. "Helluva of a match, kid. Just don't forget to have fun, you know."

The bat that Christopher got from his parents was the color of wood near the knob but shifted to a dark, shiny black near the barrel. Christopher's father told him that it was exactly like the ones that Big Papi used to use in games. Christopher genuinely thanked his father. He knew that his father was giving Christopher a piece of himself. He loved his father. He loved both his parents. Before they cut into Christopher's birthday cake, Christopher wanted to drive to Evan's house to show him the bat. Evan was a huge baseball fan. Evan's brain wasn't filled with the distractions that Christopher's was.

"Do you know how much this thing probably cost?" Evan asked Christopher as Christopher handed him the bat.

Christopher shrugged. He had no idea. "No. Do you?" Christopher asked back.

Evan paused, running his hand up and down the nearly polished wood. He shook his head. "I bet it cost a ton," Evan answered.

"Do you want it?" Christopher asked Evan. He knew that Evan wanted it. He could see the desire in Evan's eyes. Christopher didn't care. Having the bat wasn't important to him—not as important as making his only friend happy.

Evan stared down at the name signed into the wood on the beige part of the handle. He shook his head. "Your father would be really upset if you gave it away," Evan said. Christopher hadn't even thought of that. Evan handed the bat back to him. "Do you want to go out tonight," Evan asked Christopher, "to celebrate? I can probably get Tracey to get one of her friends to come out with us."

Christopher thought about it. Maybe he should celebrate. It was his birthday. He'd had fun with some of Tracey's friends before when he didn't scare them away too quickly. Christopher shook his head though. It was a Tuesday night. He didn't want to put anybody out. Christopher looked out the window. It was starting to get dark. "I should go home. My mother made a cake."

"Okay," Evan said. "I'll make Tracey give us a rain check. How about Friday?" Evan eyed his friend, never exactly sure what was going on in Christopher's head.

"Friday," Christopher agreed, knowing that it was the easiest way to end the conversation.

"Well, happy birthday, man." Evan got up from his chair and wrapped his arms awkwardly around Christopher, patting his friend on the back with one fist.

"Thanks."

"See you at school tomorrow," Evan said.

"Yeah," Christopher answered, thinking it was true when he said it.

Christopher left the house. He waved good-bye to Evan's parents on his way out the door. Evan's parents waved back, not unhappy to see their son's odd best friend go. Christopher walked across the gravel driveway toward his car. Everything seemed normal. Christopher was even relaxed. He opened the car door and threw his bat in the passenger seat. Then he sat down, started the car, flicked on his headlights and slowly pulled up to the edge of his friend's driveway. It had been light when Christopher arrived at Evan's house but it was dark now. Night came fast this far north.

Christopher had looked to his left before pulling his car out on to the long, windy road. This stretch of road was free of streetlights. Christopher would be able to see the headlights of any oncoming cars from miles away even as the light darted through the trees. Cars drove fast on this stretch of road at night, though. When Christopher looked, all he saw was miles of empty road, surrounded by trees and darkening hollow spaces. Seeing nothing, Christopher stepped on the gas and inched the car forward onto the road. The road in front of him was as empty as the road behind him appeared. His headlights cut through the darkness, reflecting off the yellow lines in the middle of the street but otherwise being swallowed by the dense forest around him. Christopher looked in his rearview mirror again. Still nothing. He looked down to turn on the radio. He began to tune it away from the station he usually listened to, the talk radio stations full of shows about UFOs and conspiracy theories where people from all over the country called in to tell strange stories about secrets hidden right in front of us. It was Christopher's eighteenth birthday. He wanted to listen to music. He found a station playing an old Bruce Springsteen song. Evan always made fun of Christopher for liking old people's music. Christopher turned up the volume and then glanced back up again. The road in front of him was still empty. Then he looked in his rearview mirror again, expecting to see darkness. Instead, he saw them. They had finally come for him.

The headlights of the car chasing him were already large in Christopher's rearview mirror and they were getting bigger, bearing down on him. The car had come out of nowhere. It couldn't have come all the way down the road. Christopher would have seen the headlights—tiny specks of light in the darkness—miles before they had gotten this close to him. The only explanation was that the car had been parked in the woods, waiting for Christopher to drive by. Christopher heard the engine of the car behind him rev as it closed the gap between them and neared his rear bumper. The moment that Christopher had feared ever since he was a child had finally arrived.

For a split second, the only emotion that Christopher felt was relief, relief that the moment was finally here, relief that the waiting was over, relief that his paranoia wasn't simply madness, relief that his paranoia wasn't worthless. Had he known them, Christopher's birth mother or birth father could have told him that there is no such thing as worthless paranoia. Christopher knew that well enough now. His paranoia had value. It was a currency that, if he were lucky, he could cash in to buy his life. The relief only lasted a split second. After that, the relief was chased away by the sudden feeling of inadequacy. Christopher began to question every decision he had ever made. Why hadn't he stuck with one fighting style? Why hadn't he trained harder? Then, after deeming the feeling of inadequacy a waste of time, Christopher was left with only one emotion. Fear. So much fear it drowned out everything else.

Christopher looked at the dark, empty road in front of him and did the only thing he could think to do. He slammed on the gas. The road wound back and forth through the dense forest. Even as well as Christopher knew the road, he couldn't floor it without risking driving off the road and into a tree. All he could hope for was that whoever was in the car behind him didn't know the road as well as he did and would have trouble keeping up. The problem was that they didn't have to follow the road. They only needed to follow Christopher's taillights. The car behind him moved in closer. Christopher felt a heavy tap on his rear fender. It jolted him forward. Christopher began turning the steering wheel later and later as he neared oncoming turns, hoping to lose his tail. He waited until the last possible second; then he would jerk the wheel to one side, barely avoiding driving into woods. The wheels of Christopher's car skidded on the road as he turned. He held his steering wheel tightly to try keep from losing control. Still, the car behind him stayed on his bumper. Whatever they were driving, it was faster and handled better than the piece of shit Christopher drove.

They pulled their car up beside Christopher's. Their car was dark with tinted windows. Christopher couldn't see inside. Then they suddenly rammed their car into the side of Christopher's. Christopher almost lost control. As long as he was on the road, he was outmatched. Christopher knew it. He had to get off the road. It was his only chance. If he could just stay on the road a few more miles, he could get to the woods close to his house, the woods he'd virtually grown up in. If he could make it that far, Christopher knew he'd have a chance of surviving.

The dark car bumped Christopher again, sustaining the contact this time, trying to push Christopher off the road and into the trees. They were going over sixty miles per hour now. Christopher clutched the steering wheel, trying to hold on, trying to keep his car from veering off into oblivion. He could feel his pulse in his hands. He could feel his tires skid sideways. Then the road bent suddenly. Christopher cut his steering wheel as the road curved. When he did, the cars separated. He heard tires screeching again but they weren't his this time. The dark car skidded, trying to stay on the road as it almost missed the turn. Christopher stepped down hard on the accelerator. His foot touched the floor. He only needed to make it another two miles or so. In seconds, the other car was back alongside him again, moving in to try to ram him off the road. This time, Christopher had a plan. As the passenger-side door of the dark car was about to ram Christopher's door, Christopher slammed on the brakes. The dark car flew by him, going at least fifty yards in front of him before they were able to pull to a stop. The dark car skidded sideways as it stopped, blocking the entire road. The car was lit up by Christopher's headlights like it was being shown in a spotlight. Christopher waited, wanting to see what the people inside the car would do. He half hoped that another car would come speeding from the other direction and slam into them but he knew that this was unlikely. People didn't often drive this road at night. He watched the car. He felt like he was watching an animal, a predator. He felt like he could see the car breathing. Then the car's passenger-side window, the window facing Christopher, began to go down. Christopher didn't wait to see what horrors the descending window would reveal. Instead, as soon as the window began to go down, Christopher floored it again.

Christopher knew that he would have to go off the road to get around them. His wheels screeched before they caught and then his car hurled onto the dirt on the side of the road behind the dark car. Christopher prayed that he wouldn't hit a hole in the ground or a tree before he was able to get past the dark car. Christopher's car rattled over the unpaved ground but it made it past them. When he could, Christopher turned back on to the road without taking his foot off the accelerator. Then he heard the screeching of tires as his pursuers once again started up the chase again. The dark car was only seconds behind him but Christopher only needed seconds. He knew where he was now. He watched the trees as he zipped past them. The other car was gaining on him again, coming right up to Christopher's rear bumper. He spotted the landmark he'd been looking for, an old felled tree, its roots sticking up into the air like the tentacles of a giant sea monster. Christopher counted the seconds. One. Two. The car behind him was about to ram him again. On three, Christopher cut the wheel hard to the left, launching himself into the darkness of the woods. He felt the wheels of his car leave the ground as he catapulted off the paved road into the wilderness. As he flew, Christopher turned off his headlights and then he felt himself plummeting into darkness.